Author's

It really is very important that the [...] of fiction. It's not history. I'm not a historian. The story takes my fictional characters through factual events. The story also at times involves real characters. I have tried hard through all my research to ensure that all of these events and characters are crafted out of well-documented fact. I have no doubt that much greater experts than myself will be able to pick holes in many of the details of the story. In the end that is exactly what 'Terrible Beauty' is – a story.

Throughout the process of writing this book I have tried as hard as I can to demonstrate absolute neutrality. I was born and raised in Lancashire. I have no God. I am neither Republican or Loyalist. If any reader detects a bias to either side in the book, I can promise that it is wholly unintentional. Some readers have commented that the book, if anything, is anti-British. Well maybe it is. I am after all British myself and many of the things that my government has done over the years I find completely unacceptable. These things were done in my name as a citizen and I claim the right to be critical.

Enjoy the book.

Mark Frankland
October 2002

Previous titles from Glenmill

NOVELS

One Man's Meat
The Cull

CHILDRENS STORIES

The Drums of Anfield
The Drums of Hampden

Terrible Beauty

Mark Frankland

A Glenmill Publication

First published in 2002

Glenmill

Dumfries

Scotland

DG2 8PX

tel: 0776 149 3542

http://www.thecull.com

British Library Cataloguing in Publication Data.
A catalogue record of this book is available from the British Library.

ISBN 0 9535944 7 5

Design & Origination by Ψasmin
Printed and bound in Great Britain

Acknowledgements

Without the absolute support of my family
I could never do this. Thanks.
Hopefully one day it will all be worth it.

Thanks also to Bik and David
for making time to see me
when the sky was falling in.

Thanks to Campbell and Gail
for your wonderful hospitality.

Contents

Prologue
The Debt

16 July 1966

There was something unmistakably fine about them. The man was no longer young. He was nearly 70 but there was nothing bowed about him. He still had the rigid straight back of a soldier. He held the hand of a boy. The boy was tall for eight years old and shared his grandfather's back and shoulders.

There was a stillness about them as they stared out over the rows of white crosses. Had anyone looked they would have been struck by the remarkable dignity of the picture. They were both Sunday-best smart with white shirts and highly-polished shoes. The boy wore a jacket and shorts. The man wore a charcoal-grey three-piece suit with a row of medals pinned to the chest.

Had anyone looked closely they would have been impressed by the medals. Impressed if they had known enough to recognise what they saw. More than impressed to see the medal that so very few men ever lived to wear.

But there wasn't anyone there to see. It was how Peter Stanton had wanted it. Two weeks before it would have been very different. Two weeks before the cemetery at Thiepval Wood had been a throng of people. They had turned out in their thousands to remember the day fifty years before when the blood of Ulster had seeped into the dusty soil of the Somme battlefield. There had been veterans and their families and politicians and reporters and mere onlookers.

Now they were all gone. A few workmen were all that was left of the great day of remembering. The silence of the place was occasionally punctured by the sound of clattering metal as they dismantled the scaffolding that had supported the temporary stands.

There had been many that had tried long and hard to persuade Peter Stanton to attend the official ceremony. The regiment had called several times to his house. A few old comrades had beseeched him to join them. The Belfast Telegraph had even offered to pay all his fares and hotel bills. Peter Stanton had been something of a local celebrity in the warren of terraced streets off the Shankill Road ever since that fateful summer's morning in the fields of northern France when he had won the Victoria Cross.

So very few men had ever been presented with the British Army's highest award for gallantry. Even fewer ever got the chance to wear it. Mostly the awards were posthumous. Peter Stanton was the exception. He had come through his wounds and lived to tell the tale. They had wanted to put him out at the front for the press to take their pictures. They had wanted him to be an icon. Here was a man who represented all that was good about Ulster. A man who had done his duty in the face of impossible odds. A man loyal to his comrades and his country and his King. A hero.

Peter Stanton hadn't wanted any of it. He had been polite, but firm. He had been grateful for the offers. He had been touched by the sentiments. He had been honoured to be considered. But he had said no. Thank you, but no. In the end they had given up asking.

He knew that he could not have stomached the speeches about glory made by politicians who had never faced a bullet in their lives. Why was it that nobody could ever make a speech without that tired old word? Glory. Always glory. Glory being the giant carpet under which they always tried so hard sweep away their mistakes and catastrophic errors of judgement. Their crimes.

He had been there. Glory hadn't.

He had been there to see men and boys from the streets where he had grown up cut to pieces by the German machine-gunners. There had been nothing glorious about those terrible few hours. It hadn't been about gallant heroism and noble sacrifice. It had been about utter confusion and terrible panic and men soiling themselves and screaming for their mothers as the German bombs and bullets reaped their terrible harvest.

It hadn't been about glory for those who fell. They had been conned. They were just good, hard working simple men. They weren't in France for glory. They had come for the great adventure. A once in a lifetime chance to break away from their grindingly long days in factories and shipyards and wet, boggy fields. They had been brought up to respect the words of their elders. Their priests and their landlords and their teachers. And of course their King.

From the cradle they had been taught that their duty was what made them special. They were the men of Ulster. They were the loyal ones. They were the ones to whom their King could always turn.

And the King hadn't had to ask twice. In his time of peril the men of Ulster had rallied to the flag. Just like they always had. Just like they always would. When they were asked they had come. They had come in their droves. They had been told that they would see the world, discover new countries, see sights that they had only dreamed of in their cramped workshops and leaking barns.

They had been promised the earth. Instead they got Thiepval Wood and the dusty fields beyond.

Peter Stanton looked down at the face of his grandson. The boy's eyes were like saucers. They had been that way for days. For the boy it had been the trip of a lifetime. Before this, the furthest he had ever been was a few miles down the coast of County Down for family holidays in Newcastle. This trip had been one long wonder to him. The ferry from Larne. The slow chugging train across the rolling farmland of Galloway. And then down through the peaks of Cumberland and Westmorland and on through the sprawling, smoking cities of the North and The Midlands. They had spent an afternoon in London to see the Palace and the Parliament and the Tower. Then across the rolling chalk to Dover and over to France.

The boy had never complained, never fidgeted. He had been quiet most of the time, gazing out of the window, drinking it all in. He had always been a quiet boy. Sometimes Peter worried that maybe he was a little too quiet. Almost reserved. Always smart. Always polite. Always dressed and ready for Sunday School. But not many friends, not much mischief. He had often felt the same concerns for his own son, the boy's father. He had grown up to be a very stiff man. Sometimes he wondered if either of them had inherited his own spark and drive.

On his return from the war he had been hospitalised for many months. When he was at last able to make his way back to his home in Granville Street, he had worked with his father in the family's small carpentry business. His father had never set his business sights high. They had never worked outside the tiny network of streets that grew off the Shankill Road like the tight packed branches of a pine tree. They did doors and windows and floorboards and roofs. Never anything big. Just small jobs for a fair price. And there had always been a living. Even through the bad times in the 1920's there had always been food on the table.

His father had died in 1931 and Peter took over the workshop. His sights were set higher. He moved the business on. He got into the finer work. They built magnificent bars for pubs and reception areas for big hotels and counters for the better shops in the city. By the mid-Thirties, 'Stanton of Shankhill' had become a benchmark for quality. The workshop had grown and was soon filled with skilled craftsmen and apprentices.

Even when things were tight, the work always came in. There was always a network that ensured that 'Stantons of Shankhill' never lacked the work. They were not always the cheapest, and occasionally they were not quite the best, but they always got the work. Peter Stanton was owed. Peter Stanton had bought his ticket in France. Peter Stanton was the one at the front with the Victoria Cross when the city remembered its dead every November. Peter Stanton had proved his loyalty in the heat of the inferno. It was never done effusively. Never brash. Never overt. It was always done discreetly. A quiet word. A subtle nudge. And the contract would go to 'Stantons of Shankhill'. It was just the way it was. The way things worked. The men of Ulster looked after their own.

Peter married in 1932 and his only child, Gerald, was born on a cold February morning in 1936. The next twenty years were a golden era for Stantons. The war meant that the great shipyards of Belfast worked 24 hours a day for seven days a week no matter how hard the Luffewaffe tried to stop it. Every ship needed a shining panelled wardroom for its officers, and the Royal Navy expected the best. Stantons worked round the clock to build them.

The war took the firm to a new level and put money in the bank. Many wondered whether Peter would take advantage of his growing wealth and move out to the suburbs. He never did. Never wanted to. The family stayed on in the small terraced house next to the workshop. Gerald joined him in the business in the early Fifties and married a local girl. In 1958 she gave birth to his grandson, David.

One of his great regrets was that his relationship with his son had always been rather distant. When Gerald had grown up through the frantic years of the war, Peter had never seemed to have the time for him. There was always another deadline to meet, always another crisis. For years he had worked eighteen hours a day. By the time he returned home to eat his food and collapse into his chair the boy had been in bed for hours. When he rose long before dawn to open up the workshop his son was still asleep. They would sit next to each other in church on Sunday morning and then share a quiet Sunday lunch. Sometimes they would walk up the Shankill Road to the park that overlooked the city below. These occasions were always stilted somehow. They never seemed to be more than strangers to each other.

Peter lived out these days on the promise that things would be different once the war was at last over. Once it was over they would have the time to take a holiday. Once it was over he would finish earlier and maybe kick a football around in the street. But when the war was at last over it was too late. The distance between them had grown too great. Gerald had become a quiet, polite boy. He did wonderfully well in school, and at an early age it became abundantly clear that he would become a master craftsman. When Gerald left school at fifteen years old there was never a minute's doubt that he would join his father in the workshop. They spent hours together quietly working away amidst the noise and the sawdust. They became a superb team. But they never became close.

When Davie was born Peter saw the boy as his second chance. He forced himself to cut down his hours. Gerald was more than capable of taking on more and more of the responsibility. Peter was able to make the time for his grandson that he had never found for his son. It soon became obvious that Davie was destined to become another quiet one. He spent hours with his bricks and his Lego and his Action Men. He started reading early, and every week he saved his pocket money to go to the newsagents to buy 'Victor' or 'Commando'. By the time he was six it was all soldiers. He would spend every spare hour in his room creating intricate battle scenes. By the time he was seven it was clear that he had inherited all his grandfather's and father's skills with his hands as he put together Airfix models of tanks and fighter planes and warships.

He was never a boy for crowds. He had two close friends and he stuck with them. They didn't go out a great deal. They were never interested in the wild games of football in the street or the expeditions to hurl stones and abuse at the Catholic boys from the Falls. They stayed in and made their models and arranged their soldiers and fought out their imaginary wars.

Davie was quiet but never a push-over. Peter was summoned to visit the Headmaster on two occasions. Each time Davie had been targeted by bullies in the playground. Each time the result had been the same, a split nose, blood all over a white shirt, outraged parents, and Davie standing respectfully with his hands behind his back giving quiet assurance that the other boy had started it. Peter hadn't reprimanded him on either occasion. He had been amazed at the parents for the silly scene they had made. It was how things were. How they always had been. If you lived on the Shankill you soon learnt to look after yourself. It wasn't that it was particularly right. It was just the way that it was.

Davie had been five years old when he had started to ask his grandad about the war. As the years had passed, and the boy's bedroom had filled up with tanks and planes and soldiers, the questions had become more frequent and more demanding. Peter had held back. Who was he to crash into the boy's dreams and games? Davie's war was a fine thing. It was the war of the cinema and the comic books and the back of the Airfix kits. It was about excitement and glamour and daring risk. It was about heroes and villains and victories achieved against all odds. And the good guys always came out on top. And the good guys always came home ready to fight another day. And there was never any mud. Never any men staring with shock-deadened eyes at the contents of their stomachs, which had slopped out on to the dusty soil.

So for years he had stalled the boy's ardent questioning. Later, he would say. When you're older. When the time is right. When you are ready. Not yet. Be patient. There is all the time in the world. The 50th anniversary celebrations had brought things to a head. Belfast was consumed with remembering its glorious dead. The long lost men of the 36th Ulster Division were back on the front pages. The schools rammed home the message to their wide-eyed pupils that they must never forget. The priests harangued their congregations. The newspapers shouted through their billboards that the lost men must always be remembered.

All the old tales started to be told. The officers striding across no-man's-land proudly wearing their Orange sashes. The men kicking footballs to each other as they walked into their doom. The songs of Loyalist Ulster fighting the terrible sound of the guns. Davie won a two-pound book-token as a prize for the best project about the heroic advance of the men of the 36th Ulster. And men in magnificent uniforms came to the house and took tea and biscuits at the kitchen table and pleaded with Peter to come and lead the processions. And the boy was so confused when his grandad kept saying no to the tall officers. And when they came for the last time, and his grandad had politely but firmly kept them waiting on the front step, there had been tears in the young boy's eyes. More than anything he wanted to see his grandad in his uniform with all his medals. He wanted to watch him lead the procession to the City Hall. He wanted to show all his friends the Victoria Cross that they never really believed in. He wanted it to be like the comics and the films and the backs of the Airfix kits.

The tears bit hard into Peter Stanton. He sat in his kitchen late into the night and pondered. He knew that he could no longer put the boy off. He was eight now. Eight was not really as old as he would have liked it to be, but he would only risk alienating the boy if he kept pushing his questions aside.

He told him one morning before the boy left for school. He told him that he wouldn't go out for the cameras with his medals because it wasn't right. It wasn't the right way to remember what had happened to all those men who came from the streets where they still lived. He told him that the two of them would travel to France once all the hullabaloo had died down. He would return to Thiepval Wood after an absence of half a century. And then he would tell his grandson about the four crazy hours when he had been a front-line soldier in the 36th Ulster Division.

It took them over half an hour to find the first grave that they sought. William Forrester. 17 years old. Died of Wounds. Beaumont Hammel. 1 July 1916. Peter's eyes were moist. His normally firm voice slightly cracked.

"That was Billy. One of my greatest friends."

Twenty minutes later they found the second white cross. Thomas Finch. seventeen years old. Killed in action. Beaumont Hammel. 1 July 1916.

"And this is my second great friend. Come on Davie. Over here. Let's sit for a while. Let me tell you what happened. It's about time."

They walked to the edge of the field of crosses and sat down on a bench. Beyond the crosses was a small wood. A few crows flapped in and out of the branches like bits of burnt paper blowing in the wind. Their harsh cries occasionally split the silence of the place. The early morning cloud was now more or less burned away, and the strong July sunshine made the horizon hazy.

Peter Stanton stared at the trees and a small smile played on his lips.

"Well Davie, that's it. That's Thiepval Wood. That's what they all talk about. Not much to look at is it. Just a wood. A wood like most other woods. Who would ever have thought that a cluster of trees could come to mean so much? So let me tell you about it. About me and Billy and Tom and all the thousands of others who were here that day . . .

"It seemed as though the three of us had always been together. Inseparable, the neighbours would say. The terrible trio. Peter Stanton, Billy Forrester and Tom Finch. We lived at numbers five, twelve and 21 Granville Street. We started playing in the street together when we were four years old.

THE DEBT

"My dad had the joinery workshop. Billy and Tom's fathers worked at the Harland and Wolf shipyard. As we got older we were often the subjects of gossip. You know the kind of thing. All the old girls with their arms folded on the doorsteps. There was never anything particularly serious. It was always just mischief. The kind of things that lads get up to. No real harm in us. Just high spirits.

"By the time that we were eleven and we had moved on to secondary school, the high spirits tended to be directed towards the Catholic boys from the Falls and the Springfield. There were times on hot summer's nights when we would be frog-marched home by the local copper. He would dump us through our front doors and leave our parents to sort us out. The beatings that we got were never the hardest. Later, I bet the men would chuckle about it over their pints in the pubs. Nobody saw any harm in bashing a few Fenians. They couldn't tell us that of course. If they'd told us that it was OK we would have got right out of hand. No, they had to give us a good hiding. But no need to get too enthusiastic. Not for bashing a few dirty little Fenians.

"The three of us grew up strong. We never knew empty cupboards. There were plenty that did, I can tell you. Plenty with no food and no heat. They were the ones who got the rickets and the whooping cough and the pneumonia. Not us. We were lucky ones. Business was always steady for the joinery workshop. Harland and Wolf had order books that were filled as they had never been filled before. The Royal Navy was ordering ship after ship to try and to keep up with the Kaiser.

"By the time that we were fourteen years old we were all tall. We ate meat twice a week and we could flatten any of the other lads when we played football out in the streets. Our reputation was growing by now. People were getting to hear about us. We were boys who never shirked a fight. Whenever things got going with the Catholic kids there would be a knock on the door and we would soon be in the thick of it all.

"By 1912 we began to feel that we had been born into great and exciting times. The whole of the Shankill was knocked backwards by the news from Westminster that the Parliament had voted in favour of Home Rule for Ireland. I'd never known excitement like it. On the Falls, the Catholics were cock-a-hoop. They were

9

almost dancing in the streets over there. On the Shankill there were always clusters of men on the streets talking. Everybody always seemed to be waiting for the papers. Everyone was always asking everybody else if they knew anything. It was unthinkable what was happening. Surely it couldn't happen. No way. Never. Not to us. The king would never desert his most loyal of all subjects. But what could we do to stop it?

"Then, just when all seemed dark, a beam of brilliant light appeared in the shape of Sir Edward Carson. He said the words that everyone on the Shankill wanted to hear. Simple words. Powerful words. Words to rally around. Sir Edward said 'No Surrender'. Sir Edward said 'Ulster will fight, and Ulster will be right.' And suddenly we could see a way out. Suddenly there was somebody to follow. Somebody to fight for.

"We marched down the Shankill Road on that great day when Carson signed his pledge of Loyalty at the City Hall. It seemed like the whole of the Shankill was there. It seemed as if the whole of the world was there. It was a day like no other. There were 100,000 people packed into the city centre. They let us into the hall in groups of 500 to sign their pledge. It went on for hours and hours. Soon we heard that over a million of our fellow Ulstermen had signed. Ulster stood shoulder-to-shoulder. We all knew that Ulster would never go down without a fight.

"One night my dad told me to get Billy and Tom to call round to the workshop at midnight. All day we tried to guess what it was all about. I begged and begged my dad to tell me what was happening. In the end he got so fed-up with me that he clouted me. Once we got into dad's van he told us.

"It was a big secret. A really big secret. Too big for us to be trusted with through the day. We were going to Larne. He told us that the Ulster Volunteer Force was landing a boatload of guns. Thousands of them. Enough to defend Ulster against anything they could throw at us. And then we realised that this all meant that we were now in. We were a part of the UVF. We weren't just kids any more. This was the real stuff. Men's stuff.

"It was an amazing night. I had never known that kind of excitement. And tension. And fear. We drove out of Belfast and all the streets were completely quiet. To get to Larne my Dad avoided all the bigger roads. He said that there might be army roadblocks. We seemed to go for hours along tiny country lanes and tracks. And everywhere looked so fantastic. There wasn't a cloud in the sky and there was a big full moon. When we arrived, the scenes were amazing. It seemed as if there were thousands of men already there. Shadowy figures in the night. It was past four when we finally got the van loaded. By the time we got home to the Shankill the dawn was just breaking. We hid all the guns under the floorboards of the workshop.

"For a while things stayed really tense. Nobody knew what the government in London would do. We were always waiting for the day that the soldiers would come. And then suddenly things eased. That was another great day. Some of the British Army officers based down near Dublin made a statement. They said that they would never take up arms against us loyal Ulstermen, no matter what the Government told them. Well, that left the men in London in a real old pickle. What could they do? If the soldiers wouldn't obey their orders they were completely powerless.

"We never took anything for granted though. No way. Every weekend my Dad would drive us out to a different place in the countryside for training exercises with the UVF. These were brilliant days. We did all sorts. There were lots of ex-soldiers who showed us everything. And we became quite an army you know. At one time they said that the UVF could call on 100,000 men.

"In the end of course it was a war that we never had to fight. By 1914 the British Government had bigger things to worry about than Ireland. It was the Germans who were the worry now. Little old Ulster just got forgotten. It was no great surprise to anyone in Belfast when the Great War started. We had been watching spanking new warships sail out of the shipyards for years. Well, you don't build them for nothing, do you?

"The word soon came down from the UVF command that we should enlist. We expected nothing different. Our whole cause was our loyalty. All we had ever wanted was the chance to stay with our own King and our own church. So when the call came we were always going to be the first to answer it.

"It was the best news that me and Tom and Billy had ever heard. This was it. This was the moment that we felt we had been waiting for all of our lives. It was amazing down there at the recruiting hall. Everybody seemed to be there – young lads, teachers, coppers, milkmen, shopkeepers, it was as if every man on the Shankill had turned out. The three of us were too young of course. We were all only sixteen and you were supposed to be seventeen. But nobody bothered about that. We were big, strong lads and everyone knew that we could handle ourselves. So we were each given our shilling from the King and we became part of the 36th Ulster Division.

"And then all the excitement completely stopped.

"I suppose in our minds we expected to be thrown a uniform and shipped straight over to France to join the fight. It wasn't like that. In fact it was the complete opposite. It seemed to take forever for anything to get organised. Everything the army did was chaotic. Eventually we were moved out into the countryside where we lived in rows of tents. We had to wait for everything. Uniforms, boots, rifles, I tell you, the UVF was far better equipped.

"Most of the time it was just plain cold and boring. All we ever seemed to do was drill. We marched up and down the same bit of grass for week after week after week. And it never seemed to stop raining. The tents were more or less hopeless and all our stuff was always damp.

"This went on for ages, right through the winter, then the spring and finally the autumn. By the time we finally got word that we were about to move, most of us were more fed up than we had ever been in our whole lives.

"At last we were shipped to France. Now we started to get excited again and all those wasted months of marching up and down were soon forgotten. Everyone was talking about the 'Big Push'. Throughout 1914 and 1915 the old armies of Britain and France and Germany had more or less fought themselves to a standstill. They had all tried to break through, but on every occasion the advances had failed. It was a massive stalemate. The soldiers faced each other from trench lines that started on the Channel Coast and ran all the way for hundreds of miles down to Switzerland.

"That was why we were there. The standing army had never been big enough for these kind of battles. That was why they had needed volunteers. They had pleaded for volunteers. They needed numbers. They needed men with real courage and patriotism. And millions of us had answered the call from all over the Empire.

"The moment that we got off the troop ship we could suddenly understand exactly what the generals had been doing. The old army had stopped the German advance dead in its tracks and they had held them back for two years, constantly attacking and weakening them. Whilst the old soldiers had held the fort, it bought time for the millions of volunteers to be gathered together and brought slowly to the front. As we made our way through Northern France there seemed to be soldiers everywhere. And we were all in such high spirits. Suddenly it was sunny every day and wherever we went there was cheering and singing. We felt that we were part of the greatest army that had ever been raised. What possible chance did the Germans stand against all of us? None. They had been battered and softened up for two years and now we had all arrived to kick them all the way back to Berlin.

"We arrived here at Thiepval wood at the beginning of June. Now that was a hard month's work. Every day we sweated from dawn till dusk digging trenches and hauling sandbags and shells. We spent hour after hour after hour unloading shells from trucks and piling them up by the artillery pieces. By this time the plan of the battle was seeping down through the grapevine. We were going to pound the German front lines with the greatest bombardment there had ever been. By the time that our guns finished their work there would be barely a German left alive. Any who managed to survive the shells would surely be wrecked and broken.

"When it started, the bombardment was not like anything I had ever dreamed of. The noise was so loud that it almost seemed to be crawling around inside you. We just huddled in our trenches and the guns just went on and on. It wasn't only a few hours. It was days. After a while we all had splitting headaches and our whole brains were numbed. You see, it wasn't as if the shells were dropping miles away. It was just a few hundred yards. Here, our trenches were at the edge of the wood there, and the shells were landing on the German lines at the top of that big field. You couldn't talk, you couldn't think, you couldn't do anything. We simply sat there and felt the ground shake and hoped like mad that nobody in the gun crews made a cock up and started shelling us.

"I think all of us had the same thought. What must it be like for the Germans who were on the receiving end? It was beyond imagination. No matter how much we hated them for what they had done, we couldn't help but feel pity. One thing that we were quite certain of, there was no way that they would be in any fit state to fight.

"At last they let us know that the Big Push would start at dawn the next morning. That was July 1, 1916. Me and Tom and Billy had joined up in August 1914. It had taken us 21 months to arrive at the war, and now our time had come. We were all in brilliant spirits. It seemed that we had been cooped-up forever, first in the camp in Ireland, then in the various camps as we made our way to the front, and finally in the trenches of Thiepval Wood. Now at last we were about to be cut loose. Once we smashed our way through the lines we would be running hard all the way to Germany. We couldn't wait.

"I can remember that night as if it were yesterday. The bombardment seemed to get even more fierce. We all huddled together in small groups of three or four. That is what our army was really. Lots and lots of small groups of mates who had joined together. Lads from the same street or village or factory. We played cards and wrote letters or just chatted about what would happen when it all started. One thing's for sure, none of us slept.

"Just as the sun came up the guns stopped. The silence seemed almost louder than the guns. It all seemed so strange. After all the endless noise it was just a quiet summer's morning in the countryside. I remember suddenly hearing the sound of the birds in the tree and the buzzing of flies. Slowly the smoke and dust that had swirled around the German trenches started to settle. The whole area was churned up like a madman had ploughed it. Nothing was moving. Everything ahead of us seemed completely quiet and deserted.

"They came round with the rum ration. That was really stupid. More than half of us were teetotal and so the ones that weren't were given double or treble rations. The rum in those days was different. It was about three times as strong as the stuff in the shops today. Lots of guys took about half a pint on an empty stomach and no sleep. They were soon drunk out of their minds. Lots of them were throwing up when we went over the top.

"Our officer came round to give us a pep talk. He was a farmer from Antrim and he was wearing his Orangeman's sash and a bowler hat. I remember thinking to myself that he looked more like he was dressed for church than battle. He told us that the battle was already won. He told us that there would barely be a German left alive after the barrage. He told us that when we got out of the trenches there was no need to run. It was better that we walked forward so that we would be sure to stay in our platoons and keep organised. He told us that the whole of Ulster would be proud of us. He told us that God was on our side.

"And then the whistles went. It was such a strange moment. After all of those months of hanging around, we clambered up the ladders and out into the open and we were at war. It was all so odd. It didn't seem like war at all. It was so quiet. We were simply walking through a field towards an area of churned up mud. It wasn't like any old field of course. There was lots of barbed wire everywhere, on our side as well as theirs. It took us quite a while to cut our way through our own stuff and then we were clear and walking forward. There were a few shots now, but not that many. I saw a lad fall a few yards away from me. I had to do a double take. There hadn't seemed to be any particular shot, he had just fallen. When I looked down half of his head was gone. Just like that. I must have stopped and been staring because the corporal came up to me and screamed in my ear and told me to keep going.

"When we came to the first trench it was just like they said it would be. It was pounded into nothing and there wasn't a German in sight. We kept on and it was much the same story when we reached the second trench. There was more shooting now. More men were falling. It seemed quite bizarre. There was no way of seeing where the shots were coming from, but men kept dropping. I saw the officer go down. As we passed him he was screaming like a trapped rabbit. The bullet had taken him in the stomach and the orange of his sash was dyed red.

"Men were starting to run now. There was no calm anymore. The shooting was getting more intense. The three of us stuck together and bent down low and ran. We made it to the third trench and jumped inside. Again it was empty. I don't know how long we had been going, no more than twenty minutes I suppose, but it already seemed like forever. The sun was beating down now and we were hot and thirsty. We took big swigs of water from our canteens and just stared at each other. This wasn't how it was supposed to have been. There was nobody to fight. Just the sound of gunfire and men falling and screaming. The screaming was really bad by now. I stuck my head up over the trench and saw that the field that we had just crossed was covered in bodies. There seemed to be hundreds and hundreds of them. Some were not moving at all. But most were still alive and screaming for help. It was a terrible sound. The most terrible sound in the whole world. Some yelled obscenities, some begged for their mothers, others just screamed.

"The trench was filling up all the time now as men leapt inside to escape the guns. Soon it was packed to overflowing and still more men were trying to get in. Then a sergeant appeared. His face was almost purple with rage as he started trying to push men out of the trench and yelling at them to get forward. Nobody wanted to go. Three men climbed out and two were immediately cut down. He started to wrestle with a young lad who didn't look like he was a day over fifteen years old. The sergeant was a big man but he couldn't move the lad at all. He was hanging onto a railing and screaming that he wouldn't go. I saw a stain appear in his trousers. The poor lad was so scared that he wet himself. We all looked at each other and didn't know what to do. The sergeant started to beat the lad around his head with his pistol butt and still he wouldn't go. I think that some of us were about to intervene when the sergeant shot him right between the eyes. Then he turned on us. His eyes were blazing. He shouted like a madman. That was the price that any coward would pay. Who was to be next? He started waiving his gun about and firing shots over our heads.

"Well, it worked. We came out of the trench at a charge. I remember howling at the top of my voice as we ran forward. Everyone was the same. We roared like animals. The air seemed as if it were filled by bullets now. Men were falling all around. The world had lost all sanity. There was no reason here. Just blood and madness. And then, by some kind of miracle, we fell into the fourth trench. But this time it wasn't empty. As I hurled myself down I landed right on top of a young German. Our faces were close together. Both of us were as astonished as each other. For a moment we just stared at each other.

"I don't suppose that he was any older than I was. He had a thin face and wire spectacles. He looked like a lad who would be top of the class in maths. For a moment I really didn't know what to do. We had been used to all kind of posters of German soldiers. These always showed them as huge brutish figures with snarling, twisted faces. Most of the time they barely looked human. And now here I was lying on top of this little skinny lad who looked as if he was about to burst into tears. Then I felt a pain in my side and I realised to my complete surprise that he was trying to stab me with a bayonet. At first I was just shocked. What on earth did he think he was playing at? What possessed him? How dare he? Then the tip of the bayonet broke through my skin and went in about and inch. This sent me crazy. I drove my knee up hard into his groin and got my hands on his throat. I was raging. Yelling and swearing. I just lost all control. I must have been like a madman because the next thing I knew Tom was there pulling me back. His voice seemed to have to go through about a mile of cotton wool before it got into my brain. And then I heard him. Peter! Peter! He was shouting. It's all right. He's dead. Leave it. He's gone. The mists cleared and I stared down at the thin face. I'd knocked his specs off. His eyes were staring straight up into the sky. And all of a sudden I felt sick. Sicker than I had ever felt before. I couldn't control it. I threw up all over his tunic. And then I felt so ashamed. Ashamed that I had killed him. Ashamed that I had been sick on him. Ashamed to have been involved in this terrible carnage. It wasn't supposed to be like this. They never said anything about it being like this.

"I was crying now. Big, big sobs. I just couldn't help it. Tom got hold of me and held me and tried to talk to me but it was no good. I felt so very bad. By now there must have been about forty of us in the trench. We were all just stunned. We were more or less paralysed. Some like me were crying. A couple were on their knees in prayer. Others were just shaking and staring at the floor. Then an officer arrived. He was only young, maybe a couple of years older than I was. He went round the men one by one. He had a kind voice and he took his time with us. He told us that the next trench was surely the last one. He told us that the Germans were almost broken. Just one more push and we would be there. Just once more. He told us that we should do it for the ones who had fallen. We should do it so that they had not given their lives in vain.

"And so we gathered by the wall of the trench and steadied ourselves for the last charge. It was almost as if we were beyond feeling fear. We had crossed a line. It seemed as if we had crossed the line into the kingdom of death itself. I remember looking into the eyes if Billy and Tom. They no longer had the eyes of boys. All their youth and laughter had been burned away in less than an hour. Now they had the eyes of the dead German boy. Nothing there. Just empty. As if they were already dead men.

"We went over. It was as if the might of the 36th Ulster had been reduced to a rag-tag bunch of walking zombies. The officer was cut down first. Literally cut to pieces. His body was blown apart. There was something strange about it. I fought to make my mind work. Then I realised what it was. We had gone too far. The machine gun was firing from behind us. I half turned to warn Tom and Billy. As I turned I saw Billy's arm ripped clean off and another bullet smash a hole in his shoulder. At the same time Tom fell as three bullets took him in the stomach. All around me men were falling. I threw myself to the ground and tried to squeeze myself into the soil.

"I could see the machine-gun nest. There were three grey helmets and yellow flashes from the muzzle. No wonder the officer had been cut to pieces, the gun was barely 40 yards away. Behind us to our left. I felt a huge rage building inside of me. They were just butchers. 40 yards. They couldn't miss. They had just cut us down. They were working the gun along the soil trying to hit the soldiers who had dived for cover. I could hear the bullets thumping into bodies and making them jump and twitch. I didn't really think about anything at all. These men had shot my two very best friends in the whole world. That was all that mattered. I got a Mills Bomb from my belt and pulled out the pin.

"I just ran at them. I was screaming again. They saw me and swung the gun around. When I was twenty yards away it was pointed straight at me. I knew that I was dead. I hurled the bomb and braced myself for the bullets to hit. Nothing. They frantically grappled with the gun, but it had jammed. One of them looked up with pure hate in his eyes. Then the Mills Bomb exploded and he was shredded. I felt a hard bang on my ankle and looked down. I couldn't believe it. The whole ankle was a complete mess. I had been shot and yet I felt nothing. Just a bang.

"It didn't seem to matter much at the time. All that mattered was Tom and Billy. The attack was over. The 'Big Push' was a joke. I didn't care about any of it any more. All that mattered was to get my friends back to a doctor. I crawled over to where they lay. They were both in a dreadful state, but still alive. Tom was the worst. The bullets had opened up his stomach and spilt out his intestines. I tried my best to push them back in and then I tied my tunic around him. Tom's arm was spouting blood where it had been severed. I managed to tie a bandage as tight as I could to stem the flow. Neither could walk. I knew that I would have to carry them. But who first?

"Tom was completely gone. He was just staring up into the sun and moaning. Billy was better. He seemed to read my mind. He spoke in near whisper. I had to push my ear right up to my mouth to hear him. Take Tom, he said. Tom is worse. I can hang on. I'll wait for a doctor.

"So I took Tom. I had to haul him onto my back and crawl. It seemed that I crawled for hours as all around me the men on the ground screamed and begged as they bled and died in the sun. It was late in the afternoon by the time that I found a medical team. Tom was barely alive. His breathing was so shallow as to be almost imperceptible. When I looked back I could see where the fourth trench was at the top of the hill. It was no more than 500 yards away. I couldn't believe the hours that it had taken for me to crawl all the way down.

"I went back for Billy. I had to crawl and scuttle and dodge amongst the dying men. I had to ignore their cries. They wanted water. They wanted their girls or their mothers. They wanted me to shoot them to end the pain. And I had to close my mind to them. My ankle was hurting really badly by now but I suppose I was beyond feeling pain. I just kept going. Half way between the third and the fourth trenches I was shot again. This time it was in my thigh. The bullet missed the bone. It just ripped all the flesh. But I didn't stop. I couldn't stop. Not with Billy still out there.

"It was nearly dark when I reached him. There was almost no life in him. Somehow I got him onto my back and hauled him into the fourth trench. As we fell over the side I landed only a few yards away from the young German. My vomit had dried in the sun. His eyes still stared at the same spot in the sky. When I leaned over to Billy he was gone. All of his blood had drained away. Slowly darkness closed in on me. I was just so tired. I felt that if I fell asleep I would never wake up. And I never, ever wanted to wake up. I had no wish to stay in this world of death. I didn't want to return to the Shankill without Billy and Tom and all the other men who lay dying out there. I just wanted to sleep and never wake up.

"But I did wake up of course. I woke up the next day in a field hospital. I had got lucky in the night when they had carried me in. They had put me down on the table of a very famous surgeon from London. He had saved both of my legs. Probably any other surgeon that night would have just cut them off and got onto the next case. Mine didn't. He patched me up and in the end I walked again. I tracked him down after the war. We sent him a beautiful Irish dresser for his kitchen. We exchanged letters for a while.

"An officer from Larne had been in the fourth trench when I charged the machine-gun post. He had seen it all and reported it to Brigade. In the dreadful days that followed the fiasco, the army were desperate to create some heroes. I suppose that I fitted their bill. I was a young lad from the Shankhill. I was tall and quite good-looking. And best of all, I was still alive. So they gave me the Victoria Cross. They said it was for being a hero. For ignoring all the odds and attacking the machine gun post to save the lives of my comrades and then carrying my two pals to safety.

"But it hadn't been like that. Not really. I was just raging mad. I'd lost it. If I had even stopped for a minute to think about it, I would never have done it. There was no sense out there. No reason. Just mindless horror. So I had charged a German machine gun like a complete madman. And the gun had jammed. Which means that I am here today.

"To this day I have never felt like a hero. I have never lost my feeling of shame. Shame about the young German boy. Shame that I came home and Billy and Tom didn't. Shame because I was there on a day when men turned into animals. Shame because I became one myself."

The old man fell into silence. The boy's head was bowed. It had been bowed for a long time. Tears poured down his cheeks. Peter Stanton felt another wave of shame as he saw the horror in the boys' eyes.

"I'm sorry Davie. I really am. I feel it is important that you know the truth. All of the talk they come out with about honour and glory is just garbage. It's a cover-up for what was little more than murder. We showed our loyalty by volunteering to defend our King from the Germans. And how did they repay us? They used us as cannon-fodder. They wiped out the best of our men."

Still the boy's head was down. Peter gently lifted up his chin and wiped away the tears with his handkerchief.

"But this is what is important Davie. This is what you must know. This is why I brought you here." His voice became much harder. "Hundreds of years ago the English king could not control his territories in Ireland. His armies did not know where to turn. And so he decided to grant lands to our people, the Protestants. We went over there and we had to fight for every acre. And we kept on fighting for hundreds of years. And we did it. Everything that you see in Ulster today is down to our forefathers – all the roads and the schools and the hospitals. All of it. And we always stayed loyal to our King. We fought his wars and we paid our taxes. Then in 1914, when he faced his greatest ever peril, he called on us and we answered his call. We answered it gladly, just like we had done before for hundreds of years. This is what happened. 15,000 men of the 36th Ulster walked onto this battlefield. 5000 were left dead or wounded. Our communities were torn to pieces. Many have never really recovered. And we did it for loyalty."

The old man's face was now as hard as stone.

"It isn't about glory and honour Davie. Oh no, not that. That is why I wouldn't walk in their parades. I'll tell you what it is about. It is about a debt. We paid our dues in blood 50 years ago. We put all of that blood in the bank. And that means that they owe us. It is a debt that can never go away. They owe us our lands and our homes and our churches. They must never be allowed to forget. This is what you must know Davie. This is what you must understand. When the time comes that people try to take from us what is ours you must always stand up. You must be like Carson. You must remind them of this debt. And if it must be, then you must fight for it. If the Crown ever turns its back on Ulster these men can never rest in peace."

The two of them stared out in silence at the ranks of quiet white crosses.

Part One
Roads to war

Chapter 2
Storm Clouds Gathering

October 1968

The voice took Sean O'Neil completely by surprise.

"I know you."

The voice came from the seat next to him. She had short red hair and sparkling green eyes and a big, big smile. She wore the tatty Afghan jacket and patched jeans that seemed to be more or less a uniform for most of the students. For a moment he couldn't think of a thing to say. A complete surprise. But then again, everything that he had experienced for the last three weeks had been a complete surprise.

"Sorry?"

"No need to be sorry. I just said that I know you." Her accent was certainly familiar enough. It was the accent that he had grown up with. It was actually an accent that he had barely heard these last three weeks. Unmistakable. West Belfast.

"Really." He said rather lamely.

"Not much for the chat are you?" She spoke with laughter in her voice. She was somehow disquieting. He felt rather awkward. Rather shy.

"It's not that. I'm just trying to remember you. Have we met?" He seemed to have met so many people in his first three weeks at Belfast's Queens University. He seemed to have met half of the country. It had been more or less overwhelming. But this girl? He felt sure that he would have remembered her.

25

This time the laughter was real. "Well, I couldn't say we have been formally introduced. I suppose I admired you from afar. About 50 yards to be precise."

He tried a smile. "Oh, I see." Not that he did, but it seemed like something to say. The room suddenly broke into loud applause. It was an emergency meeting. The night before, the Civil Rights Movement had tried to hold a march up in Derry. About four hundred of the marchers had gathered in the street ready for their protest. They had never got the chance to get the march under way. The RUC and the B Specials had blocked both ends of the street and then had proceeded to beat the living daylights out of man, woman and child alike with their batons and clubs.

Several of the marchers had travelled up to Derry from the University. Now they had returned with bandaged heads and a tale to tell. The meeting had been called in a hurry and the large room was more or less full. One by one the marchers had taken the stage and regaled their audience with tales of police brutality and imperialist oppression. The looks of horror and outrage on the faces of the young audience had quite amused Sean. Most of them were Protestants, drawn from quiet suburbs across the Province. For them policemen were friends of their dad's from the golf club. It had come as a terrible shock to watch the TV pictures of their very own police acting just the same as those in South Africa or Mississippi. It was an outrage. Things had to be done. Changes had to be made. This could never be allowed.

Sean had sat alone with a small smile playing on his lips. The TV pictures had shown him nothing that was particularly new. He had grown up in James Street, a small terrace off the Falls Road in the West of the city. The scenes on the telly were the same as those he had witnessed more or less once a month for the whole of his young life. Whenever there was any kind of problem in the Catholic enclaves of West Belfast, the RUC would come pouring in and break as many heads as they could. It was just a bit of a sport to them. Better than rugby.

He hadn't really listened particularly hard to the speeches. After the first one they had all been more or less the same. There was a lot that he would have to look into. He was quite unfamiliar with most of what the fiery young people on the stage were saying. There was all manner of stuff about the force of capitalist imperialism and the old order and how the working classes of the world had to unite. Other stuff was much closer to home. Fairer housing, one man one vote, abolish special powers, disband the B Specials. These were the things that he had grown up with. It was how it had been in West Belfast for as long as anyone could remember and nobody had ever seemed to care much. It seemed strange to him that all these young people from their nice suburbs should have turned out on a wet, windy night to swear their allegiance to the cause of justice. He couldn't help but wonder where they had all been for the last 300 years.

"It's funny isn't it?" She said "All these Prods worrying about votes and housing and us Taigs getting our faces smacked in by the B Specials."

"How do you know I'm a Catholic?"

"I told you before. I know you." Her smile gently mocked him. "I've been watching you for about half an hour. I was sitting over there. I saw that look on your face. They're all so shocked and indignant. They have no idea that none of this is anything new. Silly buggers."

He felt oddly flustered by her. It was as if she were climbing into his head. Words were seldom a problem for Sean. Words had always been his friends. From a young age he had fallen in love with words. Treasured them. Collected them. Relished putting them into the order of his choice. The nuns had seen it in him when he had just turned five. For years a series of teachers had taken joy in the boy who seemed to be able to eat books. He had always treasured the way that he could use words to make himself heard. Words were not like food and jobs and houses with inside toilets. Words were free. The library was filled with a limitless supply. But now the well seemed dry. All those hundreds and thousands of words and he could barely find two to put together.

"I'm sorry. I don't remember meeting. It's all been a bit hectic."

"Oh we haven't met. I never said that we had met. I said that I know you. That's altogether different. It means that I know who you are. I have seen you before. To be honest, I don't even know your name. I'm Mary by the way. Mary Donnelly."

She held out a hand and he took it. It was small and it sent an electric current down his spine.

"Sean. Sean O'Neil. So where have you seen me?"

"At St. Bernadette's."

"What, St. Bernadette's up in Ballymurphy?"

"That's right. I'm a Ballymurphy girl. It was last year, when St. Mary's were playing us at football."

"You like football then?"

"No. I hate it. To be honest I was sneaking a fag around the back when a couple of the girls came to fetch me. They said I had to come and watch the game. They said that St. Mary's had this gorgeous lad playing for them who looked just like George Best. Football sends me to sleep, but Georgie Best; well he's different. He's been all over my bedroom wall for three years now."

George Best? Who on earth was she on about? He racked his brain. He couldn't think of any of the lads in the team who had looked like George Best.

"So did you enjoy the game?"

"No. It was as dull as ditch water."

"And the Best look-alike?"

"Now he was worth watching. All of us agreed. We talked about him for days after. We couldn't agree whether it was his face or his bum that was making us all so frisky."

Now the words had got on a boat and left for America. Gone. Leaving empty windswept hills and abandoned cottages with no slates left on the roof.

"Oh."

She laughed. "Would you look at yourself Sean O'Neil. You're all embarrassed."

"That obvious is it?"

"I'm afraid so. I could cook an egg on that blush of yours."

"So did any of you ever meet up with your Georgie?"

"Not until tonight."

"What, you mean . . . "

" . . . I mean?" The smile was getting wider.

"Well you know, I mean . . . Well, you're saying it was . . . "

"Yes Sean. I'm saying that it was you. It was you that we all thought looked like George Best. It was you that made us go all

28

silly and girly. It was you who we decided had a simply divine bottom. And if you blush any more Sean O'Neil you'll have them all singing the Red Flag before the speeches have finished."

All of the words in the world seemed to have no use to him now. Whichever words he had thought be his were all gone. He felt completely helpless. His tongue was tied into about 43 knots. He tried a smile.

"I . . . well I don't really know what to say."

"Would I be right in thinking that you're not particularly good with the girls Sean?"

"No. Not at all. Well, a bit. It was a boy's school. Well. I suppose you know that. It's just that . . . well, well you're very forward. That's the thing. I suppose."

She laughed and a couple of earnest members of the audience who were clearly hell bent on saving the world looked around rather disapprovingly.

"You have to be a bit forward when you come from a family of nine and you're the youngest. It may have escaped your attention Sean O'Neil, but it is 1968. So when I saw you sitting there all on your own I thought I'd better get over here and grab you before any of these prim and proper Proddy girls get their nicely manicured claws into you."

The speaker was now telling his audience about a march. They were all to march to the City Hall the very next day. They were to march to show the world that the young people of Ulster would not stand for a police state. They were to march to show that the students would stand shoulder to shoulder with the working classes and the oppressed. There were cheers and the banging of feet. A wave of excitement shook through the room.

"What do you make of all this Sean?"

He thought about it for a moment.

"Television. It's all about television. Television has changed everything."

"How do you mean?"

"Well, you and I know that what happened up in Derry yesterday is nothing new. I live on the Falls and you live up in Ballymurphy. We've grown up with it. That is what the RUC and the Specials do. They always have. And if anyone had ever read any of our newspapers they could easily enough have found out. But nobody ever did read any of our papers. And their papers would never print any of it. But now it has all changed because all it takes is one camera crew to put it into living rooms all over the world.

"It is happening all over. We are seeing the things that have always been kept hidden. I dare say our soldiers did exactly the same things in Burma in 1943 as the Americans are doing in Vietnam right now. But it was private then. It was cleaned up and sanitised before anyone got to hear the official version. Not now. We can all see the GI's burning down villages and clouting women and kids the very next day. And we don't like it. We don't like it when we see Russian tanks firing on peaceful marchers in Prague. We don't like it when we see French riot police beating students in Paris. We don't like it when we see the National Guard beating demonstrators in Alabama. People can hide from words. They don't read what they don't really want to know. The television is different. It is there in everybody's front room when they are eating their tea at six o'clock. And if a picture paints a thousand words, a moving picture on a screen paints about a million."

The words had all come back home. They had hidden from him for a while but now they had got back off the boat. And when they had started he had barely been able to stop them.

"Well, well Sean O'Neil. You are a deep one to be sure."

"Not really. I just like to try and look at things. Try and understand. I always have."

"So, will you be going on the march tomorrow?"

"I don't know really. I haven't really thought about it. I can't say that I know much about the Civil Rights Movement. I just came along tonight out of nosiness."

"Well I think you should go. In fact I insist. I think that you should show yourself to be a proper gentleman and escort a wee girl from the Ballymurphy and be there to protect her from all those brutish B Specials and their big sticks."

"Do you know what time it starts?"

"Everyone is gathering at twelve. I suppose the march will get going at one'ish."

He grimaced. "That is a bit of a problem. The trials for the University football are on in the morning. Eleven o'clock. I'm not sure they'll be finished."

"Well of course changing the course of Irish history has to come second to football. I'll tell you what. I'll come down and cheer you on. We'll catch the march up from there. Date?"

"Date."

The sun had come out in sparkling autumn brilliance the next morning. As soon as he had woken up Sean had felt his mood soar. It had seemed as if he had been preparing for university for his whole life. Well, not quite that. It was more that he had been prepared. It had become clear to all around him that he was something special from an early age. He was one of those children who seemed to be able to do everything expected of them without ever having to really try. Things were changing in the Ulster of the 50's and 60's. Although the old Unionist institutions still clung on to their monopoly of power in their statelet, there were some winds of change, which they could do nothing to stop. The massive steps forward taken by successive governments in London after the war meant that for the first time there was opportunity for all in education. The Protestants were able to control jobs and housing and law and order, but higher education was beyond their grasp. If a Catholic got the grades, then the Catholic got a place.

Not many had ever made the short trip across the city from the Falls Road to Queens University. From a very early age Sean's teachers and headmasters and parents had been determined that it should be a trip that he should make. His dad was a teacher himself, whilst his mum had always worked in one of the city's many linen mills. They were both quiet, religious people. Reserved. Polite and well thought of by their neighbours, but never fully a part of life on the street. His dad was never to be seen in the pub on a Saturday night. His mum was never one to learn all the local happenings as she hung the washing out in the back yard. They were insular. A nod. A hello. Nothing more.

Sean had breezed through his school days. Schoolwork was never a chore. He was never bored by it. The teachers loved to teach him. To push him. To widen his mind. He was never allowed out to roam the area with the other boys on the street. Instead he read. Night after night and year after year. If he had been a different boy then he might well have been bullied. He might have been mocked as being a teacher's pet and a swot. But he never was. Everybody liked Sean. He was friendly and easygoing. And of course he could play football like a wizard.

Football had become Sean's social life at an early age. His weekends were always taken up with playing for the school and the boy's club and then, later, the city. There had been a couple of occasions when scouts with hats and cigarettes had called to the house to speak with his parents. They had never made it over the threshold. Professional football played no part in anybody's plans for Sean.

There had been times when the burden of expectation had weighed heavy on him. Sometimes he felt great envy for all the other boys who seemed to have endless hours to mess about and wander the area. But these regrets were never particularly serious. He developed a burning desire to set his horizons wider than the bleak borders where his community met the Protestant heartlands.

He had won a scholarship to study literature. They had all given him the kind of send off that he would have expected if he were heading overseas rather that taking a two-mile bus ride. When he had at last arrived for his first day the whole thing had come as something of a surprise. He had expected that university would be about learning and great libraries and grave professors. Instead it was long hair and hippie clothes and smoky rooms filled with a haze of dope and throbbing music. The place was alive with the electricity of young anger. All of a sudden, having lived out his life amidst a few square miles of downtrodden and besieged streets, he felt a part of something bigger. All over the world students were taking on their elders. The news seemed to carry pictures of demonstrations and riot police and clouds of tear gas almost every night. In some ways he felt utterly daunted. His own life had always been so narrow. So restricted. In other ways he felt almost permanently thrilled.

And now he felt more excited then he could ever remember. The day before he would have put this down to his football trial.

A place in the team meant travelling all over Ireland and even across the water to the mainland. But that was no longer his be all and end all. Instead he could not help but wonder whether or not she had been serious. Would she really turn up? Probably not. Maybe she had just been messing with him.

But she did. He saw her on the far touchline as they took to the field. The coach had split them into two teams in blue and yellow bibs. He took up his place in attack and gave her a wave. She grinned and responded.

A minute into the game he was flat on his back in the wet mud. A centre half in a blue bib with short hair and a big red face was leaning over him. The spittle rained down on Sean's face.

"We don't want any fucking Taigs in this team. Have you got that? Is that clear enough for you? Do I need to spell it out in big letters? No fucking Taigs. So keep out of the way. Keep out of sight. And don't come back again. Clear."

Sean heaved himself to his feet and gave the bigger student a wide smile. "Sorry. The letters are still a bit too small for me. You'll have to try and explain it better later on."

"I'll break your fucking legs you Fenian bastard."

"You'll have to catch me first."

It was a trying first half. The big centre half's love of Catholics was shared by all three of his fellow defenders. Sean seemed to spend a lot of the time on the floor and felt as if he was turning black and blue. However he showed enough when he got the ball to ensure that his own players gave him more of it. At one stage the university captain who was playing for his side came over for a word.

"Sorry about this. Sean isn't it? I'll try and sort it out."

"No don't worry. They'll soon get bored. No problem."

There were only a few minutes to go till half time when Sean scored. The ball was half headed clear from a corner and he met it with a sweet volley. There was an angry scuffle, which the ref. had to break up. At half time both sides drifted to the touchline where the two coaches talked with them. Sean's favourite centre half noticed Mary, who was standing a few yards up the line.

He nudged one of his friends and shouted over to her. "Hey darling. Why don't you give me your phone number?"

She gave him a huge smile. "My word, there's a proposition to make a wee girl go all of a quiver. I'm not quite sure you would want my number though. You see it's a Ballymurphy number. And I'm not sure that you would like Ballymurphy much. I'm afraid that we don't have any caves up in Ballymurphy and I can see you're a man who likes hanging out in caves."

Within seconds veins seemed to grow out of his forehead. "Shut your face you bitch. Fenian whore. Get back to your stinking festering ghetto. Don't you dare come and . . ."

Sean's hand was on his shoulder. He pulled him round and was about to speak. He never got the chance. A haymaker of a right hand landed him flat on his back, and within seconds a brawl erupted among the players. It was short lived and rather half-hearted. The head coach soon restored order and sent the centre half packing. He pulled Sean to his feet and gave him a sturdy pat on the back. "Good lad. No harm done. You're picked for Saturday."

Mary came over whilst Sean was still trying to shake the stars out of his vision. "Thank you kind sir. You leapt to my defence like a true Knight. I'm moved. Truly moved."

Sean rubbed the bruise on his cheek ruefully. "I can see you don't believe much in the idea of keeping a low profile then."

Her face clouded. "No I don't. No way. I won't wear all that Proddy crap. Never have. Why, do you?"

"I don't know. I suppose not. I never take it very seriously to be honest. It's just ignorance. That's all. I've always just ignored it."

"Well you shouldn't." Her face was still stern.

He grinned. "Excuse me, but am I getting a lecture here?"

"Aye, you bloody well are. Now bugger off and get changed or we'll miss the march."

In a way the argument went on for most of the afternoon. Three thousand students of all backgrounds and denominations made their way to the City Hall to protest at the Nazi behaviour of the Derry police. Several speakers condemned the brutality and demanded that the Stormont government make changes. Everybody's role model was Martin Luther King and his American Civil Rights Movement. Non violence had to be the key. As soon as they resorted to violence they would be as bad as the forces of evil that they opposed.

There certainly was no sniff of violence in the centre of Belfast that day. The police were smarting at the wave of condemnation that had poured in from all over the world as millions had watched the pictures from Derry in disgust. The atmosphere on the streets was festive rather than tense as the students cheered and sang.

"How come you're cheering so much? I didn't think that non violence was your thing" Sean had to shout to make himself heard over the noise of the crowd.

"Look. There was nothing that I did this morning that was violent. The man was a caveman and I simply told him the truth about himself. Now what's violent in that?"

He laughed. "What was violent about it was that you knew full well how he would react. You could have just looked coy and said nothing and everybody could have gone about their business. Instead you took him down a peg in front of all his mates and made absolutely sure that things got exciting."

Now she was getting angry. "I heard what he was saying to you. He was just an ignorant brute. The more we allow it, the worse they'll get, whether it's letting them march through our streets with their whistles and drums or just calling us their names. I don't care if things got exciting. I wasn't going to put up with hearing him call you all those things, that's all."

"So you're protective womanly instincts got all aroused."

"Don't you dare get sarcastic Sean O'Neil or you might just get thumped on you're other cheek."

"The thing is Mary, don't you see that by standing up for me all that you achieved was to get me laid out on the floor. If you'd just let me alone I might have got a couple more goals which would have shown him up anyway, and my face would have been intact."

She shook her head in annoyance. "Well I didn't realise that you were going to get involved did I? You make it sound like I wanted to get you thumped. If you had kept your trap shut you would have been fine."

"I never got the chance to open it. One minute I was going to say something, the next minute I was studying the clouds."

She said in a quieter voice. "Actually I am rather glad that you stood up to him, even if you did get thumped for your troubles. I must admit I would have been a bit disappointed if you hadn't."

He wasn't ready to be appeased. "That's not the point Mary. The point is if we forever let ourselves rise to the sectarian bait, then all of this will go on forever. We can march and shout and sing all day, but if in the end all we want to do is get into schoolyard arguments between Protestants and Catholics none of it is worth anything."

"School yard! Did you just say school yard!"

"Yes I did."

She glared at him for a moment. For a sickening moment he felt certain that she was about to storm off. He wished that he had kept quiet. What the hell was wrong with him anyway? She had only been trying to stand up for him. Why had he had to get on his stupid high horse?

At last she said. "Sean O'Neil, I think you better buy me a cup of coffee. I do believe that you have given me a telling off. I'm not ready to accept it just yet, but maybe, just maybe, you might possibly have a point."

October drifted on into November and life became a dream for Sean. The heady air of excitement never seemed to leave the campus. The Civil Rights campaign evolved into the radical Peoples Democracy Movement. There was never anything formal or organised about it. Meetings were regular and anarchic. Committees were elected and everyone had their say. It never took Mary long to get herself onto the platform. She was soon a favourite of the crowd. She was a firebrand speaker. She revelled in her Ballymurphy credibility as she urged her largely middle-class audiences out onto the streets to face down the brutish thugs of the RUC and the B Specials. They loved her because she was the real deal. She wasn't pretending a hard background in a hard place. She had lived it. Come from it. She had authenticity and there were many that wanted a piece of it.

Sean on the other hand tended to sit back and listen. He believed in many of the words but could never quite believe the mouths that they came from. They talked of Martin Luther King and his famous march to Montgomery. But he saw little in the students who packed the smoke-filled rooms to convince him they could ever emulate their black American counterparts. Nobody had ever made any of these people sit at the back of the bus. No

Ku Klux Klan had ever taken away any of their relatives and beat them senseless in a cotton field. They were there for things that were theoretical, not personal. He doubted whether many would have the guts to allow themselves to be beaten to the floor by a line of B Specials in the name of non-violent protest.

In the evenings he attended the meetings and sat back and watched. Whenever he found a spare moment through the day he scoured the library for anything that he could find on previous Civil Rights campaigns. He took in Ghandi and King and Malcolm X. At first he had his doubts. All the speeches said that Ulster was no different from anywhere else. But it was. It was always unlikely that the down trodden masses of the working classes would ever unite together whilst they were so split by their mutual sectarian loathing. That was what his idealistic middle class fellow students could never see. They hadn't grown up with it. They hadn't spent every Monday morning at school listening to tales of weekend scraps with the Prods from three streets away. It all went way beyond class. It probably went way beyond religion; he had certainly never heard any priests willing on their flock to beat up a Prod or two. It was just habit. Pure, ingrained habit.

Amazingly enough, there was evidence that the Civil Rights agitation all over the country were actually beginning to work. The Stormont government had been shocked and upset by the torrent of condemnation that had flowed in from all over the world. Prime Minister O'Neil was unused to this. He was cut from expensive cloth; a landowner with Eton and the Guards tucked under his belt. He was profoundly unused to being branded as a Nazi and it did not sit well. He moved remarkably quickly and it was soon apparent that he was intent on passing many of the reforms demanded by the agitators. It was all very much a case of too little too late. The blood was up right across the Province. The youngsters who had marched and been beaten up were in no mood to doff their caps and be grateful. The cat was too far out of the bag.

One night in November Sean at last made his way onto the platform. By now his hair was growing long and he had traded in his jacket and slacks for jeans and an old American army jacket and jeans. Actually, being up on the stage was an eye-opener. The audience fell unusually quiet. There was something about the tall boy with the dark, curly hair. He stood very still with his hands in his pockets and stared out at them. The girls in the audience nudged each other and giggled. The boys sat back and drew on their cigarettes and waited to hear what he had to say. Nobody would have been able to put a finger on it, but he had something extra. An aura. An electricity. There was no need for him to shout and he didn't. When he started to speak his voice was quiet, but it seemed to carry without effort into all corners of the room.

"I've been coming to the meetings for a while now. It's a good crack. Listen to a few speeches. Cheer a bit. Stamp the feet a bit. Then off to the bar. We all make ourselves feel pretty good. But I keep wondering what we are really doing here? Maybe it's all a bit too comfortable. We claim that we are standing shoulder to shoulder with our working class comrades. Are we? If we were doing that, we wouldn't be holding our meetings here. We would be hiring back rooms in pubs on the Falls or the Shankhill. But that wouldn't be a very good idea now would it? What would happen if we tried it? Well, nobody would come for a start. I know that and you know that. But why? Is it our message? Not really. The IRA is saying much the same thing as us. Some of the trade unionists are saying much the same thing. So why not?

Well I suppose I'd better tell you. I can, you see. I can tell you because I grew up on the Falls. They are my people. I listen to them at weekends when I go for my dinner at my mum and dad's. They don't like the long hair, they don't like the hippie clothes, and they don't like all the dope. They don't think that any of us go to church. They don't think that we have any respect. In fact they don't like us much at all.

Now I know this isn't really what you want to hear. You want me to tell you that the whole of the proletariat of West Belfast are waiting and yearning for us to lead them to the Promised Land. They're not. They don't think enough of us. They see us living the life of Riley and getting stoned out of our heads and screwing like rabbits. We don't know what it's like to hang off the side of a ship for ten hours in the freezing rain in February. We don't know what it's like to have our ears go numb after a shift in a linen mill. In the Russian Revolution they set up roadblocks in Leningrad. They stopped all pedestrians and took a look at their hands. If their hands were hard and calloused from a lifetime of manual work, they were allowed on their way. If their hands were smooth and soft, they put them up against a wall and shot them. Maybe there are two lessons that we should learn from this. One: How many people in this room would have been allowed on their way? Would the boys on the rifles have cared when you told them you were part of the Peoples Democracy movement up at the university? I don't think so. Two: Behaving disgracefully is something that knows no class boundaries. It is not just the ruling class who behave like thugs

So where is all this leading? Well, we should be aware that this little statelet of ours is just like a painful boil. It is full of stinking pus and it hurts like hell. For fifty years it has been growing and growing and getting more ugly. What we are really talking about is taking a needle and bursting this boil. But don't expect what comes pouring out to be pleasant. Don't expect it to be nice. Burst the boil, and we release the poison. I don't suppose Trotsky ever envisaged his working-class heroes executing passing pedestrians because their hands were too soft. But that is what happened. If we burst this boil we should be aware that there will be no quick fix. No cheering and dancing on the streets. No guarantee of a happy ending.

I just thought that maybe you all should be aware of this."

He left the podium and walked back across the hall and sat down next to Mary. At first there was a stunned silence. Then the applause and the cheering started. Mary leaned over and kissed him on the cheek.

"Well, well Sean O'Neil. The dark horse just gets darker and darker."

At the end of the meeting Michael Dennis came and joined them. The Peoples Democracy was determined to do all that it could to avoid having a leader because it didn't seem to be the democratic thing to do. In the absence of having a proper elected leader, Dennis was the next best thing.

He held out his hand and smiled warmly at Sean. "As nice a piece of balloon-popping as I've seen in a long while Sean. Nice to meet you."

That night they talked their way through a jar of coffee. By three, Mary was curled up in an old armchair and dead to the world. Sean and Dennis huddled close to the small electric fire. A big metal ashtray was full to overflowing by the time the grey light of a wet dawn smudged the window.

By then they had come up with a plan. The plan was to be a copy of Martin Luther King's march from Selma to Montgomery. King had chosen to take his people through the vicious gauntlet of the rural strongholds of the Ku Klux Klan. Sean and Michael had chosen their very own gauntlet, a 70-mile march from Belfast to Londonderry through the Loyalist heartlands of Antrim and North Derry. They would be far away from the relative safety of the cities. They knew full well that they were asking for trouble. But they wanted trouble. They wanted to show the working people from both sides of the sectarian divide that they were more than spoilt students full of their own talk. They would light a fire and prove that they could deal with the heat. They just had no idea that the fire would soon spread totally out of control. They had no idea that it would burn for 30 years.

Chapter 3
Tinderbox

January 1969

Sean pulled his jacket closer about him and stamped his feet to try and get some warmth into his boots. He checked his watch. Already well past nine. The group was still rather sparse. They had spent a great deal of time discussing how many they could expect to join the march. In their most optimistic moments the number had exceeded a thousand. More sober moments suggested maybe 400. Moments of doubt warned that there might be fewer than 200. In the cold of New Year's Day morning it was becoming increasingly obvious that they would not even make 50.

Sean checked his watch again and looked about anxiously. Where on earth was Mary? They had both been dreading telling their parents. Their worries had been different. Sean had seen his mum and dad get more and more concerned as his hair had grown and he had taken to going home in the scruffy clothes of the young agitator. His mum had said that he looked like something that the cat had dragged in. His dad was even less amused. He reminded Sean that University was supposed to be a place for study. It was all right for the rich Proddie kids whose parents were lawyers and doctors and farmers. They could afford to make idiots of themselves and dress like tramps and rub the authorities up the wrong way. They could afford it because their careers were all looked after. All it took was a quiet word over a pint after golf on a Saturday afternoon. It was all very different for a boy from the

Falls. Was he stupid? Did he not know that they would already have his name down on a file somewhere? He would already have been noted. If a nice Proddie boy from Ballyclare wanted to make a fool of himself and try to save the world that was fine. Youthful indiscretion. High spirits. Just a phase. When a young Catholic boy from the Falls did exactly the same he would be marked down as potential trouble. A threat. A subversive.

Mary's parents on the other hand had known all about protest from the time they had taken their mother's milk. They had no hang-up with any daughter of theirs shouting whatever she liked from any rooftop she chose to shout from. What they did object to was that she was doing it in the company of toffee-nosed Prods from the suburbs. The whole family had been less than pleased when she had announced that she was going to Queens University. They had thought that she should stick with her own. They had heard all about what went on in the Universities. She would wind up either pregnant or a drug addict or both. They told her in no uncertain terms that if she tried to bring any longhaired Proddie boyfriend's home they would not be made to feel welcome.

When she had landed on the doorstep with Sean one Sunday afternoon in late November their hackles had been set to rise. They calmed a little when they heard that he came from James Street in the Falls. They calmed down even more when he chatted away in a proper West Belfast voice. Her four older brothers thought he was OK. They remembered him from football. Her four older sisters were beside themselves with jealousy. Her dad thought Sean to be a decent enough lad. Her mum thought he looked like a poet. He passed the Donnelly test, even though they all agreed when Sean and Mary had left that he really did need a good haircut.

They had both known that neither set of parents would be at all happy about the march. Sean had endured the worst Christmas that he could ever remember. His father had barely talked to him. As far as he was concerned the boy was throwing his life away. Hardly anyone from the Falls ever got a real chance to pull themselves clear of the grinding poverty and unemployment. He had been given the chance to make the kind of life that most could only ever dream of. Instead he was throwing it all away for a bunch of silly middle-class prats. His dad had put his foot down. Enough was enough. He wasn't going on any stupid march and that was that. His decision was final.

And Sean had told him that he was too old for that kind of talk. He told him that he was his own man now. He told him that he was going with or without his blessing. And something had been broken between them. They hadn't even said goodbye when he had left the house.

At last he saw her. She must have borrowed a thick coat from one of her brothers and it seemed to drown her. She drew looks from pedestrians as she marched along with her big rucksack and black beret. Sean wondered if she had any idea of how comical she looked. Probably not. He grinned as she came up to him breathlessly.

"So you made it then."

"Aye, that I did. Barely." She heaved the rucksack off her back and flexed her shoulders.

"I gather that the Donnelly clan were less than supportive then."

She smiled. "You could say that. It's hard going when they all gang up. Ten to one against are rotten odds. Anyway I've got my orders. If I get beaten, bashed, bottled, arrested or interned that is absolutely fine. If I get pregnant I'm never allowed home again and my brothers will track down the father and cut his balls off. How about you?"

"Horrible. My parents think I'm going down the drain and that I'm letting everyone down who has ever known me. They wouldn't even speak to me when I left this morning."

Mary's smile faded. "That must have been rotten. Are you sure that you want to go through with it? I know how much your mum and dad mean to you."

"I can hardly drop out now. This was all partly my idea. Besides, look at us. There is hardly anyone here. About forty I suppose. We need every pair of legs we can muster. Don't fret about it. They'll come round in time."

Michael Dennis came over and lit up a cigarette. "Not great Sean. Bloody awful in fact. We won't make much of an impact with this many. Jesus, couldn't you just kick those bastards who come to all the meetings and don't show when it comes to the crunch."

Sean's face became bleak. "You're wrong there Michael. This will mean that we will make an even bigger splash. Don't worry about that."

"How do you work that out?"

"There won't be enough of us to stay safe. If we had been 500 they would have had to have raised 1000 to intimidate us. Now that we are only 40, they can get at us with a couple of hundred. What it means Michael is that we are in for a real kicking. With luck the press will witness it every time one of us gets our head split open. They are not interested in our speeches Michael. They want to see our blood. That's what will sell the papers. So worry not. We'll make a big enough splash. Its just going to be painful, that's all."

The march got under way just after ten. Their high spirits barely lasted to the edge of the square. Sean was surprised when he saw that there were Union Jack flags at the front of the procession. He moved forward through the crowd to find that a group of Loyalists had taken over the front of the march. They were being whipped up by Major Ronald Bunting who had been widely quoted in the press as being determined to do all that he could to interfere with the demonstration. Soon they were walking through the streets at the edge of the city centre. Crowds were waiting for them on the pavements. One of the marchers who were holding one of the poles of the big banner was pulled to the floor and kicked. Sean stepped forward to take the pole. Spit was raining down on them now. It seemed as if insults were coming from all directions. He pulled Mary to him.

"Now, now Miss Donnelly. Keep your cool. We've only been going a few hundred yards. Remember all those speeches about non-violence."

She sighed and pulled the huge coat up around her neck. "I know, I know. It just goes against the grain to put up with it. If my brothers were here they wouldn't get away with it."

Sean laughed. "If your brothers were here the march would have been stopped before it had even left the square."

"PAISLEY! PAISLEY! PAISLEY!" The crowds were whipping themselves up now. Groups of kids were leaping in and out of the crowds, kicking out at ankles. Time and again Sean had to hang on grimly to the banner as men attacked him in twos and threes. "Where's your Pope now you Fenian bastard! Want a vote do you! We don't give votes to papist bastards . . .."

Bunting and his supporters at the front of the march slowed down until nobody could proceed at more than a snail's pace. The crowd was pressing in from all sides now. More spitting. Kicks. Hair-pulling. A middle-aged woman lost her footing and was kicked repeatedly before the other marchers managed to pull her back up again. Dennis joined Sean and helped him to hold the banner aloft.

"How far do you reckon we've come Sean?"

"I don't know. About a mile. Looks a long way to Derry."

"Just a bit. Have you been watching the coppers?" The police were out in force. The Chief Constable had announced that the marchers would be escorted all the way to their destination to maintain public order and to ensure their safety. As the crowds on the pavements pressed in on them the policemen stood apart in small groups and shared jokes amongst themselves. They were clearly quite oblivious to the plight of the marchers.

Sean nodded. "It's nice to know that they are here to protect us."

"Aye."

At the edge of the city Bunting gave a signal to his men and they disappeared. Suddenly all was quiet. A watery sun broke out and the small group was all alone on a quiet country road.

"Think that's it then?" Said Michael.

"No chance. He's off to organise whatever he has in mind for later on. We'll be seeing plenty more of Major Bunting, don't you worry about that."

By the late afternoon they had reached the outskirts of Antrim where they were due to spend the night in a hall. Legs were aching and everyone was ready to stop. The mood darkened when they heard the sound of a large drum being beaten around the corner. Soon a crowd came into sight. Bunting was waving his arms vigorously and a middle-aged man with a bald head and an orange sash was beating away furiously on his lambeg drum. The marchers were faced by two roadblocks. At the back on a bridge were Bunting and about 200 followers. In front was a police line.

The marchers wearily came to a halt when they reached the police. Michael and Sean addressed the officer in charge, Chief Inspector Cramsie.

"I can't allow you past I'm afraid. I can not guarantee your safety. You'll have to pack it in. Nobody wants you here. Can't you see? Why not just hop it. You've made your point."

Negotiations got under way. At last Cramsie agreed to escort the marchers through in pairs. When the first pair were halfway through Bunting's men, their police escorts melted away into the crowd and the marchers were beaten. Now the officer withdrew his offer to ensure the marcher's safety.

Dennis and Sean talked with a few of the others. They decided to completely block the road. They sat down all the way across. Suddenly Bunting was rushing forward in a state of great agitation.

"Clear the way! Ambulance! AMBULANCE . . .!"

There was indeed a small ambulance. The crowd surged forward all around it. Suddenly there was chaos. The marchers were engulfed by kicking boots. Mary saw an elderly marcher being kicked repeatedly by a burly policeman. She rushed forward and tried to pull the enraged policeman away. He turned and without hesitation smashed his fist into her face. Sean pulled her clear. Eventually the police decided that enough was enough and separated the milling crowd. Again, Cramsie came forward. "You're inciting a riot. No way you're coming through."

Michael was really losing his cool by now and he squared up to the policeman. Sean eased him to one side.

"Sir, I think that you will find that this is a legally-sanctioned march that has been given permission from Stormont. Surely it is your duty to heed the advice of the government and ensure that the way is clear for us to proceed."

"Don't you dare try and tell me how to do my job you cocky bastard. I have a good mind to take my boys back to the station and leave the lot of you for a bloody good kicking . . ."

The speech was interrupted as a lorry broke through Bunting's lines and bore down on the marchers. They watched it with a sense of disbelief. Everybody assumed that it would stop at the last minute. It didn't. In fact it was only at the last minute that people realised that it was pretty good idea to try and get out of the way.

One man was not quick enough and was knocked flying. Bunting took this as a signal to send his people in for another melee.

Once again the police dragged the crowds apart. The marchers were beginning to look rather forlorn. By now there were several bandaged heads. Fear was creeping through their ranks as darkness closed in and the drum beat louder and louder. Night came and car after car arrived to add to Bunting's forces. Rocks were thrown and bottles. The marchers huddled closer and closer together.

Sean again tackled Cramsie. "It is time for a decision Chief Inspector. Leave it much longer and there will be serious casualties. Now that might just suit you down to the ground, but I doubt whether your superiors will agree. There are at least seven journalists present and you can guess what is going to be all over the front pages tomorrow. Now it might be your ambition to be remembered as the copper who watched defenceless marchers being killed whilst his men stood by and had a good laugh. If so then carry on. If not, I suggest you sort something out and fast."

Cramsie noticed that a photographer was hovering near by and shooting shot after shot of their conversation. He seemed to bridle for a moment then took a deep breath and calmed himself. "OK. I'll arrange for you to be taken to the hall in police vans. It's more than you deserve. I'll remember your face lad. Don't ever try to come back to Antrim. Not if you know what's good for you."

The last of the marchers made it to the hall a little after ten. They were bloodied and exhausted but their mood was defiant. They had been put to the test and they had passed it. The next morning the Irish papers blasted out shared outrage. Cramsie and his men were vilified. Bunting was castigated. Carloads of agitators from all over Ulster pulled up at the hall all through the night. By the time they set out the next morning they were over 100.

The next two days brought more of the same. Repeatedly the local police officers from each district blocked their way and urged them to turn back. It seemed that they spent far more time sitting and waiting than they did marching. Whenever they felt that they had at last found a stretch of open road Bunting would pop back up with his abuse screaming crowds. Progress was painfully slow. On several more occasions they had to be taken around small Loyalist towns in police vans. By the night of

Friday, January 3rd their efforts were being watched and read about far and wide. By now they had reached the small village of Claudy, and Londonderry, their journey's end, lay a mere seven miles down the road.

Their numbers had grown significantly by now. That night the hall was filled by more than 400. Outside Bunting had once again marshalled a crowd. The night was filled with the sound of an angry mob. Michael joined Sean and Mary where they had laid out their sleeping bags in a corner of the village hall.

"I reckon we've nailed it. We're a proper crowd now and the reporters are arriving thick and fast. All of the papers are on our side. The police are getting an absolute panning. They won't dare step out of line tomorrow."

Sean chuckled. "You know Michael, you're such a bloody dreamer. It's quite endearing really. When we get home from this little holiday of ours I suggest that you spend a little less time in the pub and a little more time in the library. There is an awful lot you need to learn about the people out there on the street. They don't care what the papers say or what the chattering classes say or what people in the nice circles in New York say. They couldn't give a shit. All they care about is what their own people say. They don't see us as idealistic young people who are willing to get thumped in order to help to create a better, fairer world. That is how we see ourselves. There are men out there who see us as a Papist army. Seriously! They really believe this stuff. They get told it every Sunday morning in Church. They believe that every minute of every day all that they own and hold dear is under threat from evil plots hatched in Rome.

It doesn't matter what the rest of the world thinks about the methods that they use to stop us. All that matters is that they prove to their own people that they still CAN stop us. Because if they fail, then everything in their world is under threat. Tell me Michael, have you actually considered where we intend to go tomorrow?"

"Course I have. We're going to Derry. We're going to show solidarity with our comrades in the city. There's nothing complicated about that, surely?"

"We're not just going to Derry, Michael. We are going to the Guildhall in Derry. The Guildhall is in the centre of the city. The

Guildhall is INSIDE the walls. INSIDE. That is what is important. These guys are fed stories about the walls of Derry from the cradle. You know, the siege in 1689 when the young apprentice boys heroically slammed the gates in the face of King James and his advancing Catholic army. It's folklore Michael. It is important to them. They always feel threatened. Which is why those walls are so symbolic. If we walk under those walls tomorrow they will see it as the beginning of the end. Now I know that's ridiculous. And you know that's ridiculous. And just about everyone in this hall knows that's ridiculous. But they don't. For them, stopping us is all about defending their way of life. It's about symbolism and long-cherished tales. I know it doesn't fit into any Marxist handbook Michael, but that, my friend, is what this country of ours is all about. And that means that tomorrow we will be in for the fight of our lives no matter how many journalists are there to write it all down."

For a while Michael became withdrawn and subdued. The last three days had taken their toll. He had never anticipated the sheer, mindless hatred of the crowds who had dogged their progress. He had seen too many of his own people battered almost into a pulp. He had really believed that the worst was out of the way. Now Sean had shaken him. He had spent so much of his life digesting the thoughts and dreams of revolutionaries all over the world that he always seemed to forget about Ireland. In fact, he had never really been able to fully understand Ireland. It was a place that defied all the theories. But Sean understood it only too well. He could always see into the red eyes of the beast. And yet he could always smile. Always find the humorous side in the worst of times. Maybe that was because Sean was Irish to his soul. Sometimes Michael barely felt Irish at all.

At last the small camp-lights that lit the hall were extinguished one by one. Sean and Mary pulled themselves into their sleeping bags for the night. He lay there staring up into the old beams of the hall and smoked. He was under no illusions. The next day, one way or the other, was going to be a nightmare. Mary's voice jolted him out of his musings.

"Sean. We've been on the road for three days now. We sleep in cold halls and our clothes don't get the chance to dry out. Now I don't know about you, but my sleeping bag isn't half way up to the job. I would like to remind you that your are supposed to be my boyfriend. Now, I have been waiting patiently for you to zip your sleeping bag up with mine and give me a bit of warmth. Well, it would appear that I am waiting in vain. Now if it is your wretched shyness that is holding you back will you please get over it right now and come here."

Sean laughed. "It's not shyness Mary, it's the part about those brothers of yours cutting my balls off that is bothering me."

"Well if you promise not to tell the Pope, then neither will I." She reached out to his hand in the darkness and closed his fingers around a condom.

Sean was relieved that the hall was dark enough to hide the monumental blush that engulfed his face. "I always did say that you were forward."

"If you don't want a forward girl, then you best look outside of Ballymurphy. Now stop your talk and come here."

They made love until dawn on the hard wooden floor of the hall. Outside the noise of shouts and breaking glass filled the night as the police tried to control the growing mob. The village hall was completely cordoned off and eventually the crowd vented their frustration by looting the small village shops.

Away from the noise and the vandalism, other quieter, more serious men methodically got on with their tasks. Some collected hundreds of milk bottles from the back yard of the local dairy where the final shift had conveniently forgotten to lock the gates. Others took a truck to a local quarry. They filled scores of hessian animal feed sacks with rocks the size of tennis balls. All through the night men carried the bottles and the stones into the small fields that bordered on the main Derry road where it crossed the river Foyle at Burntollet Bridge. By dawn all was ready.

Before the march got under way that morning there were speeches. Eamon McCann in particular put fire into their weary limbs. For a while all seemed well. As ever, the police held them up on the edge of the village and a small group of youths hurled a few obscenities and stones, but it was all rather half-hearted. Eventually they were allowed on their way and their thoughts started to turn to their journey's end that lay a mere six miles down the road.

As they turned a corner and the bridge over the Foyle came into view, Sean started to realise that things were about to change. There were over a hundred police with them by now. Suddenly those at the front speeded up and headed quickly for the bridge. Those behind dropped way back. He could see several men by now on the high ground of the fields that overlooked the road. They were signalling to each other. They were all wearing white armbands. White arm bands. There was something particularly ominous about the armbands. Arm bands meant organisation. Armbands meant planning. Armbands meant nothing good.

Just as he was putting these thoughts together the onslaught started. From nowhere a large crowd had materialised on the ridge. Within seconds the air was filled with rocks and bottles. The marchers pulled their jackets over their heads to try and protect themselves. They tried to huddle together. They tried to get close under the hedges by the roadside. It was futile. All around him Sean saw people going down with shocking injuries. Within seconds the quiet stretch of road had become a swirling chaos. Now there were seemingly hundreds of men with armbands in their midst. Some were simply kicking and punching. Others were armed with clubs and chair legs and lengths of wood with nails driven through. The attackers had worked themselves into a frenzy. They were screaming abuse at the cowering marchers as they hit out.

The march lost all cohesion within seconds. Now there was pure terror. This was way beyond taunting and spitting and the occasional kick and punch. This was killing rage. This was murder in the making.

Sean grabbed Mary by the arm and dragged her through the hedge. He had to get her away. There was nothing he could do back there. The police were obviously in no mood to intervene, but they could only stand back for so long. If he could just get Mary away for long enough it would blow over. There was a field leading down to a stream. All around him marchers were being chased and beaten. He closed his mind to everything. All that mattered was to get Mary away. There was nothing else he could do. She was screaming mad by now. She fought and grappled against his grip on her wrist. Then she was down. A big man in a waxed jacket felled her with a swing of his pickaxe handle. His big red face split into a grin of triumph. More men now. Two more. Now three. All big men of the country. Strong hard hands. Blood lust in their eyes. Sean crouched over Mary and stared back at them.

"Protecting the little Fenian whore are we? We don't allow Fenian whores round here. We know what to do with them. We know how to deal with the little bitches . . ."

Blows came down on him. He covered his face with his arms and closed his eyes. He turned away. He lay spread-eagled over Mary. And still the blows came down. He felt himself shutting down. His mind managed to acknowledge the fact that one of the men had carried a club with three nails hammered through it. That explained it. That explained the blinding pain in his back. Then darkness came.

It was several hours before he came round. He woke to white light and the smell of a hospital. As his eyes focused he found that he was staring into Mary's face. She looked in an appalling state. Her face was still coated in the mud of the field where she had fallen. Her cheeks were scratched raw from his dragging her through the hedge. Both of her eyes had blackened into a remarkable array of blues and purples. Her red hair was stuck up like a haystack from the middle of a bandage that was wrapped about her crown. But she was smiling. What a one hell of a girl he thought. They would have to cut her head off to take the laughter out of her eyes.

"Hi." His mouth felt as if it had been blow torched. His whole body was on fire, especially his back.

"Decided to join the land of the living then have we Mr O'Neil. How very gracious of you."

He waved weakly in the direction of a glass of water that was on the bedside table. She put it to his lips and held it while he drank. "Where are we?"

"Hospital in Derry. We made it in the end. I don't suppose either of us planned on making the last leg of the journey in an ambulance."

"And the others?"

She smiled down at him. "They got there. They bricked them all the way to the river but they made it. They breached the city walls Sean. And all the world was watching."

He lay back and felt a huge sense of contentment. He had always known that the Loyalists would try all they could to stop the march. But he had never guessed that they would ever go to quite the lengths they had tried at Burntollet Bridge. They had stuck their pin right into the middle of the boil and what had come out had been as foul as he had predicted. There was no way that even the most thick skinned of politicians could try and pretend that all was well in the state of Ulster. Not now. Not after Burntollet. Now maybe they could all force some change for the better.

Four months later Davie Stanton sat miserably at the kitchen table at his father's house in Granville Street. The reason for his misery was perfectly simple. The reason was adding fractions. There was something about the process of adding fractions that eluded every effort he made to solve them. He hated them. He hated them with a burning passion. His misery was compounded several times over.

Firstly, his grandfather was sitting at the other side of the table reading the evening paper. On occasions in the past he had managed to persuade his grandfather to let him off his homework before he had finished so that he could go out and have some time to play before tea. There was no chance of that happening on this occasion. Ever since Christmas his parents and grandad had reminded him at least three times a day that his eleven-plus exams were on the horizon. The eleven-plus was far more important than kicking a football about with Derek Shaw and Richard Green. The eleven-plus would go a long way to deciding the course of his life. Now if Derek Shaw and Richard Green's parents didn't care about their future, then that was their problem. What their parents did was their parents' business. He would sit down every night and do his studies. If he finished his work, and the work was of a satisfactory quality, and there was still time, then he could go out and play for a while. But only when it was finished.

He pushed his fists into his forehead and stared at the paper in front of him with all the concentration he could muster. The sickening thing was that there were only three sums to do. A lousy, rotten, stinking three sums and the sun was shining brightly through the kitchen window. There was a little warmth in the sun now and the window was wide open allowing the sounds of the children playing outside to drift in on the breeze. He glanced up at the clock on the wall. His heart sank. It was already nearly six o'clock. No chance of going out now.

There was a tap on the back door and his Grandad looked up from his paper.

"Who's that?"

"It's John Hutchinson. Can I come in Peter? Need a wee word."

"Aye. In you come John." Peter Stanton took off his glasses and folded his paper. Davie had not seen the man who came through the back door before. He was about 40 and wore the boiler suit of one of the welders from Harland and Wolf.

"Here. Grab a seat. This is my grandson, Davie. He's not a happy lad tonight. He wants to go out and play football and I'm making him stay in and do his maths. It's a cruel world when you're young."

The stranger grinned and ruffled Davie's hair. "That's the truth Peter. That's the truth."

Peter looked over to the boy. "Davie, me and John need to have a little talk. You go on up and finish off in your room. We won't be long."

For a moment Davie's hopes had been lifted. For a moment he had thought that his grandad was going to let him off and allow him out. Some chance. He gathered up his book and his pencil and made his way up the stairs.

"You'll have a drink John?" Said Peter.

"Don't mind if I do." Peter got up and poured two measures of scotch. They sat opposite each other across the table and took exploratory sips. "So John. You'll have talked to them about my idea?"

The idea in question had come to Peter Stanton two weeks earlier. For some time he had become increasingly incensed as he watched the government cave in to the demands of the long-haired communists who hid behind the Civil Rights Movement. It was outrageous. There was only one way to deal with these people and that was certainly not giving them everything that they wanted. Instead of firm handling it seemed that the government had gone completely soft. He could see how it had happened. Burntollet Bridge had been a fiasco organised by buffoons. He had no problem with the long haired communists getting a good hiding. That was exactly what they needed. What he had a problem with was the fact that it was all done in public.

Everyone seemed to have forgotten how these things were done. You picked them up, took them to somewhere out of sight, and then you gave them a good hiding. It was called being discreet. He found it difficult to believe that a clown like Bunting could ever have been allowed to make such a fool of himself. It had been a complete disaster. The whole of the world had seemed united in its condemnation of the Loyalists. There had been all kinds of celebrations on the Falls and in the Ardoyne. And all that their toffee-nosed, lily-livered excuse for a Prime Minister could think to do was to give away the crown jewels. Madness. Complete madness. And something had to be done.

Peter had realised very quickly that the answer was extremely simple. Prime Minister O'Neil had to go. They needed someone back in charge with a bit of backbone. One day he had grabbed his stick from the stand from the back door and marched off up to the park at the top of the Shankhill. A few hours later the answer had come to him as he sat on a bench and stared down at the warren of terraced streets below. He had walked straight back down the hill and called into a bar off the Shankill Road. Peter had called John Hutchinson from a pay phone and twenty minutes later he had walked in. Peter bought him a drink and led him to one of the private booths. His plan was simple. They had to raise the stakes. They had to get the public into a panic. They had to create a crisis. And Peter Stanton said that he knew how it could be done. They would stage a mini bombing campaign targeted against the city's electricity and water supplies. The targets were easy. They could find isolated substations up in the hills that they would blow-up to switch off the power. Water was even easier. All they had to do was to blow the pipelines. The key was to make sure that the IRA got the blame for it.

John Hutchinson was senior in the local UVF battalion. He had taken on more and more power ever since Gusty Spence had been sent down three years before. John promised that he would see that the idea was put to those in charge. He said that he knew people in the RUC who would co-operate. They were good men. Men who could be trusted. These men would let it be known that the bombs were down to the IRA. Peter had returned home and waited for news on how his plan had been received.

He looked over the table expectantly. Hutchinson grinned at him. "Well Peter, they've all gone for it. Said it was inspired. Said it was much too clever for me. Asked where I got the idea. I told them it was a little bird I know. We're doing it next week. My unit has got a substation. I just wanted to come and say thanks."

Peter looked at him evenly. "You'll do a bit more than that I think. I want in on this John. I'm not leaving you daft young buggers in charge. You'll find a way to cock it all up no matter how simple it is."

Hutchinson nearly spat out his mouthful of scotch. "Bloody hell, Peter. Don't be so daft. You're pushing 70 for God's sake. You're too old for this kind of thing."

"Don't you dare try and tell me I'm too old John Hutchinson. I intend to get hold of a car and do the driving. If you even think of suggesting that I am too old to drive a car then I'll knock you off that stool. I'll get you there and I'll get you back. It will be done properly. It will be planned and it will be organised. Nobody will be going along with drink on board. Nobody will be losing their nerve. They will do it properly because I will make damn sure that they do it properly. There are too many cowboys out there at the moment. They're all mouth and they can't keep out of the pub. This job needs a bit of experience. A bit of steadiness. And I'm going along. End of discussion."

Hutchinson scraped around his mind for something to say. In the end he could only think of one argument to try and fight his corner with. "But this is a UVF show Peter. I don't think they will want anyone along who hasn't been sworn in."

The old man gave a short, hard laugh. "Well that's fine then John. I joined the UVF in 1912. I don't recall ever resigning. So that's all covered then. I want to see you next Sunday night. I want to see the plan and I want to know who is coming along. Any cowboys get left behind. We work out the route there, the route back and the timing. We go nowhere until we have covered every single eventuality."

John Hutchinson had been desperate to argue but he couldn't think of a thing to say. It was outrageous. How could he take a 60-odd-year-old man along on a mission like this? It was absurd. But as he looked across at the fixed stare of Peter Stanton he realised that this wasn't just any 60-something-year-old man. This was a legend. Peter Stanton VC. So, OK. If he wanted in, then so be it. Maybe he had a point. There was no way he'd get all pissed up and make a bollocks of it. And there was no way that he would lose his bottle. Not Peter Stanton. And so, OK. Why not?

A few days later Davie wondered why his grandfather kept looking at his watch as they ate their tea. When they were about to start their pudding there was a dull thud that seemed very far away. Then all the lights went out. His mum had to dig in the cupboards to find candles. When she got one burning he felt sure that his grandad seemed to be smiling. It was hard to tell in the flickering light. But he seemed to be smiling.

Two weeks later Prime Minister O'Neil announced his resignation. He accepted that the path of reform had been a mistake. It was time for someone else to take on the job.

Outside, Belfast was into the fourth day of an August heat wave. The University was pretty well deserted with the students away for their summer break. The news from Derry had brought an increasing number of the Peoples Democracy people back to the Campus to try and find out more news.

The northern city had exploded two days earlier. Tensions had been steadily building for months ever since the battered and bruised marchers had staggered into the Guildhall Square from Burntollet Bridge. The outbreak of trouble had come as no surprise to anyone. Neither had the timing.

Every August 12th the Protestants staged one of their most treasured rallies. To celebrate the heroic slamming of the city gates in the face of the Catholic armies in 1689, the Derry Apprentice Boys would march noisily around the walls of the city. It was always a time of maximum tension. This year the provocation had been too much.

News from the city was sparse and confusing. What seemed reasonably clear was that the Protestant Apprentice Boys had mockingly tossed pennies down on small groups of their Catholic counterparts standing below the walls in the Bogside estate. The Bogsiders had reacted by pelting the Apprentice Boys with stones and bottles. The police had been deployed to drive the rioting teenagers back into the Bogside and away from the walls. All of this was quite normal. Almost traditional. What happened next was not.

It soon became apparent that the police had bitten off more than they could chew. Instead of dealing with a small riot made up of bored teenagers they were soon at war with the whole of the population of the Bogside and the Creggan. Barricades were erected and a pitched battle raged all through the afternoon and night. To everyone's astonishment it raged through the next day as well. Every police charge was repulsed. Word came down that Eamon McCann was broadcasting constantly on his own rebel radio station. The whole of the population was involved.

To the students who were gathering together it seemed as if this was surely the real thing. It was the beginning of the revolution. It wasn't just a few hundred agitators making a lot of noise and punching above their weight. This was everyone: man, woman and child. It was the whole population bound together to fight the ruling classes.

Michael Dennis came running into the room and all faces turned. "OK. Now listen. I've just come off the phone from Derry. Things are getting pretty hard up there, but they promise that they are not going to weaken. There are police reinforcements pouring in from all over the Province. It also looks like they're about to mobilise the B Specials. They've asked for help. They need demonstrations elsewhere to draw off some of the police. They've already got started in a few places. Now we need to get something going down here . . ."

"Did they ask for that?" Asked Sean

"Sorry? What was that?" Michael was clearly annoyed by the interruption.

"Did they ask us to demonstrate Michael? Was that a clear request?"

"Well, not exactly, but surely you can all see that we cannot sit back and watch the television whilst a revolution breaks out in Derry . . ."

"What did they say Michael. Just tell us."

Dennis blew his cheeks out in exasperation. "Bloody Hell Sean, you're like a dog with a bone. OK. They said we should hang back. They are worried we could spark off sectarian fighting, but . . ."

"Well thank God that someone at least has some sense. Jesus, Michael, they are absolutely right. West Belfast is a different world to Derry. Don't forget I live there. Things are on an absolute knife-edge. It's been like that for over a month. It will only take the slightest provocation to set the whole thing off."

Dennis turned on Sean angrily. "Exactly! Isn't that what we're supposed to be about here! We're a revolutionary vanguard. How would things have been in 1917 if the sailors on the Aurora had held back from firing their guns because they were worried that they might damage some of the statues? Revolutionaries have to seize the moment. It is our duty." He turned to the small audience with eyes blazing. "Come on comrades! This is our time. In future years when the revolution has blown away the ruling classes from our country, children will remember this moment. It's time to act . . ."

"Stop it! For the love of God stop it!" Sean's voice cut him off. The voice was hard edged with authority. "This is no game. This is called playing with fire. You won't start a revolution up there. You will start a pogrom. Unbridled religious hatred. And when it is all over the ruling classes will still be exactly where they are right now and there will be bodies on the ground. This ISN'T a game."

Dennis was steaming mad now. "And was Burntollet a game Sean? Was it just a bit of playground fun with those B Specials in their white arm bands?"

Sean stepped up very close and stared straight into Dennis's eyes. "If you do this Michael, what you will set off will make Burntollet look like a Sunday school outing."

"Nobody ever said that revolution was easy."

Sean took a long breath to try and keep his temper. "I'll say it one last time Michael. People will die. Again. People will die. Do you understand that?"

"Sometimes there must be sacrifice on the road to freedom."

"You bastard. You stupid, stupid bastard."

Sean knew with absolute certainty that he had come to a very important moment in his life. He knew what he had to do. What he should do at this very minute was to hit Michael and beat the living daylights out of him. A display of naked violence would take all passion out of those in the room. They would be frightened and embarrassed. They would not know how to deal with it. They would look at each other furtively and then go home to watch it all on TV. But Michael was his friend. They had fought through their Long March together.

He couldn't do it. His shoulders slumped and he sat down next to Mary. The moment was lost. Michael picked up where he had left off. Ten minutes later they were ready to go. They hastily produced a banner condemning police brutality. As the small group of 30 students filed out of the door Dennis came over to where Sean and Mary sat together.

"Are you coming Sean? We're going to hold a demonstration outside Springfield Road police station."

Sean looked up "Aye, I'll be along. In a while. I'll meet you there."

Michael laid a hand on his friend's shoulder. "Don't worry. It'll be all right. This is the moment. It really is. It will be fine."

Sean didn't look up. He shook his head slowly. "No it won't Michael. No it won't"

Mary was ill at ease and fidgety. "Sean, I don't really understand. I mean, maybe Michael is right. Maybe this is the moment when things will start to turn. Look at what they are doing up in Derry. It isn't just a few agitators. It's everyone. Maybe this is a bit like Russia."

He gave her a gloomy smile. "Everyone has forgotten the maths. Probably because the maths are boring. In Russia about a million members of the ruling class tortured and exploited about a hundred and ninety nine million members of the working classes. Once the revolution was under way these numbers were always going to count. In Derry there are 35,000 Catholics in the Bogside and the Creggan and 15,000 Protestants in the rest of the city. But what about Ulster? Look at the maths. The ruling class is

60

made up of a million Protestants and 55 million Brits who are on their side. The revolution can look to half a million Catholics and a couple of million down south who probably won't have anything to do with it. Can't you see? The numbers don't add up."

"But it isn't all about numbers Sean. We proved that at Burntollet. A few can make all the difference."

"Only if the few are clever. Only if they pick the time and the place. Burntollet worked because we exposed the police with the media watching. Sure, they threw stones and bottles, but it was nothing. Come on Mary, we both of us know that West Belfast is a different world. What happens when it comes to guns? What happens when the shooting war starts? Your Uncle Andy has always been involved. How many guns have the IRA got in town right now?"

"I don't know. Not many. The IRA is just political now. They've been that way for years."

"Exactly. And how many guns have the UVF and The RUC and the B Specials got."

Now she was beginning to realise where he was coming from. "Oh Jesus. Thousands."

"Who is going to protect our people Mary?"

She was quiet now. "What are we going to do Sean?"

"All we can do is to get ourselves up there and do what we can. What else is there?"

It was early evening by the time they turned off the Falls Road onto Springfield Road. The small group of Peoples Democracy demonstrators stood in a gaggle across the street from the police station. They were chanting slogans against police brutality but their voices were half-hearted. Sean could see that they were becoming edgy. Small groups of men were gathering up and down the street. 100 yards away there was a growing crowd of kids. All around were faces that Sean knew from the area. Trouble was only minutes away.

They made their way over to the students. Policemen kept putting their heads around the large doors to the station then ducking back inside. Sean joined Michael. "Time to watch your backs. Things will be going off any minute now."

Dennis was livid. "No they bloody won't. This is a peaceful demonstration. There is no way we will allow things to escalate."

Sean laughed harshly. "Jesus Michael, wake up will you? You won't have any choice. I know these people. They aren't about to listen to any wishy-washy talk about non violence . . ."

He stopped as a glint of light caught his attention from the corner of his eye. A milk bottle seemed to glide gently across the street before exploding in a sheet of flame as it hit the front door of the police station. The two officers who had been keeping station on the pavement beat a hasty retreat and slammed the doors shut.

The petrol bomb acted as a signal. A mob materialised out of nothing. All of a sudden petrol bombs and stones were raining down on the station. Dennis allowed his hands to drop to his sides. All that they had been was touch paper. He looked at the swirling mass of humanity that was now all around him. He saw faces twisted in hate and anger. He wondered what he had done.

The Stanton family were huddled up close to the small black and white TV set. This was the third evening that they had been this way. At first they had waited to see the inevitable shots from Derry of the police smashing through the barricades and chasing the fleeing mobs back into the Bogside. But it hadn't happened. Successive bulletins right through the night showed police lines that were stretched to breaking point. It soon became clear that the police were fighting for their lives. It was no longer a case of them trying to get into the Bogside to round up the hooligans. It was now a battle to keep the enraged residents at bay. It was unbelievable.

As the Battle of the Bogside entered its second day they knew that something big was afoot. This had not happened for 50 years. It was the first time that anyone watching had ever seen the RUC being beaten. Now they were watching as it happened live and in front of their eyes on the TV.

A succession of men knocked on the door and joined them in front of the screen and talked in quiet determined voices. Davie only caught snatches. His Grandad was becoming more and more agitated. At one stage he pointed furiously at the pictures of the riot. They had been joined by John Hutchinson by now.

"Come on will you John. Look at what's happening here. Every time the police try anything they are getting pelted by petrol bombs from those flats. Look. There's another one. How many do you think have been thrown in the last 36 hours. I'll tell you. Hundreds. Maybe even thousands. You don't just happen to have thousands of petrol bombs. They have to be prepared in advance. That means organisation. That means planning. And that means the IRA, probably with massive support from Dublin. This is more than a bit of a riot John. This might just be it. They might be coming."

Two other men came in and the argument became heated. Davie found it all hard to understand. His grandad clearly believed that the Irish government was about to invade. The others were not convinced. They thought that it was just Derry. The Taigs in Derry had always been a handful. Once the B Specials got in there it would all soon be over.

They soon changed their tune when the face of the Irish premier, Jack Lynch, appeared on the screen. His expression was grave and his voice full of threat.

" . . . It is evident that the Stormont Government is no longer in control of the situation. Indeed the present situation is the inevitable outcome of the policies pursued for decades by successive Stormont Governments. It is clear, also, the Irish Government can no longer stand by and see innocent people injured and perhaps worse . . ."

They were all silent for a few moments.

Peter Stanton showed no pleasure in being proved correct. "So John. Do we need it spelling out any more clearly than that?"

"No. I don't suppose that we do. What now?"

"Get as many men together as you can. Tell them to be armed. No guns. Not yet. We will know when the time is right for guns. Just clubs and sticks. We meet outside the church in an hour."

"Then what?" John Hutchinson's face was ashen.

"Then we get ready. We can't do a thing if we are not ready."

"But Peter, we won't be able to fight off the Irish Army with a few sticks and clubs, what if . . ."

Stanton's voice snapped with authority. "Don't think too far ahead. All we need to worry about now is a few thousand

Catholics 500 yards away who have been waiting a very long time indeed for this chance."

"But Peter . . ."

"DON'T 'BUT PETER' ME! What is the matter with you man? We are the UVF. Remember what it stands for. Ulster Volunteer Force. We are here to defend when our people are threatened. Not just to defend so long as the odds are in our favour. We defend no matter what. Now get out of my sight and get the men out on the street."

When Hutchinson had scuttled away Gerald Stanton turned to his father.

"What about the guns, Da? Should we be getting them out?"

The stock of guns that Peter and his father had hidden away under the floorboards after their night trip to Larne in 1914 were all still there. One night every year Peter and his son would unpack them from the cloth that wrapped them. They would take each one apart and grease every inch of it and then pack it away again. The guns were as well oiled and shiny as the day they had rolled out of the factory in Birmingham all those years before. Peter thought carefully. "No. Not yet. I don't think we will need them yet. No point putting them at risk. We may need them badly soon enough."

As the darkness gathered over the city, the mob was becoming bolder. On three occasions the police had tried to make a charge from the main gate to force the crowd back. Each effort had been repelled. The sound of shouting and explosions could now be heard across many streets. Sean and Mary were standing in the doorway of a bookmakers watching events unfurl. They were now just bystanders. The time when either of them had any influence whatsoever over events had long passed. Sean cocked his head to one side as he identified a new sound over the baying of the mob. Engines. Powerful engines. Somewhere close. He stood on his tiptoes and peered over the heads of the crowd.

"Sweet Jesus."

Mary jumped up and down to try and follow his gaze. "What? What's happening?"

"Bloody armoured cars. Three of them."

The ugly grey vehicles ground their way up the Springfield Road with their hatches battened down. One had a loud speaker. "Clear the street. Clear the street now. You will all be arrested if you do not clear the street now! Clear . . ."

The vehicle was engulfed in petrol bombs. The flames seemed to swallow it for a moment before it broke clear. A sharp, quick sound. Bang. Bang. BANG. BANG.

The sound seemed to paralyse the hundreds of bodies that swarmed all over the street. Like a freeze-frame. Like the world had come to a stop. Darkness. Flames. Dust. Smoke. And the sound of shots. An awful realisation. The crowd all seemed to realise it at the very same moment. Then mayhem. People running in all directions. People trampled on the floor. High-pitched screaming. One purpose shared by all. Get out. Get away. Escape. Real bullets. The police threw open the doors and rampaged out howling wildly as they pursued rioters in all directions. They carved through massed bodies with their batons. All was chaos. All terror. Real bullets. Sean and Mary were swept away in the crowds.

A few hundred yards away Peter Stanton cocked his head much as Sean had done. He picked out the sound of the shots. A new sound. A sharper sound over the hum of the distant shouting crowds. But who was shooting? And where were they headed? Surely the Irish army could not have arrived already? No. No chance. Stupid thought. He forced himself to think quickly.

"Now listen. We don't know what's happening but we have to assume the worst. They might be coming this way. We don't know when and we don't know how many. We need to erect barricades. Get hold of cars and vans and furniture. Anything. Block off the streets where they can get in. All of them. Pass the word."

All night they worked. Sometimes the crowds from the Catholic areas swarmed down the streets towards them. Stones were thrown. Bottles were thrown. Petrol bombs were soon arriving at the barricades in growing numbers. Peter kept darting in and out of the house to conduct quick meetings with the men of the area. He swore and he shouted and he put men in their place. He stole snatches of the news, but the news was always unclear. The night was filled with the sound of crowds and fighting in all directions. Nobody had the first idea what was going on. Rumours were flying around thick and fast. The Irish had captured Newry. The centre of Derry was ablaze. An Irish armoured column had been sighted passing Lisburn. Then, as dawn approached, one rumour took over from all the others. The Brits were coming. Stormont had requested help from the British Army. Stormont had admitted that the RUC and the B Specials could not hold the line in Derry. And Westminster had agreed. The soldiers were on their way.

By dawn the streets were quietening down. People were exhausted. Peter made a final tour of the barricades before returning home. Not a single one had been breached. For a while the Shankill had seemed to be under siege, but it had held. Once again the men of Ulster had proved their worth. Nothing had changed. He slept in his clothes for three hours and then was back at the kitchen table.

The word had spread. The legend of Peter Stanton had grown through the noise and the smoke of the night. When all had seemed lost, it had been Peter Stanton who had stood up the tallest. It had been Peter Stanton who had got the men on the streets. It had been Peter Stanton who had organised the barricades.

All that morning the kitchen was filled with smoke and hard talk. They had held the line. The morning news seemed to confirm that the threat from Dublin was hollow, for the foreseeable future at least. But they all knew that they had come close. They had been comfortable and secure for 50 years. Now the fear was back with them.

Peter thought hard about the next step. There was still much wild talk but he felt quite sure that the immediate crisis had passed. If they had been going to come they would have come that first night. And for a while it would have been all too easy for them to have done it. It had been past three in the morning by the time that the barricades had been properly in place. It had been close. Far, far too close.

"We were lucky last night. If they had made their move they would have been all over us. I don't know why they didn't. Maybe they were too busy fighting with the police. We need more time to react. We need more room. Tonight is our chance. Tonight we push them back. Tonight we give ourselves the room."

Davie had one of the best days at school that he could ever remember. At first he had been disappointed when his dad had told him that he would be walking him round to the gates. He had assumed that with everything going on the school would have been closed. No such luck. The people of Ulster would need more than a few bricks and petrol bombs to close a school. He would learn that soon enough. His mum even gave the soft areas behind his ears an extra vigorous scrubbing just to prove that life would go on as normal no matter what. However, once he was through the gates and in the playground he was glad that school was on after all.

Everyone wanted to talk to him. They had all heard. Fantastic stories were floating around about how Peter Stanton had rallied all the men to keep the Taigs out. Was it true that he shot five of them? Was it true that he stood in front of the mob with his old bayonet from the Somme? Davie revelled in it.

The only bad part of the whole of the day was when heard how all of his classmates had been out on the streets the night before helping to build the barricades and fill up the petrol bombs. He was determined that it wouldn't happen again. He arranged to meet his two closest friends, Derek and Richard, in the alley behind his house at nine o'clock. He knew that he would be able to get out of his bedroom window and down the drainpipe. He had to. There was no way that he was going to miss out again.

Sean and Mary had made their way down the Falls to his parents' house. It had been a tense time. There were heated words between Sean and his father who had been convinced that his son had been in the thick of the crowd attacking the police station. Sean had shouted. His father had shouted. In the end his mother calmed them down and each fell into a moody silence. Mary took Sean's bed whilst he slept on the couch. In the morning they tried to find out any news that they could. The battle in Derry had raged on for a third night. The newsreaders seemed more and more convinced that the British army would be called on before the day was out. The whole of West Belfast had been engulfed in the rioting. Anger built up around the streets when the news spread from doorstep to doorstep that a young boy had been killed by a stray bullet from one of the armoured cars as he slept in his bed.

There were still lots of groups of men out and about on the streets, but things were marginally calmer. By mid afternoon the news was breaking that London had acceded to Stormont's request for troops. Small numbers had appeared on the Falls Road and by and large people were happy to see them. After the armoured cars had opened fire the night before many had been terrified that the RUC and the B Specials would really lose control.

Mary left after lunch and headed up the road to her family in Ballymurphy. Sean and his Mum walked over to Bombay Street to try and persuade his Gran to come and stay with them. His mum had been on the phone constantly, but all her efforts at persuasion came to nothing. She was hoping that Sean could act as something of a trump card. His Gran had doted on him all his life. If he couldn't prize her out of her small terrace then nobody could. The scene on Bombay Street was very threatening. It was one of the many terraced streets than ran right across the invisible line that separated the Catholic Falls district from the Protestant Shankhill. About a third of the houses at one end of the street flew the Union Jack in July. The remainder of the houses sported the Irish tricolour. The night before, the UVF had overseen the construction of a barricade across the road that started level with the last of the unionist houses.

There was still quite a crowd manning the roughly constructed wall of up- turned cars and assorted furniture. They were shouting abuse and insults at the small groups of young Catholics who were clustered at the Falls end of the street. A few stones were being tossed in either direction and, on one occasion, a bottle. The air seemed thick with tension. By the time that darkness fell Sean knew that the crowds on both sides of the divide would have grown considerably. He couldn't for the life of him work out why on earth the British soldiers were deploying on the Falls Road and not in the streets where the communities faced each other over the barricades.

His Gran was not amused at all. "I stayed here right the way through everything that Hitler and his bombers could throw at us.

Why on earth should I get moved out now because of a few hooligans that are all the worse for wear with drink."

She put up a valiant effort, but in the end Sean's charm prevailed and they got her back across the Falls Road to James Street. Sean felt totally helpless. He couldn't settle. He had to do something. But what? He considered going back down to the university and meeting up with the others who would no doubt be following events. But what on earth good would that do? Things had moved way beyond the banner and protest stage. He wondered whether he should take a walk up to Mary's house, but again, he could find no decent reason why. He paced up and down the front room smoking furiously. Outside the light was fading and already the sound of distant battles was hanging in the air. He found it hard to escape a sense of responsibility for what was happening. Maybe it was all their fault. They had all felt so pleased with themselves when they had taken their beating at Burntollet and battled through to Derry. They had felt that their efforts might open up the way for Ulster to become a better place.

Instead it seemed that they had achieved the complete opposite. They had pulled the cork from the bottle and now the sectarian poison was pouring out in a gush. In the end he could stand it no more. He couldn't just wait around in the house. He had to go and at least try to do something. The greatest noise seemed to be coming from the area around Bombay Street. There was a weird glow in the sky. He wondered for a moment what on earth it could be. Then with a shock he realised that it was the light thrown up from fires. Big fires.

Peter Stanton addressed a group of 40 men who had gathered behind the barricade in Bombay Street. All around was the sound of shouting and broken glass and the crump of petrol bombs. There seemed to be hundreds of teenagers either end of the street hurling stones at each other. But the group that Peter addressed were older men, mainly in their 30's and 40's. They all leaned close in a tight semicircle to hear him.

"We are going to push them back. We will not be safe when they are this close. This is the time. If we don't do it now we might not get the chance again. We'll burn them out. We go in hard. We stick together. Stick as a group. Start at the end of the street and knock the doors in. Now let's be very clear. We check every house to make sure it is empty. We are not here to burn people to death. When each house in checked, we torch it. Start upstairs with the petrol and work your way down. Then set the fire. We don't do it in a hurry. We don't get over excited. We stay methodical. Disciplined. What we do here in Bombay Street will send out a message. This will be the first. The rest will follow. By the morning we will have pushed them back. Any questions?"

There were none.

"Good. For God and Ulster."

They all shouted out the oath.

Davie's hands slipped when he was still six feet off the floor. He crashed off the drainpipe and landed flat on his back. He managed to screw his eyes shut and swallow back a yelp of pain. He lay absolutely still and waited for the back door to swing open at any moment. He mentally counted off the seconds. The door remained closed. He pulled himself painfully to his feet and tiptoed to the back gate and slipped away.

They were waiting for him. "We were about to give you up. Come on. Let's go to Bombay Street. That's where everything is happening."

The boys turned the corner just as the men of the Shankill surged across the barricade with a mighty roar. The Catholics responded with a hail of stones and petrol bombs. For a few moments they just stood there in open-mouthed wonder. In front of them the street was one huge brawl. Davie was the first to snap out of it.

"Come on lads, let's help."

They ran forward past the barricade and started picking up stones and hurling them forward with all their might.

Sean turned the corner at the other end of Bombay Street at the very minute that Davie and his friends did the same thing. The sight that greeted him took his breath away. It seemed as if hundreds of men were stampeding down the street towards him. Their charge was stopped as they ran into a barrage of stones and bottles. The Catholics were clearly outnumbered. Badly outnumbered. They were falling back steadily. Sean saw that groups of men were smashing through the doors of houses with axes. What the hell? Then he saw a family thrown out into the street and kicked and beaten as they fled towards where he was standing. What was going on? The question was answered soon enough. There was the sound of a crash and flames started to leap out of the windows of the nearest house to the barricade. Then the next. He could not comprehend what his eyes were telling him. It couldn't be. They were systematically burning the Catholic houses. Madness. Sheer madness.

The sight of the flames enraged the Catholics and they surged forward. Sean was enraged. His temper was boiling over. It was his Gran's street. This was where he had come to tea when he was only five and his Grandfather had still been alive. This was where his mum had been born. And now the bastards were burning down the houses one by one. The rage had a full hold of him. He was screaming at the top of his voice and charging forward. Somewhere along the way he must have picked up a stick. He couldn't remember doing it at all. He bore down on two men who were attacking one of the doors with an axe. He never hesitated. He smashed the stick down onto a skull. He didn't bother looking what had happened. He raised the stick to hit the second man. The man half turned and his eyes widened in fear. As Sean slammed the stick down he dodged away and disappeared into the crowd. Bastards. Lousy stinking Proddy bastards. The men of the Shankill were falling back now. The ferocity of the counter attack had taken them by surprise. Sean looked for someone else to hit. Anyone. Young or old. He didn't care. Just as long as he could hit someone.

His frantic search for his next target was interrupted by a terrific bang on his forehead. For a moment he was completely stunned. His vision went into a blur and he struggled momentarily to stay on his feet. He put his hand to his head and felt the stickiness of blood. He looked down stupidly and saw a half brick on the floor at his feet. His thoughts were hopelessly sluggish. It took a few seconds for his eyes to focus. When they did, he found himself staring straight into another set of eyes.

Young eyes. Young face. Just a boy. How old? Ten. Eleven maybe. His mind was speeding up again. It had been him. The little bastard! Ten years old and the little bastard had hit him on the head with a half-brick. He started towards the boy who turned to run. As the boy turned, a stone stuck him a glancing blow to the head and he stumbled. A screaming, fleeing man with wild eyes and blood all over his face careered into Sean and knocked him off balance.

He righted himself and looked for the boy. He spotted him. He was still down and his face was screwed up with pain. Blood was running down his cheek. It seemed as if every person on the street had blood all over their face. The anger drained out of Sean as quickly as it had infused him. He started towards the boy.

This time he was blocked by a sheet of flame that seemed to have come form nowhere. He staggered back as it seared his eyebrows and singed his hair. Petrol bomb. His brain seemed to say it slowly. It was if it was talking to an idiot. He was finding it hard to think now. His head was throbbing. His eyes ached. So hard to keep a train of thought. The boy! That was it. That was what he had been doing. The boy. The boy was down. The boy needed help. Where was he? There. Still down. What now? Something different. Something worse. Much worse. Sweet Jesus. The petrol bomb must have landed right next to him. On fire. His arm was on fire.

Adrenalin exploded through his body. He threw himself forward and landed on the boy. The boy screamed. He rolled on the boy's arm until he was certain that the flames were all gone. He sat up and took the arm. The hand was a little burned. Otherwise, no damage. Just a charred sleeve.

He looked about. He had to get the boy away, but where? The boy probably lived on the Shankill somewhere. He didn't fancy that much. Not right at the moment. Besides the boy was clearly in shock. Probably wouldn't get much sense out of him for a while. Best take him back to the house. Get mum to patch him up. Give him a cup of tea and let him calm down a bit. Then get him home. Good plan. Good enough.

He heaved himself up and tossed the boy onto his shoulder fireman style. The walk back up Bombay Street was like a kind of burning nightmare. Bodies flailed all about him. Stones rained down. The heat from the fires burned into his face. As he reached the corner he took a last look back. It was a scene that burned itself into his memory. It seemed as if the whole of the street was ablaze. Huge flames climbed out of the rooftops and into the night.

100 yards down the Falls Road he came across a small group of soldiers looking nervous and ill at ease. When he saw the boy on Sean's shoulder, the officer in charge came over to him. His accent was pure public school.

"Are you OK there sir? Can we help? I'm Lieutenant Richards"

How bizarre. How utterly, completely bizarre. Here in the middle of Belfast and half the world on fire and the bloody Brit sounded like he was at a garden party drinking Pimms No 1.

"Aye. You can. Could one of your lads take the boy. Just around the corner. James Street. Number twelve. My mum will patch him up. Don't know if I can manage him much further."

The officer nodded decisively. He seemed relieved to be able to do something constructive in the midst of all the mayhem around him.

"Yes of course. Sergeant, take two men and help this gentleman. Sir, that head wound looks petty bad. Best get it seen to straight away."

Sean struggled to keep the young English face in focus. The blood was in both of his eyes. "Thank you. Just one thing. Maybe you should go into Bombay Street. It's on fire you know. They are burning it to the ground."

Richards looked embarrassed. "Yes I know. There have been reports. I'm afraid there is nothing that we can do. Our orders are specific. We have to maintain station on the Falls Road. I'm so sorry."

Sean looked at him a moment longer and for a moment the anger started to rise up again. Then it fell back, exhausted. Not his fault. He seemed decent enough in fact. Not his bloody country. Must wonder what the hell it was all about. He nodded.

"Orders. There's always orders. Always bloody orders whilst people get killed. Thanks for the help. I appreciate it."

Gerald Stanton was felled by a stone a little after three in the morning. Both sides had more or less fought themselves to a standstill. Peter took the weight of his son on his shoulder and they staggered back to Granville Street. As soon as they fell into the kitchen the women gave them the news. Davie was gone. He must have climbed out of the window. Nobody had seen him. Had they seen him? What could have happened? He would be all right, wouldn't he? Peter went straight back out and asked everyone he could find. One or two had seen Davie. He had been up by the barricade. He had been giving it everything. Good lad that young Davie. Brave as a lion. Chip off the old block. A credit. But nobody had seen him. His two friends were almost too scared to speak to Peter. He calmed them down and got the truth. They had all been to Bombay Street. They had all fought against the Taigs. But they had got separated from Davie when the Taigs had surged forward when the houses started to blaze. They hadn't seen him after that. They thought that he must have gone home.

Dawn was starting to break when Peter returned to the house in Granville Street. They all looked up expectantly from the kitchen table. All that he could do was to shake his head. He suddenly felt old. Very old.

Davie's eyes nearly popped out of his head when he saw the photo of the Pope over the fireplace. They were Catholics! He was on the Catholic side. What were they going to do with him? He felt almost paralysed with fear. Sean noticed and squatted down to make eye contact.

"Now calm down lad. We're not going to bite. We're just going to get you patched up a bit and I'll take you home. I'm Sean by the way. What's your name?"

"I'm Davie. Davie Stanton." His voice was very small.

Sean looked down at his hand. The burns were red and angry. It must be hurting like hell. "OK. Sit yourself down and my mum will see to that hand. You certainly must be a brave little bugger. Not a tear. I'll be sure to let your Da know."

His Gran took on the task of dealing with his head wound. She said that there wasn't much that she could do. Stitches it would be needing. He said it would have to wait until later. He had to get the boy home first. He said that the boy's Ma and Da would be worried to death. When she had finished wrapping his head in bandages she asked him the question.

"They're saying that Bombay Street is all burned down."

"Aye Gran, so it is."

"They're saying that there isn't a house left."

"No. I doubt if there is."

She shook her head. "It's a sad time our Sean. A sad time."

"Aye Gran. A sad time."

The sun was up and the streets were quiet when he found the officer and his men at the same place on the Falls Road.

"Ah. Well, hello again. Head OK is it?"

"I'll live."

Lieutenant Richards squatted down in from of the boy. "And you, young man. All ship shape and back in working order are we?"

Davie nodded wide-eyed.

"Well I'm glad that we were able to be of service. Wish we could have done more. Bloody orders."

Sean decided it was worth asking. "Actually there is one more thing I would like to ask."

"Fire away. If we can, we will."

"I need to get the boy home. He lives on Granville Street. It's not far. Just a few hundred yards. The thing is, well, it's on the other side. You never know. Someone might recognise me. They might remember me from football. Could be a problem. Maybe a couple of your lads could walk with me."

The officer looked astounded. It was all just so absurd. This was the United Kingdom and a man had to fear for his life for taking a child home a few hundred yards. Outrageous.

"Of course. I'll come myself. Not a problem"

All faces looked up eagerly at the sound of the knock at the back door. As soon as Davie walked in he was engulfed in hugs. After the hugs the telling off would soon follow. Sean stood rather awkwardly on the threshold. Outside, Richards and two of his men kept a careful watch on the alley.

Peter rose to his feet.

"We owe you thanks. Where did you find him?"

"He fell on Bombay Street. A stone got him on his head. Then a petrol bomb set his sleeve on fire. I got it out pretty quick. His hand is pretty sore. Maybe you should get the doctor to take a look. I'm pretty sure it will patch up OK."

Peter saw that blood was running down from under the bandages swathed around Sean's head. "Your head. It looks bad. Shall we look at it?"

"No. It's OK. I'll make my way to the hospital. It needs a few stitches."

"What happened?"

"Some little soldier threw half a brick in my face. This little soldier here in fact. Quiet, the young warrior is young Davie. You must be proud of him."

"Aye we are. But he'll pay a price for climbing out of his window."

"Don't be too hard on him. We were all daft at that age."

Peter smiled. "That's a fact. Will you have a cup of tea with us, sorry, I didn't get your name."

"Sean. Sean O'Neil. Thanks, but I better not. My chaperones are waiting." He nodded to the officer who was waiting outside

"And where will they be escorting you to then Sean?"

"Back home. Not far. Just back to James Street."

They stared at each other for a long moment. Peter broke the silence.

"James Street you say. Just off the Falls Road, am I right?"

"Aye, you're right enough."

Stanton nodded slowly. "Then it would seem that I owe you even more thanks than I first thought. You're quite a man Sean O'Neil."

"Not really. Just an Irishman who wishes things could be different."

He went over to where Davie was sitting with his mother and held out his hand. "So young Davie, this is where we go our separate ways. It's been a pleasure knowing you."

Davie took his hand and shook nervously. "Thanks Sean. Sorry about your head."

"Ah, no need. I think it would be fair to say you might just have knocked a bit of sense into me. Now you behave yourself. No more sliding down drain pipes. I'll see you around."

He shook hands with Peter and John and left.

Later that afternoon Richards and his men were ordered into the Shankill to ensure that no crowds were allowed to gather. There were more soldiers out now and the army was slowly beginning to find its feet. As the day had worn on he had been astonished by the hospitality shown to himself and his men on the Falls Road. He had expected hostility and resentment after their lack of action the night before. Instead it became clear that the people of the Falls saw them as saviours. They had taken cup after cup of tea, and the local fish and chip shop had given them a blank slate.

The people of the Shankill were more wary. They were not happy to find the Brits on their streets. What were they doing here anyway? It was the Taigs who were the problem. The Taigs and the IRA. Hadn't anyone told the army that this was Loyalist territory? This was where people hung the Queen's picture in the front room. They didn't need soldiers pointing guns at them

On Granville Street, Eric Fletcher came out to them. He asked if they wanted a drink of tea, and the sergeant said he didn't want to take tea with the likes of him. He said he didn't want any tea from the kind of people who had burned down Bombay Street. He said he didn't want tea from the kind of people who tried to burn women and children in their beds. And Eric had got mad and started shouting. They had no call coming and throwing their weight about in Granville Street. Granville Street was loyal. Granville Street supported the Queen. What about those Taigs? What about the IRA? They were the ones who the soldiers should be digging out. They were the ones who had caused it all. Doors had started to open and a crowd started to form. Loud accusing voices. Richards talked urgently on the radio. A stone was thrown and the soldiers levelled their guns.

Richards shouted firmly. "Enough. I want all of you back in your houses right now. Now move it . . ."

His voice was drowned out by the shouting. The crowd moved forward. A soldier stepped forward and pushed a man away with the butt of his rifle. Anger was growing now. Richards tried to make himself heard.

"Now this is the last time that I will ask. I want all of you . . ."

The crowd fell suddenly silent. Richards stooped in mid-sentence. The soldiers stared on in amazement. Peter Stanton marched slowly up to the English officer and saluted. Richards eyed the row of medals pinned to the old man's jacket. The Victoria Cross stood alone and above the rest. The sergeant saw it and whistled.

Peter Stanton didn't have to raise his voice. "I don't think that you need to concern yourself here sir. This is a loyal street. As loyal as they come. We don't break the law here. Now we'll all go back inside now. No need for any fuss. Good day to you."

The crowd melted away in silence. Richards stood and watched. What kind of a mad, crazy place had they sent him to?

"See that sir." Said the sergeant. "Bloody Victoria Cross that was. Bloody Victoria Cross."

"Oh yes, sergeant. I saw it alright."

Chapter 4
Weddings and Wakes

Easter 1970

Sean tried hard to raise his spirits as the bus worked its way slowly up from the Falls to Ballymurphy. It seemed strange when he looked back at his euphoric early days at the University. For a few short months they really had felt that they had the chance to change their little world for the better. In hindsight it all seemed so naïve.

Watching Bombay Street burn had only strengthened his own determination to become more and more active in the whole Civil Rights movement. Up till then he had never really been fully engaged. Deep inside he had always suspected that it was little more than an exciting sport for spoilt middle class students. Once the killing started and attitudes hardened he saw that it was the only hope. If the movement was seen to fail then it would be all too easy for the men of violence on all sides to have their way.

The British army was now well established in the city, and by and large they had been well accepted. There was a general feeling amongst his parents' neighbours that hundreds more families may have been burnt out if the soldiers had not arrived. However all that they had done was stabilise the situation. The August riots had been a total disaster for the IRA. The local population had been disgusted at their lack of ability to take up their traditional role as defenders of the community. It was clearly obvious to all in Republican West Belfast that the reason they were still in their homes was down to the British Army and not their traditional defenders.

It was a situation that was intolerable to the leaders of the IRA. The traditionalists had by now wrested control of the organisation from the Marxists who had run things through the Sixties. They were hell bent on taking every opportunity to stir up trouble with the British. This had made things a nightmare for the Civil Rights Movement. Increasingly they had found it impossible to stage peaceful rallies. Every attempt at protest was hijacked by the newly named Provisionals. Rallies were turned into riots with tiresome regularity.

The whole thing was beginning to wear Sean down. It had got to the stage where it was more or less impossible to persuade any moderate supporters to attend rallies and marches. Things always ended in trouble and fighting. He had tried meeting the new young commanders of the Provisional IRA and reasoning with them. They had been polite enough, sympathetic enough, even understanding. But in the end they had refused to help. They were in the business of kicking the Brits out of Ireland. That was the only objective that mattered. When the Brits were gone once and for all, then they would look at social reform. Until that goal was achieved the gloves were off. Sean had known that it was pointless to argue. Control of the IRA was back in the hands of men whose families had been fighting the British for generations.

They had been reared on tales of fathers and grandfathers and great grandfathers who had been beaten, and imprisoned and interned. He had grown up with many of these men. He knew all about their tunnel vision.

Things with Mary had been getting increasingly strained. In the wake of the August troubles literally thousands of Catholic families had been driven from their homes. Many had fled south over the border. Others had packed up what belongings they had left and had headed for the Republican heartlands. Hundreds had landed in Ballymurphy, and the local community had been stretched to breaking point trying to accommodate them. An emergency centre had been set up in St. Bernadette's school and Mary had thrown herself into the relief effort. She had attended her classes less and less and the patience of the university authorities was wearing thinner by the day.

As the months had worn on they had started to argue more and more about politics. The Donnelly family prided itself on its Republican traditions. Mary's dad, Frankie Donnelly, had been sentenced to five years in Crumlin Road jail in 1942 for his involvement in a shoot out with the RUC. Inside he had become great friends with Gerry Adams who had been one of his young comrades in D Company of the IRA's Lower Falls Battalion. They had drifted away from the organisation in the fifties and sixties, as the Dublin leadership had become increasingly Marxist. Both men considered themselves as old style Irish freedom fighters. The country came first, the Pope came second, and political niceties came a distant third. When the new generation of Belfast hard men walked away from the Dublin leadership to form the Provisionals, both men were soon back in the fold. They had moved their families onto the new estate at Ballymurphy in the fifties, and as the tension grew through the early months of 1970, they had a powerful influence over the youngsters of the estate. All four of Mary's brothers had followed the family tradition and become active IRA volunteers. For a while Mary had stuck to her Civil Rights guns and had suffered many a family row. Sean had been at the house on two or three occasions when voices were raised and tempers became frayed.

He had tried to help Mary to fight her corner, but it hadn't been to much avail. The men of the Donnelly clan were in no mood for a nice debate on the benefits of non-violent agitation for reform. They were only interested in guns. They were ready to shoot the Brits back across the water. It soon became apparent that Mary's heart wasn't really in the Civil Rights cause. With each day that she helped the shell shocked, evicted families her attitudes hardened. She stopped attending rallies and Sean stopped trying to persuade her to come along. Mary was slowly being sucked back to her roots. He knew that it would only be a matter of time before she gave up on her studies. The Donnelly clan was closing ranks and preparing for war. When the real shooting started, Sean knew with a weary certainty that Mary would man the barricades along with her father and her brothers.

Sean had been amazed to discover that Gerry Adams' son was by this time considered to be a rising star within the movement. Gerry Adams junior had been at St. Mary's with Sean and he remembered him as a particularly non-descript sort of a boy. Adams had seldom ever said a word in class and had always kept himself to himself. Sean could never remember him throwing his weight around in the playground. He had spotted Adams Jnr a couple of times at the Peoples Democracy rallies where once again he had sat back quietly and watched. His true role had slowly become clear. More often than not it was Adams who provided stewards for the marches. These stewards clearly had little wish to fulfil a peacekeeping role. As soon as any kind of trouble kicked off they would be right there in the thick of it, fanning the flames, throwing the bottles, putting the boot in. Sean had had a couple of heated run-ins over this. No matter how he shouted and demanded changes, he never got a rise out of the quiet lad from Ballymurphy. Adams would merely stare at him evenly from behind his thick black glasses and apologise politely. He could understand Sean perfectly, but there was nothing that he could do. He was, after all, only following his instructions. And his instructions were always very clear. People's Democracy had served a useful purpose. They had lit the kindling. Now that the fire was burning it was time to pass the running of the war over to the Provos. Under the quiet exterior there was always an intensity about Adams Jnr. In the end Sean had simply given up having the arguments.

As the bus trundled along Sean vowed to himself that for once he wouldn't allow politics to spoil things. It was a big day for the Donnelly clan. Mary's eldest brother Kevin was getting married to Sally McConnell. The McConnells were another Republican family of long and proud tradition. They even boasted a relative who had been inside the Post Office in Dublin in 1916. The wedding ceremony promised to be a great affair. Sean was determined to keep his head down and his mouth shut. Today was a day to have a few drinks and enjoy life for once.

As the bus turned into Ballymurphy his hopes of doing this sank down a few notches. There had been major trouble the night before. The Orange Order from the neighbouring Protestant New Barnsley Estate had staged a march the day before. The British soldiers had only allowed it on the strict promise that no provocative tunes would be played. In the morning the Protestants had set out for their traditional Easter away day to the coast in high spirits, but they had stuck to the spirit of the agreement. When they returned in the early evening they were considerably the worse for wear after a long afternoon in the pubs in Bangor. Their vocal chords were well and truly loosened and the drums beat and the flutes played. All agreements were soon forgotten as they strutted along the Springfield Road taunting the crowds that had made their way out from Ballymurphy.

The two groups were separated by a hopelessly thin line of 70 British soldiers who were totally helpless once the bottles began to fly. It had been just the chance that Gerry Adams and Frankie Donnelly and many of the other Provisionals had been waiting for. At last battle was properly joined. Now they were able to get the youngsters to throw their bottles and stones and petrol bombs at British Soldiers. It was how things were meant to be.

As the news had come in through the evening Sean had felt his weariness grow. In the time that he had spent up on the estate helping Mary with the refugees, he had met several times with Major Hancock, the Light Infantry officer in charge. He had found Hancock to be both charming and humane, and he had been impressed with his efforts to try and maintain the uneasy peace between the Catholics on Ballymurphy and their protestant enemies in New Barnsley. There had been a great deal of grumbling over the Donnelly kitchen table about the interfering Brit bastard, whose biggest crime was his popularity. It seemed like all of Hancock's efforts had come to nought the night before, as finally the bricks had started to land on top of the soldiers rather than flying over their heads.

It was eminently clear to Sean that the British Army had been less than amused by the evening's activities. He got off the bus and made his way across to Hancock's makeshift command centre. There seemed to be soldiers everywhere. Certainly many, many more than had been usual. Hancock looked drawn and depressed. He gave Sean a small nod and walked over to join him.

"Mug of tea Sean?"

"Aye. Thanks. I will."

Sean nodded to another platoon of troops who were jumping down from the back of a truck. "Re-enforcements?"

"I'm afraid so. Not my idea. The Scottish colonel was not amused that his decision to allow the march back-fired on him. He's worried about losing face. Somehow he's persuaded the powers that be that we need to be seen to impose ourselves. Apparently it is time that the residents of Ballymurphy are made to realise who is in charge here."

Sean groaned. "Jesus. That's exactly what they've been waiting for."

Hancock's smile was rueful. "Well I know that, and you know that, but we aren't the sort of chaps that anyone is very much interested in listening to at the moment. Sadly there are too many who are itching for a fight. On both sides. And as usual it looks like they will get their way."

"Is there nothing that you can do?"

The officer shook his head. "Tried the lot I'm afraid. I've made my views as clear as I can to Brigade. I've met with Adams and Donnelly. I've talked to Father Cleary. No use. Both sides want to have a fight and nobody wants to listen. Sorry Sean."

"No need Major. You're a good man. I know that well enough. I'll see if there is anything that I can do. I'll have a word, but don't hold your breath."

Sean made his way up into the estate. All around the residents were preparing themselves for battle. Men were covering their front windows with plywood sheets. Children were gathering rocks and stones into piles ready for throwing later on. Sean knew well enough that in several kitchens the petrol bombs would be getting prepared. It all seemed to him the height of madness. The community had come together with a single purpose. Man and wife, brother and sister, young and old. All of them working away together. Getting ready for a big special day. But this was no street party with home-made cakes and bunting and jugs of lemonade. This was the people of Ballymurphy preparing to do battle with a battalion of professional Scottish soldiers who were rearing to have a go at the Paddies.

By the time that he marched up the path to Mary's front door he was in a fuming temper. There was quite a crowd in the back kitchen. Mary's mum had obviously been crying. She was pouring hot water into the teapot mechanically. She gave Sean a miserable smile as he walked in. A quick glance told him the reason for the tears. Kevin had taken off his tuxedo and white shirt and bow tie and tossed them carelessly onto a chair. He was in the process of pulling on a thick woollen jumper. So the wedding was off then. Well of course it was. Who would want to waste their time getting married when the chance came along to chuck a few stones at the Brits?

Mary noticed the tensed up look on his face and gave him a warning scowl. Her father and four brothers were gathered around the kitchen table. Gerry Adams Jnr was sitting at the table drawing on a plan of the estate. All of them looked up at Sean.

"So. No wedding then."

Kevin gave him a defiant stare. "More important things to do today than getting wed Sean."

Sean laughed harshly. "Oh yeah. Really important. Just look at you all. Making your plans to go out and throw your bottles and stones like a bunch of little kids."

Kevin's face hardened. Sean continued.

"Except of course you won't be throwing the stones will you? You'll get the little kids to do that for you. How old will they be? Eleven? Ten? Hey, if you're really lucky you might even get a few eight and nine year olds into the thick of things . . ."

"You watch you're fucking mouth now." Kevin Donnelly was rising to his feet.

"Oh yes Kevin. That's the way. I better watch my mouth or else what? You knock my head in? Blow my kneecaps off? Put a bullet through my head? Is that what we're all about now is it?"

Frankie Donnelly slammed his fist down on the table. "Pack it in. Both of you. Kevin, sit down and shut your big mouth. Sean. You too. Come on. Sit down. Have a cup of tea. We're all friends here."

Mary had an imploring look in her eyes. Kevin's face had turned crimson with anger but he slowly eased himself down onto one of the kitchen chairs. Sean blew out his cheeks and sat.

"Sorry Mr Donnelly. That was uncalled for. I forgot my manners. Please accept my apologies."

Frankie Donnelly lit a cigarette from the one he was smoking and waved Sean's apology away. "Don't be so daft lad. You say what you want to say in this kitchen. You know that well enough."

Sean turned to Adams who had watched the whole episode unfold with his usual detachment. "I think it's you I should be talking to Gerry. Why don't we step outside for a moment?"

Adams nodded and got up without a word and left through the back door. As Sean got up to follow him Mary grabbed him by the sleeve. "What the hell do you think you are doing Sean? Why can't you just stay out of things. You came here for a wedding, not to stick your nose into things that are not your business."

Sean cocked an eyebrow. "Not my business is it Mary? Is that how things stand now is it? I think that you know full well what is going to happen today. But just in case you don't, I'll spell it out. These men are going to get a whole lot of kids whipped up into a frenzy. Then they will get the kids to throw anything that they can find at a whole Battalion of Scots soldiers. Now these will be protestant Scots soldiers who have been brought up on tales of dirty, nasty papist paddies who all need a bloody good hiding. And what Mr Adams out there is hoping for is that one of those eighteen year old Scottish soldiers gets a whack on the head with a piece of paving stone and loses his cool. He hopes that when he loses his cool he will fire off a couple of shots. And Gerry there hopes that one of the shots will hit some eight-year-old kid in the head and kill him. Because that will be a victory to him. He wants a nice, cute eight-year-old Catholic kid to be gunned down by some gun-toting Brit bastard. Then he can get on with writing his songs and painting his murals and sending the collection boxes over to America. Well that may be just fine with you Mary, but it doesn't wash with me. You don't get little children to fight your battles. Not in my book."

He stormed out. Mary allowed her hand to drop and fall to her side. She knew that this would be the day when he would make her choose. She had known that the day would come for a long time. She had tried to harden herself to him. She had tried to drive him away by being beastly. None of it had worked. At that moment she knew that there was nothing that she could do to drive Sean O'Neil away. He would stick with her, just as she would stick with him. She knew for certain that he loved her every bit as much as she adored him. But he would not accept the way of the gun. If she wanted Sean she would have to walk away from her Da and her brothers and her people. And she wouldn't do that. She would love him until palm trees grew at the North Pole but she would never do that.

Adams waited quietly as Sean came into the small back yard.

"I heard it Sean. Heard it all."

"Good."

Adams turned and gave Sean a long, careful stare. "And you're right. Absolutely right. That is what we want to happen. We can't drive the Brits out with our bottles and blast bombs and old pistols. No way. We can only win by propaganda. We win by making all of them over the water wonder if they really want to be here any more. And sure, every time a soldier shoots a kid they have their doubts. And in the end they will shoot one kid too many and they will pack up and leave."

Sean sighed and leant against the thin wooden fence. "And in the meantime the kid who dies is a sacrifice that is worth it in the long run."

"Yes."

"That's it, is it? Yes. You're that certain are you Gerry? You've closed down your heart and all that is left is the certainty?"

"Yes."

"Then there isn't a lot of point our talking about it Gerry."

"No. None at all." Adams face was quite expressionless.

"I'll be off then Gerry."

"Not staying then? Not even for Mary?"

"No. Mary can come if she wants. I don't want to watch it, thank you very much. I'm long past seeing anything exciting and glorious about people getting their faces smashed in. I'll see you around Gerry."

He turned to go, but Adams laid a hand on his shoulder.

"A moment Sean. Just a moment. Hear me out. This is only the start. Things will get harder. Much harder. I know your views and believe me, I respect them. That's the plain truth. We see things differently at the moment. Yours is the path of peace. Mine is the path of war. When things get worse maybe you will see it my way.

If that day ever comes, you come and see me Sean. The army will need men like you. We will always have hundreds of boys to throw the bottles and the bombs. We need men who have the brains and the heart. So remember Sean. When you are ready, you come."

Sean held the stare for a moment then left. In the kitchen he stopped briefly and looked to Mary. She stared down at the floor and shook her head. He waited for a few seconds and then pulled his shoulders up.

"Well I'll be off now Mrs Donnelly. Thanks for the tea. I'm sorry about the wedding. There'll be another day. There's always another day."

He walked off the estate and rejoined Hancock.

"No use I'm afraid Major. They're all hell bent on a fight. There's no talking to them."

Hancock nodded. "Good effort for trying. Bloody good. I suppose it was always going to come to this. We've done well out here for a few months. Kept a lid on things. Stopped the burning and looting. All change now. Look at these sods." He inclined his head to a group of soldiers devouring their cigarettes, laughing loudly. "They can't bloody wait. They'll have their fun before the night is out."

Sean patted the older man gently on the shoulder and made his way down the Springfield Road. He heard later that Hancock stayed between the lines until the very last minute trying to keep the sides apart. In the end Gerry Adams Snr had to lead him away for his own safety. Once the fighting started it lasted for two days and two nights. In folklore it came to be remembered as the Battle of Ballymurphy. Houses were wrecked, vehicles burnt and there were hundreds of injuries. This time nobody actually died. But the tide had been turned. For the first time the TV screens showed a different picture. This time it wasn't the B Specials or the RUC who were wading into a Catholic crowd with their batons crashing. This time it was British soldiers.

The war was on.

Sean felt sickened by the so-called Battle of Ballymurphy. Control had passed into the hands of the men of violence. He found it impossible to show any enthusiasm for the efforts of the Civil

Rights campaign. By now it was little more than a side show. Voting equality and fairer housing policies suddenly seemed to have lost their importance. All that occupied anyone's attention now was the ongoing battle between the Provos and the British Army.

Sean felt completely fed up and disillusioned with the whole thing. He turned his back. His tutors had been giving him an increasingly hard time over his work for several months and he decided that study was as good a way as any to take his mind off the violence that was boiling up around the city on a nightly basis. As the shots rang out and the fertiliser bombs thudded, he lost himself in the farmland of Thomas Hardy's Wessex where the sun always shone and people never got their legs blown off when they went to the shops.

His dissertation on Hardy's vision of nineteenth century politics earned him a First and the authorities soon lost all their antagonism. He was invited to candlelit dinners in wood-panelled rooms where earnest old men made encouraging noises about him becoming a professor. His father started to talk to him again.

When the exams at the end of his second year were over he took off for France with a backpack and a few pounds in his pocket. He stayed for six weeks, hitching around and sleeping in fields and barns. For a while the misery of his hometown was left behind. He found it almost bizarre to discover places where people happily lived their lives without hate or fear, or having to cock their ears to the distant rumbling sound of an explosion.

He returned in July to find the city to be seething with tension. Thankfully the army had banned most of the Orange Marches but the very fact that the calendar said that it was July was enough to put half of Belfast in a fighting mood. The Lower Falls had come to resemble an armed camp. Soldiers patrolled constantly and the days of cups of tea and fish and chips on the house were all forgotten. The young squaddies were now constantly wary. Every alley and upstairs window had become a threat. The whole of the local population had become the enemy. Pedestrians were shouldered aside on the pavement. Body searches were overtly rough and aggressive. The people had come to hate the soldiers and in turn the soldiers had come to hate the inhabitants of the Lower Falls.

Sean had bumped into Major Hancock on patrol one morning and the officer had asked him for help in working with the locals. Sean had done what he could but things had already gone too far. There were always pairs of eyes behind the lace curtains watching everything that moved out in the streets. Word soon got round that Sean O'Neil seemed to be very friendly with the Brit officer. Too friendly. Too friendly for his own good.

One morning when he was on his way to the newsagents to buy milk he was pulled into an alley by a heavy hand. Three masked men waited for him. Two of them pushed him hard into the bricks. The third thrust his masked face in close and spat words into Sean's face. The man's breath stank.

"You better watch it Sean O' fucking Neil. Just because you're a big fancy man at the University don't think we don't watch you. I don't care how much of a clever wee fucker you may be. I don't care at all. All I care about is that you're spending too much time with the fucking Brit. Now I suggest that you stop and think who you talk to in future. You won't be no pretty boy fucking footballer with no kneecaps Sean O' fucking Neil."

Sean stared with venom into the red ringed eyes inside the balaclava. "Before you speak to me about being some kind of a tout I suggest you go and speak to Gerry Adams about it. Me and Gerry know each other. Maybe we don't see eye to eye on a lot of things but he'll tell you I'm no tout. Now if you want to talk to me some more you can stop hiding behind your mask you cowardly piece of shite. Go on. No. I thought not. That's all your kind is. Scared little mediocre thugs hiding behind their masks and the kids and the women. Now get your fucking dirty hands off me."

Sean shook himself violently free. The three men seemed lost for anything to do. They were off balance from the cracking authority in his voice. He bore down on the leader, jabbing him hard in the chest with his forefinger.

"Now you listen carefully. I will continue to talk with Major Hancock because I will continue to try and clear up the shite that you and your kind leave in your wake. Now if you have a problem I suggest you take it to your superiors and get their permission to come back and do something. Until then keep out of my way. And by the way, why don't you try cleaning your teeth once in a while. You're mouth smells like a blocked drain. Now fuck off the lot of you."

Later that night the enraged man behind the mask vented his fury on Gerry Adams and two of his officers. Adams simply laughed when he heard the story.

"You leave him be. Sean's OK. He's an idealist and a dreamer, but he's OK. He's no tout. Leave him be. He'll come round in the end."

On Friday, July 3rd Sean caught a bus into the city to go and collect his exam results which had been published that morning. His tutor was delighted. He had scored a clear First and there was more talk of a Fellowship. He met up with a few friends and they headed into the centre to celebrate over a few pints. A little after nine the pub was awash with rumours that were floating down from the Falls Road. That afternoon the army had been tipped off about an arms cache in Balkan Street. The Royal Scots had sealed off the street and smashed their way into the target house. They had come out looking triumphant clutching a prize of six pistols, a Schmeisser sub-machine gun and several boxes of explosives and ammo. By this time a crowd had gathered and things started to get ugly. The nail and petrol bombs started to fly. The soldiers were in a panic. They were trapped and they frantically called in back up.

The army poured canisters of CS gas into the crowds. There wasn't a breath of wind and soon the gas was seeping through the narrow streets and into the houses. This only served to enrage the residents and drive more of them out onto the streets.

The crowds got larger and larger and the back up soldiers couldn't get through. By now the Official IRA were on the scene and the shooting started. Soon the Provos arrived and joined in. For the first time a full-scale gun battle broke out whilst the people of the Lower Falls dived for any cover that they could find. Soon there were bodies on the ground, all of them completely innocent.

Pressure had been growing on the military command from London for some weeks now. People were getting sick of seeing uncontrolled riots on the news every night. Why was nothing being done? Was there no rule of law in Ulster any more? What was the point of having the army over there if they couldn't even sort out a few kids chucking stones?

General Freedland decided that enough was enough. So they wanted to see a bit of action did they? Well, so be it. Let them have what they want. He sent three thousand troops into the Falls and imposed a curfew.

It took Sean a long time to get close to his parents home in James Street. He arrived at an army barrier a little after midnight. The only news that had filtered through to the pub in the city centre was that there had been trouble. He had no idea that there was a curfew in operation.

A voice from the darkness stopped him when he was ten yards from the barrier. North country. Harsh.

"OK sunshine. I think that's far enough. Now tell me, just what the fuck do you think you're playing at?"

Sean made to walk closer. He held his hand in front of his eyes. A bright light was spotlighting him now. He screwed up his eyes and tried to make out a person to match the voice that had addressed him.

"Is there some kind of problem?"

A short laugh. "Aye there is you Paddy twat. In case you hadn't heard, there's a curfew on. CUR – FEW. Big word for a Paddy I know. It means stay at home. It means don't come out on the fucking street or you might just get fucking shot."

Curfew! What the hell was going on? This was an outrage. He was supposed to be in the United Kingdom and yet here he was a couple of streets from his home with soldiers pointing guns and bright lights at him telling him that there was a curfew in place. In hindsight he realised that this was a time when it would have been a pretty good idea to keep his mouth buttoned.

"Don't be so Bloody daft! You can't have a curfew! Where the hell do you think this is, East Germany?"

There was a very brief silence then the northern voice cracked out again.

"Better get over here Sarge. Think we've got ourselves a live one."

Another voice. Again of the north. Lancashire somewhere. Cotton mills and wet summers.

"Right lad. Get up to that wall. Hands high please. Feet apart . . ."

Sean was outraged. "What the hell for, all I am doing is . . ."

Fast footsteps. Hands on him. A wicked pain in the pit of his stomach. What the hell was that? Rifle butt. Straight into his guts and hard. Before he got the chance to realise what had hit him, the six pints of beer he had drunk earlier were one their way up. The vomit exploded from his mouth and all over the boots of two of the squaddies.

"You filthy little Fenian Fucker!!!"

Boots now. Lots of boots. Kicking. And kicking. He made himself into a ball and screwed his eyes shut. " . . . I'll show you to try and play the clever fucker you little Mick piece of shit . . ." And kicking. And kicking.

And suddenly no more kicking. A new voice. Sharp. Clear. Very authoritative. Very firm. Very English

"What the hell is going on. Back. Get back and stand to bloody attention when there is an officer in your presence. Who is in charge here?"

"Here sir! Sergeant Morrison."

"Did nobody ever teach you to salute Morrison?"

The crashing sound of heavy boots stamping the tarmac. "SIR!"

"What is going on here Morrison?"

"SIR! The suspect refused to stop at the barrier, He turned and ran and slipped on the wet cobbles. SIR!"

"Bullshit sergeant. Save the fairytales for an enquiry. Think I'm wet behind the ears do you Sarge?"

"NO SIR!"

"Good. Now get him up and bring him over here."

Sean's head was just starting to stop spinning. His whole body ached from the kicking that they had given him. Two soldiers had to half carry him to where the officer was waiting.

"Bloody hell. Is that you Sean?"

The face was slowly becoming clear as his vision came back to normality. A familiar face. A friendly face. Hancock. He gave a small grimace.

"Evening Major."

Hancock was livid. "Get him over here. Sit him down. You're a bloody disgrace, the lot of you. Now bugger off out of my sight." He turned to Sean who was just about sitting up straight. "What the hell happened?"

"My fault I suppose. Is there really a curfew on?"

"Yes. Freedland imposed it at ten tonight."

"They said so. I didn't believe it. Told them it was crap. Told them we weren't in East Germany. They got a bit pissed off."

Hancock shook his head. "You're going to have to watch that mouth of yours Sean. It will get you in a heap of bother."

Sean grinned. "I think I have just learnt that particular lesson Major."

"Come on. I'll see you home."

Sean tried to walk on his own but he couldn't. His left leg had been kicked numb. He had to lean heavily on Hancock as they hobbled down James Street. When they arrived at number 13, the door was wide open and a soldier waited outside clutching his rifle nervously. Hancock addressed him.

"What's happening here private?"

"House search in progress. SIR!"

Inside there was the sound of breaking crockery. In the kitchen at the back two soldiers were systematically smashing every glass, cup, plate and bowl that they could find. There were more sounds of splintering wood and breaking glass coming from up the stairs. Sean was about to shout for them to stop when he saw his mother. She was down on the floor with fear all over her face. His father was flat on his back on the front room floor. His lip was dripping blood. His mum was cradling his head in her lap. Pale. He was awfully pale. Pale with a thin sheen of sweat. Grey pale. He was struggling to breathe.

His mum gazed up beseechingly. "He can't get his breath Sean. He tried to argue and they hit him and he fell and now he can't get his breath."

Hancock crouched down and made a quick examination. "Jesus." He jumped to his feet and grabbed one of the soldiers in the kitchen by the collar. "Get a vehicle. Any vehicle. Get it NOW! And if you're not back in three minutes flat you're FUCKING COURT MARSHALLED! GO!"

"SIR!!"

They had him the armoured car five minutes later. A nightmare journey. Hancock shouted his way through every roadblock. Sean held his mother's hand. Helpless. Nothing he could do. Just pray. Nothing else.

The hospital at last. Medics. A trolley. A sprint through corridors. Tubes. Doctors. Bright lights. White coats. Thumping on the chest. Electric shocks. Then sagged shoulders. Apologetic looks. Slightly shrugged shoulders.

"I really am most terribly sorry . . ."

Dead. His father was dead. No warning. No preparation. One minute he was as alive as ever moaning at the news in the morning paper. And now dead. Hit in the face. Knocked to the ground. Hit because he dared to argue with soldiers who had smashed in his front door and wanted to smash up his home. He had never broken a law in his life. He was a teacher. A professional. Someone who helped guide and educate the generations of the future. He was respected. He was respectable. He was dead.

They had smashed in his door with a sledge hammer. They had knocked him to the ground. They had spat out insults. They hadn't cared that he was a teacher. All they cared about was his address. Murdered by postcode. Dead. Murdered. Not that they would admit it. No way. Natural causes. Weak heart. Shock of the night. There would be no mention of the uniformed thug who knocked him to the ground. No mention of the two in the kitchen. Having a laugh as they smashed his mother's crockery piece by piece. The crockery that she had collected for years. Saved and saved for. Hours on end in the mill to save for her crockery and they came into the house and smashed it piece by piece.

Bastards. Bastards. Bastards.

"BASTARDS!!!!!!"

Eyes on him. All along the corridor where they sat on the hard wooden bench. Then the eyes looked away. Embarrassed. Nobody would know what to say. Such a terrible tragedy. Such a fine man.

Bastards.

Hancock gently laid his hand on Sean's shoulder.

"I'm so sorry Sean. So very, very sorry."

Sean looked up at him. He was blurred again. His eyes were filled with tears. He wiped at them but it was no good. They came out in rivers. He didn't care. Let them see. What did it matter. His

Da was dead. So what if they saw him crying. What did anything matter any more.

" . . . So sorry."

Sean swallowed hard. "I know you are Major. Not your fault. You're a good man. Really. A good man. We all want to be good men. I do. My Da did. But how? How can we?"

Hancock couldn't bear to look at his terrible grief. He stared at the notice board at the far end of the corridor. He wanted to give an answer. He wanted to tell the boy it would be all right. He wanted to tell him that he could trust the army and the rule of law. He wanted to tell him that he could still be proud to be British. He didn't because he couldn't. Who the hell could?

The army maintained the curfew for a further two days. It was to go down on the list of great British military successes alongside the Charge of the Light Brigade and the Spion Kop. Up until this point only part of the population was mobilised against them. By the time they had completed 48 hours of smashing up houses and faces alike they had ensured that they had made enemies for life. The Provos had no need to spend any more time in persuading the residents of the Falls that they should throw their weight behind the cause. The job had been done for them. The massive search operation yielded up a pathetic array of old weaponry, which the army PR people tried to use as proof of victory. Nobody really bought it.

In fact the Provos were able to win a double victory. When the curfew was at last lifted on Sunday afternoon, an army of women from the upper Falls and Ballymurphy marched triumphantly down the street with prams laden with bread and milk. It was pure theatre. The soldiers stood by and looked bemused as the provisions were distributed and the singing women marched back home again. The soldiers had failed to discover the vast majority of weapons that had been hidden in just about every nook and cranny of the Lower Falls. Unbeknown to them, the majority of these weapons were now loaded into the empty prams and taken up the hill to Ballymurphy.

The irony was that the British Army wound up doing a huge favour to the Provos. Up until July 3rd, the Lower Falls had been one of the Official IRA's greatest strongholds. In the course of that Sunday afternoon they had to stand by and watch as the Provo's collected up almost all of their weapons into prams and took them for themselves.

Once Sean and his mother had returned from the hospital they had been confined to the house along with all of their neighbours. Nobody was allowed to come and knock at the door to offer sympathy. They were alone in the house. His mother was almost catatonic. Sean paced about and smoked and couldn't settle. He was cut in half by grief and fury. The walls seemed to close in on him. He couldn't sleep. He couldn't sit down. He couldn't do anything but pace the front room like a trapped animal.

At last the noise outside told him that the curfew was lifted. They needed milk. It seemed like a task to occupy him. He made his way onto the Falls Road to find provisions. The scene was surreal. Women with prams marched down the middle of the road with their hands held high in clenched fist salutes. Soldiers looked bemused. The crowds gathered and cheered. Kids leapt about as if it were some great celebration. And all up the pavements there was the glass from broken windows, and the doors hung off their hinges. The road was strewn with the flotsam and jetsam of the Friday night riot and overhead a helicopter's rotors beat with menace.

And in the midst of it all was Mary. Her face was alight. Pure passion. She was singing with all her might. Her arm was held high like a winner at the Olympics. Her eyes were ablaze. She was radiant and vibrant and fearsome. She made his soul ache.

She saw him and came over. The passion on her face was replaced by an almost shy look.

"Hello Sean"

"Hi Mary."

"You alright then?"

"No. Not really. Not at all."

Now her face was simple concern.

"What's up? What's happened?"

"My Da's dead. A heart attack. Friday night. He's gone Mary."

She reached up and took him to her. He allowed his head to fall into the crook of her shoulder and neck.

"How Sean? Was it the trouble?"

He found it hard to speak through choking sobs. "Aye. They kicked in the front door and came in. I was out. Down in the city. He started to argue with them. They thumped him. Must have been the shock of it all. We got him to hospital but it was too late."

The sobs enveloped him and he collapsed into her. She spoke with her mouth lost in his hair.

"Oh Jesus Sean. Sweet Jesus. The bastards. They'll all bastards. Surely you can see that now."

He pulled himself clear and roughly wiped at his eyes with the sleeve of his jacket. "You're wrong. Do you know how we got to the infirmary? In an armoured car. It was Hancock. He did everything he could. He's a decent man. There are lots of decent men in Brit uniforms. Lots of bastards too. Just like our lot. It's too simple to call them bastards Mary. Can't you see we all turn each other into bastards."

She was astonished. Aghast. "How can you say that Sean? After the way they have behaved, the smashed houses, the abuse, the kickings?"

He smiled at her. Despite everything, he couldn't help it. Through all their time together she had always been the certain one. It was always black and white for Mary. Guys in white hats and guys in black hats. Good and evil. Just and unjust. Never any room for grey.

"Provo words Mary. Nice, easy, simple Provo words. Never go beyond skin deep whatever you do. Why not just think about it for a moment. Just look at these soldiers." He waved towards a group of four squaddies who were nervously clutching their rifles as the crowd milled around them. "Who are they? They are the poor kids from the poor streets in places like Sunderland and Barnsley and Wolverhampton. They joined the army because they couldn't get another job. They are not very bright. They don't have deep political understanding. All they know is that they have been sent to this god forsaken place where the people swear at them and spit at them and throw petrol bombs and nail bombs and blast bombs at them. And if they get careless for even a second there is always a guy behind a wall ready to shoot their heads off. And all the time they are expected to stand there and grit their teeth and take it. So how the fuck can any of us be surprised when they lose it when they get half the chance. I would. You would. Your brothers would. Anyone would."

Her eyes were flashing now. "So what are you saying Sean?"

"Oh I'm just the same old stuck record. I still have this naïve stupid belief that people should be able to behave better than animals. The trouble is that nobody is interested in my record any more. All anyone wants to do is to kill and maim each other. Don't try to make me hate Mary. I love you. I'll always love you. But not enough to turn to hate."

The tears were coming again now. Why did he have to be like this? He was hurting all over. Inside and out. He was broken and grieving and lonelier than he had ever dreamed that he could be. And he was crying out for the comfort of her arms and her soft eyes but still he pushed her away. "Look, you'd better go. Take your pram load of weapons back to your brothers. Just think how many Brits you can kill with what you've got there. Maybe that will make you happy. Just go Mary. For fuck's sake. Just go."

She went. She kept looking back and she nearly ditched her pram and went to him. He stood and watched. He was a bent figure. His eyes burned with despair. In the end she carried on. She pushed her pram load of guns all the way to Ballymurphy and passed them to her father.

Two days later Kevin Donnelly left the pub after last orders. He nearly tripped as he stepped out of the front door. It was raining outside. He stopped for a moment and turned his face up to the rain to try and sober up a little. A car pulled up and three men bundled him into the back. This sobered him up quicker than the rain had done. He knew them. They were Official IRA from Clonard. They were not happy punters. They wanted their guns back. His Mary had been clocked with a pram. They knew that his Mary wasn't in the family way. So it was no fucking baby that was in the pram was it? It was their fucking guns that were in the pram. And they wanted them back. All of them.

An hour later the men all agreed that young Donnelly was a tough bastard. They had beaten him with iron rods and burned him with cigarettes and he had told them fuck all. They had shot him in the back of the head and left him with the litter on a patch of waste ground.

And the war went on as if nothing had ever happened.

By November Sean hadn't been near West Belfast for weeks. He had taken his mother to live with her sister down in Newry. Once the new term had started he decided to devote all of his time to studies. He became reclusive and disappeared off into a world of books. He attended occasional rallies on the campus but he never got up on the platform. Occasionally Michael would come to his room and try and persuade him to get back involved, but he hadn't the heart for it any more. He hid away and saw nobody. He found a world that he preferred in Dickens and Tolstoy and Steinbeck. It was better that way.

He had dozed off in his chair. An urgent tapping on his door awoke him. He glanced at his watch. Past nine. Who the hell was it? He felt annoyed. Nobody bothered him any more. They stayed clear. Left him well alone. Thought him to be eccentric. A bit mad. The wild-eyed lad from the Falls. So who was it?

Mary.

He couldn't believe it. He hadn't seen her since the day on the Falls months and months ago. She was soaked to the skin and her eyes were red from crying. She looked awful.

"Jesus Mary. Come in. Sit down. Let me get that coat, Jesus girl, you're soaked through."

She tried to start speaking but he shushed her and took away the wet coat and wrapped a blanket round her shivering shoulders. He made her tea and lit her a cigarette. Then he sat opposite her in front of the rusty little electric fire and gestured for her to speak.

"I'm sorry for coming Sean. I shouldn't have. There's nowhere else I can go. Nobody else to help."

"You're fine Mary. I'm always here. You know that. Tell me."

"It's our Megan. She's in trouble. Real trouble."

Megan was Mary's nearest sister. She was a year older but twenty years dizzier. The Troubles had always seemed to pass Megan by. Megan lived for clothes and music and boys, and a few riots and bombs never seemed to distract her.

"How? Megan never goes near the trouble. It's not her."

Mary bowed her head. "The Brits have been putting on dances. In the barracks. Every Friday night. Lots of the girls started going. They said that the music was great and the soldiers were loaded. Well of course Megan went. Right up her street wasn't it. Every Friday and Megan never missed.

Well you can guess what happened next. None of it sat well with the Provies. They didn't like the idea of their women getting all those drinks bought by Brits with pockets full of cash when they have to fight their war on a Giro. Well Gerry organised a picket outside the camp and most of the girls stopped going. But Megan still went and . . ."

She wiped tears away crossly. Sean passed her a tissue.

" . . . Well she met a boy. Colin. He's from Huddersfield. And the silly bitch has gone and fallen in love with him. And my dad has gone mad and my brothers have gone mad and still she won't stop going. She sneaked into the City with me the other week and I met him in a cafe and the trouble is that he is lovely. Really nice. And any bloody fool can see that they both love each other to bits and they have got engaged and . . ."

Again she had to stop. Sean crouched down next to her and put an arm around her shoulder. "It's OK Mary. Just take your time. It will be fine."

She turned her wet face to him. Her eyes were desperate.

"But it's not Sean. She showed off her ring to the girls at work and told them all about him. One of the girls went and told the Provies. They had a meeting about it and they are going to sort her out. They're going to tie her to a lamppost and shave her hair and cover her in tar and feathers. Oh Sean it's terrible. My Da and my brothers refuse to do a thing. They've locked her in her room. They say it will serve the silly bitch right. They say it is what she deserves. Her hair Sean. She has lovely hair. She's always had lovely hair. Oh Jesus Sean."

"It's OK Mary. We're not going to let it happen. It's OK. When will they do it?"

"Tonight. At eleven. That's when they're coming. Gerry and his men. That's why I had to come."

"You did right. Come on we'd best move. We've got time."

"What are you going to do?"

He gave her a big smile. "Stop them of course. What else?"

There was quite a crowd out when they arrived. Two youths were holding the writhing figure of Megan as another tied her to a lamppost. There was shouting and jeering and hissing. As ever Adams was to one side. His face was impassive as he watched. There was no pleasure behind the glasses. It was just another distasteful job that needed to be done. It was bad for morale when the Brits had the pick of the pretty girls. And he couldn't allow anything that would damage the morale of the boys. So it had to be done. A small light of interest passed over his face as Sean strode up to the lamppost.

Sean stood very still and held up his arms for silence. In many ways the hard, lonely months had treated him badly. The weight had fallen off him and the bones stuck out of his cheeks. His hair was very long now, a mass of black curls that fell over the collar of his dark overcoat. He cut a striking figure as he waited for silence. Imposing. Almost awesome. Very still. In control. No fear.

It took a couple of minutes until the nervous shuffling silence was complete. Now there was only the rain that was coming down hard now and plastering the hair to his head. In the distance there were sirens in the night.

"OK. I'm going to cut her loose now. You're going to have to make a choice. The only way you'll stop me is if you kill me. Believe me. It's that simple. You kill me in cold blood. I'm not cutting her down because I love the Brits. I'm not cutting her down because I love the Prods. I'm cutting her down because she is just a girl. A lovely girl who loves life. Her crime is that she has fallen in love. She is one of our own. If we do this to one of our own because she has fallen in love with the wrong man then we are all lost. All of us. Lost and we'll never be found. Sure, we have our problems but we cannot do this to a girl we all know just because she has fallen in love. So I'm cutting her down. And I'm taking her away. And now is the moment that you must decide whether you're going to kill me or not."

As he spoke he took a knife from his pocket and cut the bonds. He pulled off his coat and wrapped it around Megan's shoulders. Mary stepped forward and pulled her sister close to her. The crowd parted grudgingly as the three of them stepped through. Sean walked right up to where Adams waited. They looked into each other's eyes as the rain started to come even harder.

"Don't do this Gerry. This is no way to win a war. There are more weapons you can use than guns and bombs. Compassion is a weapon. Decency is a weapon. Moral strength is a weapon. Be strong Gerry. Don't do this."

Adams stood stock-still and stared. At his side his men shuffled in readiness. At last he gave Sean a small nod.

"Take her away Sean. Take her. Go."

His words punctured the tension. The wet crowd dispersed silently. They felt shamed by the boy with the wild hair and the voice of reason. Adams stood and watched as Sean and Mary and Megan walked away down the silent street. As they turned the corner at the end he said to nobody in particular.

"One day you'll see things our way Sean O'Neil. And maybe one day we'll see things your way. And maybe one day all of this will end."

Chapter 5
Into Darkness

September 1971

Things were good for Sean and Mary by the autumn of 1971. Mary had managed to talk her way back into university for the start of the new term. The authorities had taken a sympathetic view of the case of the girl from Ballymurphy who had lost her older brother to the Troubles. Sean was still very much a rising star. At the beginning of term the two of them had found a small flat to rent just off the university campus. As the war raged around them they were able to hide away. It was a time of finding pictures for the walls and growing herbs in the back yard and learning to cook curry.

Both had made the decision to leave the Troubles behind them. Sean had no wish to spend any time at the empty house on James Street. He called in every couple of weeks or so to check on things and tried as best as he could to persuade his mother to sell the place. The Falls Road depressed him terribly. By now unemployment levels had soared. Most of the businesses had closed down and no one in their right mind would consider opening one. His contemporaries from St. Mary's were almost all out of work. He saw them in sad huddles on street corners casting malevolent looks towards the soldiers on their endless patrols. Every time he caught the bus back to the city centre he felt as if he were escaping a nightmare. Once they closed the door to the flat they could pretend that there was a different world outside.

Mary had walked away from Ballymurphy for good the night that they had led Megan away from the lamppost. Her family had completely ostracised her and she was more than happy for that state of affairs to continue indefinitely. Megan and Colin had married at the Registry office in Huddersfield. It had been a happy day and the sun had shone. Megan had sent some photos home to her mother but had received no reply. Colin's regiment had completed their tour and now the couple were starting to live happily ever after on an army base in the Rhineland.

The Civil Rights movement was still trying to make an impact, and it managed occasional successes. In August, Brian Faulkner, the new hardline Prime Minister in Stormont at last got his way and persuaded the British government to reintroduce internment. This gave the Civil Rights people a whole new lease of life. Banging people up in prison camps for months on end without any kind of trial was perfect Civil Rights fodder. When the hated policy was implemented it had turned out to be a complete fiasco. Ridiculously enough the army had been undertaking dummy runs for the big night for weeks. They may as well have sent postcards to all the IRA leadership. Dear Gerry. We are planning to smash your door down and intern you next Thursday. We were hoping to pop round at about four in the morning. Would that be OK with you?

When Operation Demetrius was at last launched, the main men were all well away. Instead the army collected up a rag-bag bunch. Some had been active in the IRA in the 1950's. One man, who was highly flattered to be lifted, had not done a day's work for the cause of Irish Freedom since 1922. The dawn raids saw over three hundred Republican suspects arrested and not a single Loyalist. The next day they had to release over 200. It was another fiasco. The army were furious with the RUC for being handed such duff information. The RUC were furious with the army for being furious with them. Everybody fell out. The buck was passed half way around Ulster and back again. And the IRA quietly got on with their work and signed up another wave of volunteers.

Sean and Mary attended a few meetings to hear speaker after speaker denounce the fascist policies of the Stormont Nazis but neither had any great wish for any deep involvement. At times they felt a little guilty to be leading such an idyllic life a mere few miles away from where the bombs went off and the soldiers darted from corner to corner. But these times were fairly infrequent. One day they told themselves it would all be over and then there would be an opportunity again for them to try and do something useful.

It all ended in the early hours of the morning of September 23rd. They were fast asleep in the flat when the front door was flattened by a big man with a sledge hammer. They came awake to shouting voices and bright lights and heavy boots. The whole thing was like a series of nightmarish freeze-frames. An image of Mary's naked body being dragged from the bed screaming and writhing and scratching. Big hairy hands pawing her. "Fuck me, wouldn't mind giving her one . . ." Trying to get to the voice. Trying to defend her. Landing on his back on the floor. A rifle butt smashing two of his front teeth. A blinding searing pain as an army boot crunched his testicles.

Two of them threw a blanket around him. Wrapped it tight. Mummified him. Marched him out. Faces in the doorways of the other flats. Looks of surprise. Shock. 'It shouldn't be happening here' looks. Then out in the cold of the street. Two Land Rovers. A last sight of Mary. Wild terrified eyes. Then the door was slammed and she was taken from him. More blows. He fell hard on the metal floor of the Land Rover. More kicks. Almost delivered carelessly. Banter from the soldiers who sat opposite each other on the bench seats. Him in the middle. Trussed like a chicken. There down on the floor. There to be kicked when they felt like it. Kicked for a bit of a laugh.

They drove for about twenty minutes. Voices. Gates swinging open. A noisy place. Lots of vehicles. Lots of lights. Shouted commands. A barking, snarling Alsatian. His toes rubbed raw as they dragged him across the concrete to a corridor. Thrown down again. A bare room. No table. No chairs. No nothing. Off white walls and a hard, hard floor.

Suddenly he was on his own. The door had been banged shut. He pulled the blanket close about him and huddled himself into the corner. He tried to put his thoughts together. He was shaking uncontrollably. What was happening to him? He was scared. Really, really scared. Absolutely terrified. He slapped himself across the face in anger.

Come on Sean. Get a grip. Wake up. Sort it out. Slowly he normalised his breathing. Slow Sean. In. Hold. Out. Hold. In. Hold. Out. Hold. Better. Much better. His heart was starting to thump a little less now. In. Hold. Out. Hold. OK. Use the brain. Think it out. Arrange the facts. They came for both of them. Door smashed in. Them taken out. Why? What had they done? Nothing. Nothing at all. It couldn't be an arrest. Internment. Of course. So obvious. Stupid Sean. Stupid. They had been interned. Obvious. Quite a few of the People's Democracy people had been lifted. They had taken Michael in August.

So no problem then. He had nothing to hide. There was nothing illegal they could hang on him. Nothing at all. But what about Mary? Had she done anything with the Provos before she had walked away? Would they have anything on her? Had there been photos of her with her pram and the guns? Had there been a tout? No good thinking about it. Nothing he could do. Just take each thing as it comes. Take it step by step. Deal with it. Keep the fear back.

The door flew open. British voices. English. London. Mocking. Amused by it all. Uniforms. The blanket was ripped from him. Three of them. One behind him, pinning his arms to his side. The others staring and laughing.

"Come on then Paddy. Let's have a good look at your tackle. Oh dear, oh dear. Not much is there Paddy? All a bit sad in the downstairs department. Know what Paddy? Know what makes me get to wondering? How do you Fenian bastards breed like rabbits when you've all got shrivelled up little dicks? Funny innit. Hey! Doreen! Here you are Doreen! Come and have a shufty at this one . . ."

Doreen came in and stared with contempt. "Not much to look at is it Paddy? All a bit sad really. I keep looking forward to seeing if any of you Provies are well hung. Not yet I'm afraid. All a bit sad really. Sad Irish bastards with sad little knobs."

Sean forced his face to stay even. He glowered ahead. Give then nothing. Nothing. Be cool. Don't let them in. Smile Sean. Just smile. Make yourself. Fuck the broken teeth. Smile at them. They'll hate that.

They did.

Kicks. Punches. Something beating his back where the kidneys were. More kicks. Pain. Rivers of pain. An ocean of pain. Endless. The door banged shut and he was alone again. The lights went out. Dark. Cold and dark. Naked on a concrete floor. Hurting all over. So cold. So damn fucking alone. So scared. He wanted to cry. No. Never. Anything but that. Don't give them that Sean. Please not that. Find some strength. Find it from anywhere. But find it.

How long? How long in the dark and the cold? No idea. Two hours. Maybe three? No idea. Just deal with it. Lights. Boots. Another kicking coming. No. Different voices. Irish. From the North somewhere. From the country.

"Put these on O'Neil. Now!"

A boiler suit. Too big. What the hell. At least a bit of warmth. A hood now. Thick material. Canvas. He shook his head but it was firm. Dark again. Clammy with his own breath.

"Right O'Neil. Walk. Now!"

A hand at his back. Pushing. Guiding. Corridors. Shiny polished floors beneath his bare feet. Outside again now. Tarmac. Cold. Noise. What kind of noise? A helicopter. Half thrown onto some kind of platform. A lifting sensation. Deafening noise. They were taking him up in the helicopter. Darkness and noise. How long? Ten minutes? Half an hour? Which way? No way to tell.

A voice close in his ear. Loud. Shouting over the noise of the rotors.

"OK Paddy. That's your free ride over with. You'll be leaving us now. No more bombing women and kids for you Paddy. Not unless you can fly Paddy. How about it? Reckon you can fly? Time to find out. . . ."

He was pushed forward. He flailed his arms around. He could feel cold air. Nothing but space. But his feet were on the ledge. His toes were over the edge. Someone had a handful of his boiler suit behind him. Holding him. If they let go he would be gone. The voice was still there but it was too far away to hear. He grasped out at the cold air of the night and screamed inside the hood.

He lurched forward. They had let go! They had actually done it. Over. Falling. Death on the way. Screaming. Terror. Bang. Only for a second. One second and he hit the floor. Bastards. Fucking stinking bastards!!!

Hands on him again. Toes dragging on the floor again. Laughter. Mocking voices.

"Got you going a bit there you Provie cunt. Shit yourself did you . . .?"

Good laugh. Great crack. Dropped him with the hood on we did. Nearly shat himself. Good crack for the bar later on. More corridors. Slammed door. A new voice. English again. More contained. Educated. No need to shout.

"Sean O'Neil, you have been interned under suspicion of terrorist activity. Please put your hands against the wall. Wider. Good. Move your feet back. That's good. Feet apart please. Good. You will maintain this position. Do not try to move or you will be punished. Nod if you understand. Good."

The door slammed. He waited. Silence in the room. Still dark inside the hood. Silence. On his own again. His shoulders were starting to ache already. Stuff them. He stood up to stretch. A hard blow slammed him back to the wall. "Move and you will be punished."

Time slowed down. Time stopped. Nothingness. Just darkness in the hood. Hot now inside. Sweat pouring down his face. An itch above his ear. Shoulders beginning to burn. Calf muscles sore. Thirsty. So thirsty. And time just stood still. Darkness and silence.

How long? Hours. Two, maybe three

How long? Maybe four. Maybe five.

How long? Almost a day. Real pain now. Shooting cramping pain. Pain all over. Pain and thirst and pain.

How long? Forever. Forever and then some.

He was starting to panic. He panicked for his sanity. He could feel madness around the corner. He worked every corner of his mind. He repeated passages from books silently. He painted pictures. He wrote essays. He considered topics for dissertations. He prepared notes for classes. Anything. Anything to hide from the pain. Anything to keep the madness away. Darkness, Madness. Darkness. Madness.

How long? No time existed any more. Only darkness.

Light.

Hood pulled off. Wonderful, perfect air to breathe. No more darkness. Pushed to a seat. Too much light. Far too much light.

Blinding sharp white light. Sitting at last. His whole body shuddering with relief. Water. A cup of water put to his lips. Perfection. More perfect that anything there could ever have been before. Hr drank greedily. Get it all before they take it away. Wonderful. Perfect. Glorious.

"So Sean. It's time to talk now. Talk and the hood will be put away. It's best to talk. Easy to talk. Let's talk."

He felt almost giddy. "Aye. Talk. We'll talk."

"When did you join the IRA Sean?"

"I didn't"

"Again. When did you join the IRA?"

"I didn't."

"Who swore you in?"

"Nobody."

"More than one was there? Quite a crowd I should think. How many was there Sean? Who were they Sean . . ."

Questions. Questions. Questions. No. No. No. Questions. Hood again. Against the wall again. How long? Ages. Forever. Hood off. Water again. Beautiful. Perfect. More questions. No. Don't know. No. Hood. Wall. Questions. Hood. Wall . . .

It lasted for two-and-a-half days. They never said a word when they took him away from the room. They took him to a doctor. The man examined him.

"You're fine O'Neil. Any complaints?"

A joke. A stupid joke. What was the point. "No. No complaints."

"Excellent. Wait here. Please O'Neil."

A chair and no hood. A table. An ashtray. Another chair opposite. A regular light. A calendar with a view of the ocean. Almost like a normal place. A normal scene. A real piece of life.

The door opened. Oh Christ. Not again. Not more. Just stop. For Jesus sake will you stop. The man was in his thirties. Late thirties probably. Smartly dressed. A tweed jacket and a silk tie and cord trousers. The man pulled out cigarettes and offered one. Sean took it and took a light and sucked the nicotine as far into himself as it would go. It made his head spin. He closed his eyes for a moment.

"I'm Edwards. Not a real name of course, but Edwards will do us well enough. How are you Sean?"

Sean managed a smile. "How do you think?"

"I dare say not so good."

"Aye. That would about sum it up."

Edwards paused and took a pull on his own cigarette. A spot of ash dropped onto his trousers and he brushed it away carefully. "I must apologise for all this Sean. There is no excuse. Absolutely none. I won't embarrass myself by trying to invent one."

Sean leered at him. "So is this the nicely, nicely part Mr Edwards? Is this the part where Mr Nice man comes in and gives me a smoke and gets me to spill all that I know? If it is, you're doing OK so far. But I'm afraid there's nothing to tell."

Edwards chuckled. "Oh I know there isn't. If those buffoons had only come to me first I could have told them as much. You're a Civil Rights supporter. You're an outstanding student. In fact I would go as far as to say that you are really a very fine young man."

"So let me go then."

"Oh I will. Very soon. Don't worry about that. This horrible fiasco is over now. I heard you speak once you know."

Sean was surprised. "When?"

"After Burntollet. Back in early 69. I was impressed. You know how to work a crowd. If you lived anywhere else you would go far. By the way, that is what brought all this on. They have a file on you. Peoples Democracy. Burntollet. All of it. They think that you are at best a subversive, at worst a fully paid up IRA volunteer. Idiots."

"And you Mr Edwards?"

"I know you are what you are. You are a man out of step with the times. You believe in decency and justice and beauty. Sadly all these things have been deported from this sad little place. I admire you Sean. Really. No bullshit. I salute you. I only wish that others could hear what you have to say."

Sean was intrigued now. He was beginning to believe that it was for real. Maybe he WAS about to be released. "Where is this leading Mr Edwards? Who are you?"

"That is two questions. I will answer the second one first. It is supposed to be a secret but I don't suppose telling you will do any harm. I work for MI6. We are the forgotten ones. We keep trying to persuade the people in Stormont and London that it would be a good idea to negotiate and nobody wants to hear us. They think that we are out of step. Everyone seems to believe that the answer to all of our problems here is to hit everything that we can find as hard as we can with a big hammer. I find it all rather distasteful. Foolish and distasteful."

"What do you want?"

Edwards carefully docked his cigarette. "Nothing Sean. Nothing at all. Well, nothing right now. Let me share my thoughts with you. Take them how you will. Maybe you will get out of here and pick up the threads of your life and simply carry on. I hope that you do. I hope that you become a professor and live out a happy and fulfilling life. Personally I don't see it. You must understand that things will get worse. Much, much worse. There are men on all sides of this tragic little war who will stop at nothing to try and win.

We are the stronger Sean. Of course we are. We are 50 million. We have the people and the guns and the money. And as things drag on, and more of our soldiers are sent home in coffins, we will fight dirtier and dirtier. It is the way that we are. We always have been. That's how we came to get such a big Empire. When things get really bad I believe that you will get off the fence Sean. I don't know when, I just know that it will probably happen. If you join the Provisional IRA you will rise up the ranks quickly. They need men like you. You are a leader. In any army, you would be a leader. One day, maybe many years in the future, there will be a time when the men of reason have the chance to end this thing. I like to think that my career will take me to higher places too. When that day comes you can call me. I will give you a number. You can memorise it and store it away. When they answer the call say that you would like to enquire about 'The Terrible Beauty'. If I can help, I will. That's all Sean. Nothing else. I will organise your release now."

"One thing Mr Edwards."

"Yes?"

"Mary. Mary Donnelly. My girlfriend. They lifted her at the same time. Could you get her out?"

"I already have. She will be at your flat when you get there."

"Thank you"

Edwards got to his feet and extended his hand. Sean shook it. The Englishman seemed to hesitate for a moment before speaking.

"I better prepare you Sean. Mary didn't bear up too well. She is . . . she is changed. She is going to need some time. Some patience. I'm sure you will know what to do."

Edwards left and Sean pondered on what he had said. So many people seemed so sure that there was a kind of inevitability that he would join the IRA. It annoyed him intensely. No matter what he was put through he found himself no nearer wanting to take up arms and kill people. And yet both Edwards and Adams seemed so sure. Such very different men, and yet with their similarities. Both were trying to look beyond the misery of the first horizon. Both were working away for things that lay years in the future. He pushed the thoughts aside. What was of much greater concern was Mary. Edwards had been elusive, but his words had somehow carried a heavy threat. What had he meant? What had they done to her?

Two soldiers came for him an hour later. They brought a set of civilian clothes that they must have dug up from somewhere or another. He pulled them on. One passed him a piece of paper to sign. He read it three times over with great suspicion. In the end he could not find any hidden agenda. It was a simple discharge note. He was in no mood to kick up a fuss. He just wanted to get back to Mary.

They took him out to a yard full of military vehicles. The fences around the compound were high and guarded by watchtowers. He hadn't the first clue where he was. Two plain-clothed policemen took him into their charge. They sat him in the back of a Cortina and drove out of the barracks.

It was quite late and the dusk was falling. The streets were quiet. It was raining softly. He gazed around and realised that he had ended up in Malone Barracks in Portadown. It could have been the dark side of the moon for all he knew about it.

The policemen never said a word all the way to Belfast. They sat in the front and smoked incessantly. When they pulled up outside his flat one of them tossed him a set of keys. He checked them. They were his own. He realised that when he had left the flat he had been bollock naked and wrapped in a blanket. How considerate.

"Go on. Fuck off out of it."

Nice meeting you too, he thought to himself. He felt a sense of unease as he made his way up the two flights of stairs to his flat. He unlocked the door and went in.

"Mary. You home?"

Nothing. Just quiet.

"Mary!"

Lounge. Nothing. Kitchen. Nothing. Bathroom. Nothing. He opened the bedroom door and he saw two terrified eyes. She was sitting bolt upright on the bed. One arm was pulling her knees up into her chest. She was sucking her thumb hard. Her hair was stuck up in all directions. She was rocking herself forward and back, forward and back.

"Sweet Jesus, what have they done to you Mary?"

He crossed the room and made to take her in his arms but she shrank back from him. She was shaking violently. Her arm tightened around her knees. Sean raised his hands slowly and backed himself away.

"Hey, it's OK. It's fine. I won't hurt you. It's Sean, Mary. It's Sean."

Her wide eyes stared at him without a trace of recognition.

"Tell you what, I'll make us a cup of tea."

As he made the tea his stomach was churning. What in the name of hell had the bastards done to her? He didn't have to think about it much. He knew what they had done to him. Maybe he was stronger than Mary. It had taken every bit of resolve and bloody-mindedness that he possessed to get himself through the nightmare. A cold rage took him when he remembered how the soldiers had pawed at her nakedness when they had been lifted. Surely not. Oh Christ not that.

He took the tea into the bedroom and tried to pass it to her but she backed away again. He tried to talk to her softly and soothingly, as if she was a bird on the roadside with a broken wing. Nothing. He felt terribly helpless. In the end he put the tea on the bedside table and softly closed the door.

When he returned half an hour later the cup was empty and Mary was back in the same position rocking herself back and forward. He repeated the procedure with a plate of sandwiches. Later he took in hot chocolate and biscuits and her night-clothes.

He tried to talk, tried to get through, but every time he got too close she started to shake and tense up.

In the end he left her for over an hour and when he returned he found that she had put on the night-clothes and was fast asleep. He sat late into the night smoking cigarette after cigarette, just staring into space. In the end he fell into an exhausted sleep in the chair. It was past noon when he at last awoke. He made his way to the bedroom with a gnawing hope. Maybe after a night's sleep she would be a little better. Maybe she would be ready to speak.

She wasn't. The day followed the same routine as the one before. And the next. And the four days that followed. By this stage he was beginning to feel that he was becoming unravelled. There was no sign of improvement whatsoever. He was torn by indecision about what to do. Mary had not spoken with any of her family for months on end. He felt that he really should get in touch, but was not at all sure what good it could come of it. He couldn't see what her mother could do that he wasn't already doing himself. What he was certain about was that the pitiful state of their sister would send her remaining three brothers demented. If they turned their rage into some idiotic attack on the soldiers and got themselves shot he would not forgive himself.

In the end, after a week, he went to his tutor. It turned out to be a sound move. The professor was appalled at what he heard and immediately took Sean to a colleague in the Psychiatry Department. Doctor Hughes was a kindly man in his late sixties. He accompanied Sean back to the flat and stayed with Mary for well over an hour. When he emerged from the bedroom his face was grave.

"I'm sorry Sean, but the news is not very good. Of course it is far too early for me to give you a proper diagnosis, but I am certain that what we are looking at here is shock. Not just regular shock. Serious shock. Very deep-rooted. You are going to ask me questions that I cannot answer I fear."

Sean felt almost physically sick. "How long will she be like this?"

"That is the very question that I was alluding to. There is no answer. It could be a day. A week. A month. It could be anything. Can you give me some kind of clue as to what Mary has been through?"

"We were both lifted by the army. Interned. Of course we were separated straight away. All I can tell you is what happened to me. I have no way of knowing what they did to Mary"

The old man's face hardened as Sean took him through the abuse and degradation and mental torture that he had endured. When Sean finished he could barely speak.

"My God. I can scarcely believe it." He saw that Sean was about to rear up. "No. Please. I'm not saying that I don't believe what you have told me. Of course I do. I just cannot comprehend that this is happening right here in our country. It is diabolical."

Sean spoke quietly. "There may be more. When they came it was four in the morning. We were in bed of course. We were naked. They . . . well they were groping her . . . all over....when they took her . . . one of them had his hand between her legs . . . they could have . . . might have . . ."

His voice trailed off. He stared miserably at the wrinkled old face. And there were tears in the old eyes that looked back.

"What can I do professor?"

"Maybe all that she needs is rest and care. Just what you have been doing. Maybe. Sadly I fear things are rather more severe. I think that she will need professional attention. It is not widely available. The field is somewhat specialised."

"Is there anywhere in particular?"

"There is a clinic in California that has been conducting ground breaking work. The Americans have an awful lot of their soldiers coming home from Vietnam in a dreadful mental state. They show many of the symptoms that Mary exhibits. I have heard outstanding reports on the work that they are doing. But of course that is out of the question."

"Why? Would they not take her?"

"Oh they would take her. That is not the issue. In America it is the dollar that rules admissions. I don't want to be rude, but I can only assume that the costs involved would be prohibitive for you and Mary's family. We are talking many, many thousands of dollars over a long period here."

" Would you make the calls Professor. Set it up?"

"Of course I would Sean. But how? They will want to know

about money. I'm sorry. It sounds awful. But that is how they are."

Sean gave a grim smile. "I'll get the money."

The next day a taxi took Sean from the railway station and dropped him at the main gate of the huge barracks that held the British Army Headquarters in Lisburn. He went up the small office by the heavily armoured gates.

"I'm here to see Brigadier Kitson please."

The soldier looked at Sean's long hair with suspicion. "Do you have an appointment sir?"

"No."

"Then there's no chance. You mad or something?"

Brigadier Kitson had been in charge of British forces for several months now. He had made a name for himself in Kenya during the Mau Mau emergency in the fifties. It hadn't taken him long to establish himself as enemy number one in the eyes of the Republican forces. London had wanted a hard-liner to crack the whip. Kitson had started to deliver. He wasn't a man to ask to see without an appointment.

Sean smiled easily at the soldier. "Listen. Why not go and fetch an officer. I can assure you that the Brigadier will be keen to hear what I have to say. Maybe I should start a little higher up though. Security and all that you know. Now be a good chap and run along will you."

For a moment the soldier's face reddened with anger. Then he visibly made the effort to control himself. "Wait here please."

Ten minutes later he was led to a room and joined by a captain. The officer sat down at the table and took out a notebook.

"So Mr O'Neil. How can we help you?"

Sean smiled pleasantly. "Actually it's the other way round. I think that I can help you. If you check your records you will find that I went through St. Mary's school with Gerry Adams Jnr. I expect that Gerry is pretty high on your list of targets for internment. Can't find him can you? Well maybe I can help you there. The thing is, I will only deal with Kitson. The top man for a top man. So to speak."

It took hours. Sean spent the day being passed from officer to officer in a variety of bare rooms. In the end he was shown into the Brigadier's office a little after seven. Kitson was a small man. Sean was struck by brass and medals and red flashes. He had bright eyes and a surprisingly engaging face. He jumped to his feet and reached across the desk to shake Sean by the hand.

"Ah. Mr O'Neil. All rather unorthodox, but you're welcome. Most welcome. Tea? Coffee? Something stronger maybe?"

"Coffee would be nice."

Kitson nodded to his batman who had been hovering at his side. "Make that two would you? Splendid. So Mr O'Neil. I gather that you feel that you can assist us with Mr Gerry Adams Jnr. At school with him I gather."

Sean smiled easily. "Yes I was. I can tell you that Gerry wasn't up to much at school. He was very quiet, sat at the back, wasn't all that bright and never said boo to a goose. Other than that Brigadier I'm afraid that this is all a bit of a con."

A small frown creased the little man's brow. Sean was relieved. He had expected him to go ballistic. "I see." Sean could tell that he was about to leap to his feet.

"It's OK Brigadier. Don't fret. I'm not about to attack you."

"Really."

Sean widened his smile. "I'm not that daft. Look I do have a proposal, it's just not about Gerry. Gerry and I have our differences, but I wouldn't dream of shopping him."

The Englishman seemed to relax a little. He leaned back in his chair and eyed Sean. The coffees were served and the batman slipped quietly from the room. Kitson carefully stirred his coffee. "Well Mr O'Neil. You'd better get on with it."

"Two weeks ago my girlfriend and I were interned. You came for us at four in the morning and took us away. I wonder how much of what is going on out there you are actually aware of. Just in case you are not fully in the picture I will tell you."

The soldier sat very still as Sean walked him methodically through the nightmare that he had endured. It took several minutes and when Sean was done the soldier drummed his fingers softly on his desk. He seemed to think for a long time before he spoke.

"I am sorry to hear that your girlfriend is so unwell Mr O'Neil. I genuinely am. You were right to come to me. There are things that I will look at. You have my assurance."

"I'm wanting a lot more than sorry Brigadier."

Anger flickered in the older man's eyes. "I advise you not to push your luck young man."

"I'll push as hard as I have to. Mary and I were involved in Civil Rights. Everything that we did was completely legal. We have the right to free speech in the United Kingdom. Oldest democracy in the world we are told. In return for exercising our rights we were subjected to the kind of treatment that you expect behind the Iron Curtain. I will not accept this Brigadier."

"I dare say you won't. I agree. It is you're right not to."

"Let me spell a couple of things out. I am a student at Queens University. Rightly or wrongly, the authorities there see me as a high flier. I have been offered a junior fellowship at the end of this year. Now I can assure you that if I cut my hair and put on a jacket and tie I will become the sort of person that the media is going to believe on both sides of the water. Mary was examined by Doctor Jonathan Hughes. Jonathan is one of the most eminent experts in his field in the UK. He is hopping mad about what was done to Mary. I can assure you that he will have no qualms about saying exactly what he thinks to the media."

"Your point?"

"My point is that we will make impressive witnesses. You will find it hard to rubbish us as yobs and thugs."

"So?"

"So it can be avoided. We can make a deal."

"Go on."

"The best place in the world for a case like Mary is the McDowell Institute in California. The US Army has pioneered research into victims suffering from stress related shock. A lot of their guys are coming home from Vietnam in a hell of a state. Doctor Hughes is convinced that their work is groundbreaking. He has convinced me that it is the best place in the world for Mary. He is happy to refer her."

Kitson nodded slightly. "Excellent. It sounds ideal. You must go ahead."

Sean laughed. "It isn't that simple. One, the Institute is a wholly military affair. Two, even if they could be persuaded to accept a civilian, it will cost many thousands of dollars. This is why I am here. I want you to pull the strings with your allies over the pond Brigadier. I want you to get them to take her in. And I want the British Army to pick up the bill. In return I say nothing. And Hughes says nothing."

"How do I know that you will keep your word?"

"Simple. If I start shooting my mouth off about what was done you simply stop paying the fees."

Kitson drummed his fingers again and fixed Sean with a long stare. "You must really love her."

"I do."

"Very well." He extended his hand. Sean shook. "We have a deal. Give me Hughes's number. It will be arranged. Off the record Mr O'Neil you have my personal apology for what was done."

Mary was put on a plane west ten days later. Sean was left alone with emptiness all around him. Once again he was alone in his chair. The hours drifted by and he couldn't find the energy for anything. He just sat and stared at the orange light of the electric fire. Late into the night, long after the sun had set and the autumn chill had settled over the city, he was startled by the distant roar of an explosion. He strained his ears. It was somewhere up on the hill in the West of the city. Maybe even James Street. He felt thankful for the umpteenth time that his mother was well away from the Falls.

Whose side of the line? The Falls or the Shankhill? IRA or UVF? More bodies on the ground. More horror on the TV screens. More tears and anger and funerals. He found that he was shaking. Only slightly at first, but then more and more. Tears were building up in his eyes and suddenly he could do nothing to hold them back. Soon huge sobs were jerking through him. It seemed to go on and on. When at last he managed to calm himself he realised that he had not had the time to come to terms with his own experiences. Mary had filled every minute of his time since being released.

Now all the fear and loneliness and misery seemed to break out of him. He felt as if he had been raped. Now that Mary was gone there was nothing that he wanted to do. He felt as though life had been drained from him. His whole soul had been stripped bare and rubbed raw. All his strength was lost. All purpose. All belief. All fervour. He was nothing more than another victim. Damaged.

Soiled. Scared. He just wanted to hide. He just wanted to curl up into a ball and hide.

The explosion was so close to the house in Granville Street that several cups were bounced off the top shelf of the dresser to shatter on the floor. Peter and John Stanton leapt straight to their feet and started pulling on the coats, which hung on hooks on the back door. Davie reached for his coat too.

"Put that down Davie. You're going nowhere son."

"Oh please mum. I'm thirteen now. I'm big enough. They will want all the help they can get."

Davie's mum looked grimly to Gerald Stanton. "Get him told Gerald. Tell him he's going nowhere."

Gerald looked across to his son and opened his mouth to speak. Then he stopped. It was almost as if he were seeing his son for the first time. The boy had pulled on his coat and was standing next to his grandfather looking defiant. Where on earth had all the years gone? The boy was already nearly five foot ten and his shoulders made the seams of the old coat strain. Two weeks earlier he had been selected to represent the Ulster under 14's Rugby side as a lock forward. The boy was right. The time had passed when he would be told to stay at home.

"It's all right love. We'll keep an eye on him. Come on, let's go."

Outside, crowds of people were pouring up the Shankill road to where the sound of the blast had come from. The men of the Stanton family only had to cover a hundred yards. The Four Step Inn on Ainsworth Avenue had been reduced to a pile of rubble. The air was choking with dust and everyone was coughing and fighting to see what was happening. Already over a hundred figures were heaving away at the pile of shattered concrete that had once been the pub. Davie and his father joined in immediately. After a few minutes Davie's hands were raw and he could feel the blood sticky in the dust. Every now and then someone would shout for silence and all work would stop as the diggers cocked their ears to catch the sounds of those who were buried beneath.

A faint cry came to Davie. He looked across to where his dad toiled away next to him.

"Hear that Da?"

"Don't know. Maybe." His father silenced those around them. Davie got down on his knees and pushed his ear close to the bricks. This time he was definite. The cry from below was muffled but unmistakeable. Others joined them as they ripped at the rubble. Slowly a body became visible. They were more careful now. Once the man's face was clear he spat the choking dust from his mouth and started to scream. A medic cradled his head and tried to calm him whilst the rescue party cleared the remaining rubble. Davie dragged a large chunk of concrete away and nearly gagged. The man's leg was horribly shattered. Below the knee there was nothing but a mess of torn flesh and bone. For a moment Davie couldn't move. He was frozen; he found it impossible to tear his eyes away from the appalling sight. His father gently took him by the shoulder and eased him away.

"Come on Davie. Let's give the ambulance men a bit of room shall we? Come on. He's going to be fine. You'll see."

They fell back from the bombsite as the emergency services took control. Peter Stanton was standing away from the crowd. His son and grandson could hear that he was having a heated argument as they approached. When they got closer they saw that he was with John Hutchinson who was shouting loudly.

" . . . Don't start getting all righteous with me Peter. This was no UVF pub. There can be no justification. They came here to the Shankill and set their bomb to kill Prods. This isn't Brit soldiers. It's not even UVF or UDA. This is just men out for a pint or two. Our men Peter. Our people. I tell you, they're going to fucking pay, so they are."

Peter Stanton was every bit as mad as Hutchinson. "So what will that do John? What message does that send out? The IRA commit pure bloody murder on innocent men so we're going to do the same? We're going to prove that we can be just as good as them at killing innocent men and women? That it? That the message you want to sent out to the world for Christ's sake!!"

Hutchinson leaned in close. "I don't give a shite about messages to the world Peter. Not a lousy shite. I only care about sending a message to those Fenian fuckers on the Falls. They need to know that if they dare to come here we will pay them back twofold. That is the only message I am interested in sending."

"Oh for Christ's sake John will you grow up. Don't be so bloody naïve, can't you see . . ."

"Shut it Peter." Hutchinson prodded his finger hard into Peter Stanton's chest. "Don't try and order me about. In case you hadn't noticed, you're an old man. The days of chivalry are all gone now. This isn't 1916. This is here. This is now. And those bastards will pay . . ."

He was prodding harder now. Davie darted forward and grabbed his wrist.

"Get off me you little wee shite." Hutchinson writhed and pulled but Davie's grip was too strong for him to break. In the end he stopped struggling. "OK. OK. Let go will you. No need to get carried away. We're just arguing . . ." The look in the boy's eyes pulled him up short. Davie was very still. He had Hutchinson's wrist clamped between his fingers. His eyes bored into the older man. Hutchinson had never seen such eyes. Not a flicker. Not a blink. Impassive. But scary, Really scary. Jesus, and only thirteen. This would be one to watch.

Davie released his wrist eventually and the older man edged away uncomfortably. "You OK Granda?"

Peter Stanton nodded. "Aye. Fine. Thanks Davie."

There wasn't much else they could do. They returned home and dusted off their jackets and shoes in the back yard. When they were inside Davie at last decided to say what had been on his mind for several weeks.

"I want to join the YCV."

His mother threw the dishcloth into the sink splashing water onto the floor before making an angry exit from the kitchen. The Young Citizens Volunteers was the junior wing of the UVF and already many of Davie's friends had been sworn in. His father gave a non-committal shrug. Peter Stanton stirred his tea slowly. Eventually he spoke to his grandson in an even tone.

"If that is what you want then there is nothing we can do to stop it. If you mention this because it is advice that you are wanting, then I will give you some. Don't. Our people have faced many a crisis over the years. This is not one of them. Things looked bad for a while in '69 but we held the line when it counted. Things are hard now. We will have years of bombs and shootings. But Ulster is not under threat. The British Army are here and they won't leave in a hurry."

He took a slow sip of tea and put his words together carefully.

"Going out and throwing a few bottles and stones won't do much for our people Davie. All that it will do is put you into the RUC files. One day things will be very different. One day the very fabric of everything that our people have done here will be under threat. That is the time when you should be ready to step forward. When that day comes you need to have everything on your side. You will need to be a stranger to the security forces. You will need to be fully trained in what you do. So my advice? Stay out for now. Get your head down at school. Get your exams. Get yourself to university. And keep on with your plan to join the army. Take the training. Learn all there is to learn. Then when the day comes you will be ready."

Davie stared down. At times his grandad made him feel quite miserable. He always cut through to the truth of things. Joining the YCV was nothing to do with defending Ulster. It was about going out with the lads on a Friday night. It was about the crack. It was about the girls who were attracted to the YCV boys like bees to a honey pot. Why did his grandad always have to put things on some kind of higher plane? Why did he always have to talk about defending Ulster in its moment of need?

All Davie wanted to be was like all the other lads.

But in the end Peter Stanton's advice was taken. Davie never did join the YCV.

As autumn drifted into winter the depression weighed heavily on Sean. Internment had sent the violence levels in the city spiralling out of control. A few months before riots had been occasional and death very rare. Now the riots raged in part of the city every night and the death toll was rising fast. Internment had been another catastrophe for the British. Almost to a man the leadership of the IRA had gone into hiding and by-and-large the new camp at Long Kesh was filled with low level players. What the policy had achieved was a tremendous upsurge in the number of IRA volunteers. This in turn panicked the Loyalist population and their

Para-military organisations started to flourish. More volunteers on both sides just meant more and more killing.

Sean had no wish to socialise. Once he had finished his lectures and tutorials for the day he would disappear into his flat and escape into his books. Almost every night he would look up from the pages as the night air shook with yet another bomb.

The Internment issue had breathed new life into the Civil Rights movement. The new students who had started in the autumn flocked to meetings. Once again the university was a hot bed of discontent. Michael Dennis had been lifted by the security forces the month before Sean and Mary. He had been rather luckier. They had held him overnight and let him out the next morning. Michael's dad was a solicitor from Coleraine. A few phone calls had done the trick.

When Michael came to call on a rainy night in October, Sean found his old friend in tremendous spirits. He was certainly much changed from the near broken lad Sean had comforted after his ill thought out rally had unleashed the pogroms of 1969. Sean could not help but smile as Michael marched about his room talking ten to the dozen.

"Hey. Slow down, will you. You're making me dizzy. I thought that people were dying out there and the whole place is falling apart. Yet you are acting like a man who has won the pools. What's going on Michael?"

"Internment. That's what's going on. It is just what we needed. They couldn't have given us a bigger boost. We're back in the thick of things again. You should see the numbers at the meetings now. Unbelievable. Better than back in '68. Honestly man, it's fantastic. You've got to start coming again. You'll love it."

Sean chuckled. "It sounds more like a party than revolution in the making."

"Aye, well that's not far off the mark. I'll tell you what Sean, once we get down the pub after a meet all I have to say is that I was interned and that I was at Burntollet and about 50 of the first year girls all drop their knickers in unison."

This really made Sean laugh. "Jesus Michael, that's typical. Long live internment so long as it helps us all get laid."

"If these young women of Ulster want to open their legs to me because they see me as Coleraine's answer to Che Guevara then you won't find me complaining. Revolutionaries need their perks. Seriously Sean, you want to come down. They'll be all over you."

Sean's smile froze. "I have a girlfriend, Michael."

"Oh shit. Sorry Sean. What a prat. How is Mary? Any news?"

"Bits and pieces. Nothing much. She isn't speaking yet but they seem to think that they are making a bit of progress. All we can do is hope."

Thinking about Mary popped Michael's enthusiasm. "You've never talked about what happened Sean. Was it really bad?"

"Bad enough I suppose."

"I wish that you would come and share it at a meeting. Christ man, you were always the best speaker. Come and lay it on the line. All of it. Let people know."

"Come on Michael, we've been over this before. What happened, happened. I'm not about to stand up and shout about it."

Dennis could never understand. "But why the hell not?"

"I've got my reasons Michael. Good ones. Trust me on it." He saw the disappointment on his friend's face. He always seemed to be a disappointment to people these days. "Look Michael. Tell you what, I'll come along tomorrow and I'll speak for you, but no nitty-gritty, no lurid details. OK?"

"Bloody magic."

The next evening Sean had to wait for several minutes as the cheering and whistling of the crowd died down. Michael was right; things were clearly on the up again. The room was packed with sweaty bodies and young faces shining with excitement. It had only been two years since he had caught the bus down from James Street. He had been just like them. So young. So full of passion and hope. And there had still been laughter and mischief in Mary's lovely eyes. Now she was gone along with his youth. He had only just turned 21 and he felt 60.

Michael had given him a huge build up. They were about to be addressed by a legend of the Northern Ireland Civil Rights Movement. Here was a man who had been there and seen it all, battered at Burntollet, bruised by internment, but still out there fighting against the terrible injustice of the imperialist/fascist British State. It was heady stuff and the young audience lapped it up. Michael even got so carried away that he yelled out "So here he is, a Civil Rights legend . . . the ONE AND ONLY . . . SEAN . . . O . . . NEIL!!!"

At last the room fell silent. Other speakers had shouted at the top of their voices. It seemed that voice loudness was the only measure of depth of passion. Sean didn't buy it. He spoke quietly.

"Michael wants me to tell you horror stories about being interned. Makes it all sound exciting and glamorous I suppose. Well it isn't. What happened to me isn't particularly important. In fact it is irrelevant. So if it's horror stories that you're wanting you'd best be off now."

He waited a moment, rather theatrically.

"OK. Staying on? Fine. Two names for you. Alexander Andrews and Ernest Bates. They went for a pint in a pub a few hundred yards from when I grew up. It was a few weeks ago. They're dead now. Both of them. There was a bomb outside the Four Step Inn on the Shankhill. The reason that they are dead is that the IRA has picked up the violence since the introduction of Internment.

So who were these guys? They must have been something big in the internment machine? Lawyers? Prison guards? Special Branch? No. None of these. They were just ordinary, run of the mill guys who went out for a quiet pint and wound up getting blown to bits. Why?

Come on. Hands up.

Why?

Nobody out there know why? Well, you do of course. All of us do. Everyone in the room. You're all just too embarrassed to stand up and say it . . .

They are dead because they were Protestant.

Got that. Registered is it? One more time to be sure. They are dead because they are Protestant. Here is the other statement that none of us wants to hear. This was cold-blooded sectarian murder.

Now all of this is important, believe me. Because it is the way that we react to issues like internment that will decide our future. The boys up on the Falls decided that it gave then carte blanche to go out and commit naked homicide. The Brits bang us up without trial so we decide to take the chance to blow a couple of completely innocent prods into about a thousand pieces. And yet have I heard any speeches tonight about how disgraceful it was that these two completely innocent men are dead? No. Have I heard any speeches about how those who planted the bomb must be rooted out by their own communities and made to pay? No.

Why not?

To the best of my knowledge the Brits haven't managed to kill anyone yet in internment. The Brits lift innocent people and intern them without trial. It's wrong. They ignore our basic civil liberties and freedoms. Sure, it's wrong. That is why we are here. But whilst we're here, we can't simply stick our heads in the sand when it comes to all the other stuff. Who looked after the civil liberties of Alexander Andrew and Ernest Bates? Nobody. Who looked after the civil liberties of all the poor sods in McGurks Bar the next day when the UVF took their revenge? Nobody.

What would Martin Luther King have done in this situation? Let's just say that the Alabama police lifted some of his people and gave them a kicking. Well of course they did. What would he have done if his people had gone out and killed a couple of white people? Any white people. Come on now, we all know the answer. He would have gone mad.

So I'm sorry. I'm sorry that I am spoiling your night. But this is where Civil Rights cannot afford to lose. It is much more fun to stand up and have a go at the Brits because, by and large, they will simply take it. It's a bit different having a go at the boys in the IRA and the UVF because they may just take offence and come down and break your legs. But these self-branded hard men are every bit as big a threat to civil rights as the government in London. If we haven't got the guts to stand up and say it then we might as well not bother turning up at all.

Our job is to try and persuade everyone out there that things can get better without violence. For the last two years all we have managed to do is to fuck things up. We are on our last chance. If we fuck it up again nobody will remember that we even exist. Then it will be the hard men who will call all the shots. So think about it. Think about it long and hard."

Michael was fuming when Sean sat back down. "You bastard Sean."

"Not a bastard Michael. Just a realist. If these kids want to find an excuse to come out and smoke dope and fuck like rabbits, then fine. If on the other hand they have any interest in making a political difference, then thy might as well know the truth."

"Jesus, what happened to you Sean?"

"Life happened Michael. Shit happened."

Two days later a very official envelope was waiting for Sean when he returned from his lectures. Inside was extravagantly fine paper with the ornate letterhead of Brigadier Frank Kitson.

> "Dear Sean,
>
> I have just read the transcript of your speech.
> You are a man of your word. Please accept my respect.
>
> Best regards
> Frank Kitson."

Inside was a return airfare to Los Angeles.

The next time that Sean saw Michael was at the end of January. Sean had spent a bizarre Christmas in California. Mary had still not spoken but she was past the stage of always flinching away from him. They had gone for long walks through the dry, sun-baked hills around the Institute. They had held hands. There was still a long, long way to go, but he knew she was coming back. The sun and easy going Californians had a re-invigorating effect on Sean. He started the new term in better spirits than he could remember.

Michael on the other hand had clearly slipped down from his pre-Christmas high. When he came into Sean's room he had a huge black eye and a pronounced limp.

Sean grinned when he saw him. "She must have a big brother."

"Who?"

"Whichever fresh-faced young first year is the latest to lose her cherished womanhood to a Civil Rights legend."

This at least brought a small smile to Michael's face. "Some chance. No. I was up at the march. You know, Magilligan Point, where they're building the new internment camp by Derry."

"Aye. Saw it on the telly. What happened?"

"Fucking Paras. That's what happened. We were all on the

beach. There must have been about 3,000 of us. It was all a bit of a crack. They'd put a load of barbed wire fences down to make sure that we wouldn't be able to get too close to the camp. Some of the lasses found that when the tide had gone out there was a gap between the water and the wire. So we all decided to have a go at paddling through. It was more of a laugh than anything else. Not for the Paras it wasn't. Jesus Sean, they just went absolutely mental. It made Burntollet look like a picnic. Rubber bullets, batons, fists, the bloody lot. It was a miracle nobody was killed."

It was a lousy development. The Paras had made a name for themselves all over Belfast. Whenever the going got a bit too tough for a local commander he would call in the Paras who would pile in like men possessed. There was something of an argument for this role in the heat of a West Belfast riot. However when they started using these tactics against peaceful Civil Rights marchers it was an ominous development.

"What about Sunday?" Said Sean "Is anyone having second thoughts about the big march?"

Michael shook his head. "No. It's still on, though I don't suppose there will be much of a turn out after Magilligan."

Sean grinned at him. "You sill have a lot to learn my friend. The march on Sunday is guaranteed to be huge. Firstly BECAUSE of Magilligan, and secondly because it has been banned. The surest way to get a big turn out for any march is for the government to ban it."

"Aye. Suppose you're right. Anyway, that's what I'm here about. The Derry people are of a similar mind to you. They are expecting thousands. They are desperate for stewards. They asked me to bring as many people as I can. We'll be needing a few cool heads. Experienced lads. You know what the kids up there are like. The first sign of anything they'll be rioting for all they're worth."

Sean nodded. "That's fine. I'll come. No speeches though."

Michael gave a dismissive laugh. "Do you seriously think I'll ever ask you to speak again. You must be nuts. I'm taking the car up on Saturday afternoon. I'll pick you up about lunchtime."

"Yeah, grand."

The premature darkness of a cold, wet January day was already wrapped around Derry by the time they arrived. It took a long time to make it through to the Bogside. There seemed to be army checkpoints every few hundred yards. The soldiers seemed very up tight. Twice both of them were made to leave the car and were searched roughly by the roadside. The welcome was not a great deal warmer when they passed through the IRA checkpoint that marked the border to what had come to be known as Free Derry. The men under the balaclavas were obviously extremely unimpressed by long hair and student cards.

The Civil Rights crowd had made their HQ in the City Hotel. There was an overwhelming feeling of excitement. Sean felt his spirits climbing for the first time in ages at the prospect of going on a march. The rooms full of naïve students seemed a long way away now. These were the Civil Rights veterans. In Derry it was very much the real thing. The people of the Bogside and the Creggan had never taken their barriers down. The big gable end mural announcing 'Welcome to Free Derry' was no idle boast. The barricades had kept the RUC and the British soldiers out for over a year. To all intents and purposes the people of the Bogside and the Creggan had declared their own independent little state.

Sean was soon down to his shirtsleeves and fully involved in all the preparations. He was delighted to be back in the company of many of the veterans from Burntollet, particularly Eamon McCann and Bernadette Devlin. The only organiser who seemed to lack high spirits was the charismatic local MP, Ivan Cooper. He seemed harassed and flustered, endlessly on the phone. A little after ten he disappeared into a private room to take a call. He emerged looking pale and drawn. Sean went over to stand with him.

"You OK Ivan? You don't look too clever."

Cooper shook himself and forced a smile. "Oh, I'm fine Sean. Just a few worries, that's all. I just got a call that isn't great news." He looked around to make sure they would not be overheard. "It was Lagan."

Chief Superintendent Frank Lagan was almost unique in the whole of Ulster. He was both a very senior policeman and a Catholic. It was largely down to his efforts that the undoubted mayhem that had engulfed his town for two and a half years had never descended into an orgy of bloodshed as it had in Belfast."

"What's the news?"

Cooper shook his head angrily. "Shite. As shite as it gets. The Paras are in town. They'll be out and about tomorrow."

"Jesus, that's all we need. Did Lagan know anything about what their orders are?"

"No. No idea. He's going to try and find out more. He wants us to cancel. He reckons it could be too dangerous."

Sean nodded. He could see the Chief Superintendent's point. "Look Ivan. Let me make a call. I might be able to find out something. Can I use your room?"

"Sure. Be my guest."

The phone was answered on the second ring. Sean spoke slowly and carefully. "I would like to speak with Edwards. I would like to enquire about the 'Terrible Beauty'."

"Just a moment please." The line clicked a couple of times. Then there was a silence for over a minute. Then Edwards was there.

"Well Sean, this is rather sooner than I anticipated. Nice to hear from you. What can I do?"

"Don't get all excited Mr Edwards. I'm not an IRA man. I'm still just a peaceful mug, marching for Civil Rights. Anyway, that's why I'm calling. I'm helping to organise tomorrow's march. The word here is that the Paras are in town. What I need to know is why? What are their orders? Should the march go ahead?"

For a few seconds the line was silent. "You have a cheek Sean O'Neil, I'll give you that. I will need to make a call or two. Ring me back in half an hour. I must admit, I rather fail to see what is in all this for me?"

"You can take pleasure form being on the side of the angels for once."

Edwards was in sombre mood when Sean called him back. "It isn't good Sean. I can't give you anything tangible. Just gut feelings. There are a lot of hyped-up people up there in Derry. What is pretty certain is that our lords and masters in London are sick to the back teeth of seeing permanent barricades manned by masked gunmen on the streets of a British town. There are a lot of people who want to use the march as an excuse to smash through the barricades and reclaim Derry for the Crown."

"So is that why the Paras are here?"

"I cannot say for definite, said Edwards, "but I would be highly surprised if they are going to be used for traffic duty. I think you should call it off Sean. Call it off if you possibly can. I'm afraid I have a really bad feeling in my bones. Nothing I can put a finger on. Just a sense. Something in people's voices. It will take next to nothing to send the whole thing way out of control. Try and be safe."

"Thanks Mr Edwards. I'll do what I can. See you now."

"Best of luck. Cheerio."

The ensuing argument turned out to be a spectacular. It went on almost all night and most of the following morning. Sean was a lone voice in wanting to cancel the march. He could see the point of everyone else's argument. If they cancelled the march then they would be more or less throwing in the Civil Rights towel. Once the authorities figured out what had happened, all they would need to do to stop any future marches or rallies would be to deploy a couple of companies of Paras. Eamon and Bernadette were the most forceful. They were adamant that the march should not waver an inch from the proposed route. This would mean that they would try for the Guildhall, which of course would mean that they would have to break through the army barriers that were there to stop them. In the end Sean and Ivan persuaded the rest that this would be far too risky.

At last, a compromise was reached. The march would simply head down from The Creggen estate and finish at Free Derry corner in the Bogside where the speeches would be made. With luck the route would stay well enough clear of army positions to avoid trouble breaking out. A foreboding had filled Sean from the minute that he had put the phone down after talking to Edwards. He had barely slept when he had at last crawled into a sleeping bag a little after five. It stayed with him as the hours of the morning flew by as they all tackled a seemingly unending list of last minute preparations.

However, when the crowd started to gather on the Creggan Estate much of his feeling of impending doom started to fall away. The rain had at last let up and there was a buoyant atmosphere among the thousands who came together. These were different people to the Peoples Democracy crowd back at Queens. They carried no intellectual airs and graces. They were just plain Derry folk who had finally got sick and tired of being kicked in the teeth. For two years now they had been kicking back. Things were very different to Belfast. There had been a concerted bombing campaign in the city for several months. Unlike in Belfast the IRA had set out sensible, well thought out goals. Their intention in Derry was to wreck the Protestant dominated economy of the town. To do this they had planted a huge number of bombs and more or less paralysed the town centre. What really set the campaign apart was that warnings were always given and to date civilian casualties had been avoided. The Protestant ruling class of the city had been squeezed until the pips had dropped to the floor.

Sean began to feel confident that the big march could be another example of how things in Derry could be done better. What he found particularly encouraging was that there seemed to be an impressive number of camera teams there to film the events of the day. Surely their presence would discourage the army from being too heavy handed.

At last the crowd was ready and the rally followed a coal lorry down the hill into the Bogside like a giant unravelling snake. Everyone was amazed at the size of the turnout. It seemed as if the whole of Catholic Derry was there. 'We Shall Overcome', the anthem of the Movement, rang out loudly and small children leapt and danced in excitement.

As they approached the bottom end of William Street, Sean felt the tension in his stomach. A hundred yards further back the crowd had spotted the unmistakeable red berets of Paratroops at the top of a wall. The mood had darkened. If things were going to go wrong, this was where it would happen. There was a barricade off William Street, which blocked a road leading into the city centre and the Guildhall. Every afternoon it had become a custom that the young tearaways from the Bogside would gather to throw stones at the soldiers who manned the barricade. This event had become so established that it had almost become a sport. The kids would hurl bottles and stones and abuse, and the soldiers would respond with abuse of their own and fire off rounds of plastic bullets. Every time a bullet was fired there would be a wild scrum of kids trying to retrieve it. Used plastic bullets had become the souvenirs that all visitors to the city wanted to take home to show off to their friends. The going rate was £5, and this made sure that there was always a major financial incentive for the kids to make their way down to 'Aggro Corner' for the afternoon riot. For the soldiers it was a welcome relief to the boredom. They had christened the kids as the YDH – Young Derry Hooligans – and if both sides had been entirely honest, they would have said that the daily afternoon riot was a pretty good crack.

The organisers had spent most of the morning trying all they could to persuade the YDH to take a day off. The kids had agreed and nodded and made their solemn promises. Everyone had been quite convinced by them. Sean had his doubts. £5 for a plastic bullet was a hell of an incentive. Sure enough, as the march reached Aggro Corner and made a turn towards its destination, small groups of kids started to break away. Soon there was a healthy crowd of them chanting "BRITS OUT! BRITS OUT!"

Sean and the other stewards didn't bother with the kids. There was little point in trying to persuade them to give up the excitement of a good riot to come and listen to a load of boring speeches. However there were many marchers who had not been made aware of the changed route. Some of these were livid when they heard that the Guildhall was no longer the destination. These needed lots of persuading to join the main body of the march. Others were easier. They saw the logic of the decision and moved along happily. Eventually Sean was happy that anyone who could be persuaded to re-route had been so persuaded. All that was left now was a group of three or four hundred rioting kids.

He quickly made his way to Free Derry Corner and joined Ivan Cooper on the back of the coal lorry. Bernadette Devlin was in full flow and the crowd were lapping it up.

"What's happening back there Sean?" Ivan asked.

"Just the kids. They don't seem to want a march get in the way of their afternoon riot."

"Little bastards. How's about the soldiers?"

"They seemed OK to me. They were just starting on the plastic bullets as I left. With luck it will all be business as usual. Did you see the Paras?"

Cooper nodded. "Aye. Top of the wall when we were coming down William Street. I don't know what their bloody game is"

It was now obvious that the soldiers on the barricade had moved on to firing CS gas. Small clouds were spreading from the ground where the kids were throwing stones and the marchers at the back of the crowd were beginning to cover their mouths and noses with handkerchiefs.

Bernadette's voice was getting louder and louder as she competed with the noise of the riot and the sharp cracking of rifles firing plastic bullets. Then she stopped and stared out from the back of the wagon with her mouth open in surprise. Kids were fleeing wildly across the waste ground. They were being pursued by three Saracen armoured cars, which bumped and bounced over the rough terrain. For a moment the crowd was in shock. This was the first time in nearly two years that the security forces had entered the Bogside. Everyone watched in anger as the doors at the back flew open and helmeted soldiers spilled out.

For a while the scene resembled a kind of anarchic episode of Tom and Jerry as soldiers ran in all directions chasing fleeing rioters. They were catching them in ones and twos and forcing them to the floor at gunpoint. The marchers were shouting their protest. Anger was growing. A few at the back of the crowd had turned and were throwing stones towards the soldiers.

Crack.

Crack. Crack. Crack.

Crack. Crack. Crack. Crack. Crack. Crack. Crack. Crack. Crack.

"JESUS CHRIST!" Shrieked Devlin "THEY'RE FIRING REAL BULLETS!!!"

Utter mayhem broke out. The whole of the rally started running in all directions. Sean maintained his spot on the back of the wagon and tried to make some sense of things. It was impossible. Not real bullets. They couldn't. They just couldn't. There was no kind of order. Just a madness of confusion.

He saw a soldier drop to one knee and aim his rifle.

Crack. Crack. Crack.

A young boy of about seventeen seemed to be lifted and tossed to the floor. Jesus Christ. He shot him. He actually shot him. Running away. In the back.

Crack. Crack. Crack.

Shots were everywhere now. Sean could see more very inert looking bodies down on the ground. It suddenly occurred to him that he was standing all alone on the wagon. He jumped down and took cover with a group of people by the back wheel.

Crack. Crack.

On and on. It seemed like hours but a glance at the watch told him that it was only twenty minutes. Everyone was more or less hidden now. In every alley or doorway there were clusters of cowering people. The soldiers were dragging people to walls where they were made to stand with hands held high.

Crack. Crack.

Further away now. Somewhere in the flats.

Crack.

Sean felt totally numb. It was beyond anything he had ever believed could happen. He had heard it in Edwards' voice. They had decided that enough was enough. They had taken their most ferocious soldiers and ordered them into the Bogside. They had wound the Paras up into a killing madness. It was as plain as day what the plan had been. The plan was to shoot the young stone-throwers down. Send out a message. Teach them a lesson they wouldn't forget in a hurry. Show them who's boss. And now there were bodies on the ground. He hated to think how many. The shooting had gone on and on. It could be a hundred.

He tried to convince himself that he was indeed awake. He screwed his eyes shut and then opened then again. The scene remained unchanged. Soldiers. Bodies. Saracens. Groups being herded away with their hands on their heads. It was real. It seemed impossible, but it was real. He had just witnessed a massacre. Pure, unadulterated, premeditated murder.

And everything was changed. Completely changed. It wasn't about Civil Rights any more. It wasn't about fairer housing allocation and the right to free speech and the neutrality of the RUC.

It was war.

The Brits had declared war in as clear a way as they could have chosen. It was unequivocal. It was beyond discussion. Beyond argument. Beyond all doubt. They had come out onto the streets and gunned down kids because they were throwing stones. Shot them dead.

It was war. Plain and simple war.

He walked over to where two men were laying the Civil Rights banner from the lorry over a spread-eagled corpse. Most of the man's head was blown away. His skull was left open like the shell of a soft-boiled egg. As soon as the cover was in place the blood from the head wound started to seep through the cloth in a huge red stain.

Civil Rights was as dead as the corpse on the ground. Everything had changed. Now there was only war. The long war.

When he returned to Belfast he had to wait for a week before he was taken to Gerry Adams. He waited on a street corner and was picked up by a car. A hood was pulled over his head and he was pushed down to the floor. A few minutes later he was frog marched through a door. When the hood was pulled off he saw that he was in the back kitchen of a small terraced house. He was probably only a few yards from home.

"Hello Gerry."

"Sean."

"I'm here to volunteer. You were right. It was always going to happen."

Adams merely nodded. "You were up in Derry?"

"Yes."

"We've had thousands of volunteers ever since. It will be the turning point. We have an army now. The Brits will come to regret what they did in Derry. Please. Have a seat. Have a cuppa."

"What do you want me to do Gerry?"

Adams smiled. "I think you'll be surprised. I don't want you on the end of a rifle Sean. You're too valuable for that. There is more important work for you. I want you to carry on absolutely as normal. Get the exams. Take the Fellowship. It is perfect cover. We want you for your brains. We need strategists. Analysts. We have any number of lads who are itching to fire the guns.

You will be perfectly placed. You have the library at your disposal for research. You have plenty of reasons to travel. Most of all you will be in their blind spot. You'll be a university don. Who would ever see a guy in a gown and mortarboard as a terrorist!

Just one thing. When you start on your PhD, choose something

American. Find a reason to make lots of trips to the States for your research. The battle to win support in the States will be the most important battle that we have to fight. I want to put you in the front line Sean. That will be your first war zone. America."

An hour later Sean O'Neil slipped out of the back door of the small terrace off the Falls Road.

He had been sworn in.

He had become a volunteer in the Provisional Irish Republican Army.

He was at war.

Part Two
Heart of War

Chapter 6
Spectacular

March 1979

Sean turned his back to the wind and cupped his hands to his chest to light a cigarette. He managed it just as he was about to despair. The smoke wandered pleasantly through his nose and throat. The waves of the Atlantic crashed down onto the deserted beach. Overhead several oystercatchers flapped busily towards the ranks of sand dunes.

A feeling of almost complete peace filled him. He often felt that the wild coast of Connamara was the edge of the old world. 3,000 miles to the west lay the frantic energy of America. Such a young country. A naïve country. Immune from the festering old hatreds that tore at the old civilisations of Europe. Here was where it all ended. Here was where the New World began.

He was often struck by the ludicrous irony that marked his seven year career in the IRA. Whilst he had devoted his efforts to the non violence of the Civil Rights Movement he had been beaten up, interned, tortured and nearly killed. He had been threatened and bullied by the RUC, the B Specials, the IRA and the British Army. He had seen his father more or less murdered, his mother and grandmother driven from their homes and the woman he loved almost destroyed.

From the moment that he swore his oath of allegiance, things in his life had completely settled down. He had studied ferociously hard for the remainder of his third year at Queens and had been duly rewarded with the impressive First that all his tutors had hoped for. His Fellowship had been duly offered and accepted. From that point on he had been on a fast track of academic achievement.

He had enjoyed regular promotions and the year before he had become a senior lecturer. His lectures had become very popular. The speaking talents that he had first discovered in the early days of the Civil Rights campaign stood him in good stead. The senior dons all liked him because he epitomised much that they held dear. They never tired of telling visiting dignitaries the story of the young boy from the war torn Falls who had made it to the top before he was thirty. The young male students liked him because he left his hair long, dressed down and kept hold of his radical views. The girl students liked him because he looked like a film star. Everybody liked him.

He had maintained all his connections with the Civil Rights movement. To all intents and purposes the movement had ceased to be of any importance the day that the Paras opened fire on Bloody Sunday. The war and the world had moved on. The heady optimistic days of the Sixties had disappeared out of sight. The last bastion of the old dreams were the small crowded meeting rooms in the university. Young students still clung to the belief that they could change the way things were. They made their speeches and passed resolutions and not a soul outside the campus gave a damn. But Sean always made an appearance. He was the star turn. He became glamorous. He was the in house Civil Rights legend. He never failed to get them all on their feet with hands clapping and feet stamping. His speeches were radical to the point of being outrageous. He had the knack of peddling utter pipe dreams with such passion that everyone could not help but get into them. No doubt as soon as the cold night air-cooled the listeners down a little, they wondered what on earth they had been so ecstatic about. But they didn't care. Sean was eccentric. A real working class hero. A visionary. Who cared if he was a bit off the wall at times.

Sean quite amused himself with the utter nonsense that he came out with. Early on he had decided that the best cover he could possibly find was to become an outrageous radical. It tickled him when he thought of the earnest trainees from MI5 who would have the job of writing up the contents of his raging speeches for the consideration of their superiors. Somewhere there would be a file on him that would make hugely entertaining reading. Along with his early efforts with Peoples Democracy there would be evidence of his involvement in a stunning variety of causes. Over the years he urged his ardent student followers to campaign against injustice all over the world. They should avoid buying products developed by animal testing. They should boycott all goods coming from the foul and evil apartheid regime in South Africa. They should write letters via Amnesty International to help political prisoners in Chile and Burma and the Soviet Union. They should march to ban the bomb. They should champion gay rights. They should campaign for abortion to be legalised south of the border.

Sean not only kept the watchers bemused with his speeches. He went out of his way to meet up with any radical who turned up in Belfast. He even wangled invitations to be a guest speaker for Militant Tendency in Liverpool and the miners in South Yorkshire and the CND pickets at Greenham Common. It seemed as if he was drawn like a moth to a flame to any anti-establishment organisation that he could find. There was only one exception. He was never seen in the company of the men from the IRA. In fact they were the butt of his anger in many of his speeches. He derided them for their small 'c' conservatism. They were men of the past, forever rooted in their outdated Catholicism. They were reactionary terrorists. Who in their right mind would wish to live in an Ireland governed by these men?

Maybe if he had been living in London or Paris or Berlin his wild views might have caused a small alarm amongst the security services. Maybe he would have been seen as an extremist. A subversive. A potential enemy of the state. Not so in Belfast. In Belfast he was a breath of fresh air to the men of MI5 and the Special Branch. He was up-front, out in the open, demanding working class revolt from the rooftops. This was their type of guy. They were more worried by the guys who lived painfully normal lives as farmers and milkmen and never said boo to a goose. These were the guys who slipped out in the middle of the night to dig up Semtex from hidden caches in the fields. They were the dull ones. The boring ones. The non descript ones with three kids, and who went to Mass on Sundays. They were the ones who blew up policemen and removed kneecaps. Compared to these guys, an outrageous nutter like Sean O'Neil was a breath of fresh air. Leave him be. Commie bastard. Silly sod.

Sean was always careful never to push the University authorities too far. They didn't mind an eccentric, but only if he did the job with the students. Once he was in the lecture hall or the tutorial room he was all business. He had a way with his students. He could get them to achieve to the maximum of their abilities. He had the rare knack of making everything that he taught seem interesting. His students barely noticed that he got them working through the night. He inspired them and his inspiration was reflected in their results.

For seven years his work with the IRA had been largely academic. After the wild west year of 1972 things had started to go badly for the Movement. The Army at last started to find its feet in the Province and to get the measure of the task. By 1973 it was starting to take the IRA apart. The old structure of Brigades and Companies was woefully easy to penetrate. A single informer was able to point out more or less the whole pyramid of command in any given area. And they did. Soon the Movement was being dismantled.

Gerry Adams was one of the first of the leaders to see what was happening and he managed to persuade his colleagues that the Movement would have to change, and change fast. By this time he was interned in the old Nissan huts at Long Kesh. He got word out to Sean and set out the problem. Sean took months carefully studying the workings of numerous terrorist groups from all over the world. Eventually the two men came up with a new structure for their army. The Movement was drastically slimmed down and broken up into small four-man teams. These teams were to have little or no contact with each other thereby ensuring that each volunteer knew very few of his comrades. When the new structure was adopted the organisation became much tighter. The wholesale arrests dried up. The hatches were battened down.

Adams also used Sean as a trusted sounding board for policy. By the mid-seventies it had become eminently clear that the

British were not about to throw in the towel and give up. By this stage there were well over 20,000 troops in the Province and the government in Westminster seemed happy to offer the security forces a more or less open cheque book to fight the war. There was not a hope in hell of short-term success. Both men saw that there were no easy solutions. They started the task of bracing their colleagues and the communities that supported them. They had to gear everyone up for the conflict lasting for many, many years. The concept of The Long War was born.

Sean had been successful in building up a small academic reputation on the other side of the Atlantic. Every summer he spent six weeks on lecture tours around universities on the eastern seaboard of America. He delivered them the fierce passion of hundreds of years of Irish literature to the Americans and they lapped it up. And once he was away from the lecture halls and the polite drinks parties he quietly got on with the business of the IRA.

He tossed his cigarette into the water and checked his watch. Time to move. He strolled back along the beach and down a small country lane to his Bed and Breakfast. He had first found it four years previously and had become a frequent visitor. The wild emptiness of the west coast of the Irish Republic was the perfect place to work quietly, far away from the distractions of Belfast. The bars in the tiny villages along the coast were ideal for discreet meetings where he would be issued with his orders by representatives of the Army Council.

For the last two years his regular contact had been Brian Docherty, a tough no-nonsense farmer from the hills of East Tyrone. Docherty had been active in the Movement for over twenty years and had never been picked up by the security forces. He was cautious to the point of obsession which suited Sean perfectly. If Brian was to be found sitting in the appointed bar at the appointed time it meant that he was a 150 percent certain that he had not been followed and that all was safe. If he wasn't there it meant that he was only ninety nine percent sure. One percent was unacceptable to Brian Docherty.

Sean got into his car and drove for an hour along small country roads. He took a tortuous route and by the time he reached the small bar that doubled up as a hardware store he was more than happy that he was alone. Brian was waiting. All clear.

Sean bought a Guinness and joined him.

"You well Sean?"

"Aye. Fine. Yourself?"

"Not so good. Things are going hard for us. Touts, undercover surveillance, bounty hunters, soldiers behind every bush, it's getting so we can barely move in Tyrone. We just keep losing people Sean. Good people. Hard to replace. Morale's lousy."

Sean nodded. It seemed to be the same story everywhere. Success was hard to come by. The security forces always seemed to be a step ahead.

"Anyway Sean. How have you got on? Have you come up with anything?"

Sean grinned. "You bet. We're going to get the guns, make a bob or two and conserve energy all at the same time. And to cap it all the British government is going to help us with the bills."

"What you on about?"

"Loft insulation comrade. We're getting into the loft insulation business."

Docherty shook his head. "Jesus Sean, I worry about you at times. I'm going to need another pint for this one. Want one?"

His task had been to find a secure route to bring in Armalite rifles from America. Buying them was no problem at all. The Irish community in the States were contributing hundreds of thousands of dollars to the cause and the guns could be purchased over the counter. The problem was getting them over the water and into Ireland. The Brits had been getting more and more successful in their efforts to intercept shipments. The Army Council had decided that the losses had become unacceptable. Sean had been passed the problem six months earlier.

Docherty returned with two pints and lit a cigarette. "Come on then you crazy bastard. Let's hear it."

Sean took a cigarette for himself. "OK. 1973. The Arabs attack Israel and the Six Week war sends oil prices through the roof. A year later the miners bring down the Tory government. These events have made governments very touchy about energy. They have woken up to the fact that it has got expensive, it is largely owned by dodgy Arabs, and one day it is going to run out.

So. What are they doing about it? They are appealing to the great British public to start to be conscious of their problem and to do their patriotic duty and start to save energy. Sadly we live in an era when public-spiritedness is hard to come by and so the boys in Westminster have decided that they need to offer financial incentives to get the people to do their duty. Now, in a house with no insulation, 25% of all heat is lost through the roof because, as we all learned in school, heat rises. Now that's a fair lot of wasted energy. So to encourage the public to insulate their lofts they are offering grants of £50 per house. The average terraced house in northern Britain uses about £150 worth of heating a year. If you can save a quarter of that you save just under forty quid. The going rate to put in loft insulation is about £70 of which you get £50 back from the government. So in a nutshell, the punter pays out £20 and saves £40 a year. A sure-fire winner.

It is pretty good business for the companies who are doing the installation as well. The cost of the job is about £45 giving a profit of £25 per house. Now on the mainland there are companies setting up right, left and centre. But not here. Not yet.

So how does it all work for us? First we set up a company and take one of those new sheds they have built at the top of the Falls. West Belfast is a 'Less Favoured Area' so we'll get the place rent and rates free for three years and a cash grant for every man that we employ. Then we put the word out in the Falls and the Ardoyne and the Bogside that insulating the loft is a good thing and that people should do it. Nothing too heavy, just gentle persuasion, we're actually doing people a favour. With luck, in a year we should be able to do about 10,000 lofts. That should clear us the thick end of a quarter of a million profit, all of which is basically coming out of the pockets of the government in Westminster.

Lofts are insulated with fibreglass. It is bloody horrible nasty stuff that you have to handle with gloves. I have found a company in Michigan that manufactures the stuff, and a few boys on the night shift have never forgotten their Irish roots. Basically, it means that we can buy our guns and these lads will take them into the plant and wrap and pack them in with the fibreglass. The rolls get packed into containers and shipped into Belfast. Now if there is one thing that the peelers are not going to fancy digging through, it's fibreglass. Why should they? The whole thing will be completely legit and above board. Once we unload the rolls we can redistribute them to depots in Derry and Newry with the guns nicely wrapped up inside.

You have to admit it's rather sweet. The company will make more than enough profit to pay for all the guns. The reason we can make the profit is because of grants from the Brits. Which of course means that the Brits will be paying for the guns. Now that can't be bad."

Sean tossed an envelope onto the table and grinned. Docherty shook his head and smiled. "All in here is it?"

"Aye."

"You're worth your weight in fucking gold Sean."

Sean went for more Guinness.

"So what's next? Any orders?"

"Aye. Different this time. A new field for you. The Council met last week. Nobody quite knows what to make of this Thatcher woman who they've elected. She talks tough, but fuck it, she's a woman. The Council feels we need to give her a warm welcome to the hot-seat. Something to show us what she's made of. Something big. Something to help with morale. A spectacular. A real spectacular. They have collected in lots of snippets of intelligence from all over the place. Little things. Just tiny pieces of information. Somewhere in the middle of all of it there will be a piece of gold. They want you to find it Sean. Find the piece of gold. Find the spectacular. I've got a bag full in the car and there will be more next week. It's a blank piece of paper. Find something."

Outside the bar Docherty pulled two carrier bags from his boot. Inside each was a mass of paper. He grinned at Sean. "Told you there was a lot. Should keep you off the streets for a day or two. Best of luck. I'll have more for you next week."

They made arrangements for their next rendezvous and went their separate ways. When Sean got back into his room he upended the two bags onto the bed. He had to smile as the hundreds of scraps paper spilled out. It could only happen in the IRA. The word had been sent out for information, any information, nothing would be considered too small. And the response had been overwhelming. And now they expected him to sift through the lot of it and find them a spectacular.

He spent long hours arranging the papers into a kind of order. Then he tried to analyse each piece of paper one by one. It generally meant referring to the relevant ordinance survey map and getting a feel for the ground. After five endless days he came to the conclusion that there was nothing there. It was all too small. Routes used by RUC officers to drive home. Pubs sometimes frequented by UDR men. Hotels which offered potential bombing targets as part of the economic war against tourism. Suspected UVF fighter's homes or workplaces or golf courses. It was all just small stuff. Nothing more than the bread and butter little acts of violence that had come to make up the routine of the Long War. There was nothing big. Nothing to test the mettle of the new lady in Downing Street. Nothing spectacular.

A week later he set out to make the two-hour drive to Monaghan where he was due to meet up with Docherty to collect another batch of information. When he walked into the smoky pub in the centre of the town there was no sign of the man from Tyrone. The one-percent must have rung alarm bells. Sean decided to have a drink and wait for a quarter of an hour just in case he was late.

He had just taken a place at a table at the back of the room when he was joined by a stranger.

"Fuck me Sean, it's you! How the hell are you?"

Sean was struck dumb for a moment. Who the hell was this? "I'm OK. Sorry, but I don't remember you."

The younger man laughed. "I'm not surprised. It's been years. We were at school together. You won't remember me. I was just a snotty nosed little bastard two years below you. Jimmy Flynn"

What was this? Was it just a co-incidence? "Oh, got you. So what you doing down here Jimmy? Work is it?"

"Is it buggery. I've been sent to meet you. Got a bag of stuff. Course, I never knew it was you. They just told me the time and the place and to look for a bloke with long curly hair. Jesus, I can't believe it. What can I get you?"

Sean was furious. It was totally unprofessional. "No. Nothing. Why the change?"

"Hell, I don't know. Other guy couldn't make it I suppose. It was a rush job. Short notice. Come on Sean, have a drink."

"No. I won't thanks. Lets just make the switch shall we?"

Flynn seemed disappointed. "Oh, OK then. Fair enough."

Sean took even more care than ever on the drive home. He had no real reason to feel so worried. There was probably a perfectly innocent reason for Docherty not making it. And what else were the Council to do? They didn't have the time to mess about. They wanted something fast. If Docherty couldn't do the drop they would obviously have to get someone else. In the end he relaxed a little. He was getting thoroughly paranoid in his old age.

He found it after three days. He found it when he was just beginning to despair. It was a small crumpled up piece of paper. A note was attached to it explaining that it had come from a litter bin at the army base in County Down. The document was a short British Army memo ordering the availability of two, four tonne trucks to move a company of the 2nd battalion of the Parachute Regiment from their base in Ballykinler to Newry where they would relieve the Queens Own Highlanders. They were due to travel on 27th August.

Sean opened the map and felt his pulse quicken. The obvious road that they would use hugged the East Coast as it wound around the mountains of Mourne. It then ran alongside Carlingford Lough more or less due west into Newry.

"Jesus" He said it quietly. Way down under his breath. Two trucks. How many would that be? Had to be 40. Had to be. Now that would be a spectacular. A real spectacular. They had all waited for seven long years for a chance to get revenge on the Paras who had murdered the fourteen on Bloody Sunday. Here was a chance. A real chance. He knew the where. He knew the when. And he was certain that there was something else. Something buried deep in the back of his mind that would tell him the how. It was close, but he couldn't quite reach it. He decided to turn in and drive up there early in the morning.

He set off at dawn and the drive across Ireland was achingly beautiful. For once June was turning out to be a proper summer month. As the morning wore on the sun burnt away the mist that cloaked the fields. The countryside had erupted into a spectacular array of vivid greens. The smell of cut grass swept in through the open window. There were times when he wondered why on earth he was doing what he was doing. Dark times when every bit of news was bad. Times when he yearned for a simple, ordinary life with a house and a garden and a job and maybe a wife and children. If he were just a simple lecturer the wife could be Mary. She had been doing really well for two years now. She had stayed out in California and he always visited her on his trips to America. She was working as a teacher in a kindergarten out in the suburbs of San Francisco. Her mind had learnt to deal with all that had happened and there was now a serenity about her. She wanted them to be married. To settle down. To begin life in earnest after so many bad years. She didn't care where. Belfast, California, it made no difference.

Telling her had been the hardest thing he had ever done. He had told her that he could not move out to America because he had commitments. Responsibilities. Not work. Not the university. Not his mother. None of these. Responsibilities to the Cause. The Movement. The IRA. And he would not allow her to come to Belfast. Because one day it would happen again. The soldiers would come and take him away. But this time it would be different because this time he would be guilty. Maybe he would just get a good hiding. Or maybe he would be one of those who never saw the inside of a courtroom. One of those who got a bullet through the head for resisting arrest. He told her that he could never put her through it again. She would never be strong enough. Maybe when the war was over it would be different. But not before. And it was a long, long war.

These were the bad times. Times when he would hide away for a while and drink. Times when all the memories would come flooding back and tears would wander down his cheeks. Times when the endless futility of their battle with the Brits would seem impossible to deal with. Dark times.

This promised to be a better time. The gorgeous morning reminded him of what it was all about. This was his own beautiful Ireland. Perfect. Unlike anywhere else in the world. And home. And they had been bullied and murdered and beaten and raped and robbed by the bastard Brits for seven hundred years and it was time that they were sent home. It took a perfect summer morning to emphasise just how simple it all was. 700 years was just too long. It was time that they went. And if that took guns and bombs then so be it. And if young men had to die, then so be it. And if he couldn't go and live happily ever after in California with Mary, then so be it. Sometimes his life became far too complicated. A world of books and theories and strategies and endless complication. Then there were times when it all seemed so simple. Fields. Mountains. Rivers. Home. His home. A home he was happy to fight for. And if the fight was a long one, then so be it.

He drove out of Newry in the late morning and was soon on the dual carriageway that ran alongside the water. And it came to him. The small fact that had been buried deep in his memory. The stretch of water was so narrow. On one side was the Republic of Ireland and on the other side was Great Britain. And the water was less than a hundred yards wide. And that was the how.

Things moved remarkably quickly. His report was rubber-stamped by the Army Council within days. In early July he was instructed to make his way down to a small farm a few miles outside Dundalk. He arrived a little after ten in the evening and was met by two big men who said next to nothing as they sat him in the back of an old Land Rover and drove him along twenty miles of winding country roads to another farm. He was ushered into the kitchen where another big man was waiting for him at the table. It was the first time that he had met with Brendan Conner.

Conner was a man whose reputation had grown fast within the Movement. He owned a farm that straddled the border a few miles from the Republican stronghold of Crossmaglen. Ever since the Troubles had erupted ten years earlier he had run the South Armagh Brigade with an iron fist. As virtually every other Brigade had been penetrated and betrayed and almost paralysed, the men from South Armagh had gone from strength to strength. They were hard rural men from wild countryside and they had been a thorn in the British side for hundreds of years. Merlyn Rees, the Northern Ireland secretary in the mid-seventies had famously labelled South Armagh as 'Bandit Country'. It had become the land where the British Army feared to tread. There was never any information. Never any informers. Never a chink of light. Just dead soldiers on a regular basis. And Conner was the man who made it all tick.

He nodded Sean to a chair and poured him a tumbler of whisky without asking.

"So. You're O'Neil. Gerry's blue-eyed boy. Thinks the sun shines out of yer arse, Gerry does."

It was no less than Sean had expected. It wasn't the kind of place where Fancy Dans from the big city were welcomed with open arms. He decided it wasn't worth replying. He took a swig of whisky instead. Conner continued on.

"I don't much like the idea of the likes of you coming down here telling us our business. Been in many fire fights have you?"

"No."

"Been in any?"

"No."

Conner looked over to his two colleagues and smirked. "So what the fuck are you doing here then?"

Sean sighed. "Look, why don't we stop fucking around. You're the big tough farmer and I'm the soft nancy-boy from the city. That's fine. Let's just agree on it shall we. As far as I am aware, we are both soldiers in the same army and we both take orders from the Army Council. Now, they asked me to come up with something big and I reckon that I have found it. No, I'm not going to pull the trigger because, yes, I'm just the soft fucker from the city. You lot will pull the trigger. That is if you want to. So do you want to fuck about all night in a who's got the biggest dick contest or do you want to look at the map."

Conner laughed happily. "Aye, I'll look at your map O'Neil."

It took over three hours to batten down the finer details of the plan. When they were done Conner was content. He poured out two more big measures of whisky and lifted his glass. "For Bloody Sunday."

Sean mirrored him. "Aye. For Bloody Sunday." He took a swig and said. "I was there you know. Saw it all from the back of the coal lorry. It's why I joined. It was when I saw what they were capable of."

"Bad as they said was it?"

"Worse."

Conner nodded and stared down at his glass in silence. When he spoke he didn't lift his head. "They say you're the one with the brains. You and Adams and Morrison and McGuinness. What do you make of this Long War stuff? Are we pissing in the wind?"

"No. They'll break. It will take years, but they'll break in the end. Like a tree in the wind. The wind will blow forever. The tree will only live for so long."

Conner nodded slowly. "It gets hard at times. All the young lads away in the Kesh or just straight gunned down. You wonder if it's right at times. Young farm lads up against the SAS."

"It's right Brendan. It's never easy and it's never nice but it's always right."

Conner had lost all of his bluster by now. "This is where the war will finish up you know. Little by little the bastards are winning everywhere else. Touts, spooks, death squads. They'll win in the end everywhere else. Not here. Not South Armagh. They've done their worst for hundreds of years down here and they're still no closer to winning. In the end it will be down to us and our few hundred square miles. You can come down. When things get too hot up there you come down. You're alright O'Neil. You can come down and join us for the last stand."

Sean smiled. "Now there's an offer that's hard to refuse for a soft bastard from the city."

It was time to go. They shook hands and Sean made his way out of the back door. For a brief moment his face was lit by the light of the kitchen. Fifty yards away there was the soft click of a camera shutter. As the car drove out of the yard one of the men in the wet ditch whispered to the other.

"Did you get him?"

"Think so. If we're lucky."

The photos were developed two days later in the Army stronghold in Bessbrook Mill a few miles outside Newry. The chief intelligence officer stared down at them for several minutes before shaking his head in annoyance. "No. Haven't a clue. Never seen him before. I'd swear he's not local. Send them up to Lisburn. Maybe they'll have more luck."

The grainy photo was at last recognised a week later. The MI5 officer whistled as he made the match with a two-year-old photo of Sean addressing a CND rally. "Well, well, well Professor O'Neil. Who's a dark horse then? What's a harmless commie like you doing meeting Brendan Conner in the dark of the night. We're going to have to watch you."

Sean agonised constantly for the whole of the week before the attack. He knew that he really should be professional. He had completed his part. They had given him a mountain of papers and he had used his academically trained mind to find a plan. That was the end of his part. He had found it. He had prepared it and he had sold it to Conner. And that was it. He was the ideas man. That was his value. That was where he was needed.

But he couldn't settle. What was about to happen was down to him. It was his creation. One way or another men were going to die. Maybe it would be the Paras or maybe it would be the boys from the South Armagh brigade. Whichever way the cards fell it was down to him. For the first time in his war there would be blood on his hands and it seemed cowardly to stay away and watch it happen on the news. In the end he decided on a compromise. On the morning of August 26th he left his flat and drove down the main Belfast to Dublin Road. Once he was south of the border he found himself a guesthouse five miles away from Carlingford Lough. He went to great lengths to tell the elderly landlady all about his passion for ornithology. She must have been suitably impressed because when he arose at dawn the next day he found a bag of sandwiches large enough to feed an army on campaign. He walked for three miles until he came to the top of a small hill. A mile and a half away he could see the light traffic moving along the dual carriageway on the northern side of the water.

He checked the view through his binoculars. Sure enough he could get a clear view of both the lay-by and the ornate gatehouse of Narrow Water Castle. He squeezed himself into a gap between two gorse bushes and settled down to wait. A little after lunchtime a small hay wagon drew up and parked in the lay-by. The driver got out and was picked up by a blue car. It was getting closer. There was sweat now on his palms as he scanned the eastern end of the dual carriageway. Somewhere on the south side of the border the trigger team would be in place now. They would be like him. Wound up. Tense. Sweating. Waiting for the small convoy. What if they didn't come? What if the intelligence was old and out of date? Well, if it was then the operation would simply be aborted. Part of him was beginning to hope that it would be so. Out here in the summer sunshine with the skylarks darting and looping overhead it all seemed so very different. On paper it was easy. But this was real. A real summer's day and men were about to die.

There they were. His heart seemed to double its speed. A Land Rover in front. Two trucks behind. How far to go? Not far. Just a few hundred yards. A few seconds. His mouth was completely dry. His skin felt suddenly cold. His body was like stone. How far now? Nearly there. The Land Rover level with the hay wagon. Past it. The first truck level now and . . .

Unbelievable. The truck took off as if it were a rocket. Straight up into the air. The hay wagon just disappeared in a blinding orange flash. How high was the truck? Christ, it must have been 40 feet. And all done in silence. Not a sound. Then the roar of the explosion carried across the mile and half of warm shimmering air. It made the hairs of his neck stand on end. Even at this distance the explosion seemed to rock the air in his throat and push at his ear drums. The truck reached the top of its arc and then seemed to pause for a moment to take in the view. Then it toppled and hurtled down to the tarmac below. The sound of grinding metal as it smashed down into the road floated across to him.

"Oh Christ what have I done?"

There was no triumph. No feeling of primal joy at the death of an enemy. There was only horror. Sheer appalling horror. And it was all down to him. Sean O'Neil. Killer. Bringer of death. And it wasn't over. Not nearly over.

The men from the second truck and the lead Land Rover were out now. Running around. Frantic. Like blind men. Jerky. Shocked. Lost for something to do. Cars were stopping. And a bus. And two lorries. Clusters of people. Lost. Shocked. Staring at the mangled lump of metal that had once been a truck full of living breathing men. Now the thumping beat of a helicopter. Circling. Watching. Assessing. And now landing. Landing in the field behind the gatehouse. Just like he had guessed it would.

More soldiers from the helicopter. One of them taking charge. A tall figure. Straight back. A commanding figure driving order into the chaos. Land Rovers with more men arriving fast from the west. Stretchers. Impossible to believe that any could have lived through the explosion. And just like he had thought, the stretchers were being carried to the field by the gatehouse. Suddenly the field behind the gatehouse was the centre of all activity. A command area. An emergency medical area. An evacuation zone. It was the place chosen by the tall officer in charge to restore some order. To get a grip of the situation. To save as many men as he could. Just like Sean had guessed. Just how he had predicted. He had predicted it because he had put in the hours studying the way the British Army handled itself in the wake of a bomb attack. By studying how they did it in the past he had predicted how they would do it in the future. He had guessed what was said in their book. And now the tall officer was doing everything by the book. Just like Sean had guessed he would.

He glanced down at his watch. Jesus. 28 minutes gone already since the bomb. The time had passed in the blink of an eye. He had a terrible feeling inside now. A feeling of dreadful, horrified guilt. What was going to happen was not about glory. It wasn't about being brave. It was about clinical, cold-blooded murder. It was an atrocity. He had guessed where they would take their wounded. He had guessed where they would set up their command post. He had guessed how long it would take them. And they had done it. Done it like men sleepwalking to their doom. And Sean O'Neil sat and watched through his binoculars from a safe distance and watched as the second orange flash scarred the sky. And he felt the shudder of a second rolling thundering sound. And he shook as he imagined the horror that would be found in the field behind the gate house where they had hidden the second bomb set to go off half an hour after the first.

He got up and walked away. He moved slowly. Like a robot. His legs seemed as if they belonged to somebody else. He felt as if part of his soul had withered and died. He was a killer. A murderer. And nothing could ever change it.

Later as he sat and watched the news with his landlady he heard that eighteen soldiers had been killed. It was the worst day that the British Army had known since the Second World War. Sixteen of the dead were members of the hated Parachute Regiment. And yet what had happened was almost a side show. That morning as he had walked through the fields to his lookout point on the hill there had been another bomb far away on the western coast of Ireland. This bomb had been placed in a small fishing boat and had killed a mere four people. However this was the bomb that rocked the world because one of the four was Lord Louis Mountbatten of Burma.

The IRA had their spectacular. In fact they had two of them. Celebrations went on long into the night in pubs and bars all over the places where the Irish tricolour flew from the lampposts. The Army Council also had the chance to observe and assess their new adversary in number 10 Downing Street. The MP from Finchley North emerged from a helicopter in Bessbrook Mill in South Armagh the very next day. A senior soldier threw down the epaulettes of the tall officer at her feet. He told her that was all they had been able to find. The lady never blinked. By the time she flew out the army knew that here was a leader who would let them take off the gloves. The IRA came to know Margaret Thatcher as 'Tinknickers'

The Long War suddenly got a whole lot longer

That evening Davie Stanton was out with friends in the centre of Leeds. They had all just got the results of their finals. Davie was a happy young man. After three years at Leeds University he had come out with a 2:1 in English. Any pass would have been good enough for him to take up his place at Sandhurst. But a 2:1 was great. A 2:1 was more than he had expected. Most of the lads who were out with him were teammates from the University rugby team. He had been their star. He had played in almost every game for three years and he was the one who would be remembered. They had been out since five that evening and the pints had flowed like water. He had watched the news in amazement but it had not dampened his party mood. He was just less surprised that the rest of them. They wanted to talk about it. They wanted to ask him how it could be. But he had waved them aside. Tonight was not the night. Tonight was a time to celebrate.

He went up to the bar to order more drinks. Beside him three skinheads with Leeds United scarves clocked his accent. The abuse started. The spitting hatred. A space cleared. One of them smashed a bottle on the bar and lurched towards Davie. Davie fixed his eyes. Stared deep into them. Never blinked. Very slowly he took off his jacket and wrapped it around his arm. The skinhead seemed to hesitate for a moment. He was unnerved by Davie's stillness. The he sprang forward. Davie parried the blow with the bottle easily and used the momentum of the man's charge. He stepped lightly aside and got his arm around his assailant's neck. He slammed the face hard into the wood of the bar. As the man dropped he took the face hard with his knee and felt the bone splinter.

He turned slowly to the remaining two. "OK boys. It's up to you. Before you do anything you shouldn't be confused by my accent. Sure I come from Belfast. I come from a place called the Shankhill. My dad and grandad are both in the UVF. They've been killing the IRA bastards for the last 60 years. So don't get yourselves hurt on account of what happened today. Because you would be getting hurt by going for the wrong man. Now make your minds up boys. Do you want to sleep in your own beds tonight or is it to be a ward at Leeds General?"

He smiled as he waited for them. The smile froze them. It froze everyone who saw it. At last one of them gave a small shake of his head. Davie nodded. "Good decision boys. Very good decision. Now I think you'd better find your mate some medical attention."

He carried the pints back to his mates. "Sorry about that lads. A little local difficulty."

They laughed a little too loud. Davie Stanton was a good lad. Davie Stanton was a laugh. But Davie Stanton was a bit of a headbanger when he got going. There was always something a bit dark about him. Nothing to put the finger on. Just something.

Jimmy Flynn felt as if his whole stomach was knotted with excitement as he made his way down the Falls Road. It had been three years since he had joined the Movement and now at last the day had come when he was to go active. He had no idea what the job was going to be. But it was something big. He could tell that by the phone call.

There were four of them. They were a self-contained active service unit. Their leader was Terry Nish, a 37-year-old painter and decorator who had been active since 1971. The other two were still teenagers. As a team they were woefully inexperienced. They were not alone. It was the same everywhere. Too many of the experienced men were behind the wire in the Kesh serving ten and twenty-year stretches. More and more operations were being handled by inexperienced kids.

Jimmy made his way up a back alley and knocked at Nish's kitchen door. The others had already arrived. Nish nodded to him.

"Alright Jimmy. You OK?"

"Aye. I'm grand."

"Sit down. I'll go through the plan. We're going into the Ardoyne. We've good intelligence on this one. We've got the address of a senior UVF man. He works nights. We go in at one o'clock. His wife will be out at work and the kids are at school. He'll be in bed upstairs. This is a very, very simple operation. We park outside. The driver stays in the car with the engine running. One takes out the front door with a sledge hammer. The other two go in, up the stairs and we whack him. Quick. Easy. Simple. No need for cowboy stuff. In. Do it. Leave . . ."

Both the doors into the kitchen flew in at the same time. Before any of them even had the chance to stand up there were guns pushed hard into their temples. The soldiers were screaming at the top of their voices. The table was thrown to the corner of the small room and the four volunteers were pushed face down on the floor and roughly searched. Jimmy had a boot on his cheek and the lino floor felt greasy and smelt bad. Within seconds they were dragged to their feet and pushed out of the front door. It had all been so fast. A few passers by were looking on open-mouthed. He hit the floor of the Saracen armoured car hard and within seconds they were away.

All four of them were constantly beaten as a police Land Rover with siren blazing lead them across the city. Jimmy curled himself up into a ball and took it as best he could. A quarter of an hour later they were dragged out of the Saracen and dragged inside the Castlereigh Interrogation centre. All the way they were kicked and punched. His head was spinning as they made him stand against the wall and took his photo front and side on. More kicking. His clothes were stripped from him. He was thrown into a bare room. He huddled into a corner and waited.

They all knew about Castlereigh. That was where the men of the RUC and Special Branch would break them down. They heard the stories of Castlereigh in the pubs on a Saturday night. They heard the stories of Castlereigh when men gathered on street corners when yet another boy had been turned into a Supergrass. They heard the stories of Castlereigh when defence lawyers pleaded to the courts that their client's confession had been obtained by means of physical and mental torture. And now he was here. They hadn't even made it out of the house. Fucking touts. Always the fucking touts. The army had known the lot. Who they were. Where they were. What time they would be there. Bastard fucking touts. All he wanted to do was cry.

A big man in an ill-fitting suit came into the room half an hour later. He walked over to the quivering figure in the corner and stood over him for a moment. He then kicked him viciously in the ribs and spat down into his face.

Jimmy tried to make himself into a ball but the big man just laughed at him.

"Let me fill you in you wee Fenian twat. You're fucked. Not just a wee bit fucked. I mean 150 percent fucked. One of your pathetic little crew told us all about it. I've got his signed statement locked away safely in my desk drawer. We had a microphone in the kitchen and we recorded the whole thing. We've got two Armalite rifles and a sledge hammer. We've got you trussed up like a scrawny little Taig chicken and all we've got to do now is hang you upside down and cut your throat. We've got membership of an illegal organisation. We've got possession of guns. We've got conspiracy to murder. One, two, three Jimmy boy. And one, two, three will get you at least a twenty, maybe even a thirty if we're lucky."

He paused to light up and strolled casually to the other side of the room where he leant against the wall.

"I suggest you take a while to think about it. You're 25 now. By the time you'll get out you'll be 40. Think about all those years away from the sun Jimmy. It's a long time. It's forever. Now I've got you for a week here. I'll get you some clothes now and then we'll be spending a lot of time in the interrogation room. There's no need to shite yourself. Everything is on film these days. We can get round that of course, but for you there's no need. I don't need a confession from you Jimmy. I've got you bagged up tight. Now, we can just sit opposite each other for a week and you can play the big hero and say fuck all. Aye, we can do that. Makes no odds to me. I've got a good book. A nice long boring week sitting in silence and then you get put in a place away from the light until you're 40."

He picked at his fingernails and took another hard pull at his cigarette.

"Or there is another way. I can't say I'm very optimistic because it seems to me that you are just a low-grade toe rag. But you never know. Sometimes there can be surprises. Maybe you can give me something. Maybe you can give me a bigger fish who is worth more to me than a little shite like you. You never know. You're a single lad Jimmy. No ties. No commitments. No wife. No kids. No job. It wouldn't be too hard for you to chuck it all in and start over. I could see you away over the water with a new name and a nice house and a steady job and a few quid in the bank. Oh yes, I could see to that. No problem. I could sort it all out in a day. But the price is high. It is only an option if you can give me a bigger fish. So think on Jimmy boy. Think on."

Jimmy cracked half way through the fourth day. He had barely slept and the solitude of his cell had been eating him up. He hadn't been able to stop himself from crying all the time. Every day in the cell seemed like a lifetime. How could he stand it for fifteen years? Over 5,000 lifetimes. He wanted to talk to someone. He wanted someone to tell him what to do. But there was nobody. Just hours on end sitting across the table with the big RUC man who chain-smoked and read.

In the end he just cracked. There was no fight in him. He wasn't cut out for it. Never had been.

"Sean O'Neil."

The big man looked up sharply. "What was that Jimmy?"

"Sean O'Neil. It's the only name I know."

"Tell me Jimmy. Tell me and you might just get your 'Get out of jail free' card. Because I know that name as well. And if we are talking about the same Sean O'Neil, I might just be very interested.

Sean was awake when the door to his flat flew in at three in the morning. It seemed as though he had been constantly awake ever since the bombs had gone off across the narrow water. As soon as he drifted off into sleep the images of the mangled soldiers flew into his dreams and he would jump up in a sweat.

He was sitting in front of the small electric fire with a book on his lap. He was half way through 'Crime and Punishment' for the second time. The book was killing him. The book was making his whole soul crawl with guilt. But he kept forcing himself to read on. It was page after page of torture. So when the door flew in it almost came as a relief.

They piled into the room with all the usual aggression and shouting. Sean held his hands up. "OK. OK. Calm down. I'm coming. No need to trash the place."

This earned him a smack in the face.

"If we want to trash the place, we'll trash it. What the fuck do you care anyway. You won't be seeing it any time soon."

Strangely enough his seven days in Castlereigh were a whole lot easier than he would ever have imagined. They beat him and abused him and screamed at him but it was nothing compared to what they had done when they had interned him all those years ago. In a way he almost enjoyed it. Part of him welcomed every kick. Part of him craved punishment. He had allowed the dark side to take a hold. He had become a killer. Not just small time. Big time. An eighteen men dead killer. A mass-murderer. A cold blood killer. He deserved it. Every kick. Every punch.

For a while he was scared. Not scared about what was going to happen. Scared because this time he had something to tell. This time he wasn't innocent. This time he could tell them things that would tear the Movement apart. He was sacred that he may not have the strength to endure it. Scared that they might drug him or hypnotise him. Scared that they would find a way of dragging out what he knew.

But this fear didn't last long. It soon became clear that they had been reined in. The British Government had been tried by the

European Commission for Human Rights and it had been found guilty. This had caused acute embarrassment to the world's oldest democracy. It had been bad for the image. Bad for the tourist trade. Bad for business. And the security forces over the water in the Province had been told in no uncertain terms to put the gloves back on.

And so he spent the long hours in the interrogation room with a small smile playing on his lips saying absolutely nothing. It was easy to smile. He smiled in sheer relief. He filled his mind with images that made him count his lucky stars. He could have been held by the KGB in Moscow or the South African police in Pretoria or the Ayatollah's merry men in Tehran. Then he would have had a problem. Then he would have been forced to tell. In comparison Castlereigh seemed easy. So he just smiled and never uttered a single word for a whole week.

At last he was transferred on remand to the Crumlin Road jail in the centre of the city. The charges became clear. He was to be charged with being a member of an illegal organisation. A lawyer came to see him. The lawyer was in confident mood.

"First things first Sean. This is important. Vital. And you have to be truthful. This comes straight from Gerry. Did you tell them anything? Don't worry. If you did, everyone will understand. It's hard in there. We all know it. But we need to know. We need to make arrangements."

Sean smiled. "No. Nothing. I never said a word. And tell him that they won't find anything in the flat either. All my paperwork is safe. They'll never find it. I don't keep much anyway."

The lawyer blew out his cheeks in relief. "Good man Sean. Bloody good man. Gerry said you wouldn't say a word. He knew it. Now. These charges. They're shite. They've got a surveillance photo of you with Brendan down in the south. That's not worth shite. I can raise plenty of reasonable doubt that it was taken illegally in a foreign country. They won't want to admit that they had people south of the border so they will be forced to withdraw it. All that leaves is the tout. It's Jimmy Flynn. He says he made a delivery to you in Monaghan."

"Aye, that's right enough."

The lawyer looked about the empty room nervously.

"Cut that out Sean. Now he says that he got the impression that the orders had come from on high. Now we can clean him up on that. You just need to say that you met accidentally, shared a pint and had a crack about the old days at school. It boils down to your word against his. I think we'll beat it. We also reckon we can get at Jimmy Flynn through his family. We'll send a couple of boys around to have a word with his mum and dad."

"Well it all sounds very nice, but I'm afraid I won't be saying anything. Please leave Jimmy's mum and dad alone. I know them. I grew up two streets down from them. They're good, decent people. Leave them out of it."

The lawyer tossed his pen down on the table in annoyance. "Oh come on Sean, don't give me this shite."

Sean folded his arms and stared at the agitated man evenly. "I shall simply refuse to recognise the court or its authority over me. I am a member of the Irish Republican Army and I will never recognise the right of any British court."

"For Christ's sake Sean, that is exactly what they are charging you with. Don't be so bloody stupid."

Sean flared in anger. "Don't give me stupid. We are an army. We are fighting for the right to be free in our own country. We are fighting a war. And it better bloody well had be a war, because if it isn't, we're out there murdering a hell of a lot of people. If it's war, these people are casualties of war. If it isn't a war, then it is pure cold-blooded murder. Now I believe that it IS a war and that I am a soldier. I got caught. I demand to be treated as a prisoner-of-war under the terms of the Geneva Convention. I will not stoop to using the loop-holes provided by the British legal system simply because it is to my advantage. Now is that clear."

"Yes Sean. Crystal. It means five years you know."

"I know."

The lawyer packed his papers away. "I'll tell Gerry."

"Yes. Do that"

The lawyer left and Sean was taken back to his cell. He hadn't told the man everything. He would never tell a soul. The real truth was that he craved to be put away somewhere where he could arrange his thoughts and come to terms with what he had done. He craved to be sent to a place where he would not be expected to be responsible for any more death.

It was Davie's second week at Sandhurst. They were still at the stage when the NCO's were trying to run them into the ground. It was the time of being kicked out of bed at three in the morning to be sent on a four mile run in the rain with a full pack. It was the stage when the hard faced sergeant major from Rotherham screamed into their ears from two inches away. None of it particularly bothered Davie. The physical stuff wasn't a great deal harder than the university rugby training had been. The rest more or less washed off him. He was different to most of the other recruits. They had come from nice comfortable backgrounds and found the abuse hard to take. He had grown up on the Shankill and for him it was just part of the furniture.

The jibes had started up across the dorm exactly on cue. The jibes had started on the second night. There were four of them. They had been together since the age of thirteen when they had gone on from prep school to Marlborough. They had all gone on to Oxford together and now they were together once again at Sandhurst. They were men for whom bullying was a way of life. It meant that the quiet Irishman in the bed across the dorm was always going to be their natural target.

Davie just ignored it. He never registered any of it. He just got on with whatever he was doing at the time. Tonight he was polishing his boots ready for the morning. Let them go on. It made no difference to him

"Few problems coming up I fear Paddy. We'll be all finished with the hod-carrying stuff by the end of next week. There'll be a bit of the old reading and writing after that. I should think it might be a bit on the tricky side, won't it Paddy? Never been a strong suit for you chaps has it, the old reading and writing? Shame they couldn't change the course a bit. Just for you. Put in a spot of potato eating or having a shit with the use of paper. That kind of thing. The right kind of level for a Paddy boy."

They fed off each other's laughter. Others in the dorm turned away, embarrassed. Maybe enough was enough. It wasn't really fair on the others. Maybe he better call a halt. He put the newly-

polished boot down next to the one he had already cleaned and
swung himself round so that he faced them.

"OK lads. I think we better clear up a couple of things."

"My god, it speaks! It actually speaks!"

Davie smiled. "Now all of this stuff is a bit tough to understand
for an Irish boy like me. It seems that there are two possible
reasons for this odd behaviour of yours. One. Maybe you are
being sarcastic. Possibly. Making jokes about Irishmen being a bit
thick is a well-established tradition. I have heard that. Goes back
years, so it does. Well, if that is the case, then fine. You just carry
on. That's OK. Just so long as it makes you happy. It makes no
odds to me. Simple pleasures for simple minds and all that. I just
think that the rest of the room is getting a little bored with it all.

On the other hand, maybe what you are doing is threatening
me. Possibly. If so I don't know how happy I am about that. You
see where I come from we don't take too kindly to being
threatened. You might have read about it. Or watched it on the
tele. So if you are threatening me, you better make it clear."

The four of them rose slowly to their feet. Their faces were
reddened with anger. They weren't used to being spoken back to.
It wasn't the way things worked. The Irish bastard was going to
pay. Davie got up slowly. He allowed his arms to hang at his side.
He still smiled. He waited.

Then there was another man at his side. "Hi Davie. I'm
Hamilton. James Hamilton. I was in two minds. I feel rather
confident that you don't need any help with these silly wankers.
But then again, that in itself could cause a few problems. One
against four means that you will have to resort to levels of violence
that you might wish to avoid. We don't want to see any of these
clowns in the infirmary now do we? You might just get thrown out,
and that wouldn't do at all. So, two against four is probably better.
Two against four means we can just give them a good thumping
and they'll be fine for the morning. OK with you Davie?"

"Aye, that's fine with me. How do you want to do this? Should
we pile into them and get it over with or should we wait and see
if they have the bottle to come to us?"

Hamilton grinned. "Ah yes. Good point. You mean they may
just shit themselves and sit back down."

"Well they might."

Hamilton smiled across the room. "Well chaps. What is it to be? A good hiding or shit yourselves and sit back down?"

Others in the room were laughing now. Everyone knew they would sit back down. Even after a week it was clear to all of them that Hamilton would finish top of the year. He had it all. He was tall and athletic and the born soldier. He came from a family whose men had been soldiers since the dawn of time. His father had been at Arnhem, his grandfather had been on the Somme and his great grandfather had fought in the Khyber Pass. They made an odd pair. The total Englishman and the quiet man from the Shankhill. There would be no fight. The four bullies sat down and looked crestfallen.

Davie turned to his new found comrade. "Appreciated."

"The pleasure was all mine."

Chapter 7
A Dark Corner of Hell

January 1980

The courtroom was full. Sean looked around carefully as he made his way to the dock. His gaze landed on his mother. He gave her a small nod and saw her dab at her eyes with a tissue. His barrister looked moody. The reporters scribbled away idly. It wasn't one of the big show trials. It was small time. Nobody had been blown up or shot or executed. Just a membership of an illegal organisation. Routine. Mundane. A conveyor belt.

They were reading the charges now. It was as if he wasn't there. He had to shake himself to start concentrating.

" . . . How do you plead?"

He waited. He allowed a silence to settle over the court. It was second nature to him. Working an audience was what he was good at. He had been doing it to packed rooms and lecture halls for years. So what was so very different this time. Nothing really. Just a fancier room and guys in wigs. He allowed a small smile.

"I won't be registering a plea because I do not recognise the rights of this court. This is a British court that has no jurisdiction here in Ireland. This court has no authority to judge me or any of my fellow citizens. I will not dignify the court by offering a plea."

After that it was all a mere formality. He might as well have turned up with sunglasses and a black beret. He might as well have clenched his fist and yelled 'Up the Provos'. They went through the motions. Flynn took the stand and a torrent of abuse

171

came down from the public gallery. He was so afraid he could barely speak. He stumbled through his evidence and departed like a terrified animal. There was no jury present. The judge didn't take long over it. He found Sean O'Neil guilty of the charges brought and sentenced him to the maximum penalty available: five years. He asked Sean if there was anything he would like to say.

"Not a great deal. There is just one thing. Jimmy Flynn is not a very strong man. He is just ordinary. Whatever was done to him in Castlereigh was too much. He broke. Cracked. Couldn't take it. It could happen to any of us. I appeal to anyone who cares to listen to let the matter rest. Leave his mum and dad alone. Treat them with respect. They are fine, decent people. Leave Jimmy alone. Let him be. He will suffer enough for what they have made him do. Please. Let's show that we can be better than those who make us do these things. That's all. All I want to say."

The van was dark and cold. There was no brutality as he was taken from the court and loaded into the back. He imagined the sheer ordinariness of the landscape outside. It was only a half-hour drive. Out through the south west of the city and onto the motorway. A few short miles across the grey winter countryside to Lisburn. He sensed the van going round roundabouts and stopping at traffic lights. Then out of the town and into the dull flat farmland alongside the motorway. The van stopped several times as it made its way through the various security barriers until it stopped for a final time.

They got him out of the back. He was in a yard. The rain had started now and the January wind was cutting cold. He glanced up and saw that he was being watched from the towers. All was quiet. Rain. A few rooks in some distant trees. High walls. Wire. Bored guards with sub-machine guns. All brand new. Soulless. Functional. He had always known it was where he would end up. Her Majesty's Prison Maze to the British. The Kesh to the prisoners. It was supposed to be the best-appointed, most modern prison on earth.

The Brits had shown it off to anyone who cared to look when they had opened it. It had the lot. Comfortable cells. Education rooms. Recreation rooms. Chapels. Laundries. Workshops. They spent more millions than they could count to show the world what decent people they really were.

The problem was that they took away what the prisoners had held most dear in the old leaky army huts that the new prison had replaced. When prisoners had been interned they had been allowed to wear their own clothes and associate freely in the various huts. The Brits had rightly realised that their internment camp soon became little more than a university of terrorism. Once they had finished building their new model prison they changed the rules. They said that paramilitary prisoners were no different from common criminals. They insisted that every prisoner in Northern Ireland should abide by the same rules be they an IRA bomber or a fraudster or a burglar. They had known that the prisoners would not like it, but assumed that they would have to lump it. What the hell else were they going to do? How wrong they were.

The first prisoner admitted under the new regime was a young man called Kieran Nugent. When it was time to put on the prison uniform he refused. He said he was not a common criminal. He demanded POW status. So they gave him a blanket and a towel to wear and laughed their heads off. But soon he was not alone. As the months went by more and more prisoners joined the blanket protest. Not wearing prison uniform meant a breach of the rules. A breach of the rules meant that almost all privileges were taken away. No exercise. No recreation. No association. Only one visit a month. Only one letter a month. Only a mattress in the cell. The Brits were pretty confident that it was mere petulance. It would soon blow over.

It didn't. It escalated. The prisoners were only allowed one towel. They demanded two. One to hide their nakedness as they made their way to the showers and one to dry themselves with. The authorities refused. And so the prisoners refused to wash and the dirty protest began. Hair grew long. All the prisoners had the beards of wild men. They refused to slop out their cells. They poured urine under the crack of the door and flung their shit out of the windows. The warders started to throw it back in. The prisoners responded by getting rid of their waste by smearing it onto the cell walls. And the problem just got bigger. The world's media started to take an interest. Men in towels and blankets was hardly earth shattering news. Men with long hair and beards refusing to wash was a bit better. Christ like figures locked down for 24 hours a day in cells with the walls coated in shit was bloody tremendous.

Sean was marched into the reception compound. He was fingerprinted and photographed and made to strip and shower. Once he was washed he was examined by a doctor and made to stand in front of a senior warder. This was the moment that the warders looked forward to. This was the would he or wouldn't he moment. As soon as the prisoner got out of the van they would start laying bets. It was hard to tell. Some of the real hard-looking bastards would surprise them. Some of skinny ones who didn't look like they could kick their way out of a paper bag would surprise them. This one was interesting. Tall. Pretty fit. But he didn't really look like a hard case. In for illegal membership. Probably not daft enough. And yet there was that little smile on his face. Nothing much. Just a small smile. As if he wasn't phased by it all. As if he didn't give a shite. Maybe he would be daft enough.

The warder got slowly to his feet and walked around the table. He picked up a uniform and boots which were neatly folded and held them to Sean.

"Uniform O'Neil. Put it on."

Sean shook his head slowly. "I am not a common criminal. I have broken no laws. I will not wear the uniform of a criminal."

"One more chance O'Neil. Will you put on the uniform?"

"No. No I won't."

The warder shook his head and put the uniform back onto the table. He resumed his seat whilst the others winked and nodded to each other.

"Have you any idea whatsoever what it's like in there O'Neil?"

"I bit. Probably nothing like the reality."

"Well it's your choice. You can move blocks at any time. All you have to do is inform a warder that you are willing to wear uniform. I'm sending you to H4. We have a vacancy for you. Know why?"

Sean shook his head. He kept the smile in place. "No. Actually I don't."

"McCann. Tommy McCann from Cookstown. Fancied himself as a real hard case. Kept having a go when he first came in. Right tearaway he was. We took him away yesterday. He'd only been on the blanket for ten months. Went clean out of his head. Absolutely lost it. He's a gibbering wreck now. We had to have him committed. Third one this year. I hope that you are strong enough O'Neil."

"I suppose only time will tell." Smiled Sean

"Go on. Take him down." The warder started scribbling at a form. It was always the calm ones who knocked him off balance. Jesus, this one was a university professor. So sure of themselves. So bloody downright certain. These were the ones that scared him.

They put him in a van to move him across the compound to H4. Again there was no kicking. Just blank faces. The smell hit him as soon as they led him through the door. The warders wore handkerchiefs over their mouths. The smell was appalling. Overwhelming. Old rancid sewage. He felt vomit rising up the back of his throat and it took all of his willpower to keep it down. The corridor was soaking wet with urine that had been tipped under the doors. He flinched at the thought of paddling through all the piss in his bare feet. There was banging on the doors as he made his way down. Greetings in Irish. The warders smacked the doors hard with their batons and yelled for the prisoners to shut up. Two thirds of the way down the corridor the warder opened up a cell door. Inside a man with hair down over his shoulders and a long wild beard was sitting on the floor in the corner. The warder stared at Sean for a moment. He passed him a blanket. "Welcome to Hell O'Neil. Welcome to H4." He then pushed him inside and the door slammed shut.

Inside the cell the smell was even worse. Sean struggled to overcome an overwhelming claustrophobia. The walls were covered in shit. It came down from the ceiling halfway to the floor. The cell was completely bare except for two mattresses. It was beyond belief. Beyond anything he had even begun to imagine.

The scarecrow figure rose up from the corner and held out a hand.

"So comrade, welcome to our five star apartment. I'm John. John Conner." His smile was infectious. Sean couldn't help but return it.

"Sean. Sean O'Neil."

Conner's smile got even broader. "Fuck me, it's the Prof. I've heard all about you from my Da."

"What, are you Brendan Conner's lad?"

"Aye. One of them. We're eight altogether. Five lads, three lasses. There's two of us lads in here on the blanket, two still at the farm and one shot dead by the Brits. He was impressed with you Prof. Dead impressed. That's rare for Da. Don't panic yourself about the stink. I know it's fucking awful to kick off with, but you'll get used to it. Honest. I can't smell a thing."

John showed Sean the ropes, such as they were. They had two buckets for their piss. In the corner was a pile of damp old bread and waste food. John explained that when the buckets were full they would send out word. Every cell would co-ordinate the emptying of the buckets under the doors. Sometimes the screws would just mop it away. Other times they got mad and pushed the piss back in. That was what the old food was for. As soon as the piss was away they would mould the old bread into a damn. They got rid of the piss at dinnertime. By the time the screws got back the dams would be in place. He explained that the shit got rubbed onto the walls when it was fresh. They used a piece of sponge from the mattress. He explained that they always threw the dregs of their tea up at the harsh neon lights on the ceiling. It helped to cut the glare.

Over the next two days Tom guided Sean through the routine of the Kesh. He had been in since early 1978 and he had been on the blanket ever since. That was the year when the screws had make the biggest effort to break them. They had hurled the doors open and thrown buckets of boiling water into the cells. Almost all the prisoners had suffered for weeks with severe blisters. Next they had introduced forced washing. The prisoners were dragged out of their cells and forced into boiling baths. The screws attacked them with vicious stiff brushes and nearly rubbed their testicles raw. This was the time when they smuggled out the address of Governor Miles. The boys outside had whacked him. After that the screws backed off.

There was no consistency to the screws. They had good days. They had bad days. The bad days usually coincided with news from outside. After Narrow Water and Mountbatten there had been beatings for a week. Other times they were just bored.

"One thing Prof, we look for different attributes in here." Grinned John. "I know that you are a brain box outside, but in here we need other bits of your anatomy than the brain."

"Like what?"

"Like yer foreskin and your arsehole. I hope to fuck you're not circumcised."

"No. Where are we going here?"

John's grin got wider. "It's our communication system. Comms we call it. Every month you get a visit. Now wherever possible we encourage our families not to come. Instead they send young lasses. Volunteers who pose as our girlfriends. Now as soon as you get in the room she'll give you a huge great tongue sandwich. She will have messages written on cigarette paper and wrapped in Clingfilm which she pushes into your mouth. And you do the same to her. It's quite an art. Once the transfer is made you sneak the comm out of your mouth and either shove it up yer arse or stick it in yer knob. We've got it down to a fine art. The record's 42."

"42 what?"

"42 comms under the foreskin in one go. The man's a fucking donkey."

Sean collapsed onto his mattress in laughter. Only the Irish. Only the bloody Irish. Even when they were reduced to shivering nakedness in cells covered in shit they still fought back with their foreskins.

"Know what John? There is no way on God's earth that we're going to lose this war. Those poor bastard Brits really have no clue what they're up against."

It was a superb day. Perfect. Perfect in the way that only England in the summer can be. The sky was blue from edge to edge. The Sandhurst grounds looked absolutely magnificent. The crowds were gathering. It was a day for photos to go in albums that would never be misplaced. A day when mums and sisters and girlfriends attacked the plastic with complete abandon to get an outfit to match the occasion. It was a day when dads and grandads stood an inch taller and remembered their own wars and the days when they were young. It was a day when younger brothers stood with eyes like soup bowls and vowed to follow in their older brother's footsteps. It was the day that the first class of 1980 were invested as officers in the British Army. It was a day of ceremony that the Army had practised for hundreds of years, and like most similar events, the British had honed it to perfection.

For Davie it seemed to go in a whirl. It was the moment that he seemed to have been waiting for all of his life. He could barely believe what he saw in the mirror as he got himself ready in the morning. The man who stared back at him in the dress uniform was a stranger to him. He hadn't noticed as the boy had become a man. He had never thought it possible to feel so proud. Proud that he had made it all the way from the Shankhill, through university, and now here. David Stanton. Second Lieutenant. Scots Guards. It was true. Real. Nobody could take it away.

However the best moments of all were when the formalities were all done with and the new officers mingled with their families in the grounds. These were the best moments because he could watch the faces of his fellow cadets as they came up to be introduced to his mum and his dad and his grandad. The best moments because he could watch their faces as their eyes were drawn to the Victoria Cross pinned on Peter Stanton's jacket. He watched them as they went away and nudged shoulders and pointed. The word spread across the garden party. The sergeant major from Rotherham marched over and saluted stiff as a board.

He shook Peter's hand. "An honour sir. Not many like you left. Good to have you here."

Peter smiled. He was well into his 80's now and his back was no longer ramrod straight. He leant slightly on a stick. Yet he still cut a dash. Still had presence. "Pleasure to be here. How was he? Play up at all"

"Pardon my French, but I kicked his arse from pillar to post and all I wound up with was a sore foot. I'd say he did you proud sir."

"He always has Sergeant Major. Always has."

James Hamilton came over. It had been no surprise when he had been unveiled as the best recruit of the intake. He had done the rounds, always easy, always with the right words, the generous smile, the infectious laugh. He was a man born to garden parties. He shook hands with Davie's mum and dad and turned to his grandfather.

"It is an honour sir. Truly." They shook hands. "Bloody dark horse your Davie. Never said a word about this." His glance rested on the medal.

"Good. I've always told him not to. Hate to make an issue of it. Only wore it today because he nagged me to. Wish that I hadn't bothered now. Bloody fuss over nothing."

Hamilton smiled. "Hardly sir. My grandfather was on the Somme. I wish the two of you could have met. He died a few years back. He was a fine man."

"Davie wrote us about you. Said that you had army family going back to the Dark Ages. Said that you have been a good friend. I thank you for that."

Peter laughed. "I'm afraid we Hamiltons have always been too thick for anything but soldiering. Please, don't thank me. Davie was a good friend to me. I hope we stay in touch."

"So. Where now?"

"Parachute Regiment."

Peter Stanton raised an eyebrow. "Paras? Thought you more of a Guards type."

"Plum in the mouth? Chinless wonder?"

The old man was suddenly embarrassed. He shuffled and made a grumping sort of noise.

"Sorry sir, only jesting. I can see where you are coming from. I just think that if one decides to be a soldier one may as well try to be a proper soldier. Don't you think?"

"Aye. I wouldn't disagree. You'll be heading for our neck of the woods I dare say. Call in to see us when you do. We're easy found. Halfway up the Shankhill. No need to worry. I'll let the people know who need to know. You'll be fine."

"You can be sure that I will take you up on that."

Peter assumed a fierce expression and forced his back straight. "And don't you give those IRA bastards an inch. Never. Not an inch. Shoot them down."

Davie's mum reached across to him. "Peter. Please. For heaven's sake. Really."

James Hamilton just smiled. "Oh I intend to do just that sir. Exactly that."

"Bears in the air!!" The call rang down the corridor. From inside the cell Sean could hear the sound of heavy boots outside. Was it him? Probably. Must be about time. The door opened. "On your feet O'Neil. Visit."

It was the one time in the month that they got to breathe fresh air. A few minutes as they walked across the yard. This was his sixth visit with the girl from Belfast who posed as his woman. They marched him into the examination room in the administration area in the middle of the H Block.

"Sorry about this Prof, but it has to be done, even for a professional type like you."

They pulled the blanket away from him and forced him to squat over a mirror. This was always the worst moment. Most of the time they only gave the reflected view of his arsehole a cursory glance. He didn't blame them. He stank to high heaven. They all did. Usually all the screw wanted to do was to give him a quick once over and get him dressed and out into the fresh air.

Sometimes, when there was a flap on, they donned gloves and conducted an internal examination. If they did he hoped they wouldn't probe too far. He had six comms wrapped and packed up his back passage and one under his foreskin. There had only ever been one warder who had gone as far as to peel back the foreskin. He was remembered as a perverted bastard. He had taken particular care to examine the younger prisoners. They had sent out his details. The boys the other side of the wire had taken care of the rest.

It was an easy day. They barely glanced. He pulled on the over large uniform and they took him outside. It was warm and sunny and he closed his eyes with pleasure. What would he give to be able to sit out in the sun for an hour or so? Just an hour of real fresh air and sunshine and the soft breeze on his face. Instead he got about three minutes.

There were four other prisoners in the waiting room. Three of them were not on the dirty protest and they made a great play of holding their noses dramatically. As Sean sat down two of the prisoners stood up to stretch. The warder looked on without interest. Using them as cover he removed the comms from their internal hiding places and put them to the side of his mouth.

He saw her across the room. She was called Brenda. Her family lived in the Ardoyne area of Belfast and she had been a volunteer for three years. She was a hairdresser by trade and most of her clients thought her to be a quiet girl who was never one for the gossip. She wasn't one for discos or girl's nights out. She kept herself to herself. She had always been quiet. At school she had got her head down and studied hard. She was never part of the banter. In fact she was barely noticed. She had never given a thought to politics. The Troubles were something that had raged around her for most of her life but she had never been remotely involved. Her parents locked their doors and hid from it. Lots of the girls in her class would come in on a Monday morning filled with tales of riots or gunfights over the weekends. Brenda never joined in. Hers was a family that drew the curtains and watched the TV and hoped and prayed that one day it would all be over.

It all changed for Brenda one day in 1978. She finished work and walked for half a mile to a community centre to pick her young brother up from his karate class. On their way home they rounded a corner and walked straight into a full-scale confrontation between rioting youngsters and a company of soldiers. She immediately caught him by the shoulder and made to turn around and take an alternative route home. As they turned he fell. She assumed that he had tripped and made to help him back to his feet. He was all limp. His eyes were vacant. There was a plastic bullet beside him on the pavement. Hours later a grave doctor came to Brenda and her parents and informed then that there was nothing else that he could do. The bullet had caused massive damage to the brain Her brother was in a coma. It was impossible to say how long it would last. It was now three years later and he had still never moved.

It had torn something deep inside her. It was just so unfair. Her family had never been involved. They were quiet people. People who would never dream of breaking the law. And yet it had meant nothing. A soldier had disobeyed every rule, every instruction, every guideline. He had let the situation go to his head and he had fired a plastic bullet above the legal height and it had hit her brother in the head.

Two months later she had walked across the city and volunteered her services in the Sinn Fein offices on the Falls Road. They had given her a 'boyfriend' to visit every month out at the Kesh. The first 'boyfriend' had been released in late 1979 and Sean had been his replacement. To start with it had been almost more than she could stand. She would meet her contact in a local park during her lunch hour. She would be presented with the tiny rolled up comms wrapped up tightly in Clingfilm. Sometimes there were other items to be taken in. Refills for pens or small packs of tobacco. Initially the shame of pushing it all into her vagina was almost too much. She had to brace herself and focus on the image of the pale unmoving face of her brother and all the tubes attached to his shrunken body. She hadn't liked her first boyfriend much. He was coarse and crude. He took far too long over their kiss when the comms were passed. He pawed her and made her sit on his knee. She hated it. Every minute of it.

Sean was different. The first time she saw him she was nervous. She was chewing hard on some gum. As she sat down opposite him he asked if she had any more. He took a couple of pieces and chewed on them frantically. She wondered what on earth he was up to. He noticed her confusion.

"Sorry . . . Brenda. That's it isn't it? Brenda?"

"Aye. Brenda."

He looked rather embarrassed. "I've been worrying about this for days. We haven't any toothpaste you see. I hate to think what kind of state my mouth is in. I've been swilling water about all morning and scraping at my teeth. They've all been taking the mick. I just can't stand the thought of how bad it will be for you having to kiss me. Hopefully the gum will help a bit. Make sure you always bring some in."

She giggled. Kissing Sean was a whole lot better than kissing her first boyfriend. When they had managed to swap their loads she found that she was blushing.

He looked awkward. "Sorry. That must have been horrible."

"No. Not at all. I'm used to it. Really."

"Well, it's good of you to say so. So. Come on. We'd better find something to talk about. Let's see. Tell me where you are from . . ."

That had been six months ago. This was her sixth visit. On their second meeting he had discovered her love of books. The teacher took over and he gave her a reading list of three books to get through before their next meeting. The visits became tutorials. After five meetings he persuaded her to enrol for night school. He told her that he was determined to see her in college before he was released. Brenda found that she had come to look forward to the monthly trip to Long Kesh. And, even though she would never have admitted it to a living soul, she rather looked forward to the kissing.

Sean smiled as he took his place across the table. He too looked forward to their meetings. She was a lovely girl and life had treated her poorly. She passed over three sticks of extra strong gum and he chewed hard.

"You don't have to do this you know. I really don't mind."

"Well I do. Christ knows what I must smell like. Six months now. Six months without a bloody wash. It doesn't bear thinking about."

"Honestly, it's not that bad. You're paranoid." She seemed to hesitate for a moment. "I read what the Cardinal said. It's all over the papers you know. He said that the conditions you are all living in are worse than anything he has ever seen. He says the only place where he has seen anything that comes close was when he saw people living in the sewers of Calcutta. Are you sure you are all right Sean?"

"Aye, I'm fine. People always exaggerate things. It's amazing what you can get used to. It's not all that bad. We keep ourselves busy. I never seem to have a moment. Rushed off my feet so I am."

She couldn't help but smile. He always made her smile. She knew that he was lying through his teeth but she didn't care. She gave it one more try. "Isn't six months enough Sean? Surely you have done your bit. Can't you come off now? Give up the blanket and have a proper cell and clothes and things."

"So kissing me really IS getting hard work!"

"NO! That's not fair . . ."

"Hey, calm down. I'm only teasing."

She looked down. "I worry about you. That's all. I just worry."

He reached over and took her hand. "Well don't. I'm fine. They breed us tough on the Falls. Anyway, I couldn't think of leaving my other prize student, could I?"

His other prize student resided in the cell next door. Bobby Sands had never had much in the way of formal education. He, like so many others, had been sucked into the Movement in his late teens as his family saw themselves ethnically cleansed. Bobby had been interned in the early seventies and it was during his time in the makeshift cages of the old Long Kesh that he had discovered his love of literature. He devoured book after book about revolutionary politics from all over the world. But it was poetry that became his greatest passion. He read everything that he could get his hands on and became a talented poet in his own right. Once he discovered that a professor of literature was residing in the next door cell his demands were immediate and considerable.

Sean spent several hours of each day presenting lessons through the shit covered walls. He had started with Chaucer and after six months he had reached W.B.Yeats. It had caught on. The occupants of the cell on the other side wanted lessons too along with John Conner. Then he had responsibilities for the whole of the wing. Storytelling was a favourite pastime. Prisoners would stand by the cell door once the block had gone quiet for the night and remember books that they had read as well as they could. It didn't take long for Sean to be everyone's first choice. He found that he had a clear memory of his favourite books and discovered an acting ability that he had never been aware of. Night after night he would perform the parts of numerous different characters as he took on the works of Hardy and Dickens.

Sands was everyone's inspiration. He was second in command for all of the Republican prisoners locked up in Long Kesh. These men were a battalion in their own right. In the overall Army structure they were the fourth Battalion of the Belfast Brigade. This of course meant that Sands was a senior officer in the overall command structure. It was his task to do all that he could to maintain the morale of his men in the midst of the stinking hell that they existed in. No matter how desperate things became, Bobby never seemed to lose his infectious enthusiasm for life. He made sure that all prisoners exercised vigorously every morning. He organised Irish classes. He co-ordinated the comms that went out of the prison. He was their talisman. Their inspiration. Their hope.

Brenda hung on to Sean's hand. She was annoyed with herself. Livid. How could she have said that? It was her job to give encouragement. To boost him. To put determination into him to carry on with the protest. And what was she doing? Acting like some silly mother hen and doing the exact opposite. She felt like kicking herself.

"How is Bobby?"

"Oh, as amazing as ever. We'd all be lost without him. Still my star student. Well, after you of course. Anyway. We'd better get on with the business of the war. Brace yourself. Give me a kiss and then you can tell me how you have got on with "The Mayor of Casterbridge.""

He had all the usual joshing as he was led back down the corridor. The joking voices shouted out from behind the doors.

"So how was she Prof?"

"Poor old girl. Christ knows what she sees in an old fart like you!"

"Let her know that there are real country men who are happy to step in if she ever gets fed up with a soft city boy wimp like you . . ."

The door slammed behind him and his shoulders sagged with relief. They all felt it. Up his back passage was word from the outside world and an unusually large consignment of tobacco. Getting caught on the way out was bad enough. It meant a week or two of naked solitary on the cold concrete bed in the detention block. But at least the comms could be written again and another would get them out. Getting caught on the way in was the real catastrophe. That meant no word. No news. Nothing to smoke. Sean had never known a much better feeling than making it back to the cell with his arse stuffed with goodies.

Sands shouted through the wall.

"You OK Prof? Everything fine and dandy?"

"Aye. Piece of cake."

"Grand. Well come on man. You've had your little break. Time for work. It's taken six months to get to the good stuff. Let's get started. W. B. Yeats. Easter 1916.

> *"MacDonagh and MacBride*
> *And Connolly and Pearce*
> *Now and in time to be,*
> *Wherever green is worn,*
> *Are changed, changed utterly;*
> *A terrible beauty is born."*
>
> *Let's get on with it!"*

The words stirred in Sean's mind. They took him back nearly nine years to the time when he had been interned. Christ. It seemed more like a hundred years. Edwards. Edwards and his code. Ring and say you want to speak about the terrible beauty. He wondered what had become of him. Was he still in Ireland? Was he still working for the government? He had certainly been right about Sean and the IRA. They all had. He wondered if he would ever make the call. Maybe. Maybe one day there might just be a chance to help stop the madness that was all around him. The madness that he had become a part of.

40 or so miles to the south, Brendan Conner had called a meeting. Four men had been summoned. They stood in the midst of Conner's herd of dairy cows as they chewed away at a trough full of silage in one of his farm buildings. He was confident that the mooing and shuffling of the cows would render any hidden microphone ineffective. It was how things were. You couldn't even have a quiet yarn in your own kitchen in case the bloody Brits had sneaked in with a mike. There were eyes and ears everywhere.

He looked at the faces of the other men. He was lucky. It was what made South Armagh different. He doubted if there was anywhere else in the province where a commander could have called on men of this kind of experience. He had grown up with these men. Grown from boyhood all the way to the gates of middle age and they had battled the Brits every inch of the way. That was what made South Armagh different. Special. No touts in South

Armagh. No cosy places for the security forces to hide. Never the time of day from the locals. South Armagh was tight. A fortress.

"Right lads. We got some intelligence in this morning. We heard that they were doing a change over. Well it's done. The Scots Guards are back. Fucking orange bastards."

The others murmured their agreement. Conner continued on.

"There's more. One of the lads got stopped at a checkpoint yesterday. Whilst he was waiting he heard the Lieutenant on the radio. Guess what? The Lieutenant's an Orangeman."

"What, Scottish Orange or Irish Orange?"

"Irish. Accent sounded like Belfast."

They stood in silence, amazed by the news. It wasn't a question of whether or not they should kill the new officer. That went without saying. No way was any Loyalist bastard from Belfast going to lord it around the square in Crossmaglen. No way on earth. The only questions to be answered where, when and who. These were the only issues at stake.

They decided on a sniper. A diversion and a sniper. That would be the way. They decided to go in two days when the patrol came out of the barracks for the afternoon patrol.

Davie took deep, deep breaths. He slowed his breathing down. Two minutes to go. He gave his platoon a last check. All seemed in order. The young faces were stretched with tension. The police station at Crossmaglen had become legend in the British Army. The sprawling structure had grown over the years. Now it was ringed with high metal fences topped with layers of razor wire. A high watchtower gave a view of the small market town spread out below. Like all good forts it was built on top of the hill. On top of the fences and all around the watchtower were huge wire cages to keep out mortar rounds or rockets. The quarters inside were cramped and miserable. The army had long given up travelling the surrounding countryside in vehicles. It was impossible. The local IRA were expert in placing bombs under bridges or in drainage ditches and culverts. The only way in and out of the fortress was by helicopter. The soldiers stationed inside only forayed out on foot. Twice a day patrols would check all the areas which could be used for placing a mortar to attack the station.

The army had learned the hard way that a patrol was at its most vulnerable at the very moment that it came out of the main doors to the station. They had developed tactics to minimise the risk. As soon as the doors were opened the whole platoon would come out at the run, fanning out, finding cover. Once they were all out they would move in short bursts, men covering whilst others moved forward. It was lethal ground. The town was entirely Republican. The soldiers could feel the hate all around them. Every corner promised a booby trap or a sniper or a hidden bomb. A half an hour patrol could seem like a lifetime. They knew that they would never get the chance to see their enemy. Death would come from nowhere. Death was always waiting out there in the nondescript little streets. And the British army was no stranger to death in Crossmaglen. It was without doubt the most dangerous couple of square miles on the planet to be a British Soldier.

It was Davie's third patrol. Before Crossmaglen they had been posted in Lisburn. It had been nothing. Just training. The occasional patrol through friendly streets to get accustomed to the ground. No real threat. Just preparation for the real thing. Crossmaglen was as real as it got.

He glanced at his watch again. 30 seconds. He gave his sergeant a nod. The small wiry man from Fife took control. "OK wankers. Get ready. I want the same again. Same as yesterday. We go out fast. Don't worry about how your hair is looking. Just go. Go like fuck. Out. Find cover. Get your guns up. Scan and study. It's simple. Ready. On three. One . . . two . . . three . . ."

The doors opened and they went through in a rush. The adrenalin poured through Davie. It seemed as if he floated for 50 yards before ducking down behind a low wall. His heart was pounding. He checked through 360 degrees. Nothing. Silence. The locals could always seem to sense when a patrol was due. The streets would empty as if by magic. OK. All set. He nodded to the sergeant. All hand signals now. The platoon split in half. Half one side of the road. Half the other. They moved forward in short rushes. Men covered. Men ran. Checking. Watching from behind the sights of rifles. Nerves jumping. Ten minutes in. About half way. Keep the concentration. Don't ever let the mind wander.

A soldier was up. Pointing. Shouting. Where to? Davie looked fast. A figure. Average height. Jeans. Parka coat. Balaclava. Gun in the hand. Running. Running away fast. The facts rattled into his brain. Something wrong. Running fast. Running away. A gun. But no shots. No shots and running away . . ."

"Shit!" He threw himself at the soldier who was standing and shouting and pointing. "Down! All of you! Down!"

He felt a disturbance in the air behind him. The air that he had just left as he dived at the pointing soldier. Two sounds. Hard upon each other. The nightmarish splat of a high velocity bullet flying into flesh. Then the loud crack of a rifle shot.

His brain coped with it well. He stayed analytical. As he crashed into the soldier and knocked him to the ground he had registered the yellow flash from behind the graveyard wall. He fell well. Fell and rolled and came to his feet and was running, just like he was emerging from a ruck on the rugby field. He zig-zagged and kept low. Twice more he felt the movement in the air around him. Two more loud cracks. Two more yellow flashes from the wall. 40 yards. Thirty. He fixed his eyes on the spot.

Then the sniper's nerve cracked. He was suddenly up and running for a revving car waiting at the other side of the graveyard. Davie stopped. Lined him up. Took a long slow breath in. A slow breath out. And his finger squeezed. The rifle thumped into his shoulder. One. Two. Three. Four. The runner was pitched forward and onto the floor. He lay twitching. The car sped away. And then silence descended.

Davie remained stock still for a moment. Still exhaling his killing breath. "Never run straight arsehole. Never run straight. Straight gets you dead."

He turned and dodged back to where his platoon had secured a position around the soldier who had fallen. Please let him be OK. Please let be a leg or an arm. Oh no. Oh fuck. Nineteen year old Donald Maclean from the picturesque border town of Peebles had lost half of his head. His brains were all over the pavement. His body was as still as stone. Three days. Three lousy stinking days and he had lost one. He wanted to howl and scream with rage and rake the walls with a sustained burst of fire. But he gritted his teeth down hard and kept his voice level and even.

"Corporal, call in support. Sarge, keep the area secure and throw a cordon around that fucker in the graveyard."

He stripped off his flak jacket and covered what was left of the young face of Donald Maclean. He knew it would earn him a bollocking. Stuff it. He could see the curtains twitching. There were eyes all over. Silently cheering. Silently rejoicing the death of a nineteen-year-old lad from the small picturesque border town of Peebles. And later the pints would flow like water and all the old songs would ring out of the pubs and bars around the square in Crossmaglen.

Three days. Three lousy, stinking days

Later he stood ramrod straight in front of the colonel's desk.

"At ease Stanton. Please. Sit down. Drink?"

"Yes please sir."

The colonel poured. The whisky tasted like nectar. The colonel prided himself on serving the best dram in the British Army.

"I've read all the reports Stanton. Excellent. Truly excellent. The man you shot was Gerald Docherty. He is on every list that the RUC has. Active since 1969. Accomplished sniping skills. Suspected of at least five previous shootings. No kid throwing stones this one Stanton. This one was a player. A real player. It will rock them back on their heels will this one. They don't like losing men like Docherty. Not one bit. Brendan Conner will choke on his dinner tonight."

Davie wasn't sure if he was supposed to speak. The colonel continued.

"There were no errors in the patrol Stanton. None. You reacted with speed. You were decisive. I do not hold you in any way whatsoever responsible for the death of young Maclean. I want that to be very clear."

"Thank you sir."

"In fact I will be referring your actions further. You will be at least mentioned in dispatches. Maybe more. I don't know."

"Thank you sir."

The colonel took a ponderous drink from his tumbler. "However there is something else. The intelligence boys have studied the reports and the photographs carefully. Look at this. This is what they have come up with. See. This is the ground. This was where the shooter was waiting. This was the line of fire. See? Now if you hadn't dived to get Gregson down the bullet would almost certainly have hit you. Almost certainly. The intelligence boys are pretty sure that you were the target. They think that someone must have heard you talking and have passed this on to the Brigade command. Lets face it, you hardly sound as if you come from Edinburgh. They believe that what happened today was a specific assassination attempt on you. It would certainly be no surprise. An Ulster Loyalist in a Scots Guards uniform is bound to be a prime target for them.

Basically, Stanton, what I am saying is that we believe that your are in an unusual amount of danger. Maybe more than is acceptable. Should you wish to be transferred you can be sure that you would have my full support. I can categorically assure you that it would in no way affect your future career."

So that was it. Davie had already guessed. He had guessed a few seconds after he had gunned down Docherty. He had been hoping that nobody else would put it together. Well they had. Sod it.

"Actually sir, I am quite happy to stay on. I wouldn't want to leave my platoon at this time. Maybe this situation could even prove advantageous. We can expect another attempt. It might give us the chance to get another one."

A slow smile spread over the colonel's face. "It may indeed. Good man Stanton. Bloody good man. Have another drink. Time to celebrate I would say."

Later Davie found sleep hard to find. The bunk was hard and all around him were snoring men. The events of the afternoon rolled through his mind over and over. The image of young Maclean refused to leave him. Surely there must have been something he could have done. There had to have been. If the colonel was right, then what the hell were they doing here? They were setting themselves up for target practice. Like every other British soldier who had ever lain awake inside the ugly fortress in Crossmaglen his thoughts turned inevitably to one particular subject. They knew full well who all the main players were. They knew where they lived, where they worked, when they collected their Giros, what time they got up for their morning shit. And yet they could not touch them. Day after day they would send out the young soldiers as targets and hope to flush out a player. They were forever on the back foot. There had to be another way.

Sean soon discovered that summer was the worst time in the H Blocks. It was warmer in the cells, which was an improvement. However he would have taken the cold any time. Summer meant maggots. They were everywhere. Whenever they awoke from sleep there would be maggots all over their faces. The maggots more than any other factor made men give up and accept the uniform. It had been the maggots that had sent two prisoners clean out of their minds and into the asylum. Sean hated them. Hated them more than anything he had ever hated in his whole life.

He found it almost impossible to sleep. Just as he would be slipping away he would sense the maggots coming for him and he would jump up. He wondered whether he should mention it to Conner. Maybe they could sleep in shifts. He would be able to sleep if he knew that Conner was there to brush the maggots off him before they had the chance to wriggle into his nose and his ears. He had been considering bringing it up for days. The trouble was that it was weakness. He hated the thought of showing any weakness. They all did. Especially since it was only about a few little maggots.

He sat up against the wall and muttered under his breath.

"Fuck. Fuck. Fuck."

"You awake Sean?"

The voice came in softly from the cell next door.

"Aye Bobby. That I am. Fucking bastard maggots. What time do you reckon it is?"

"Don't know. Back of two I suppose. I'm the same. Can't abide the wee fuckers."

Maybe this was the time. After all Bobby was the man in charge. "I was wondering whether I should have a word with John. See if we could sleep in shifts. One could brush the bastards away whilst the other gets some kip."

"That's sound. Good thinking Prof. I'll put the word out tomorrow. Lots of the boys struggle this time of year."

They sat in silence for a while. The ward was totally quiet.

"You know what Bobby?" Said Sean eventually.

"What?"

"It's not just the maggots. I never seem to be able to sleep. Even before I was in here. It's been months now."

"How come?"

Sean wondered whether he should say anything. Maybe it was insecure. On the other hand Sands was a senior man. He had to talk to someone. Had to try and unburden himself.

"Did you know that The Narrow Water attack was down to me?"

"Aye. I heard whispers."

"I watched it happen. I was going to stay away but it seemed cowardly. So I went down and watched it from a mile away. It was terrible. I can't clear it out of my mind. Every time I close my eyes I get the pictures. They just won't go away."

There was silence from the other side of the wall for a few moments. In the end Sands spoke. "They were Brits Sean. The enemy. That's how it is."

"Hell, I know that Bobby. But look at it this way. When we win this war and we have our United Ireland, we will have a proper army. And young lads from Belfast and Derry will join up because they can't find a job anywhere else. And they might get sent overseas somewhere. They won't be the government. They won't be fanatics. They will just be lads. Lads who probably flopped their exams and want a job. That is all the Brits at Narrow Water were. Just lads. And their faces won't leave me alone."

"Christ Sean, you're talking to the wrong guy here. We fucked up our operation. We were going to bomb a showroom but we got caught. Complete cock-up. I've never killed a man in my life. I don't know how I'd be if I had. But if it's amateur psychology you're after, I'll try a bit."

"Please do. Anything."

"I think you're feeling bad for feeling bad. We try and live up to the image of being superhuman. Men who will kill for freedom without a second thought. Bullshit. We're just lads too. I guess it has always been the same. I guess soldiers from any war that has ever been fought have always felt the same. Well, the decent ones probably have. The nutters will always get their rocks off from killing. It's OK to feel bad Sean. Nobody would expect any different. But what choice is there? Every time we've tried to ask them nicely they have kicked us in the teeth. We either fight or we get kicked in the teeth forever. And if we fight people will get killed. And it's shite. The ones who sing in the pubs don't know anything. The ones at home never do. It's the poor bastards who pull the trigger who have to live with it. I don't know if this sounds like a load of bollocks, but it's the best I can come up with."

Sean chuckled. "So the key is to feel good about feeling bad instead of feeling bad about feeling bad."

"Spot on."

"That's just daft enough to make some sense."

Again they allowed the silence of the night to settle over them. It struck Sean just how odd life could be. Here he was in a place that to all intents and purposes was in the lower depths of hell. And yet he had built up a friendship that he had never known before. In his months in H4 he had never actually seen Bobby Sands face to face. All he knew of his friend were glimpses through the bars as he made his way across the yard for visits. Their bond had been built as they sat and talked for hours either side of the stinking wall. It wasn't just the two of them. It was every prisoner on the blanket. The sheer misery of their existence drew them closer together than any of them would have thought possible. But the summer was beginning to prove too much. It had been a long time. Years. And the longer it went on the less likely it seemed that they would prevail. Thatcher was the problem. Anyone else and it would have been different, but Thatcher was impossible. There was never a crack. Never a chink of light. The woman was implacable. This time it was Sands who spoke.

"Things are going to have to change Sean. I can't keep the lads morale up for much longer. We're going to have to move this thing along."

"What the hell else can we do?"

"I suppose we'll have to take the road that Irishmen have been taking for hundreds of years. Hunger strike. There's nothing left. Living in shite isn't going to move Tinknickers. Some of us are going to have to die. Just like always"

It was nearly a year later that Bobby's words proved to be prophetic. The first hunger strike had been called in the Autumn of

1980. By this stage there were over five hundred prisoners on the blanket and the impasse with the government in London was total. The overall commander in Long Kesh, Brendan Hughes, led a hunger strike consisting of seven men who represented the six counties of the Province alongside an INLA prisoner. Bobby Sands was promoted to become the new commander. The leadership of the IRA was dead against the action. They feared that it would be a distraction to the armed struggle. More than this, they feared that it would be a disaster for the Movement were the strike to fail. However by this time the army command had more or less lost control of the men behind the wire. The Dirty Protest had hardened them. They were not ready to step back. They were hell bent on going forward. It became clear that a hunger strike would go ahead with or without the consent of the Movement's leadership.

170 of the men on the protest put their names forward for the strike. Sean was one of them. Bobby chuckled when he received a comm regarding this from the Belfast command.

"Sorry Prof. If you're planning a diet you'll have to find an alternative. I'm afraid our lords and masters are not amused. You are too valuable to be wasted they say. The tone of the order isn't particularly cordial. The gist of it is 'stop fucking about O'Neil!'"

The strike reached its climax in December. It was to prove a hard lesson for the prisoners. They realised that they had made a big mistake. The mistake had been to put all seven men on the strike at the same time. They had forgotten the old truism about eggs and baskets. The British played a devious game. They made assurances and promises but everything was in too much of a hurry. Hughes found himself in an impossible position. Weakened by two months without food it seemed to him as if the British had capitulated. One of his men was within hours of dying. There was no time to confer with the leadership outside. He gambled and called off the strike. Within a matter of hours it became clear that the words of The British had been hollow. When the relatives of the prisoners brought in clothes they were turned away. Instead the government announced that all convicts in the Province, be they political or regular, could wear 'civilian type clothing'. This meant clothes from Marks and Spencer that looked remarkably like a convict uniform.

For the leadership it was everything that they had dreaded. The Brits had out flanked them. They had tied them up in words and made them look foolish. The men inside the wire were enraged. Sands immediately announced that another strike would begin. This time he would lead it himself. This time they would learn their lesson. Volunteers would join the strike at fortnightly intervals to ensure that the pressure would be maintained. Once again the leadership did all that they could to stop it. Once again the men in the H blocks were beyond their control. When the first strike had started in October, a rally of 10,000 had marched through the streets of West Belfast. When the second strike got underway a mere 3000 marched. It seemed as if nobody was convinced any more. But everything soon changed.

It was one of those historical quirks of fate that come from nowhere to change the world. At the beginning of March, Frank McGuire, the MP for Fermanagh – South Tyrone, dropped dead. There was to be a by-election. Slowly the bones of an idea emerged. The flesh was soon on the bones, and the hunger striker Bobby Sands was announced as a Sinn Fein candidate. Against all odds and expectations he actually won. That had been a night to end all nights in H4. All the prisoners had been on tenterhooks waiting for the result. At one point there was a mighty cheer from the warders down the block and their spirits had collapsed. The only reason for such joy could be a defeat for Sands. Or so they had thought. In fact the warders had been listening to an International football match and the cheers were to celebrate a Northern Ireland goal. It was in fact the warders who were to make the mistake. The rumour mill had convinced them that Bobby had lost. They were so confident that they switched their radio up high to rub it in.

" . . . Harold West, Ulster Unionist party . . . 29,046 . . ."

The warders were cheering. Already celebrating. No way 29,000 ever going to get beaten. No way at all. What they hadn't reckoned on was the turnout. The turn out had been a staggering 87%

" . . . Sands, Robert, Sinn Fein . . 30,492 . . ."

The cheering spread down the corridors of H4 and all across the Maze. The cheering went on and on and on. Sean completely lost himself. He cheered until his throat felt as if it would tear. He gasped in deep breaths and cheered some more. Outside the warders went ballistic. They hammered on the doors with their batons and screamed threats. But nobody gave a damn. Bobby had done it. Their Bobby. Their talisman. The quiet, nobody lad from Twinbrook Estate had managed to poke Tinknickers in the eye. Robert Sands MP. Unbelievable. Absolutely unbelievable.

And it had seemed as if all was at last about to change. Once the hunger strikes had got under way the Dirty Protest had been called off. Sean still could not get over the sheer unadulterated bliss of washing and wearing clean clothes and sleeping on a bed in a cell with no shit on the walls. And now Bobby had won the greatest victory they had ever had. Things simply had to move now. There was no way that the Brits could do anything else. Allowing a hunger striker to die was one thing. Allowing a fellow MP to die was another thing altogether. Their whole strategy had been smashed into tiny little pieces. From the moment that they had taken the special status away from the prisoners in the Kesh they had justified all of their actions by doggedly arguing that these men were no more than common criminals. They had never missed a chance to label them as gangsters and racketeers. They likened the IRA men to little more than Mafia type mobsters who relied totally on violence and bullying and had no support whatsoever among the ordinary, decent folk of their communities. Well 30,492 voters from Fermanagh and South Tyrone had shot the whole policy down in smoke. They were left with no choice. They would have to negotiate.

The euphoria did not last long. It soon became horribly clear that the lady in Downing Street was not for changing. There was no movement at all and the horror of the situation began to dawn on the prisoners. With each desperate day of April the grim reality of what was about to happen began to sink in. By the time May arrived things were desperate. On May 5th the news filtered out. It was the news that every man in the blocks had been dreading. Bobby was gone. Bobby was dead.

For a while Sean wondered if he would ever be able to deal with it. It was as if his heart had been kicked one time too many. For twelve years he had known little but pain and grief. His whole life had been slowly destroyed by the nightmare of his country.

Time and time again he had picked himself up and forced himself to keep going. But each time it got a little harder. Each time the temptation just to give up and leave it was stronger. This time he felt was one time too many. The war took away everyone that he loved. But for the war, his father would still be with him. But for the war, he and Mary would now be married and probably have children. But for the war, he and Bobby might have met for a few pints in the pub where they would have put the worlds to rights. Instead he had only ever known the best friend he had ever had through the shit covered walls of a cell.

And now he was gone. The day when they could meet like real ordinary human beings and have a drink or take a walk or watch a film would never come. Bobby Sands had become a legend all over the planet. His picture was to be seen on bedroom walls and magazine covers and T-Shirts from New York to Moscow, but for Sean he was gone for ever.

As the spring turned into the summer and the summer moved into autumn nine more men died. For the other prisoners it was a time of drawn out torture. Even though they now had clothes and clean cells and water to wash with, their morale had never been lower. One by one they heard the news that their comrades where dying. Wasting away. And still the lady never moved an inch. Still there was not so much as a glimmer of hope. It descended into an ultimate battle of pride. They would never, ever allow her to win. Not if every last one of them had to die. And she would never allow them to beat her.

Sean entered a twilight world. The days of storytelling and literature classes were long gone. Nobody had the stomach for it. The blocks had become a place where men waited for their turn to die. With every night Sean found that the pictures in his head of those who had perished at the Narrow Water became more and more blurred. In the end they disappeared altogether. The only picture now was that of Bobby. Bobby who had shown them all the way ahead. The sheer mindless evil of the Brits was more than he could comprehend. Even after twelve years he had never believed they would stoop so low. Bloody Sunday had been a few soldiers running amok. Maybe their orders had come from higher up, but not the top. But this was different. This was coming from the very top. They were willing to let men die horrible lingering deaths rather than allow their pride to be compromised. They would not admit that after 700 years of occupation and suffering that his people even had the right to want to change things.

The level of hypocrisy was stunning. They were fulsome in their support and admiration for the heroic Muhajadeen fighters who fought to throw the Russian invaders out of Afghanistan. They sent them weapons and medical supplies and food. They made speeches in the UN raising Holy Hell about the invasion. It was the same with Lech Walesa and his Solidarity movement in Poland. And yet the Russians had only been in Afghanistan for about ten minutes. The bloody Brits had been in his country for 700 bloody years. And all they wanted was for them to accept that they had the right to fight a war for their own freedom. They were not asking to be let out. They were not asking for forgiveness. All they wanted was the right to be treated like other soldiers all over the world. All they wanted was to be treated as prisoners of war under the terms of the Geneva Convention. And even that was too much. Instead they were willing to let men starve to death. For the first time a black rage started to grow inside Sean. Bloody Sunday had been enough to make him join. The death of Bobby Sands hardened his soul. He would fight The Long War. He would fight with whatever weapons he could find. And if British soldiers died, then he would no longer find sleep hard to find. Not now. Not after Bobby. Never.

The Colonel looked cold. Cold and wet and suddenly a lot older. They were all cold. A damp miserable cold. And still the rain seeped down out of the leaden sky.

The officers of the regiment squatted down in a rough semi-circle. The meeting had been convened in an old sheep shed that had lost its roof years before. The shelter it offered was meagre to say the least. The rain still soaked them but at least there was some respite from the wind. He had finished what he had to say. There was no way of sweetening it up. It was crap. Pure undiluted crap. No way it could be sweetened. One or two of them glanced uneasily over their shoulders to where the high grey hill climbed up into the mist. Complete crap.

"So chaps, that's about it. We go at seven tonight. Won't be easy. Not a lot of point pretending otherwise. But they've given us the job so we'd best get on with it. Good luck"

Some of the officers made their way out of the ruined shed in groups of two or three. Davie preferred his own company. Before returning to where his platoon waited by a low broken wall he took a long hard look at the mountain that rose up into the clouds. It looked so ordinary. Just another hill. It could have been anywhere. It certainly could have been in Ireland. Somewhere out west. Rotten, boggy shitty ground that was no good to anyone. A few sheep, a few curlews, a few harriers and a broken heart for any poor sod trying to scratch a living from farming it.

But it wasn't Ireland. It was umpteen thousand miles south. It was the Falkland Islands. It was Mount Tumbledown. And on top were an unknown number of soldiers from the Argentine Army. And that night he and his men were expected to attack and capture it. And it was crap. Just crap.

The whole operation had been a scratch job. They had been stationed in Germany when the shit had hit the fan. It had been a mad scramble to get men and equipment back over the Channel and onto the boat at Portsmouth. For days the journey had been nothing but slow and tedious. Then the word had filtered around that ships were sinking. The Argentinean Air force had Exocet missiles and they were working. Royal Navy ships were being sent to the bottom of the South Atlantic. Boredom had been replaced by terror. The hours seemed to crawl by. Time after time the air raid claxons would ring out and men would throw themselves into life jackets. False alarms. Day and night, false alarms. And his men were wrapped far too tight. There was nothing that any of them could do. They couldn't fight back. They just had to sit and wait and pray.

When they arrived and disembarked there was more chaos. Nothing had been properly planned. Nobody seemed to know what the hell was happening. Nobody seemed able to find where equipment was stored. They made their camp and made do. And waited. And all the time it rained. Soon they were all soaked through. The cold was worse because they were always wet. The countryside was drab and grim. The enemy was nowhere to be seen most of the time. Occasionally jets would fly in low. But that was all. They just sat about and got wet and got cold. Really cold.

At last orders came through that they were to be moved. The plan was crazy. The plan was bordering on the lunatic. The regiment was packed into landing craft and ferried around the coast. It took ten hours. They had no protection. All it would take was one aircraft to get lucky and the whole regiment would be defenceless. Davie had never known ten hours could pass so slowly. But in the end they made it. It couldn't be put down to great tactics or being decisive and bold. It was just stupid. Plain bloody stupid. They had sent them out like sitting ducks and only sheer luck and lousy weather had saved them from disaster.

And now that they had arrived it had just got worse. Much worse. Worse than he would ever have believed. He wasn't daft. He could read the bits between the lines that the colonel had decided to keep to himself. The whole army was pretty well at breaking point. The operation had been crazy from the very start. They had only got this far because of the sheer bloody-mindedness of the soldiers on the ground. But now things were becoming critical. Supply lines were stretched. The weather was getting worse by the day. And the endless wet and cold was slowly bleeding the spirit from the men. Ammunition was running low. Morale was running low and the winter was getting close. The only way out of the mire was to somehow go forward and win. Port Stanley or bust. Between the British front lines and Port Stanley was a line of grey mountains. The night before, the Paras had managed to capture the heights of Mt Longdon. That left the brooding hulk of Mt Tumbledown as the last obstacle to overcome. And that was their job.

The Colonel had laid it out clearly enough. The attack broke just about every military rule that they had ever been taught. They had been taught that an attacking force must always have at least a three to one advantage in numbers to take on a well dug-in enemy. If the enemy were in possession of high ground, then both heavy air support and artillery would be needed. These rules were gospel. These rules were the result of hundreds of years of experience. And now the rule book was being torn up.

They would have no advantage in numbers because there were not enough men. There would be no air support because there were no planes available. There would be no artillery support because they could not spare the ammunition. There was no scope for tactics and manoeuvre. The plan was simple. Climb the mountain at night. Engage the enemy in a firefight. And find a way to win. Crap. He had spent months and months of his life training his platoon in the careful methods of modern war. They all had. They were good at it. They understood command and control. They knew how to co-ordinate an attack with air and artillery support. They knew how to work in conjunction with helicopter troops. There was a way to do this properly. But not this time. This time there were no guns and no planes and no helicopters. So it was back to the Middle Ages. Run in headlong screaming and fight it out with bayonets if necessary. Crap.

His sergeant was waiting for him a little apart from the men. The little man glanced up at the mountain and raised an eyebrow. Davie nodded.

"Fraid so Sarge. Get the men to fall in please."

They were on their feet fast. Davie was pleased to see there was no muttering and groaning. He was proud of his platoon. Crossmaglen had made them. Before Crossmaglen they had been a group of well-trained professional soldiers. After Crossmaglen they were a unit. And Davie was the absolute core of them. Even before he had shot down Gerald Docherty they had taken to him. He was a different type of officer. Most of the Lieutenants in the Guards were public school. They tended to come from families with brighter brothers and sisters. They were the sporty ones. Good on the rugby field. Good at the point to point. They were dedicated enough. Professional even. But always apart. Always outside of the loop. It was always the sergeants who made things tick.

But Davie Stanton was different. He came from the kind of streets that they had all grown up in. He never said a lot. He never let them off with a thing. But he was always fair. And on that afternoon in South Armagh he had shown himself to be a warrior. The men who had been on the streets of Crossmaglen that day were never shy in telling the story over a few jars to anyone who would listen. You should have seen him. Their Rupert. Something else he was. Never even thought. Just rolled and he was up. Ran straight at the bastard until he bottled it. Then he just stood there calm as you like and took him down. Fucking brilliant it was.

The Colonel had discreetly leaked the fact that he had given Davie the option to be moved out. They all knew it. When they couldn't sleep in the miserable cramped quarters inside the fort they would talk about it deep into the night. No way were the Provos going to get their man. No way in hell. Just let the bastards try. And they became tighter. Closer. And Brendan Conner was never allowed to get anywhere near.

As Davie approached they stood stiff to attention. Jesus, what a state. They were all soaked to the skin and their faces were drawn and tired. They had been with him for two years. Two years of endless preparation and training. Training that was now more or less of no use at all. They were supposed to be ready to work in careful co-ordination with massive technological support. Instead it was to be about sheer, downright fighting rage. That was all they would have. They had to be crazy enough. Stupid enough. Proud enough. It would only be these things that would get them to the top of the hill.

"At ease lads. Sit down if you can find anywhere." Some squatted, some sat on rocks. They formed a semi-circle around him.

"OK. I'm not going to try and butter this up. What we have lads is a bag of shite. I don't suppose the army will like me saying this, but you deserve it straight. It seems as if the whole force is just about running on empty. The weather is closing in and our momentum is more or less gone. If we don't manage to take these hills in the next day or two we'll probably not get the chance again. So there are no options. We take it tonight. The whole regiment is going up at 1900. We'll get just about no support. Nothing from the air. Not much from the ground. There is no easy way to do this. All we do is go up there and fight for it."

There was some shaking of heads. Some bowing of heads. Cigarettes were lit and pulled at hard. Overall they were taking it well. As well as could be expected.

"I'm not going to pretend it will be any good up there. It's going to be a right bastard. And we're going to take casualties. Maybe a lot. There is only one way to do it. We show more bottle than them. No matter how bad it seems, no matter how impossible, we keep going. No matter what. With me?"

There was no wild cheering and stamping of feet. There were just nods. But he liked the way their faces looked. They knew it would be crap. It was in the open. But their faces told him all he needed to know. They would keep going.

By midnight Davie felt as if he had entered Hell. The first three hours had not been too bad. Firing from the heights above them had been little more than sporadic. The hardest thing was the terrain. The hillside was covered in thick, tussocky grass and it was grindingly hard to make headway. The rain had intensified and there was no shelter from the slicing cold of the wind. By ten o'clock the firing was much heavier. The whole of the mountainside had become a crazy firework display of streaking tracer bullets and floating flares. The sound of guns was all around them. It was incredibly hard to pinpoint where the fire was coming from. The angles were awful and now that they had reached the upper slopes of the mountain there were numerous rocky outcrops that provided perfect cover for the Argentinian firing teams.

Their progress ground down to a crawl. He split the platoon into squads. They would pinpoint a firing position and then one squad would pour in fire whilst the other moved up. He had to constantly emphasise the crucial importance of using as little ammunition as possible. By eleven they had ground to a halt. Every effort they made to burst forward was driven back. He had lost four of his men by now. Three were wounded, one badly, and one was dead. The platoon was cowering behind the rocks as the enemy poured down a constant level of fire.

Davie screwed his eyes shut and forced himself to think. There had to be a way. There had to be a way fast. He could sense the morale leaking out of his men. There were bad odds and there were impossible odds and there was plain bloody suicide. It seemed as if the Argentinians were grouped around one particularly steep outcrop. How many? Fifteen. Maybe twenty. At least one machine gun. Maybe two.

After several minutes he knew there was only one way. He would have to commit more men. He would attack with three-quarters of the platoon leaving just a couple back with the walking wounded to provide support fire. They would take hits. No way to avoid it. But hopefully enough of them would get through. No other way. He crawled over to his sergeant and gave the order. The tough little man nodded and scurried around the others to pass the word. They would go in five minutes.

The adrenalin started to pump through Davie. This was probably it. He knew there was not a lot of hope of his making it through the next few minutes. His brain started to wander. It occurred that he would probably never see sunlight again. Never see his mum and dad. Never drink another pint. Never eat corn flakes. He cursed himself. Stupid. Get the mind on the job. You wanted it. You've got it. So get the bastard done. He remembered the gateway from the police station in Crossmaglen. He started his breathing. Christ the streets of South Armagh were a bloody cakewalk compared to this nightmare. That was danger. This was sheer madness. How long? Seconds now. He could feel them leaking away. The same boring, ordinary seconds that had patiently timed the whole of his life. Couldn't be many left now. Twenty. Maybe ten. He took a last big breath and braced his legs ready to go. Five?

"GO! GO! GO!"

Moving. Moving in dark slow motion. Ahead was yet another outcrop. 50 yards. Maybe 60. Six seconds on a running track. Maybe ten seconds in full pack. Maybe twelve seconds at night on rough ground. The noise simply swallowed him. He realised that he was screaming as hard as he could but he could not seem to find his own sound. His own sound was lost amidst the roar of the guns. The air seemed to be bouncing and shaking with bullets. The tracers screamed in at him and then past before he could register them. He was conscious of men falling. One. Now two. And still another 30 yards to go. Three. No. He's back up. Twenty yards. A huge bang took him in the arm. It threw his balance but somehow he corrected himself and continued to go on. Ten yards. What the hell had that been? Must have been a bullet. He dived the last five yards and rolled into the hard wet granite of the outcrop. The Argies seemed as if they were almost on top of him. As he looked up he could see the tracers shooting out and away down the hill.

He forced himself to concentrate. Assess the position, Strength? He looked left. He looked right. Nobody. Fuck it. Only him. Only one. He looked back. Two bodies. Both trying to crawl. Two more bodies 30 yards back. Very still. And nobody else. Fuck. Only him.

Don't think. Just do. He darted out and reached the first man. It was the sergeant. He heaved the small man up and the two of them managed to drag themselves back to cover.

"How is it serge?"

"Ah it's fuck all. Just the leg. Only good for support fire now. Can't run."

The man's face was contorted. Davie could see the pain all over him. Morphine. Get the morphine in. But not yet. One more. Get the other one back. Then the morphine. Don't think. Do.

The second time they were ready for him. The bullets were everywhere. Then he sensed his own men open up with everything they had and the level of fire eased a little. He reached the second man. Irving. John Irving. Big mess in his stomach. Big mess. The lad was gone far away. No sense in him. Delirious. Screaming. Gone.

The pain in Davie's arm was beginning to kick in. Christ it hurt. Waves of pain were shooting through him. Don't think. Just do. Somehow he got the injured man onto his back and started to crawl. How far. For fuck's sake it was only yards. Ten lousy stupid yards. So how could it take so long? He felt the body on his back jump and jolt. The body was not alive any more. It was just meat. Irving had caught six rounds in the back. Davie rolled out from under him and clawed his way back to the rock.

"You OK sir?"

"Aye. Not bad. Taken on in the arm I think. Hurts like a bastard. I'll give you morphine then you do me. OK?"

He bound up the sergeant's leg as best he could. The sergeant reciprocated with his arm. He told Davie that he was one lucky Irish bastard. The bullet had gone clean through the flesh at the back of his arm. He didn't feel lucky. He felt just about all in. There was nowhere to go. He had had his last throw of the dice and it had come up with two ones. So what now Davie? Curl up into a ball and feel sorry for yourself? Have a sulk? Have a moan about how unfair it all is. Grow up. Get real. Don't think. Do. Check the ground. Consolidate the position. Secure the perimeter. He worked along the left side of the outcrop. Six yards. Then open ground. Maybe another fifteen yards to the Argies. Would they come? No way. Why should they? No point. They held all the cards. Go the other way. More rock this side. Maybe twenty yards. He moved along slowly and then froze solid.

It was a voice. Close. Really close. Inches away. A voice from the rock.

"Do not move. Not a muscle. You've got five seconds to tell me your British. Do it."

"Well it would hardly be a Frenchman crawling about on this fucking hill would it?"

"Fucking Hell Davie, is that you?"

The figure detached itself from the crevice in the rock where he had been hiding. His face and hands were smeared black. All Davie could see in the light of a flare that hung overhead were the eyes.

"James? No way. Is that you?"

Now there were white teeth to go with the white eyes.

"Bet you're bloody life it is. You should be thankful for that distinctive Shankill brogue of yours. Might just have shot you otherwise. Want a drink?"

James Hamilton dug for a moment inside his jacket and pulled out a flask. Davie took a swig and felt the warmth of the whisky burn down to his stomach.

"What in the name of Christ are you doing here James?"

"I'm forward recon. Got up here yesterday bloody night. My job is to assess the strength and position of the enemy and to report back. Then once the fun stated I was to co-ordinate support fire. And that would all have been hunky bloody dory if my radio had decided to work. But the bastard packed in this morning so I've just been sitting here like a lemon watching the world go by. Was that attack your idea?"

"Aye."

"Hope you don't mind me saying, but it was hardly Napoleon."

Davie chuckled. "What, you don't think it was one for the textbooks."

"Not quite. The words crazy Irish bastard spring to mind."

They both laughed and took another swig at the flask before Hamilton put it away again. Davie tapped him on the shoulder.

"Come on. Better get back. My sergeant is up there."

For a while they just sat huddled against the wet granite as the sound of the battle raged all around them. Soon the frustration got the better of Davie.

"Come on James. You're the high flier. What are we going to do? We can't just sit here all night."

"There are times when the best thing is to do nothing. All about odds this game. We are three, two wounded. They are about twenty. They have the high ground. We are bottled up. Nothing to do but wait. Hopefully some of the other guys will be getting on better and they will get past and come in from behind. We'll give it an hour. See how things pan out."

Davie rested his head back on the rock. The morphine was beginning to kick in and his arm was at least bearable now.

"Anyway James, what the hell are you doing here? I thought your lot were on Mount Longdon."

"I moved away from the Paras. In 14th Intelligence now. They figured that our skills at hiding in wet ditches could come in handy out here. I'm amazed you haven't joined to be honest."

14th Intelligence had been formed in the early seventies specifically to work under cover in Northern Ireland. Their job was to track and watch suspects, to locate arms caches and to guide either the SAS or the RUC into their targets. After a rocky beginning they were beginning to make serious inroads into the IRA.

Davie was amazed. "Jesus Christ James, how the hell do you blend in with that plummy accent?"

"I grunt. Never speak if I can help it. Not ideal, but lots of you Irish are morose bastards. I've got away with it so far. Seriously Davie, you should be in. You could blend in anywhere. I can set things up. No problem. Proper soldiering."

Davie laughed. "Don't you think this conversation might just be a little academic. From where I sit our chances of seeing tomorrow morning are not exactly bright."

"Don't be so bloody morbid. We'll be OK. Something will turn up. Stop avoiding the issue "

"Hell, I don't know. You're not the first to ask. I'm an obvious candidate. I just don't like the idea of leaving the lads. We've all been through it the last couple of years. Especially South Armagh. It would seem a shitty trick to walk away from them."

The sergeant chipped in. "Don't be so bloody daft boss. We've got two-and-a-half bastard years in Germany to come once we get out of this place. You've not been there yet. Boring as fuck. You'll be climbing the walls. Don't bother about us. Get yourself into the Det."

The 'Det' was the nickname by which the men of 14th Intelligence were known throughout the Province. Davie relapsed into silence. The sarge had hit on a sore point. The prospect of the Germany tour had been weighing heavily. Lots of officers looked forward to the slow days and endless sport and parties in the Mess. Not so Davie. He hated all that stuff. He was in the army to be a soldier. The nitty-gritty work of the Det was much more up his street than cocktails in the Mess.

"Aye, well maybe. You sure you can sort it out?"

"Of course. Couple of phone calls. Don't get too excited though. The training course is a pig."

"Yeah. So I heard. Run by the SAS. The fun part is when they assess your ability to withstand interrogation I hear."

"You'll be OK. You're probably daft enough to quite enjoy it."

They lapsed back into silence. There was sporadic firing from the rocks where the remnants of the platoon had retreated to cover. Each burst of firing up hill was met by an angry fusillade from the rocks above them. It was impossible to make any sense of the overall battle. It was a world of darkness and noise. There was no sense of order.

A little after 2 a.m. Hamilton again checked his watch. In the preceding hour the sergeant had deteriorated quite badly. The morphine that he had taken was failing to keep pace with the pain. He was a tough man but it was becoming too much. Time was almost up. He would need help soon. James made his decision.

"OK lads. Enough is enough. Time for a bit of fun. I have a plan. I'm afraid it is out of the same locker as the Charge of the Light Brigade, but it will have to do. Have a go at shouting to the platoon Davie. See if they can hear."

It took a few minutes. At last his corporal heard them and they were able to communicate. Davie managed to make himself heard. "We're doing a William Wallace at 02.30. All the covering fire you've got!"

The three men prepared themselves. The plan was maybe just crazy enough to work. They collected grenades from the dead soldier who Davie had failed to save. The sergeant passed over his grenades. Davie and James shook hands with him and made their way to the far end of the outcrop. The sergeant crawled painfully to the opposite end and waited.

Once again Davie's stomach was in a knot. Again death was waiting a mere few seconds away. He watched the hand on his watch work its way inexorably round the luminous face. As it reached vertical his men opened up. At the far end of the rock the sergeant rolled out of cover and poured continuous fire into the rocks above. At that instant Davie and James tossed six grenades one after the other into the area where the Argentinians were returning fire at the platoon.

And they moved. They had decided that they would have to risk the shrapnel from the grenades. It was a gamble. The gamble was that the rocks above would protect them. As they scrambled up the rocks they felt the first grenade blast. Two. Three. Still going. Four. Scratching at the rock to get forward. Five. Almost at the lip. No firing yet. Five feet more. James pulled him down. Six. The rock and debris and shrapnel flew over their heads. Up again. Over the edge. Utter mayhem. Bodies blown into pieces. Others dazed and numb from shock. Fire. James was already shooting. Bright spurts of blood exploded out of a soldier's chest. Another reaching for his gun. Then his head burst apart as if it were a piece of ripe fruit. There was a movement in the corner of his eye. He swung round. A soldier. Coming out of the shock. His hand was already moving for the place where he had dropped his rifle. Davie swung round smoothly and pulled the trigger. Nothing. Not a damn thing. Bastard blockage. The gun was almost on him now. Any second. He threw himself forward and felt his bayonet sink in. The man's eyes flew open in shock. He still tried to bring his weapon to bear. Davie put all of his weight in. Pushing. Twisting. Driving. Kill. Kill. Kill . . .

"DAVIE!! DAVIE!!" The voice seemed to come from a long,

long way away. Hamilton's hand was on his shoulder, gently easing him back. "Davie. It's OK. He's gone. Look. See. He's gone. They're all gone. All of them."

The rage seeped away from Davie. His spinning brain slowly settled down. He found that he was breathing short shallow breaths. He found that he was shaking like a leaf. He found that he was burning hot even though the night was still wet and cold. He found himself surrounded by dead bodies. He found himself alive.

James took him by the shoulders and stared hard into his eyes. "OK? You there? Yes? Good. Come on. Call up the rest of the platoon. We need to move whilst there is still a breach."

By the time that the miserable grey light of the dawn started turn the blackness to grey they were sitting on the top of Mount Tumbledown. All along the summit of the hill small clusters of men sat and gazed down at the meagre spread of Port Stanley a few miles below. It wasn't much of a place. Not much more than a village. A grey little town in a wet, grey world.

"Jesus Davie, just look at it. End of the fucking world. What in the name of God are we doing here. That is what they sent us half way round the world to kill for. Just look at the bastard place."

Davie said nothing. He just stared ahead. A degree of shock was settling into him. He was trying to come to terms with what he had become. For a while he had been little more than an animal. All humanity had left him. There was no training or preparation or tactics or planning in the end. In the end it was back to the jungle. The caves. The oldest instinct of all. Kill. He had never believed that he would have been capable of it. He knew that he would fight on a battlefield. He had done it. Done it when he allowed a long slow controlled exhale as he gunned down Gerald Docherty. This was different. This was just plain madness.

" . . . hey, Davie, are you with me?"

He shook his head angrily. "Aye. Sorry. Mind was elsewhere. What were you saying?"

"I was saying that this just about wraps it up. The white flag will be out before tomorrow. Another war won. Another mighty chapter in the British Empire. Another colony defended."

"I suppose it is.

"Well, I best push along. Want me to make the call to the Det?"

Davie thought for a moment. He couldn't face the idea of Germany. Not now. Not after this. Two-and-a-half years of drill and brooding. No way.

He turned to Hamilton. "Yeah. Thanks James. Make the call. I would appreciate it."

Chapter 8
In the Shadows

May 1987

Sean stared back at the reflection in the mirror. Who was it? Where had this tired old guy come from? He had never carried any weight. His face had always been bony. Once upon a time with his long hair and bright eyes it had been a face that had got the girls going. Age had brought lines. Deep, angry lines that spoke of years of frustration and disappointment. The flowing, curly hair was long gone too. Now it was cut short and there was more than a smattering of grey. It was the face of a tired man. A disillusioned man. A man who had been on the losing side too many times.

He was just turned 37. It had been a birthday that had gone by unmarked. No cards had come. Nobody had taken him out. He doubted whether anyone even knew. His mum had died two years before. Mary had married a postman in San Francisco called Gus and when Sean had last heard they had two young children. The Movement was never big on pretty details like sending birthday cards to volunteers.

"Jesus Sean, will you look at yourself. 37 going on 60"

He carefully straightened his tie and smiled at himself. So where is the young rebel now? Not here. All there was here was Sean O'Neil the middle-aged schoolmaster. Sean O'Neil the English teacher who did a good job with the kids but would never become head of department because of his record. Sean O'Neil who pretty well kept himself to himself and was the subject of rumour and gossip.

He had been released from the Kesh in 1984. He had received instructions to head south to the Republic. It made no odds to him. His days at the university were categorically over. There was nothing for him in the north. Gerry Adams met him in a bar in Dundalk. They had pulled strings to get him a job as a teacher in a school in Monaghan. This time he was to keep a low profile. This time he was to play the part of a man who had been beaten. He was to become grindingly ordinary. They told him that the Brits would keep an eye on him for a while but it would not last long. They didn't like operating in the Republic if they could help it. Just so long as he played the part out they would get tired of it soon enough.

He rented a small terraced house and got on with it. He settled into the new life for a year until everyone was happy that it was OK for him to resume an active role. Monaghan was just a few miles over the border from Brendan Conner's territory in South Armagh. His prime task for his first year was to help organise, distribute and hide the three massive shiploads of weapons that were presented to the IRA by Colonel Ghadaffi's regime in Libya. The fourth boat was intercepted by the French secret police but the IRA were still left in possession of more sophisticated weapons than they had ever known before.

This led to considerable debate amongst the senior commanders. For the first time in the war they had the kind of arsenal that could inflict serious damage on the enemy. The question was how. The Movement had changed in the years that Sean was locked away. There were two reasons for this. On the one hand the security forces had become more and more effective. The Brits had learned many hard lessons through the long, hard years of the Troubles. They had absorbed these lessons. Most had been learned the hard way, but they had been learned all the same. By the mid-1980's the security services had become superbly effective at their work. The Province of Northern Ireland had become a terrorist's nightmare.

Out in the open for all to see were police stations that looked like medieval fortresses. The soldiers on the streets moved with precision and practice. The RUC had become every bit as professional. There were no more easy targets to be found. Of even more concern was the array of forces that could not be seen. The Government had invested millions in new technology. Literally thousands of bugs and tiny cameras monitored the whole of the country. Undercover units were constantly in place watching suspects. The Special Branch had built up an army of informers. And the SAS were always waiting for the opportunity to intervene with massive force.

The net result of all this for those commanding the IRA was that it was getting harder and harder to carry out any operations in the Province at all. The only targets that they could reach with any degree of success tended to be civilian. They killed prominent Loyalists and contractors who undertook work for the security services or part time UDR men. And all too often their units got things completely wrong and killed completely innocent civilians who more often than not were Catholics.

These mistakes had always caused disputes within the Movement. Now these disputes were more heated than ever. The reason for this was that there had been a second major change. This had been a change that Sean had witnessed at first hand. Bobby Sands' stunning victory at the 1981 by-election had awakened many in the Movement to the real potential offered by following an increasingly political road. It was in this period that the theory of the having an Armalite in one hand and a ballot box in the other had emerged.

There were those who hated the idea of all things political. They had seen it all before. They saw no point in trying to talk to the Brits and the Orangemen nicely. It had all been tried before for hundreds of years. In the end the Brits always wriggled out of any deal. The time for talk was passed. The only way that they would ever get their country back was at gunpoint. However many others saw things differently. They saw that the longer the war went on the stronger the Brits were becoming. They saw with increasing clarity that in a straight fight there would only ever be one winner. Gerry Adams was the leader of this group and Sean had no problem at all in supporting his old mentor every step of the way.

His time in prison had put a weariness into Sean. Too many

good young men were being killed and it was becoming increasingly clear that these deaths were in vain. They had entirely underestimated the sheer stubbornness of their enemy. Sean realised that this was a mistake that he had made himself. He had always believed deep down that the Brits would surely see sense. What on earth was the point in going to such lengths to hang on to a colony that really was worth nothing to them any more? He had been convinced that they would be pragmatic. Surely in the end the accountants would have their way. A Government balance sheet for the Province would have made painful reading. Countless millions of pounds headed over the water in one direction and a pitiful amount of tax revenue headed back the opposite way. It wouldn't go on. Couldn't go on.

What he hadn't reckoned on was the crazy pride of a nation that could not come to terms with not being great any more. The moment that Thatcher had sent a fleet out of Portsmouth to defend the rights of a few sheep farmers in the South Atlantic his heart had sunk. It had sunk even further when the lunatic venture was received with flag-waving joy by the British people who had duly rewarded Thatcher with another five years. If she would go to these lengths to defend a worthless colony 12,000 miles away there was little doubt that she would do almost anything to hang on to Ulster.

During his endless days in the Kesh, Sean had plenty of time for reflection. He came to the conclusion that perception and propaganda were everything. They could never force the Brits out of their country. The only way would be to embarrass them out. Shame them out.

A whole new strategy started to emerge. Military operations simply had to be directed against the security forces, and civilian casualties had to be kept to a minimum. Every military operation had to be staged with propaganda value first and foremost. They had to sell themselves to the world as being heroic freedom fighters battling away against impossible odds. They had to be able to demonstrate that they enjoyed the overwhelming support of their own people. Bobby Sands had shown that the best way by far to do this was to take on the Brits at their own game and beat then at the ballot box.

Hitting the Brits on the battlefield was an altogether more difficult task. They needed targets that were not impossible but were still unequivocally part of the security apparatus. Sean had studied the Vietnam War carefully. For him it was an ideal model. The Americans had enjoyed an almost ridiculous superiority in terms of firepower but they had lost. One measure that the Viet Cong had employed was to create Safe Havens for their fighters. This involved targeting police stations and small army bases in certain vulnerable areas. By claiming areas of territory for themselves they proved to their people that they were still a force to be reckoned with even though the targets that they chose were more or less inconsequential.

Sean saw the many tiny police posts in the villages of Armagh and Tyrone as ideal targets. In reality they were more or less worthless to the security machine. They only tended to be occupied by two of three policemen for a few hours each day. They were merely symbolic. Attacking these posts was almost risk free, unlikely to cause any civilian casualties, and yet would be of disproportionate propaganda value.

Several successful attacks had been staged in 1986. The Movement had lost no men and morale had been lifted. They steered clear of the major outposts such as the forts at Crossmaglen and Newtonhamilton and the large barracks at Bessbrook Mill. It was little more than a fleabite on an elephant. But it made the elephant angry. And when the elephant got angry it made itself look silly. However these careful successes always seemed to be negated by other operations that tended to undo much of the good work. One bad side of the reorganisation of the Movement into small, self-contained cells was that in many cases it allowed teams to operate without discipline. All too often units took it on themselves to carry out sectarian killings or poorly planned bomb attacks that led to civilian deaths. Every time this happened it made the job of Sinn Fein more difficult. The British on the other hand responded with glee. They would put their publicity machine into overdrive and tell the world that they were trying to deal with gangsters and maniacs and cold-hearted murderers.

These were the times when Sean felt most despair. He had given everything to the Movement. He had sacrificed all that he held dear. He harboured no regrets about this. It just enraged him that whenever they managed to take a few tentative steps forward some bloodthirsty cowboy would always undo all the good work with yet another act of sectarian savagery.

The face in the mirror saddened him. It was a face that spoke of constant disappointment. There was no joy there any more. No mischief. No humour. Just disappointment. And fatigue. Mind numbing, bone aching fatigue. The prospect of the day gave him a small lift. The hours spent teaching were the ones he now enjoyed the most. He still had a flair for it. He could still pull the kids out of their lethargy and enthuse them. He allowed some of their hope and youth to rub off on him. His own life had drifted away long ago, but theirs could still be different. Better. Worth having.

For a few short hours he could clear the business of the war away from his mind. Then once the bell would ring at the end of the last period it would be time to go back to the war. The lonely Long War where the end was never in sight. Later that night he was due to meet up with Brendan at a small farm to plan the next op. Then it would be details of personnel, spotter cars, required weapons, escape routes. But first it was the poetry of Ogden Nash.

"You well Prof?" Brendan Conner never seemed to change. Maybe he was a little heavier around the waist. Maybe the hair wasn't quite so thick. But his face was still brown and his eyes still burned with violence.

"Aye, Can't complain. Getting old, but aren't we all."

"Bollocks. You're no age Prof. Just a lad. You take things too seriously, that's all. Too much politics. Too many books. You need to get out more. Just say fuck it and get a few jars down the neck. Find a bloody woman for Christ's sake."

Sean smiled. "Bloody hell Brendan, I never thought you the type for a bit of fatherly advice. I'm touched."

"Ah, fuck off."

They both lit up and Sean pulled out papers from his briefcase. "OK, let's go over this shall we."

He spread a map out on the table. It was a large scale Ordinance Survey map for North Armagh. In the centre was the small village of Loughgall. He had been looking at the small village police station for several weeks and had finally recommended it as a target. Sean was about to start speaking when Conner waved him silent.

"Forget it Prof. They've taken it off us. Given it to those wankers from the East Tyrone Brigade."

"You're kidding."

"No. Fraid not. We had a right old bust up, but it's no go. They say they need something to give them a boost. Say that South Armagh gets all the best ops. Say that things have to be spread about a bit."

Sean felt annoyed. He could see some logic in the decision. The East Tyrone Brigade had taken a beating for the last three years. They certainly needed a lift. That was fine. He could live with that. He just wished that people would keep him in the loop.

"So when do they want to see me?"

Conner shook his head disdainfully. "They don't."

"What?"

"They say that they can manage everything themselves. They say they don't want any interference. They say they know what they're doing."

Sean was livid. "Are they mad? They've been getting their arses kicked for months because they plainly couldn't plan how to take a shit in the morning. This is bloody stupid."

Conner laughed. "Hey Prof, you don't know the bloody half of it. They want to make it into a proper spectacular. They want to send eight men including their Chief. It's like a fucking Christmas outing."

Sean sank back into his chair. Typical. Absolutely typical. "Nothing you can do Brendan?"

"Not a fucking thing. They won't listen to me. I'm just a thicko farmer from the bog. You might get further. The sun never ceases to shine out of your arse as far as the Army Council are concerned."

"Stupid bastards. Can I use the phone here?"

"Sure. It's secure. We checked it."

It took Sean a few moments to be connected to Gerry Adams.

"Sean. Long time. How's things down South."

"Bloody crap Gerry. That's how. Crap and shite and then some. Have you heard about this Loughgall business?"

There was a moment's silence at the other end of the line. "That line of yours OK Sean, sounds a bit fuzzy to me."

"Yeah it's fine. Just checked. Yours?"

"It's OK. Keep it brief though. I know a bit."

Sean took a deep breath to compose himself. "You need to intervene Gerry. Those boys can't plan. They've proved it. If they have to get the job, then fair enough, but at least make them use me to plan it. Jesus Gerry, the morons are sending eight men out."

"Sorry Sean. Can't do a thing. Politics."

"Oh fuck the politics Gerry. This is just plain stupid. The Special Branch and the Det are crawling all over them up there. The chances of this not leaking with eight lads going out are next to zero. This could be a disaster."

"Don't over react Sean. There's not a thing I can do. The Council has made the decision and that is that. Done. Finished. Don't get so up tight. It'll be fine."

"Yeah. Sure. See you around Gerry."

"Bye Sean."

He stared at the phone for a while. Conner smoked quietly and sipped at his tea. "Come on Prof. Chin up. You never know, they might just show us all up. Take a look at these."

He tossed down a pile of papers. Sean didn't pick them up for a moment. He had a bad feeling in his bones. Really bad. But what could he do? Not a damn thing. Not a damn thing.

The room was packed. Just about everyone was smoking and there was no ventilation. Davie wondered whether there was any group of people on the planet with a higher percentage of smokers than the security services in Northern Ireland. The room was too small and there were not enough chairs. Some leant against the wall at the back; others lolled on the floor. It was the war as Davie had come to know it. Miserable windowless rooms with cheap plastic chairs and central heating turned up too high. The barracks that he worked out of changed, but soulless institutional rooms were always the same. Good show today. Bigger than normal. It seemed that everyone had a piece of this one. There were Special Branch and RUC and regular army and his own crowd, 14th Intelligence. And then there were the men with the long hair and the torn jeans and the dirty sweatshirts who hadn't shaved for a while. As ever they seemed as if they were a little apart from everyone else in the room. They were the ones who would do the killing when the time came. The executioners. The SAS.

The door opened and the Colonel in charge of the sector marched in briskly with his adjutant close behind. He was all business. Papers dropped on the desk with a bang. A quick clearing of the throat.

"Evening gentlemen. I think everyone knows each other. No need for introductions. We know why we are here. Let's get on with it shall we? Doyle, you start."

Bill Doyle was Special Branch. He was a big bald man who had hair sprouting from his ears and a shirt at least two sizes too small. He was the man who had started the ball rolling. He was the one with the man on the inside. He had the source, and he knew it. It was his moment and he was enjoying the limelight.

"We spoke with our man this morning. It's a go. On the ninth he says. Evening sometime. There will be eight of them. He doesn't know the exact plan. He just says it is going to be a big one."

There was a buzz around the room. Eight! Unbelievable. This was unheard of. No wonder the room was so full.

There were a few questions but there was nothing much more for Doyle to contribute. The Colonel nodded towards Davie.

"Stanton. You next. What is your situation."

Davie stood up. "We've got three teams out. Team One is on around the clock watching the arms dump. Team Two are eyeballing the Chief and Team Three are on the Quartermaster. Nothing to report as yet. Nothing moving."

A nod. Nothing more to say. The SAS officer was next. He looked the absolute opposite to any popular image of the elite soldier. He wasn't particularly tall. His long hair was greasy and lank and he wore a grubby yellow sweatshirt with 'University of Minnesota' emblazoned across the front. When he spoke he had a rather quiet voice with a Yorkshire twang.

"We'll dress two of our lads up as coppers and put them in the station the morning before. Inspector Doyle will give us one of his men as well. The rest of the team will take up position the evening

before and dig in. No real problem otherwise. The ground is fine.
Fields of fire are good. We'll be ready."

"How many of you?" It was one of Davie's lads that asked the
question

"30."

The Det man whistled. 30 SAS troopers was unusual. They
generally operated in teams of no more than four. 30 was a full
wartime deployment. Something was going on. The Colonel's face
was set hard. Davie felt his pulse quicken. Something was
happening here. Something new. The Colonel stared about the room.

"The plan is simple. We have decided to let them run. We
monitor them all the way into the village. If the opportunity for an
arrest presents itself, it will be taken. This option will only be
considered once the players are in place outside the police station.
If this option should lead to any risk to any of our people
whatsoever then it will be discounted."

He stared them all out. There wasn't a man in the room who
didn't realise what it was that he was saying. There would be no
sensible opportunity to make any arrests once a fully armed team
of eight men had been allowed to make it all the way to the gates
of the police station at Loughgall. The only place for an arrest
would be at a roadblock where they could take them unawares. No.
Arrests were not part of the agenda. Nobody was even considering
arrests as a possibility. They were going to guide them in and gun
them down. And they were deploying 30 SAS troopers to make
sure none of them walked away. This was no local operation. This
had been sanctioned from on high. Very high.

Davie glanced down at the clock on the dashboard of the car for
the umpteenth time. His colleague lit up a new cigarette from the
one he had just finished. It was more or less dark now. Their part
was almost complete. Davie had decided to join the team at the
arms dump. Three players had come early in the morning. They
must have nearly emptied the cache. They had taken three large
heavy holdalls and heaved them into the back of an old van.
Team's Two and Three reported that the chief and Quartermaster
of the East Tyrone Brigade had left their houses a little after seven
in the evening. Davie had ordered his men to cut them both loose.

It was too risky to try and tail them. What was the point. They knew exactly where they were going.

Now he and his colleague in the 14th Intelligence team had only one task remaining. They were cruising the area looking for a sighting of the IRA team. They would not follow them. No point. All they were required to do was to radio ahead to the SAS ambush squad. Then their part would be done.

"Hang on Davie, look at this."

Ahead was a pair of red lights. Something strange about them. Not usual. As they got closer Davie could see why. It wasn't a car. It was a JCB digger. They reached the slow moving machine at a straight stretch of road. Davie indicated and pulled out to overtake. He spoke quietly. "Don't stare now. Don't be obvious. Wouldn't want to scare them away."

As he gently cruised by the digger he registered a man in overalls. In front was a transit van. Digger. Van. Digger following van. Blue overalls. Conclusive. They took a corner and Davie picked up the radio from where it lay between the seats.

"Charlie One this is Rabbit. One JCB. One Ford transit van, blue. Moving at approximately fifteen miles an hour. Three miles east of destination. ETA twelve minutes. All rabbit units clear the area. Over."

"Rabbit, this is Charlie One. Understood and out. Over."

Davie tossed the radio back down and indicated to turn left. He spoke half to himself and half to his colleague. "OK. That's us. We'll just drive about the perimeter and make our way in when it's done."

He felt no great elation. His teams had operated superbly. They had watched the IRA team all the way in. They could have made arrests at any time. They had the photos. They had the evidence. But it had not been required. For whatever reason nobody wanted these men arrested. He felt sorry for them. Little did they know as they approached Loughgall at a snail's pace that they had already been betrayed by one of their own. It wouldn't be a very fair fight. Wouldn't be fight at all. Even if there had been a hundred of them they would have been no match for a well-hidden ambush team of 30 SAS men. But there weren't a hundred. There were only eight. It would be a slaughter.

Davie just drove. Better not to think about it much. Not his problem. It was for others to decide how the war should be conducted. The politicians. Always the bloody politicians. He was just the simple soldier who did as he was told. They were about a mile to the south of the village when the sound of gunfire broke out. There was the crump of an explosion and a yellow flash lit up the sky. The guns roared for a little over a minute and then they fell silent.

Breathless voices on the radio. A few minutes later he heard. "Clear. All clear."

He didn't hurry to get into the village. He had no voyeuristic urges. What would be there was something he had seen before. When he parked up there were men running in all directions. A helicopter hung low overhead and flooded the scene outside the police station in white light. The JCB had half disappeared through the front wall of the station, which was massively damaged by the blast of the bomb that had been carried in the digger's front bucket. There were bodies all over. Soldiers were emerging from the woods and staring down at the corpse in small groups of three and four. Two more helicopters landed on the road and the SAS team jumped aboard. Then they were gone. It was a police show now. Land Rovers were arriving, cordons were being put into place, order was being imposed. The scene would be arranged in nice tidy order ready for the arrival of the TV cameras. This one would be played for all it was worth. This would be hailed as a great victory. A team stopped from committing yet another horrific outrage.

Of course it was all bullshit. The bullshit made him tired. Bullshit and lies and more bullshit. Never honesty. Never the simple truth. Never say that with eight of them gunned down very dead the Provos might have the odd problem getting new volunteers. Of course not. That wouldn't do at all.

They got back into the car and headed for the Barracks. His colleague was dying to talk all about it but he had the sense to recognised Davie's high-strung tension. They went back to the same room. All the same faces were there. The same cloud of smoke made a fog. The ashtrays spilled the same ash onto the same lino surfaces. But this time everything was different. There was booze stacked on every surface. Some of them must have started early. These were the ones who had been stationed within the barracks. They had sweated it out and put it all together from the radio transmissions. By now they were the ones with the red faces and the sleeves rolled up and the voices already too high. The SAS men had beaten Davie by a few minutes. They were throwing down cans of beer and winding themselves up for the singing. Everyone was hyped up. Ready for an absolute skinful. Ready to drink until they dropped. Ready for a celebration party that would be talked about for years to come. It was what they had all waited for. What made it all worthwhile. All the endless hours hiding in ditches or in battered old cars where the heater never seemed to work,or trying to read in miserable bleak rooms waiting on orders.

Davie picked up a can of beer and took a sip. He didn't remotely feel like joining in. He found it all rather pathetic. All he really wanted to do was to leave. To find a bit of space to call his own and allow the brain to wind down. He couldn't abide the thought of the rugby songs and the backslapping and the vomit on the toilet floor. But leaving wasn't much of an option. It was the sort of thing that would be noticed. Commented on. Considered to be evidence of bad form. Lacking in team spirit. So he would have to stay and fix a silly grin on his face and put up with it.

The Colonel was doing the rounds. The granite expression from the middle of the day was long gone. He was all smiles now. Everybody's favourite uncle. The proud leader of men. A man who had delivered what his lords and masters had asked for. Davie watched him as he pumped the hands and slapped the backs and filled his glass with trebles of whisky. It would be his turn soon. Time to get the mood right. Time to show the face that the army expected.

He had always managed it before. He had even managed it when they had hopped and hobbled their way into Port Stanley. When he looked back on the moment in time to come he could never really understand why he had not managed it this time. The big man came over and threw an arm around his shoulder.

"Now then Stanton. Bloody marvellous effort. Would never been possible without you and your chaps. Worth your weight in gold you are. All of you. Never get the credit you deserve."

Davie looked at the red nose and the eyes that were becoming bleary. Sod it. Why the hell should he always tow the bloody line? Sod the old pratt.

"May I ask Sir, why is it that we are celebrating?"

The colonel's face showed a trace of suspicion. "Don't be so bloody stupid Stanton. Because we took them down. Eight of them. Most of the big wheels in the East Tyrone Brigade. All in one hit. Course we're bloody celebrating. Why shouldn't we be?"

"I would have thought that we would only have been celebrating if we had managed to arrest them."

Now suspicion was turning to anger. "For Christ's sake Stanton. Not some bleeding heart fucking liberal are you? Spare me that. It's a war. They want to fight, so let them. They can't moan about it when they lose. It's that simple. I won't risk a single one of my people on them. We took no risks today. We played safe. We won. They lost. Game over."

"Oh come on Sir, don't give me that. We executed those men because the orders came through from up high. It was policy. Kill a few and send out a 'we're getting tough message' to the voters. Nothing like a few dead terrorists to win a few marginal seats in election year. We'll be out on the High Street giving out brochures for the Tory Party next."

"You'd better remember who you are talking to Stanton." The colonel's voice was rising now. He pushed his beetroot red face close in to Davie. Conversations were stopping all around the room. A silence was settling. Heads were turning. Some faces were amused. Some were concerned. All were interested. "If you don't like it I suggest you reconsider your career. This is the army son. The British Army. It might not always be pretty, and it might not always be nice, but we get the bloody job done. Now if it is a bit rich for your blood, then you know what to do!"

Davie looked him square in the face and laughed. "Jesus. Have you any idea how pathetic that sounds. I've spent the last four years of my life tagging players. I've done Londonderry. I've done Belfast. I've done Tyrone. Call it a war? Don't be so bloody soft. We know who these people are. All of them. We know who they are, where they are and when they'll be there. If we fought like real soldiers we would just go in and take them out. All of them. One by one. But we don't. We don't because it might just cost votes. Instead we wait for an excuse to gun men down and dress it up in fancy clothes. You want me to celebrate Sir? I'll celebrate when we fight this war properly. I'll celebrate when we are allowed to fight with both hands. Identify them. Locate them. Take them out. Win. That's how simple it is. Every man in this room knows it. That would be the way a soldier does it. Today? Today was a massacre that happened because the PR men found an excuse for the headlines."

He knew that he had said enough. Too much. Far too much. The colonel was struggling to find words like a goldfish on the lounge carpet. Time to put an end to it. Quickly.

"I apologise sir. I feel I have been rather too frank. Forgive me. Emotions are running high. I will leave now."

He turned and marched through the door. He shuddered to think what damage he had just done to his career. Terminal in all likelihood. He should have felt wretched. He should have felt desperate. He didn't. A smile played on his lips as he marched down the corridor. He felt as if he had just taken off a heavy rucksack. So what if there were repercussions. Sod them. Sod the lot of them.

Sean spent the night alone. And he paced. He had learnt from many previous similar evenings that there was no point in trying to sit and read. It was hopeless. He would sit gazing at the same page without any focus, reading the same line over and over without registering a word. He had learnt that pacing was the only way. Pacing and smoking and working his way down a bottle. The radio wittered on in the background. It was some kind of farming programme. An attempt at sanity. Normality. The pretence that all could be normal in a land consumed by madness.

He stiffened when the programme was interrupted. The tone of voice said it all. It was that 'you are about to hear something important so pay attention' tone of voice.

" . . . *We are interrupting this programme to bring you a Newsflash from the studio . . . an hour ago the security forces foiled a major IRA raid on the police station in Loughgall in County Armagh. Information from the scene is still sketchy, but early reports indicate that at least eight terrorists have been killed. No casualties are reported from any of the security services involved in the action. We will bring you more information in our nine o'clock bulletin . . ."*

The vomit came from nowhere. He clamped his mouth shut as he rushed for the bathroom. It exploded into the toilet. It came and came until his stomach muscles cramped. He collapsed into a heap; his back propped up by the bath. He weakly lifted his arm and flushed the toilet. Tears were pouring down his cheeks. He was shaking. Shaking with no control. Eight. All of them. Executed. Gunned down. And for what? Would it never end?

Peter Stanton pulled on his raincoat. It was a slow process. Everything had become slow. Even the act of lifting his arms into the coat was taxing. His daughter-in-law made to help him but he gestured her away impatiently. Christ he was getting old. Old and decrepit and good for bloody nothing. In a few months he would be ninety. Unbelievable. 90 years old. And 71 of those years were borrowed time. 71 years more than Tom and Billy and all the others got. It was getting harder to feel positive about it. There was not much that was good about life any more. His son was a shadow of his former self. The Troubles had all but annihilated the business. Now there was only Gerald and one other man in the old workshop. He had watched Gerald age a few years every time he was summoned to the bank. It could only be a matter of time now. They had been hanging on and hanging on and their savings were more or less drained. Soon 'Stantons of Shankhill' would be a name consigned to history. A half-forgotten name that the older men in the pubs might just remember from time to time over a pint on a slow Thursday night. At least there was no mortgage on the house. At least that would still be there.

He collected his stick and made his way out. The rain had stopped and it was a pleasant spring evening. A few kids were kicking a football about in their Glasgow Rangers shirts. They all looked warm enough. Of course they did. It was a nice warm evening in May. But Peter wasn't warm. He pulled his raincoat close about him. Always cold these days. His blood felt as thin as water. Old and weak and slow and not worth a bloody light.

A miss hit shot sent the football clattering into his stick. For a moment he struggled for his balance. A boy trotted over and picked up the ball and turned back towards his friends. Not a word. Not a bloody word.

"Hey. You. Come here."

The boy turned. There was a look of contempt. Contempt at his age and his bent back and the stick that he needed to be able to walk. The boy wasn't coming anywhere. No way. Peter was angry. "Ever heard of the word 'sorry' have you?"

The boy looked amused. He turned to his mates to make sure that he had an audience. He turned back to Peter. "Ah fuck off you old twat."

They all had a good laugh. They all thought it was a good crack. And Peter knew there was nothing in the world he could do. He was imprisoned by his skinny creaking body and the stick that he needed to walk with. He was imprisoned by his 90 years. Nothing to do. He turned and made his way along the pavement with the laughter ringing in his ears.

He found it hard to come to terms with the fact that this was the same Shankill Road where he had lived out his long life. All was changed. Most of the shops were gone. Where there had once been thriving little businesses there were now only boarded up windows covered in graffiti. Unemployment had rocketed. Nothing was certain any more. The shipyards had all but closed down. The place was filthy. Litter strewn. It had become a ghetto.

These days he could hardly bear to walk about. Everywhere he went was haunted by the ghosts of better times. They had all been so proud. Proud of their land and their culture and their loyalty and their achievements. Now it all seemed like a sick joke. These were the acres that he had fought and killed for. What a waste. What an absolute, complete waste. There were days now when he never made it out for his daily walk. He would say that it was too cold or too wet or that his bones were too sore. But that wasn't the truth. The truth was that there were days that he hadn't the strength to face up to what the Shankill had become.

It was past seven now. The street was quiet. There were a few dog walkers. Courting couples. Men making their way to the pub. Kids taking home the chips for tea. Thin traffic. And suddenly the picture seemed to disintegrate. Like a stuck video. Time stopped. The air was sucked away. Gravity lost control. A balloon blown up too far.

Then the storm broke. The walls of the Wheatsheaf pub exploded out. There was a boy. Not very old. Maybe twelve. Possibly thirteen. The walls of the pub seemed to fragment into him. Just for a moment. A fractional moment. For a moment there was a boy with his arms cradled around the chip supper for the family. Then the walls moved out to meet him as his head started to turn towards the pub. Just a moment. A fractional moment of near peace.

Then he was gone. Engulfed in dust and smoke, and the roaring rage of the bomb split Peter's ears. The force of the blast threw him backwards onto the pavement. The world seemed to roar away over his head. And then as quickly as it had come it was gone. He was on his back. There was silence now. His hearing was all gone. A silent movie. Just pictures. Smoke. Dust. And the boy. The boy had been thrown twenty yards across the street. He was down. Like a broken doll. There were chips on the road all around him.

Peter dragged himself up. His legs barely worked. There was pain. Pain that he would not accept. Wouldn't admit to. Wouldn't bow to. He forced himself to the boy. Only a few yards. Not far. No problem. His legs wouldn't work. He had to crawl the last few yards. The boy was confused. He stared down at the road, at the chips that had been thrown from his hands.

"My Ma will kill me. I've dropped them all. All of them . . ."

Peter crawled up to him. He managed to pull the boy close to him. He pulled him into his chest and wrapped his arms tight about him. It was easy to lift the boy. It was easy because he had only half a body. There was nothing left of him below his waist. The blood was pumping out of him. But still his eyes were fixed on the chips.

"It's OK son. No bother. I know the man at the Chip Shop. He's a mate of mine. He's a good lad. He'll understand. We'll go and have a word. He'll give you some more. You'll see. Your Ma will never have to know. No problem. He's a mate of mine . . ."

There was noise now. Sirens. Shouting. Screaming. Police Land Rovers. Army. A soldier came over. He looked down at what was left of the boy. A stump of a body in a huge pool of blood. He looked into the face of the old man who held the boy tight and told him of how he knew the man at the chip shop as the tears streamed down his pale face.

"Sir. It's no good sir. He's gone. I'm afraid he's gone...."

For a moment they were a picture. The soldier from Coventry, squatting down, leaning in, imploring. The old man with the tired thin face streaked with tears. And the boy, already dead, blown in half, sent by his mum for the chips. None of them knew anything when the second bomb blew. It was only feet away. 200 pounds of fertiliser stowed away in the boot of a VW Golf. The blast more or less vaporised them. Reduced them to little pieces. And Peter Stanton's 71 years of borrowed time ran out.

Later that night the Provisional Irish Republican Army claimed responsibility for the two bombs on the Shankill Road. They said that was revenge for the SAS murders at Loughgall in County Armagh.

Davie was into his third day of hanging around. Maybe it was to be expected. Maybe not. He had known this before. One mission would finish. Then he would wait. Report in and hang around. Wait for the next mission to come along. The theory was that a bit of time between operations gave them all the chance to wind down and recuperate. Bullshit. They just got bored and irritable and lost their edge. Cigarettes and magazines and endless games of cards.

This time it was different. Davie had no idea what the consequences would be following his outburst at the Colonel. Maybe they would just let it drop. Put it down to a surplus of tension. Maybe. But not very likely. They were always on the look out for signs of stress in the men and women who undertook the murky work of 14th Intelligence. The slightest clue would send you into the psychiatrist's office. They were neurotic at the prospect of men cracking under the strain. Cracking and making a mistake and getting caught and spilling the beans. Davie had never put a foot wrong before, but it probably wouldn't count for much.

There was nothing to read in the face of the officer when he came. Not that there ever would be. He was just the messenger. He led Davie down the undecorated corridors with their tube lighting. He opened the door of the office and stood to one side to allow Davie in. His commanding officer glanced up over his glasses and nodded Davie to a chair. There were open files on the desk.

"Good evening Stanton. Thanks for coming."

"Sir."

The officer took off his glasses and rubbed at his eyes. He tossed the glasses down onto the files on the desk and entwined his fingers together.

"You ruffled a few feathers the other night Stanton."

"I'm aware of that sir."

"And your explanation?"

Davie picked at his words with care. He didn't like the tone of voice at all. Not one little bit.

"I was rather wound up sir. It had been a tense night."

"Yes. A tense night. A tense night indeed." The officer let his voice trail away and flicked at the pages of the file. "Well I'm afraid that really will not be good enough Stanton. Not really. You have got people worried. Alarmed. Your background has its good points and its bad points you see. On the credit side it means that you can blend in where others can't. You know the ground. Of course you do. It's where you come from. On the debit side we're always worried that you may become . . . how can I put this . . . over-zealous? Yes. Over-zealous."

"Over-zealous sir?"

"Yes. You see Stanton; the Government in London has made it policy that Her Majesty's Forces in Ireland must always be seen to be following the rule of law. To the letter. When we first came over here in the early Seventies there were lots of cowboys who were given a free rein. And it backfired. Badly. We were made to look bad in the eyes of the world. And the Government doesn't like that. Not one little bit. So now we are all paranoid about cowboys. We are more paranoid about cowboys than we are about the IRA. You see the people who run this war are more concerned about bad PR than they are about guns and bombs and people getting shot. Our job is not to try and win the war. We can't. We know that. Our job is to contain. Keep the bad guys bottled up wherever possible. Keep the Irish Troubles on pages four or five of the papers. Not on the front.

Now you're not alone in your resentment, Stanton. Not alone at all. I expect most of the army feel much the same. But we keep it to ourselves. It is not for us to say. We are merely civil servants with guns. We don't have opinions. We simply do as we are told. And we don't express those opinions. And if we do we are discreet. We don't do it in front of a room full of people. We don't do it in the face of a senior officer. I'm afraid you've blown it Stanton. They are saying that you may become a loose cannon. They are saying you could be a liability."

So there it was. A decision already made. No point in arguing. "I see."

"Well, I hope you do Stanton. I hope you do. I have reviewed your file this evening. There is little doubt that you are a very fine soldier. Exceptional in fact. We just feel that 14th Intelligence is the wrong place for you at this moment in time. I have arranged for you to rejoin your Regiment with immediate effect."

"Thank you sir."

"Don't be too disappointed Stanton. It will no doubt turn out for the best."

He was packing his things when there was a knock at the door. "Yes."

It was one of his fellow officers.

"Sorry Davie . . . I'm afraid there's been news . . . bad news . . . there's been a bomb. Two in fact. On the Shankhill. It's your Grandfather. He's dead. I'm so sorry."

Davie nodded slowly. The officer hovered for a moment and then realised that he wasn't wanted. Davie sat down slowly. His eyes were fixed on the stark bare wall of his room. For a long time he never moved a muscle. Just stared. And then for the first time in more years than he could remember tears came. He saw the picture of an old man and a young boy with a wood where crows sat high in the branches. He saw the clear blue skies and rows of neat white crosses.

Gone.

The funeral was to be a large affair. The family hadn't wanted anything spectacular. It wouldn't have been Peter Stanton's style. He had always hated fuss. They had planned a simple ceremony. No frills. Just a quiet send off for a man who had been much loved. But Peter Stanton was no ordinary 90-year-old. He was one of the great ones. A legend. A man who had marched with Carson. A man who had been there with the UVF from the very start. A man who had gone with all the rest to the Somme and had come back with the Victoria Cross. Men like Peter Stanton did not have quiet funerals. Not in West Belfast.

Hutchinson came to the house the night before. Davie's father had taken it hard. The years had taken their toll on Gerald Stanton. He had never been a strong man. All he had really wanted was to wile away the days in his workshop. He had tried to do his bit for the UVF. It was what was expected. But he had never been fully engaged. He just wanted to get on with his life. The Troubles had made it impossible. His business had collapsed and now his father was dead. He took it hard. Davie could barely get a word out of him. He just sat and stared at the television without taking anything in.

Hutchinson looked at him for a moment. "Hello Gerald. You OK? Bearing up?"

Nothing. Gerald's eyes were fixed firmly on the grinning white teeth and false tan of a game show host. Davie shook his head and guided Hutchinson into the kitchen.

The older man sat down at the table and accepted a drink. "Taking it bad is he Davie?"

"I'm afraid so. It's just the shock. He'll be OK. What can I do for you John?"

Hutchinson looked carefully at the man across the table. He was impressive. Young Davie Stanton was always going to be impressive. He remembered the night of the bomb at the Four Step Inn when Davie had faced him down. Christ, he must only have been thirteen then. He had filled out since then. The man at the other side of the table had grown to over six feet and Hutchinson could feel the power of him. He didn't know much about Davie's career in the army. Just bits and pieces. Once there had been something in Crossmaglen. Hutchinson had known lots of hard men over the last twenty years. He had seen them come and go. He had seen them kill and be killed. Some were all muscles and tattoos and mouth. Others looked as if they would never hurt a fly. They came in all shapes and sizes. But this one was different. It was something that he couldn't put a finger on. Just different. Just something. Something that made him wonder whether this one was the hardest man of them all. Something. Something that sent a chill through him.

Davie said nothing. He had never liked Hutchinson much. Never trusted him. There was too much of the gangster about him for Davie's taste. But he was straight enough. Davie had checked out his files. Hutchinson was a believer sure enough. Cut him in half and he would be orange. But he was bent. Too much into the drugs and the rackets. He was in no mood for small talk.

"Well?"

Hutchinson was uncomfortable. It was usually he that inspired the fear. It was usually that he would make men shuffle in their seats and sweat. "We want to do something at the funeral Davie. Something to show our respect."

"Like?"

"Four soldiers. A volley over the coffin. He was one of ours Davie. One of the first. Peter was UVF back in 1912."

Davie had been half expecting it. It was too good an opportunity for them to pass up. There had been a lot of negative talk about the UVF. Drugs and punishment beatings and racketeering and assassinations of randomly chosen Catholics. No wonder they wanted to make a bit of a show at the funeral. Peter Stanton was the respectable side of the UVF. Davie wondered what to do. His own instincts were to take the man by the collar and toss him out onto the street. But his Grandfather had worked with the man. He had always been there to advise and counsel Hutchinson. Right to the very end. Peter had always been proud of his membership of the UVF. Maybe he would have wanted it. Maybe he would have liked to have been recognised as a soldier in the only army he ever really believed in.

"OK. He would have liked that. Nothing too showy. Let's have a bit of dignity shall we? Discreet. Respectful."

"Aye. Of course. I'll make sure."

There were more people than Davie would ever have imagined. The word had spread through the Shankill. When the hearse made its way out of Granville St there were hundreds out and waiting. A steady rain fell and a helicopter hovered overhead. The crowd seemed to walk beneath a moving roof of umbrellas. At one point Davie looked back and the crowd filled the Shankill Road from side to side for as far as he could see. It was a quiet mood. The only sounds were the crunch of walking feet and the distant thumping of the helicopter. At the graveside the priest gave a short address. Nothing over the top. A brief outline of the life of a proud man. And then, out of nowhere, they were there. Four of them in the their trademark green combat jackets and black balaclavas. They raised their guns to the sky and shot. Then they were gone. The umbrellas closed in tighter to cover the gunmen from the eyes of the helicopter as they moved away.

Once it was over, the throng slowly moved away: away back to the poor terraced houses in the streets off the Shankill Road. Soon Davie stood alone. He wore no hat. The wind was up now and the rain plastered his hair to his head. He struggled to come to terms with the fact that he would never again have the chance to talk with his grandfather. A fertiliser bomb in the boot of a parked car had succeeded where the machine guns and the howitzers of the Kaiser's army had failed. Peter Stanton could have cheated death for a second time. Everyone in West Belfast knew the dangers of secondary devices. But his Granddad hadn't thought twice. He had made the same decision in his 90'th year as he had made when he was eighteen. He had gone to an injured boy. A dying young boy with no legs and so very scared as the life was bleeding out of him. Peter had ensured that a boy had not had to die alone. And he had paid the price.

There was a fact that was burning hot in Davie's brain. It was a fact that he had kept to himself. A simple fact. As simple as any fact could be. He knew who had done it. He didn't know who had placed the bomb and who had driven the car and who had triggered the bomb. But he knew exactly who would have sanctioned the operation. The identity of the commander of the Belfast Brigade's Lower Falls unit was Eugene Quinn. He was a man with a fat file. Davie had helped to compile the file. He had spent long days sitting in his car down the street from Quinn's house. He had been part of an observation team who had watched the house from the loft of a disused factory once their cars had been spotted. He had noted down the comings and the goings and he had seen the information from Special Brach informers. He knew all about Eugene Quinn. He knew the man better than the man's own mother.

Eugene Quinn was good. One of their very best. He was careful to the point of paranoia. He had been interned for six months back in 1973 but since then the security forces had never got close. He had been one of the top ten targets all through Davie's time with 14th Intelligence. They watched him, filmed him, bugged him, photographed him, lifted him, interrogated him, they left no stone unturned. But they could never find a thing that would stick. It had become a waiting game. One day he would make his mistake. Everybody did. Nobody was perfect. And when he did, they would have his cell in the Kesh all ready for him.

But now everything had changed. Davie was no longer a part of 14th Intelligence. He had been over-zealous. They had worried that he might become a loose cannon. He was on leave for the funeral and then he would be joining the Regiment in Cyprus. His grandfather had always said that he would let Davie know when the time had come. Davie had been happy to abide by his decision. He had been guided by his grandfather all his life. But now that time would never come. Eugene Quinn had seen to that. Eugene Quinn had ensured that Davie would never speak with his grandfather again. Eugene Quinn had forced the issue. He had brought forward the moment. He had forced Davie to make his choice. And it was a choice that he would have to make alone.

He could get on the plane and desert his country and pursue his army career. Or he could stay. He could stay and take up the place that Peter Stanton had vacated. He could stay and fight the war on his own terms. As he stood and stared down at the soaking wet soil of the grave he knew that the choice was an easy one. All his life he had known that in the end he would join the war. He had known it from the sunny afternoon in the cemetery at Thiepval Wood all those years ago. It had never been a question of would he join the war. It had only ever been a question of when.

Eugene Quinn had provided the answer. And Eugene Quinn would pay the price.

As Davie emerged out of the cabin he felt more at peace than he had known in years. Maybe more than he had ever felt before. The red light of dawn tinted the snow capped-peaks of the Rockies a deep pink. The sky was a rich blue. He stood for a moment and shivered slightly as his body adjusted to the chill of the dawn. Above him an eagle turned lazy circles as it waited patiently for its prey.

It had been a long journey that had taken him from Army HQ in Lisburn to the mountains of Montana. Resigning his commission had not been easy. They had fought and pleaded with him every inch of the way. They had told him that he was one of their rising stars. They had promised that a long and successful career lay ahead of him. They told him that he had what it took, that they had been watching him for a long time, that they were desperate not to lose him. Davie kept his cool. He fended off a series of officers with quiet determination. He told them that his father's health had deteriorated after the death of Peter Stanton. He told them that his dad could not manage any more. He was needed at home. There was nothing that he could do. He couldn't walk away from his family.

He had worked away in the workshop for a few months just in case they checked up on him. He even found a new route for the business to take. A chance conversation put him onto the fact that there was a tremendous demand for reconditioned period furniture in America. 'Stantons' placed advertisements and the response was pleasing. He spent several weeks driving their van the length and breath of Ulster collecting antique tables and dressers. Once they were back in the workshop his father restored them to their former glory. Having Davie in the business to deal with the bank and the creditors worked wonders for his dad. Soon his health was more or less fully restored and he was happier than he had been in years doing the kind of work that he had been trained to do.

Davie was able to find three outlets on the eastern side of the United States and for the first time in many years 'Stantons' started to turn a profit again. Once Davie was happy that the business was well and truly back on its feet again he took the boat to Scotland. He rented a small warehouse on the outskirts of Ayr to handle the mainland UK side of their business. He registered a new company called 'Ayr Furnishings Ltd' and once again placed ads in the local papers for period pieces. This time the response was not as great as it had been in Ulster but he wasn't greatly concerned.

Having established the Scottish depot he took a plane from Glasgow to New York. He introduced himself to the distributors who had taken the first shipments from 'Stantons' and found that the new customers were more than happy with what they had received. He was able to identify three further outlets: two in California and on in New Orleans. By the time he had spent a month in America the order books were full for several months.

At last he was able to turn his mind to the real purpose of his visit. There was a bar in New York that he had often heard mentioned during his time in the army. It was a bar for ex-soldiers. It was a bar where ex-soldiers could plug into a network that spanned the globe. When Davie walked in one Thursday evening he was pleased with what he found. There were no body-building types with Special Forces tattoos. Instead there were men who looked like plumbers or electricians or the managers of hardware stores. Finding the information that he needed took a few nights. It was not the kind of place where anything would be volunteered easily. They were all careful people. Credentials needed to be checked. This wasn't difficult. There was a web of unofficial information that flowed around the armies of the world. Davie came up clean after four days. Then they told him what he wanted to know.

He could have had almost anything. There were excellent opportunities for a man with his track record in South Africa or the Middle East. They weren't pushy about it. They pointed out the chance of big pay and no tax but they didn't take offence when Davie informed them that he wasn't really interested. For a thousand dollars Davie was given an address. It was the address of a man called Gus who lived alone on a small ranch in the Rocky Mountains in Montana. Gus had once been a Green Beret who had served out three tours in Vietnam. When the war ended Gus took the same route as many of his battle scarred comrades and he lost himself in the wilderness of the American west. As far as his few neighbours and the residents of the local town were concerned, Gus Bennett ran hunting trips in the high woods. There was an advert on the notice board of the hardware shop in the town. And there were small ads in the classified sections of several hunting magazines. And every summer clients flew in from the great cities of the east and Gus Miller would take them high into the forests to hunt deer.

However, Gus Miller had another side to his business for which there were no small ads in national magazines. This was the side that his neighbours and the people of the town had no idea about. In Vietnam Gus Miller had been a sniper. During his time in Asia he had 37 kills. They were not just any kills. They were all carefully targeted. They were senior officers in the Viet Cong or political officers of the North Vietnamese Army. Gus was one of the ones who was handed the wettest of wet work. His targets were often miles behind enemy lines. A mission would involve living rough for weeks with his team of two South Vietnamese guides. With tortuous precision they would slowly close in on the location of the target, dig in, watch, wait, make the kill and allow the jungle to swallow them.

Like many others Gus Miller felt a keen sense of betrayal when he came back home. America was desperate to pretend that the work that he and his kind had done was not for public consumption. There were no ticker-tape parades. No civic receptions and glowing tributes on the front page of the local paper. There was only obscurity. The deniable Ops that Gus had carried out on the orders of his Country were duly denied. They offered him a training position at Sniper School. Gus declined. He'd had a bellyful. He walked away and found himself a place high in the hills where he could live life on his own terms.

They had warned Davie to be careful when he arrived. Gus didn't take kindly to visitors. When he drew his hire car up in front of the cabin, Davie had opened the door very slowly and made a play of keeping his hands up high as he stepped out. A voice came from the trees that surrounded the small clearing.

"Figure that's 'bout far enough. Who are you? What are you?"

"I have a letter. In my pocket. It's from Slinger. I won't take it out."

Gus emerged from the treeline cradling his rifle casually. He talked relaxed and low.

"OK. You just keep those hands up nice and high and I will come and get the letter. It's probably a good idea to keep completely still for a while. That's good. That's fine . . ."

He was quite a small man. Five eight. Maybe five nine. He carried no weight and the jeans hung off his waist. He was largely bald with a heavily lined and weathered face. A quick examination of the letter was all that he needed.

"OK. Fine. Let's have coffee."

The inside of the hut lacked all frills. A wood burning stove kept the place warm and the furniture was basic and comfortable. There was little by way of decoration, no moose heads or triumphant photos. The coffee was on the stove and Gus poured two cups. He put sugar and milk on the table and sat down without ceremony.

"OK. I don't want to know your name. Not the real one anyway. Charles will do. You can be Charles. What is it that you want?"

"Sniping. Up to a thousand yards."

"You ex-military?"

"Yes."

"British Army?"

"Yes. Seven years."

"Done much shooting?"

"A bit. Nothing long range."

"Any good?"

"Above average."

"Combat?"

"Yes."

The small man nodded. Davie liked him. No frills. Nothing macho. Just business. "I'll need a weapon too."

"Anything in mind?"

"No. Whatever you suggest."

"Barrett 50. It's as good as anything. It's available in all the best hunting shops. I've got a couple here. You got plenty of money?"

"I think so."

"Three weeks and 10,000 bucks. That includes the Barrett. If you're no good after that you're wasting your time. We got a deal?"

Davie nodded and extended his hand. He was relieved that in his time in 14th Intelligence he had barely spent a penny of his salary. He had never bought a house and had never incurred any costs in his life. He had needed to draw heavily on his savings once he had resigned his commission.

As the eagle floated silently overhead Davie felt sad that his time in the mountains was almost done. He liked the way that Gus lived his life. Simple. Solitary. Far from the greed and madness and hate of the human race. In another lifetime he might have been able to do the same. The course had been fascinating. Davie had soon realised that it was much more about mathematics than marksmanship. Gus was soon more than happy that Davie's basic weapon skills were excellent. He taught him how to breathe, how to train the mind to keep its focus whilst concentrating on the same thing for hours on end. He taught him the tiny muscle exercises that were needed to stop the body from cramping as it lay prone for long periods. And then there was maths. Lots and lots of maths. How to adjust for wind speed. How to adjust for temperature. How to judge the trajectory of the bullet over distance. These were all sums that had to be done instantly and in the head. Gus explained that there were machines that could do the job but they should be avoided. If the brain was up to it then the brain should be used.

By the end of the second week they moved off the firing range and into the woods. Gus took Davie to positions hundreds of yards away from the tracks where the deer moved. He learnt to wait behind the scope for hours in the cold. He learned to keep his concentration focused. To drain his mind of everything bar the task in hand. All the while Gus would point out targets at different distances and make Davie do the calculations for each different shot.

It took him a week before he made a kill. It was his sixth shot. Already he could hit a target on the range ten times out of ten at 1,000 yards. But it took a week before he could hit a living target at the same distance. He had waited for seven hours for the deer to come. Gus had selected a site where the deer would only be in range for a matter of two or three seconds. The wind had got up and the cold had eaten into Davie's body. He had more or less given up on the prey. It was already almost dusk. But unlike the other days he managed to maintain his concentration. When the brown shape of the deer wandered into his telescopic sight he took in a slow breath without conscious thought. As he allowed the air back out he gently caressed the trigger. It seemed to take forever before the animal shook slightly then fell.

Gus nodded. "That's good. Nice shot. Let's go get it."

Davie killed a further four animals over the next few days. For the last shot Gus chose a spot where the animal was only visible for two seconds. Davie hit it after a wait of five hours.

The American got to his feet and announced that the course was complete.

Over dinner that night Gus broke out the beer to accompany the venison steaks. They worked their way through the case and Gus told Davie about Vietnam. They were easy and relaxed together but Davie knew that this was still part of the programme. There was something more to come and it came a little after midnight.

"Ever killed Charles?"

Davie nodded. "Twice."

"Close or distance?"

"Both. One at 40 yards with an SLR. One close up. A bayonet."

The other man's eyes widened for a split second. "I just wanted to check. All the technical stuff isn't worth a thing if you can't pull the trigger when the moment comes. Not everyone can kill a man."

Davie nodded and stared into the fire. There was no more to be said. They both saw what they had known already. They were both killers. It was what they had done. Neither felt good about it. But neither was eaten up by it either. It was something that they had done because it had been necessary.

The cabin door swung open and Gus walked out with his hands deep in his pockets. He looked up at the clear blue sky for a moment then came to stand with Davie.

"All packed?"

"Aye."

" Well, that's it then."

"It is. Thanks Gus. You keep well."

"I will."

They shook hands and Davie climbed into his car. Gus tapped on the window and Davie wound it down.

"You won't miss."

" I know."

Gus thumped the roof of the car with the flat of his hand and Davie drove away from the quiet place high in the hills where he had found peace. He had one more job to complete before returning to Ireland. He drove back east across the flat Prairies to Pittsburgh where he purchased a new lathe for the workshop from a small engineering firm. He carefully repacked the equipment along with the Barrett 50 and the telescopic sight and the ammunition. He arranged for the heavy crate to be shipped to Ayr Furnishings Ltd in Scotland.

As he had stared down at the bleak greyness of the Atlantic Ocean on the flight back home, there had been two crucial decisions that Davie had battled with. Thus far he had done everything alone. All his instincts urged him to continue to do so. He had seen at first hand during his time with 14th Intelligence that weakness always came from too many links in the chain. He tried every which way he could to find a way that he could continue to work completely alone. Regretfully he realised that it wasn't feasible.

On his return he spent several weeks organising the work that he had gathered during his time in America. His father had taken on two new apprentices and the workshop had come alive again. His worst moment had been when he had driven his car off the ferry at Larne with the Barrett 50 hidden in a false compartment in the boot. It was always going to be the moment of maximum risk. He knew full well that the odds were stacked heavily in his favour. His record was clean and there was no reason on earth why he should be stopped. Even if he was, it was unlikely that the security forces would submit his vehicle to the kind of rigorous examination that would be needed to find the Barrett. However there was always the chance. The chance that everything could be undone by the gut feeling of a bored policeman at Larne docks. As it turned out they never gave him a second glance.

He had wondered what to do with the gun once he got it into the country. For a while he had considered hiding it with the other weapons that his Grandfather had stashed away in the workshop all those years before. He had decided against this. Instead he had bought a static caravan on a large site a few miles south of Belfast on the coast of County Down.

Once the gun was safely hidden away it was time for him to break cover. The following Saturday night he made his way to one of the many clubs on the Shankhill. He worked his way through a couple of pints and passed the time with faces that he had known from school or the workshop. It was after ten when he noticed John Hutchinson making his way to a table in one of the pub's small wooden booths.

Hutchinson had had a remarkable run for his money. The Loyalist paramilitaries had often done more damage to each other than the IRA over the years. Vicious turf wars were forever breaking out as rival factions of the UVF and the UDA shot it out to determine the right to control different streets or estates. As the years of the Troubles had worn on, there had been many cases of the paramilitaries abusing this control. Their guns meant power, and the power in turn gave unique opportunities to deal drugs and extort protection money. There were times when things became blurred as men who had originally set out as defenders of their communities slowly turned into gangsters. Peter Stanton had raged about this turn of events in the years before his death and on several occasions he had buttonholed Hutchinson out in the street to let him know exactly what he thought of the direction that the UVF was taking. There were not many others who would have dared to do the same, though many supported everything that Peter had said. Peter had felt immune from any consequences. The local community would never have forgiven the paramilitaries if anything had ever happened to him.

Hutchinson looked mildly uneasy as Davie made his way over to the table. He wouldn't have put it past the grandson to follow in the old man's footsteps. The two big men who sat at the table with him sat slightly more upright. Davie diffused the tension with an easy smile.

"Evening John. You'll have a drink?"

The tension dropped out of the minders. Davie felt only contempt for them. Pathetic amateurs. If he had wanted to drill Hutchinson it would have been ridiculously easy.

"Thanks Davie. Pint."

When Davie came back he sat down next to the older man in the small booth. "Could you get the lads to take a walk for a few minutes. I could do with a word. A private word."

Hutchinson hesitated for a moment then gestured his men away with a casual nod. They heaved themselves up from behind the table and took up station a few yards away. Davie glanced round carefully. When he was convinced that it was impossible for them to be overheard he started to talk.

"OK John. I'll be brief. I'm going active. I will only work one way. Alone. Completely alone. I will be taking no orders. I'm not interested in territory or command structures. I'm not interested in any of these random sectarian killings. I'm not interested in drugs or protection or punishment beatings. I'm in this for one thing and one thing only. I will take out senior Provos. Not kids. Not stone-throwers. Not couriers. Just top men. Battalion commanders and above. When these guys die the Provo command will have no choice but to give them a full military funeral. Nothing else will be accepted . . ."

Hutchinson had put his pint down and lit a cigarette; His mouth was slightly open. This was unexpected. Davie drove on remorselessly.

"I choose the targets. I complete the operations. Nobody will know until it's done. I don't need money, I don't need intelligence, I don't need weapons and I don't need back up. When the job is done I will call you from a public phone box and say the word 'Snapdragon' and the name of the target. You can then claim the kill on behalf of the UVF. It won't be regular. It doesn't have to be. I anticipate one or two kills a year. I expect you to ensure maximum publicity. You will tell the papers that the execution has been carried out by 'The Ghost'. Got that. 'The Ghost'. Do this properly and every one of their top people will be shitting themselves every time they step out of the front door. This isn't a negotiation John. It's an offer. If the UVF don't want it I'll go down the road to the UDA. It's your call."

Hutchinson's mouth had gone dry. The man scared him. Really scared him. It was the certainty. The complete implacable certainty. John Hutchinson was not much used to fear. But Davie Stanton frightened him. He struggled to retain his composure. The unblinking brown eyes seemed to see right inside him.

"Sure Davie. Why not? The Stantons have always been UVF. Right back to Carson. Wouldn't want you going down the road now would we?"

"And the terms? You agree the terms?"

"Aye. No problem. I can live with that."

Davie leaned in closer. His eyes were only inches from Hutchinson's. He could feel the man's fear. He kept his voice very even. Very low. "There's only you who will know this John. Only you. So if I'm betrayed there will only be one man to come for. Understand what I'm saying John?"

Hutchinson tried to swallow but couldn't. All he could do was nod quickly and look away. Christ he was scared. He wondered what the hell he had just agreed to.

Suddenly Davie's face changed completely. A smile was on his lips. The eyes were now quiet and relaxed. The moment had passed. "Good man John. I knew you would be sound. You always have been. Lets have another shall we?"

A couple of nights later he waited in another pub. He looked up from his table to see Derek Shaw and Richard Green come in together. He had always stayed in touch his two old mates from Granville Street. They had come over the water a couple of times a year when he had been at university and the three of them had hit the pubs and night-clubs in Leeds. When he had come home for his leave during his years in the army the three of them had always started up where they had left off. Strangely they had always had an unwritten rule that they would leave the Troubles alone when they spent time together. These were times when they could forget it all and just be ordinary young men. It was something that Davie had known little enough of.

During his time in the army he had often checked the computer to see if either of his friends had become in any way involved. There were a few small mentions, but nothing firm. Certainly neither had ever been arrested. Derek Shaw had always hoped to follow his father into the Harland and Wolf shipyards, but by the time he left school the great old company was more or less on its last legs. He had drifted from job to job but never really found anything permanent. For the last three years he had been working in a bar in the city centre. Richard Green had never had these problems. His dad ran a small building company and his son had joined immediately on leaving school.

Davie knew that talking to his two oldest friends was a huge gamble. When they had been kids they had done their share of rioting and stone throwing. There was no doubt that Richard and Derek both came from backgrounds that were fervently Loyalist. Davie knew for a fact that Richard's father was a long term UDA man. However this was different. This was a step up into the serious business of the war. This was where a small mistake could easily mean a bullet in the head or a twenty year stretch in the H Blocks. He really didn't know how they would react. He just knew that there was absolutely nobody else that he could trust. It was a gamble he felt that he had to take.

They drank a couple of pints and chatted away happily. Davie suggested that they should go for a drive in the van. The others looked slightly confused but went along happily enough. They made their way down the Shankill and picked up the inner ring. Once they were out of the city Davie took a deep breath and started to speak.

"OK boys, I'm going to drop a bombshell on you. A bloody great big one. The real reason that I left the army is that I'm going active. The Brits aren't here to win this war. All they want to do is to keep a lid on things. They want out but they can't find a way yet. If they could, they'd be gone. They don't give a shite about us. They know exactly who the Provos are. Most of the time they know exactly where they are. I saw it lads. First hand. Up close. I was five years in 14th Intelligence."

Richard let out a long whistle. "Fucking hell Davie, you never said anything about that."

Davie chuckled. "Well it's hardly the kind of thing you advertise on the radio is it?"

"No. Suppose not. It's just bloody amazing that's all."

"It wasn't. Most of the time it was just plain old boring. Watching. Bugging. Tailing. Containing. Always bloody containing. With what we knew we could have stripped their command structure to the bone in a week. But we didn't because that was not how London wanted to play it. All those bastards care a shite about is their PR. Most of the time they want to be seen as the heroic upholders of law and order. They are scared stiff of ever looking bad in Europe or America. But sometimes, at election time, they can see there are a few votes to be had by getting tough on the terrorists. This is when the gloves can come off. Look at Loughgall. Look when it happened. And look who got elected for a third term in Downing Street a couple of weeks later. It's Bullshit. All of it. And in the end they'll hang us out to dry."

The three of them were quiet for a while. They meandered along small country road with fields full of dairy cows on either side.

Derek Shaw spoke at last. "So what are you wanting from us Davie?"

"I intend to attack them where they hurt the most. The top. Right at the top. I want to hit the Battalion commanders and intelligence officers. At the moment these bastards feel indestructible. The Brits simply watch and monitor and the loyalists are more interested in killing completely innocent Catholics and dealing drugs. It's time it changed."

His two friends had gone pale. Davie could see that he hadn't handled things particularly well. "Jesus Davie." Said Richard. "You're bloody nuts. You can't just go round topping top Provos. There's no bloody chance."

Davie grinned. "Don't be so daft. It's what I'm trained to do. It's what I've been doing for five years. I've done everything but pull the trigger. These are not supermen. In any real war they wouldn't stand a chance. The only reason that they are safe is that the Brits haven't got the political bottle to get out there and take them out. These guys aren't Special Forces. They're plumbers or milkmen or farmers or just unemployed."

"Look, that's all very well. Sounds great. But how? How do you propose to do this? How can three of us make a difference?" Richard could not hide the interest in his voice now that the shock was wearing off. Davie pulled the van into a lay by and turned towards them.

"OK. Here's how. Number one. I know the first three targets. I know everything about them because I spent hours of my life watching their every move. I know what they look like, where they live, their routine. That gets me close. So, what then? Number two. I have just finished a three-week intensive sniping course in the States. I can hit a deer from a thousand yards. That's how it's done. Number three. The object is not to kill every single IRA commander. That would be impossible. You're right. The thing is we don't have to. Think about it. Think about the psychological impact. If we start taking out their men at a distance of half a mile just imagine what it will do to the rest of them. How would you feel? How would you feel every time you walked out of your front door? You look up and down the street and it all looks OK. But what about that building over the rooftops? What about that clump of trees on the top of the hill? Imagine their fear. Every one of their senior people will live in fear every day of their lives. We don't have to be in action all the time. That's the whole point. Once or twice a year. That's all that will be needed."

"So what about us?" said Richard "Where do we fit in?"

"Back up. I don't want you to pull the trigger. That's my job. I need you to get me in and get me out again and help with surveillance. That's it. I will train you. Don't worry about that. I'm good at it. I was taught by the best in the business. It's not the soldiers who are fucking things up. The soldiers are the best there are. It's the bastard politicians who are leaving us in the lurch. Can't you see where this is all going? Every year our people are getting more and more demoralised. Every year the Catholics are taking a little bit more and a little bit more. All the bloody British are waiting for is the day when enough of our people pack up their bags and leave. For the time when there will be a Catholic majority. Then they will shrug their shoulders and say that democracy will have to run its course. That will be the day when they will pack up and leave us to it. Now I'm not saying that we can stop that day coming. It's probably too late already. But what we can do is have an effect on who will be our opposition. If we can hit the hard men and make them cower we give the reasonable ones the chance to take control.

Not all Catholics are bad. Course they aren't. Anyone who says they are is an idiot. Just like all Germans aren't bad. The point is that some of them are. And if we allow the bad ones the chance to be the top dogs when the Brits pack up and leave, then our people will be in the same position as the Jews were in the 1930's. I won't have that. We are all very good at painting heroic murals and marching with whistles and drums and going out and gunning down innocent civilians. But that does nothing. It doesn't hurt the enemy. It just makes it easier for those in charge to find the next generation of volunteers. It's time that our people had proper soldiers to defend them. Like my Granddad and the old UVF. That's exactly what we can be."

Derek suddenly laughed. "Fuck me Davie, you should have been a politician, or a bloody preacher. OK. You win. I'm in. How's about you Rich?"

"Aye. I suppose so. I couldn't really let you daft bastards out or your own could I?"

It was the third Sunday in a row that Davie had waited. As a set up it simply could not have been better. Eugene Quinn lived in a small estate on the south side of the Falls Road. His house was near the edge of the development. An area of litter strewn waste ground separated the houses from the Falls itself. A hundred yards to the north of the Falls the high peace wall kept apart the warring clans who lived either side. On the Shankill side of the wall was an old disused factory that had last heard the hum of machinery many years before. Davie had found a spot on the fourth floor. From the broken pane in the filthy cracked glass he had a clear line of sight all the way to number two Simpson Close, the small maisonette where Quinn lived with his wife and two children.

When Davie had marked Quinn for 14th Intelligence the target's routine had been reasonably regular. Most Sunday's Quinn would leave the house after Sunday lunch and make his way to the local club for a few pints. He tended to leave between two and three and walk through the estate. Davie doubted that anything would have changed. When Quinn had not come out on the first Sunday Davie had not been much concerned. It was not unusual for him to miss. When the same thing happened a week later he became a little worried. Maybe he had changed his routine. Now it was already close to three and still there was no sign.

Davie mentally ticked himself off for his agitation. What good would it do? If he didn't come, then so be it. He would simply return for as many Sundays as it took. It wasn't as if he had to wait for hours. It wasn't as if he was out in the open in the wind and the cold. He was well hidden, he was dry, he was safe. All he needed was patience. He started his breathing exercises for the umpteenth time. He concentrated on draining his mind of all unnecessary thoughts. He focused his whole self into the view of the non-descript two storey house with the peeling green window frames and the grey pebble dash walls.

His heart skipped a beat as the front door opened. A man emerged. About 40. Overweight. A thick bush of dark curly hair. A blue anorak. Grey slacks. Work shoes. The man turned back to the open door. He shouted something. He closed the door and walked down the ten-foot long path through the overgrown patch of front garden. He stopped to fiddle with the catch on the gate. It must have been stiff. Probably rusty. It annoyed him. He gave it a sharp kick and the gate swung open. He walked through the gate and stopped whilst he zipped the anorak up to the neck to keep out the sharp wind. He looked up to the sky to see what the weather held in store. He was still looking as Davie allowed the long breath to slowly ease out of his mouth. His finger closed on the sensitive trigger of the Barrett 50 as gently as if it belonged to a concert pianist. The split second it took for the bullet to ark its way over the peace line seemed to last for hours. Davie was so deep in concentration that he barely noticed the roar of the gun. He never moved. Never blinked. He stayed completely still to see the burly figure thrown to the pavement. He let out a second long breath and sent the second bullet over 900 yards of West Belfast into the prone figure of Eugene Quinn. There was no need. The first bullet had taken him squarely through the back and had passed through his heart before smashing its way through the rib cage. Eugene's career with the IRA had come to an end.

Davie did not hurry. This time there was no need. It would take forensic 900 yards from the other side of the peace wall. Right now nobody would have a clue. There was no rush. He took care to leave the dusty concrete floor exactly as he had found it. Richard was waiting outside. They hid the gun in the compartment in the boot and made an uneventful journey to the caravan on the coast.

Davie used a pay phone in a pub.

"Snapdragon. Eugene Quinn. This afternoon."

He replaced the receiver before Hutchinson had a chance to speak. He bought more beers from the bar and joined his two friends. They raised their glasses to each other in a silent toast.

Chapter 9
Ghost

January 1989

Davie was cold. Really cold. Probably as cold as he had ever been before. To start with it had been just inconvenient. Annoying. Uncomfortable. But now it was becoming serious. He had taken up his position in the clump of hawthorn bushes an hour before dawn. For a while the position had been a joy. The hard, cold spell of January weather was now into its fifth day. The ground all around him had frozen as hard as iron. Above him the sky was almost impossibly clear and the stars shone out as if they were in a Disney movie. The bright moonlight lit up the frosted white of the fields and made them glow. Davie could not remember a stillness that was so complete. There was not a sound, not a movement, not a breath of wind. The tune of 'Winter Wonderland' rolled around his brain.

If the landscape of the moonlight had been spectacular, the world that unwrapped itself with the dawn was awe-inspiring. The deep red of the sun crept slowly over the craggy low hills with their lattice work of small fields and dry stone walls. There were clutches of sheep with breath steaming in the cold air. A couple of crows flew high across the deep blue of the sky. The world seemed at peace with itself. Time had stopped.

By the time that the red ball of the sun nudged over the eastern horizon the cold was beginning to really get to Davie. It seemed that it crawled out of the frozen ground and seeped into every bone in his body. He tried to concentrate on the tiny muscle exercises that he had been taught in the mountains of Montana. He drained his mind of the discomfort. He forced his chilled eyeballs to focus on the small farm that sat across a shallow valley just over a thousand yards away.

An hour after dawn and he was becoming concerned. The rest of his body didn't matter much. It was the fingers that gave cause for alarm. He was wearing fingerless gloves and they were next to useless. The fingers of his right hand were stiffening with every minute that passed. He made the decision and put the gun down and he rubbed them vigorously for a few moments. A rush of pain made him wince as the blood started to circulate properly again. He checked his watch. 7.35 Almost time.

He resumed his position and once again fixed his gaze on the white back door to the farmhouse. His mind ran through the calculations for the umpteenth time. It was his easiest shot to date. Visibility was magnificent. There wasn't a breath of wind. There was only the coldness of the air that he needed to take into account. But for the cold it would be perfect. But the cold in his bones made him nervous. Would he be able to ease the trigger down when the moment arrived? There was no way to tell. All he could do was wait.

The minutes dragged by and with a sinking heart he felt the numbness returning to his fingers. Maybe he should abort. There was no need for it to be today. Better to wait than to fail. Better to be sure. Always look for a hundred percent. He knew what Gus would have said. Gus would have told him to abort. Gus would have reminded him that the greatest weapon that a sniper possessed was patience. The sniper set the agenda. The sniper chose the moment. The sniper chose the place of execution. The sniper never allowed any doubt.

He was on the verge of giving it up when he felt a jolt of excitement as the back door began to open. His mind raced. He tried to be objective. Tried to come up with an honest evaluation of his state of readiness. The door was fully open now. The figure of a man emerged. Tall. A well worn waxed jacket. Thick tweed trousers. Woollen socks. A flat cap covering wiry ginger hair. Thick features. Wide nose. O'Hara. Michael O'Hara. Michael

O'Hara stooping to pull on the first of his Wellington boots. Michael O'Hara with his lips moving in a silent curse at the coldness of the boot. Second boot next. Soon it would be on. Then he would stand up.

Decision Davie. Decision. He's there. Perfect. Right in the centre of the cross wire of the telescopic sight. Easing himself up now. Probably stiff with the cold. Aching joints. Not as young as he had been. New lines on the face. Decision time. The decision came from instinct. The adrenalin was flowing now. Somehow the chemicals in his body had wiped away the cold. He felt the breath easing out of his mouth in a steady stream. His instinct had made the decision. Autopilot. A machine. His finger depressed the trigger And it was done.

The shot rang in his ears as the figure of Michael O'Hara sank to the floor leaving splashes of red on the white paint of the back door. He took the second shot. The body twitched as the bullet thudded through the thick coat. The sound of the shot had sent a clutch of crows flapping into the sky. Then silence once again clamped down over the frozen fields of South Armagh.

Brendan Conner was in a towering rage as he paced the kitchen. He turned angrily to Sean as he entered the room.

"Where the fuck have you been Sean?"

Sean raised his hands in a calming gesture. "Hey, take it easy Brendan. I got here as soon as I could. I can't fly you know. Calm yourself down."

Telling Conner to calm down was much akin to pouring petrol on a bonfire.

"Don't tell me to fucking calm down Sean. Don't even think about it. Just remember who you're speaking to here. Just you remember that. Don't you know what's happened here?"

"I know."

"So don't tell me to fucking calm down."

"OK. I won't. Stay mad if you like. It won't bring Michael back."

Conner sprang across the kitchen with a speed that belied his bulk. He was on Sean. Pushing him back into the sink with his big hard hands on his throat. It took two men to pull him off. He slumped down to the chair at the table as Sean straightened out his shirt collar. The anger drained out of him. He waved for Sean to sit down.

"Ah fuck it Sean, sorry about that. I was out of order. We go back, you see, me and Michael. We were at primary school together for fuck's sake. Twenty years we've been fighting together. Twenty bloody years and now this. It would have been bad enough if it had been the Brits. SAS or Paras or something. But this. This is hard to take. I never thought the day would come when some UVF fucker could come down here and kill our Michael. Fuck it Sean, this is getting serious."

Sean nodded. He didn't need Brendan Conner to tell him. The emergence of the so-called Ghost had done the Movement more damage than anything he had seen during his time in the IRA. When Eugene Quinn had been killed it had been a shock. The shock had been magnified when the news leaked out that the shot had been fired from a distance of 900 yards from the other side of the peace line. Nothing remotely like it had ever happened before. The Loyalists had killed before. Of course they had. But never like this. They would send teams of men to smash in front doors with sledge hammers and kill from point blank range with shotguns. More often than not they got the wrong man. And when they did get the right man he was only ever a junior volunteer. In the bigger picture it only ever helped the Movement. These killings mobilised anger in the communities and ensured that new volunteers continued to come forward.

It was the same when the SAS carried out their executions. Unlike the Loyalist paramilitaries they tended to hit the right guys. There was damage. Of course there was. But the propaganda gains always compensated. Whenever the SAS shot any of their people dead, the funds from America would flow in with new vigour. This was different. Terribly different. Quinn was one of the old guard. He went all the way back to 1968. They had to give him the full military funeral in Milltown Cemetery. Nothing else would have been acceptable. But instead of being another martyr murdered by the Brits he was the victim of a clinical strike from the UVF.

When the statement was issued claiming responsibility Sean felt a chill run through him. They announced that Eugene Quinn had been executed by 'The Ghost'. They said that any senior member of the IRA should live in fear of a similar fate. There were those who laughed it off. They said it was just typical Loyalist talk. There was no Ghost. Who would believe in a Ghost? They said it was all bullshit. Sean kept quiet and waited.

Four months later Terry Rogers was shot dead as he delivered milk on an estate on the outskirts of Cookstown. The RUC established that the shot had been fired from a small wood on a hillside twelve hundred yards away. The UVF once again claimed responsibility for the killing. They said that the Ghost had struck again. Rogers had been one of the only senior officers of the East Tyrone Brigade who had not been involved in the ill-fated attack on the police station at Loughgall. He had been appointed as the new Brigade commander more or less by default. All the other candidates were filled with holes care of the SAS. He never got the chance to impose himself in his new position.

In the late summer the Ghost struck again. Once again the East Tyrone Brigade provided the victim. In many ways the IRA career of Robert McNeil mirrored that of Sean. Robert had been a high flier at school in Dungannon and had gone on to achieve an excellent Engineering Degree from Queens. He had joined a firm of chartered surveyors and impressed everyone. He was made a full partner before his 30th birthday and was known as something of a yuppie in the town as he drove about in his Mercedes car. Very few knew that Robert had been a member of the IRA since the age of seventeen. He was seen as a man to watch. He provided the East Tyrone Brigade with cunning and intelligence. Sean had heard that he had been bitterly opposed to the huge raid at Loughgall

There had been many in the Movement who had been surprised when McNeil had been appointed as the new commander. He was the new breed. Young. Intelligent. Pushy. There were those who doubted if he would ever be accepted among the hard men of the countryside who had traditionally filled the ranks in Tyrone. Sean had lobbied hard for the appointment and looked forward to great things.

As it turned out McNeil never got the chance to prove his worth. The Ghost picked him off from 700 yards as he was unlocking the door of his car in the office car park. The RUC established that there was a narrow line of sight to the car park from the space under the roof of a disused church. The funeral had caused vigorous debate within the IRA. Nobody in Cookstown had the first idea that McNeil had been a senior Provisional. His death had been greeted with outrage and shock. The claims of the UVF that the Ghost had once again struck at the heart of their enemy were widely rubbished. There were those who said that giving him a military funeral would only benefit the UVF. Sean had argued this point strongly. He had urged the Leadership to be pragmatic. He tried to emphasise the critical importance of propaganda. His words had fallen on deaf ears. The traditions of the Movement were not to be tampered with. The military funeral was something that was not up for discussion. There was an air of astonishment at the funeral when the four masked gunmen appeared at the graveside to fire off their volley of shots.

It had been a disaster. Complete and unmitigated. The Loyalists were jubilant. The killing of Robert McNeil was the moment when the legend of the Ghost really took off. Within weeks the murals started to appear all over the Province. There were images of the cartoon Ghost wrapped in a Union Jack. In some it stared down the barrel of a sniper's rifle. In others it held the rifle aloft. In others it stood in triumph over the bloody corpse wrapped in the Irish tricolour. The Ghost became a legend. A talisman. A hero. The Ghost was the centre of excited conversations in playgrounds and workshops and pubs. There was a new mood of confidence in all the places where Union Jacks hung from the lampposts. At last they had a true defender. At last there was a real soldier who was taking the war to the very heart of the enemy. A pop group from Ballyclare even released a record dedicated to the exploits of the Ghost. The Government promptly banned it but it sold like wildfire. Every Saturday night it became a favourite in the pubs and clubs.

The effect on the IRA was disastrous. There wasn't a senior officer in the Movement who didn't know the chill of fear when they stepped out of their houses or cars. They could not help but scan the horizon for places where the Ghost could be hiding. It took weeks before the Army Council had been able to find anyone willing to take on the job of commanding the doomed East Tyrone Brigade.

After the Rogers killing, Sean had been given the job of investigating the new threat. He had done what he could but it hadn't been much. His report did little more that state the obvious. He suggested that it was clear that the assassin was highly trained. He pointed out that the assassin must have had access to excellent intelligence for him to be able to identify and locate his targets with such a high degree of accuracy. Realistically the only viable source for this information had to be the security services. He doubted whether the Ghost was working directly for the British Government. They may well have been happy enough with the job that the Ghost was undertaking. It was unlikely however that they would ever risk using a trained sniper assassin directly. Were such an operation ever revealed it would be a propaganda catastrophe.

Sean had concluded that the Ghost was a highly trained, motivated and capable individual who had access to security service files. He guessed that he was either working entirely alone or with a small team. He felt it unlikely that he would be operating as part of any larger grouping within the UVF. In conclusion, he could see no feasible way that the Movement could realistically hope to identify the Ghost. They simply did not have the resources. Their only feasible course of action was to ensure that all senior officers took whatever precautions they could. The Council had not been ecstatic about his report. He would have been surprised if they had been.

The Ghost had been quiet for several months. The tension within the ranks had at last started to ease a little. Maybe something had happened to him. Maybe he had been run over or got a girl. Anything. Anything so long as he went away. But now he was back. And this time he had come to haunt the men of the South Armagh Brigade. Sean knew better than to suggest that Brendan should hold back from giving his old friend a full military funeral. There would have been no point anyway. Michael's involvement was hardly a great secret within the local community.

Conner had been silent for a while. At last he raised his head and spoke. The anger was all gone now. It had been replaced with resignation. Sadness.

"There must have been collusion. Had to have been. If they had wanted to bottle him up they could have done it. We know they could. Just look at how hard we find it to get the boys away after an operation. And we don't have to leave the area. We just need to get our lads away a couple of miles or so. He must have had to drive all the way out of Armagh. On quiet roads just after dawn? No way. He couldn't have done it. They must have left him a clear passage. The bastards must be pulling his strings. There's no other explanation."

"Yes there is." Sean's voice was flat. He hadn't seen it until Conner had spoken. Then the reality of what had happened had jumped vividly into his mind. The Chief looked up with interest.

"What?"

"Christ Brendan, I think the bastard went and read our book. He's turned the tables on us."

"Stop talking in riddles Sean."

"Look at where Michael's farm is. 300 yards from the bloody Border. He didn't have to worry about them blocking off his exit route. He never went near them. The Ghost took his shot from the Republic. The cunning bastard. As the Brits were scrambling to lock him in he was probably sitting down for breakfast in his B&B. It's hardly a new idea is it Brendan?"

"What are you saying?"

"Think man. Narrow Water. It is exactly what we did. He's taking the piss."

The colour drained from Conner's face.

"So what do we do?"

Sean gave a short laugh. "What can we do? You'll have to move. That's for sure. So will all the boys who live on the border. That's about all there is. He's got us on the run."

It took a moment to sink in. Conner could not believe it. The Brits had thrown everything they had at him for twenty years and they had never been able to move him out of his farm. They had even built one of their towers a few hundred yards from his house but still he had spat in their faces. But now everything had changed. He was being moved out by a lone UVF gunman who had killed with a shot from the Republic. He considered arguing the point. He was tempted to be stubborn but it was no good. He was important to the Movement. He could not allow himself to be risked.

He moved out of his farm the next day. The soldiers in the watchtower laughed and cheered when they saw the suitcases being put in the back of the car. One of them threw a white sheet over his head and made cartoon ghost noises. It was a bad day for Brendan Conner.

Sean would have been rather surprised if he could have seen the true situation of the Ghost. Davie had always been aware that the first few kills would be the easy ones. The problem was that the further away he got from his time in 14th Intelligence, the more his knowledge and intelligence information would be out of date. He had no doubts whatsoever about Eugene Quinn. The man was a player and he always would be. He had been in charge of his territory for years. He was sure-fire.

Terry Rogers was more of a gamble. In the months leading up to Loughgall, Davie had gained an in depth knowledge of the personnel and workings of the East Tyrone Brigade. He had felt pretty certain that Rogers would be the only viable choice to take control. It was a small gamble, but it had paid off. Robert McNeil represented a much bigger gamble. In many ways he was always going to be an unlikely choice to be given command. It was gut feeling rather than hard logic that had convinced Davie to target him. Even if he was not the new commander it was pretty well certain that he would have been moved up the ladder in the wake of the Loughgall killings. There had been something about McNeil. There was a danger about him. The designer suits and the thirty grand car only seemed to enhance his threat. Davie had often sensed the killer inside McNeil during the long hours of surveillance. His instincts told him that McNeil would be a particularly good man to get rid of. Once again his gamble had paid off handsomely as the evening news had shown the four gunmen send McNeil off to the next world with a volley of shots.

Once the McNeil operation was complete Davie had used up all of the knowledge that he had gained from 14th Intelligence. The

O'Hara kill had come from his time in the fort at Crossmaglen. O'Hara was one of the men whose picture had been on the wall. It had been on the wall since 1968. He was part of the furniture. They had known all about him but he was as slippery as an eel. He had initially discounted trying anything in South Armagh for all the reasons that Conner had identified. The idea of the cross border shoot had come out of the blue. The trouble was that it was a tactic that could only be used once. So far his plan had worked better than he could ever have imagined. Wherever he went people wanted to talk to him about the Ghost. The murals were the cause of huge amusement between Derek and Richard and himself.

In many ways, his two years as the Ghost had proved to be a strangely wonderful time for Davie. Life was better than it ever had been. The business had started to thrive and the orders kept flowing in from the other side of the Atlantic. Davie realised that he had been isolated for years. His accent had always marked him out at University. It had never caused him any particular problems. Nobody would have dared. But he had always been one step removed from his contemporaries. This wasn't just because of the way the others viewed his Irishness, although it did have an influence. Every time the news headlines were filled with the familiar images of burning Belfast he noticed that heads would turn to stare. More important was the way that he viewed everyone else. They had all come from nice easy conventional upbringings in pleasant English towns. They had never seen plastic bullets being fired or clouds of CS gas blowing down the streets where they lived. The world for them was a comfortable place where death only visited occasionally and naturally. Many felt the need to fight the comfort of their lives and became punks or modern anarchists. Davie thought them pathetic.

The army had been little different. Soldiers of the British Army were accustomed to men from West Belfast being the enemy. The very sound of the accent brought out their aggression. Davie had soon been accepted. Respected. Sometimes viewed with a kind of awe. He was the man who had stood in the face of the bullets in Crossmaglen and never flinched. He was a man who had killed with a bayonet on the slopes of Mount Tumbledown. He was accepted. Readily accepted. But he had never fitted in. 14th Intelligence was different. It was a place where everyone was a loner. The life didn't attract gregarious types. Teams were small and self-contained. Most of the time the work was grindingly boring but the threat was always lurking. There was no Officers Mess. No social life. Just the business of tracking and tagging the IRA.

Once he had resigned his commission Davie was soon filled with a sense of belonging. The Shankill Road was his home and he was back among his own people. He had no problem living out his double life, and being a part of the Ghost team gave him a greater sense of comradeship than he had ever known in the army.

More than all this he had a sense of victory. He had not known this in the uniform of the Queen. The war in the Falklands had been a moronic, idiotic exercise that had won a woman he despised a second term in office. He had never felt any sense of victory from any of his time with the army in Ireland. Crossmaglen had been an exercise in hanging on. Loughgall had been a turkey shoot. It would have been different if the day had ever come when the Red Army tanks rolled over the Rhine. That would have been a war with no grey areas. A war that could be fought for all the right reasons with no politicians to get in the way. Now he had his own war. It was a war that made complete sense to him.

There was nothing complicated about it. His own people were facing the extinction of their way of life. All his life he had been preparing for the fight that he now waged. He had no doubts. Only certainties. And now he was no longer a man apart. He was back amongst his own.

He was waiting for Terry and Richard in the caravan by the coast. He had grown oddly fond of his hideaway over the months. It tended to be rather busy in the summer, particularly on the rare occasions that the sun shone for any length of time. But in the winter the place was deserted. He found that the grey emptiness of the beach was the perfect place to marshal his thoughts. He had put in many miles over the last couple of days and to his consternation he had come up with a big fat zero. He had always assumed that something would turn up once the well that he had filled in his time in the army ran dry. Now that time had arrived and it suddenly didn't seem so easy at all. The IRA was the world's tightest knit terrorist army and even the might of the British security services with their bottomless pockets found it tough to get inside. It was suddenly very clear that for the small Ghost team the task was bordering on the impossible. He had called the lads in to have a brain storming session. Maybe something would come up.

They arrived a few minutes after seven with an Indian takeaway and a carrier bag full of beer. Soon the small table was covered with the debris of fast food and docked cigarettes. Davie decided to cut the small talk.

"OK lads. We've got a few problems. I thought it would be a good idea to kick them around a bit and see what shakes out. I never mentioned it before, but O'Hara was the last target from my army time. There's nothing left. Everything else I know will be way past its sell by date. We're in the cold now. We need to find a way of digging out senior Provies."

They bounced ideas around the table but nothing showed much promise. It was close on midnight when Richard suddenly remembered something.

"Hang on lads. Maybe I might have something."

"Go on."

"It was a couple of weeks ago. I was down the club on Saturday night. There were a few of us sitting together. The talk was of the Troubles and all that. Something came up. I never thought much about it at the time. I was a bit pissed to be honest. We all were. There were a couple of guys there who are supposed to be UDA. They were getting a bit mouthy. You know how they do. Showing off for the women. Anyway one of them said that they were getting all the stuff they needed now. The business. The name Brian Nelson came up. Then the talk moved on again. It was something and nothing. I never gave it a second thought."

"Brian Nelson? Who's Brian Nelson?" Asked Davie.

"You know him. He's a mini-cab driver. He was pretty active in the seventies. Went down on an eight for kidnapping. He fucked off to work in Germany. Came back a couple of years ago."

Davie tried to search for the name and the face. There was something there. Nothing much. Then the image hardened

266

slightly. "Oh aye. I know him. Little bloke. Always pissed up. Mouthy. I always thought he was a bit of a tosser."

"He is. But when you think about it there are a few things that are a bit fishy."

"Like?"

"Well the way I heard it he came back from Germany and straight away gets himself a nice house and a new car. He's always buying everyone drinks. Likes to play the big man."

"So how does he afford all this? There's not a lot of cash to be had driving a mini-cab."

"He said he won the German Lottery when he was out there. That was how he was able to afford to come back home and buy the house."

A slow smile spread across Davie's face. "Bingo."

"What?"

The smile was now huge. "Come on. Look at the odds. Won the German Lottery! Bollocks. Toe rags like Brian Nelson don't win the lottery. I can't believe they could come up with such a tonne of bullshit." He couldn't help but laugh.

"What's so funny?" Asked Derek.

"It's just so typical. This isn't MI5 and it isn't Special Branch. Those lads would never come up with anything so bloody stupid. They're too cute. I know exactly who this is. This is the bloody army. This is some plum in the mouth Colonel's idea of playing James Bond. Now come on. Try and remember everything about what was said. The lot."

Richard struggled. It had only been a snatch of conversation and there had been eight pints of lager swilling around inside him.

"Christ Davie, I just can't remember clearly. There was nothing blatant. It was just hinted at. The impression was that Brian was something to do with UDA Intelligence and he was coming up with the goods. You know. Targets."

Davie drummed his fingers on the table. What the hell were they up to? Whatever it was it warranted looking into.

To start with Davie had been worried that they might have given Nelson some anti-surveillance training before they brought him back. That would have made life difficult. He had wondered whether or not to involve Richard and Derek in the watching but had decided that they were more likely to give the game away. The only way was to do the job himself. After the first couple of hours he relaxed. Nelson was taking no precautions whatsoever. The mini-cab was easy to follow. The target drove around slowly and obeyed traffic lights and speed restrictions like a model citizen.

It had been ten days now. Ten days of meandering around the streets of the city following Nelson's Mazda. There was nothing suspicious. Just another mini-cab plying its trade. Many would have become frustrated and impatient. Davie didn't. It was work that he was used to. He had done it for nearly five years of his life. He had done it on the very same streets that they now drove through. Patience was never a problem for Davie. He had been born patient.

There was nothing to excite him as the Mazda pulled into a small suburban street in the south of the city. There were trees and neat gardens and semi-detached houses. For the millionth time in his life Davie was struck by the contrasts of his home town. The street was no more than two miles from the Shankill Road as the crow flies but it might as well have been on a different continent. No murals. No litter. No peace wall. No hard faced kids hanging around waiting for a fight. Instead this was a place for junior managers or dentists who changed their cars every other year and took their holidays in Tuscany. Two miles. Mad. Two miles from war zone to suburb.

The Mazda indicated and pulled up in a space between a Saab and a Renault. Davie pulled up a hundred yards back. Another fare. Maybe a housewife left without the car. What was the cab for? A trip to the hair salon? An appointment at the school? A rendezvous with a lover? It was the way the watcher passed the time. Taking tiny pieces of stranger's lives and guessing.

He sat up slightly in his seat as the door of the Mazda opened. Maybe something here. Probably not. Probably Nelson was just going to knock on the door. Maybe the punter wanted some help with bags. Maybe she was packing up and leaving for good. Maybe she was heading out to Rio with her lover.

Yes. It might just be something. There was something about the way that Nelson got out of the car. Nervous. Shifty. Looking up and down the street but trying to look as if he wasn't. You're a poor man's James Bond thought Davie with amusement.

Nelson made his way to a front door and rang the bell. Seconds later the door opened. Nelson went in. Davie was fully alert now. What was next? Maybe he would come out, struggling under the weight of the suitcases that were on their way to a new life in the sun. Or maybe he would stay inside. The seconds ticked by. A minute. Three minutes. Ten minutes. Davie relaxed and sat back in his seat slightly.

So. This was it. Maybe Brian had a bit on the side himself. Stranger things had happened. But Davie doubted it. If Brian was to find a woman she wouldn't live on a street like this. Surely not.

Davie had been in these kind of houses before. A quiet street. A nice part of the city. A place where neighbours would go out of their way not to talk to each other. Discreet. It had 'Army' written all over it. Twenty minutes. He ran through his options. What did he know? Not a lot. Maybe Brian was something in UDA intelligence. Maybe he was being paid by the Brits. Maybe they were passing him target information. Lots of maybes and just possibly this was the confirmation of the maybes. So what next? The address was pretty meaningless. It was just a meeting point. If Brian was to be worth anything it was that he had led Davie to his handlers. So what did that give him? Hard to say. Maybe a way in? No point thinking about that now. What was important was to decide on the next course of action. Surely that was obvious. Follow the handler. Find a location for the handler. He could plan the next stage once he got that far. It was a bit thin, but it would have to do. Maybe the handler would simply drive to one of the barracks. That wouldn't get him very far. On the other hand they might work out of a safe house somewhere and that could be useful. He made his mind up. Follow the handler. That was assuming that there was a handler. He could be completely wrong. Even as he watched Brian might be in the middle of the sexual experience of his life.

40 minutes. The door opened. Who would it be? Brian. Brian pulling up the collar of his anorak. Brian looking even more shifty. Brian at his car door. Brian getting in. Brian driving away.

OK. So there he goes. So wait. Let the cards fall. Five minutes. Maybe a lover after all. No. He couldn't believe it. Maybe this was the safe house where they actually stayed. No. That would be taking idiocy to new levels. Ten minutes. Just wait Davie. Sit and wait. Just like you have a thousand times before.

Twelve minutes. The door was opening. One man. Two men. Ordinary clothes. Very Marks and Spencer. Very upright. You can't hide the bearing can you? All that drill. Never goes away. Both look pretty fit. How old? Thirty'ish. That would be about right. Which car? Of course. The Escort. Blend in boys. Except that you haven't blended in. OK. It's time to play follow the red Escort. Time to see how well trained you are lads . . .

The door again. Opening. Must be another. That buggers it up. Come on Davie. Decision time. Two of them in the Escort about to leave. The fumes already coming out of the exhaust. Or do you wait? Wait and have a look at the next one. Play the odds Davie. Take the Escort. Bird in the hand . . .

"Jesus H Christ."

The next man was outside now. He was turning to lock the door. A long grey coat. Probably a suit underneath. And cufflinks no doubt. You look like a City banker thought Davie. You look like a senior consultant thought Davie. He smiled and eased his foot off the clutch. Everything about the third man was familiar. The way he walked. The way he unconsciously pushed back his thick mop of blond hair. The way he cupped his hands around his lighter to block out the wind. The way he allowed the smoke from the first draw to run out through his nostrils. He knew every move because he knew the third man.

The third man was James Hamilton.

"Bingo" He said it softly. The decision made itself. There was no point trying to tail James. Not on his own. Even with a team of six it would be tough. Doing it on his own would be a complete waste of time. There was only one way to do it. The Escort was at the far end of the street now. It was indicating right. A bus passed by. A gap. The Escort eased itself away. James had walked over to a Peugeot. He was unlocking the door. Davie drew up level with the car. He felt James tense and saw his hand already moving inside the banker's coat.

"Easy there James. Don't go shooting me now. That's no way to treat an old mate."

He wished that he could have bottled the look on Hamilton's face. Total and utter shock. One second he had been instinctively reacting to an assassination attempt. The next he was staring into the smiling face of Davie Stanton. It wasn't often that James Hamilton was ever lost for words. But he was now. Completely. He looked like a rabbit in full beam headlights. A ten-year-old caught by Mr Singh with a stolen Mars bar in his pocket. Davie found it quite amusing.

"Cat got your tongue James? Come on. Hop in. Let's go and get a pint."

Hamilton climbed into the passenger seat and tried to compose himself. When he managed to speak he was more or less as smooth as ever. "Christ Davie. I don't believe it. You jumped me out of my skin there. Thought you were a bloody Provo for a minute. How the hell are you? It's been ages."

"Sound. I'm sound. How's Brian?"

Davie had to give his old friend credit. The recovery was magnificent. A small frown. A slight shake of the head. A vaguely troubled look. "Brian? Who's Brian, Davie?"

"You tell me James. You know best. Mr Brian Nelson. Long time toe rag who returns from Germany with a pocketful of cash from the Lottery. There are some who think that it might all just be a bit of a fairytale. Some whisper that Brian is in UDA intelligence. Some whisper that he is the man who has the names and addresses of Provie targets. Now I got to wondering how that could be. You see, Brian has always been a bit of a dickhead. He's not the kind of guy to come up with the goods. He's a pisshead. One of life's losers. So how? I asked myself. How? So I decided to come and take a look, and, well here we are James. Here we are."

The colour had drained from Hamilton's handsome face. He chewed at his lip. He was completely off balance. He sensed the smoking ruins of his career.

"What exactly is happening here Davie? I heard that you were out. Gone. Who the hell are you working for? Not those bastards in MI5 surely."

Davie laughed. "That would be the ultimate nightmare wouldn't it. Better the Provies than those bastards." It was time to take the moment. It was no time to hesitate and try to box clever. It was a time to follow the feeling in the gut. He went for it. "Don't panic James. Your career is safe. I did leave. I'm out of it. The only person I work for now is me. And it's your lucky day old friend. I'm your dream ticket."

"So what the hell are you doing following Brian Nelson?"

"You better take a big deep breath James. Hang on to your seat and all that. It's bombshell time. I'm the Ghost. Yes. Me. Davie. A real life Ghost. You heard they killed my Grandad?"

Hamilton's voice was little more than a whisper. "Yes. I heard. I'm sorry."

"So was I. That was when it was enough. I got fed up with containment. I decided it was time to fight my own war. That's what I've been doing. Your lot aren't bothered about winning this war. I saw it. I was on your side for years."

"Christ." Still Hamilton was reeling. Davie saw it was best to press on.

"I'll cut to the chase James. I've used up my target list. I have a blank page in front of me. Hence the interest in Nelson. It seemed pretty obvious that you lot were running him and passing him target information. Christ knows why. The man's a bloody joke. I need targets James. This can work for both of us. We know the score. There are men who need to be put away. Permanently. The bad boys. The killers. The nutters. I'm not daft. I know as well as you do that one day you lot will pack your bags and leave. When the day comes my people need to be able to deal with politicians, not the hard men with the chips on their shoulders. I'm the tool. The method. I can make the real bad boys go away. For good. If you lot want to do this, use a proper soldier, not a useless twat like Brian."

Hamilton sat very, very still. His mind was running at full speed trying to arrange his thoughts. The shock was wearing off. He was slowly coming to terms with the facts that been revealed. He could see the opportunities. All of a sudden his future career was bathed in golden light. Davie Stanton was the Ghost. Wonderful. Fantastic. His voice now had all its usual composure.

"Tell me about your set up Davie?"

"Me. That's it. I work alone. I have one contact in the UVF. He knows nothing of targeting or planning. When it's done I call him, and he makes the claim. That's it. One man. And now you. And that's how it stays. If you're interested."

"Don't believe you Davie. No way you do all this alone. There must be more. A small team I would guess, but you don't want to tell me about them. Which of course is only right and proper. I wouldn't want to tell you either." He was smiling now. Sometimes life could just be so bloody perfect. "I assume that you will work anywhere? Down south? Overseas?"

"Of course."

"I think we have common ground, Lots and lots of common ground. I will have to go upstairs with this. Up to the top floor in fact. I expect a rather good reception. There are people who have been waiting many years for you to come along. It's a bit like finding a cleaner when you live in a big dirty house that you can't seem to stay on top of. I will need two weeks. Then we'll meet. OK by you?"

"Fine. You are my contact James. Nobody else. Anyone else and I walk. Understood?"

"But of course. You don't seriously suggest that I would pass you on to someone else do you? I'm still rather a nasty ambitious bastard in case you hadn't noticed."

James was true to his word. Their next meeting was arranged two weeks later. They met in a small Italian restaurant in Soho. Davie arrived first and was amused by the lavish surroundings. It was so typical of James. The clandestine meet up in a rainy lay-by would only ever be a last resort for James Hamilton. A quick glance through the menu was enough to demonstrate to Davie that having a reliable arms length killer on the books was something that was something worth opening the public purse for.

James breezed in ten minutes after Davie. The shocked pale face that Davie had seen in the car in the street in South Belfast seemed to belong to another lifetime. The man for all garden parties was back in the saddle. He greeted the owner effusively and planted a gracious kiss on the cheek of his wife. James was always the master of the careless laugh and the easy smile and the cheery slap on the back. Every restaurateur's favourite customer. Every killer's favourite handler.

They were ushered to a table in the corner. The next two tables had 'reserved' signs on them. Davie nodded to them and said "Yours?"

"Of course."

"I can see that you have managed to get your expenses sorted James."

"Of course. That is lesson number one. Never embark on a project until the expenses are adequate for the job. I look at it like this. You and I do our bit for Queen and country. It isn't asking a great deal to expect Queen and country to do a bit for us. Decent food. Nice drop of red. Pleasant ambience. And all for less than it costs for a rifle to be carried around by some worthless eighteen-year-old from Walsall. Value I call it."

They didn't rush into it. They ate and reminisced. A second bottle of wine duly arrived. Pudding came and went. Then coffee. James passed over his open packet of cigarettes and Davie took one. That sat for a while in easy silence. Eventually Davie stubbed out his cigarette.

"So James. Stop being coy. What news?"

"All good I'm glad to say. You have many friends in this town Davie. We have been receiving all kinds of intelligence over the last few months. Do you know it took the poor sods nearly three months to persuade anyone to command the East Tyrone Brigade? The poor dears are laying eggs. The Ghost has got right under their skin. People here are jolly pleased. Really jolly pleased."

"I'm delighted to hear it."

"There is a weight of opinion that we should move things along. There are a few dissenting voices of course. Aren't there always. Toes have been trodden on. Turf is threatened. Like schoolboys most of them. However there is a degree of will. We don't feel that it would be particularly appropriate to give you a whole list of targets. That would be rather risky. To start with we will give you one. Take it as something of an exam. People want to see if you deliver. If you do there will be more. At that point the final choice will of course be down to you. We are quite aware that anything that you do must have a proper propaganda value for your people. I will make sure that you have a proper choice."

"But not the first time."

"No. Not the first time. The first time we need you to prove your credentials. Prove that you're up to it and all that. I don't think that you will be in any way disappointed. Not in the slightest."

"Go on."

"Jimmy Madigan."

Davie leant back and smiled. "No I'm not disappointed. Not in the slightest."

"Oh, and there is another bit of good news."

"Go on."

"Money Davie. Lots of lovely money. I got them to agree 50 thousand. 50 thousand for the head of Jimmy Madigan."

Davie had said that he was interested in helping to get rid of the bad boys. That was why his smile had been so wide when he heard the name Jimmy Madigan. Jimmy Madigan was just about as bad as a boy could get. There are all kinds of men who find their way into the world of terrorism. Some are born idealistic. They crave a better world. They have a vision of the way things should be. If bullets and bombs are the only way to make this happen, then it is a price that has to be paid. They find their way to the ramparts through their books and buzz of conversations in coffee shops. Others come to the cause because of personal experience. Often they will have never dreamed of becoming involved. Then the police come and smash their mother in the face or the army shoot a younger brother with a plastic bullet or they get lifted themselves and get the insides of their arseholes scrutinised by mocking policemen in rubber gloves. They are turned by a single incident. They come to the Cause to channel their anger, to exact their revenge.

Then there is always the most dangerous of minorities. The nutters. The head cases. The ones who want nothing more than a sanction to be violent. This was the cloth from which Jimmy Madigan was cut. He grew up hard in the Bogside estate in Derry. His Dad went to work in England when he was only five. He never came home. His mum was left to raise a family of seven as best as she could. It was a task that proved too much. Soon the only way she could face life was through the bottom of a gin bottle. It was a time when there was always another man from the pub who came home with his mum every night. Jimmy came to hate these men. He hated their loud laughter. He hated their stinking breath. He hated the grunts and groans that kept him awake along with all his brothers and sisters.

When he was eight it got worse. Micky was the man from the pub who became a permanent fixture. Micky was a postman. Micky was a big pot-bellied loud mouth with teeth like broken tree stumps. Micky soon got fed up with fucking his mum and started to beat her instead. Then he worked his way through the kids. One by one. Male and female. Micky didn't care about age or gender. And all his mum could do was to drink and cry and hide away in the bedroom and then drink some more and cry some more.

By the time Jimmy was eleven the rage had hardened inside him. He took it out on everyone and anyone he could. He was shunted from school to school. His mother was beyond caring. The schools found him uncontrollable. It was the era when the belt and the stick were the preferred methods of control. They beat Jimmy until their hands ached and the balance of his mind slid away over the edge.

He was sixteen when Derry exploded in the summer of 1969. It had been years since he had been in a school. It had been months since he had been home. He slept where he could. He stole when there was a chance. He ate when there was food. He was more or less running wild.

Jimmy had spent his whole life as the squarest of pegs in a world of perfect round holes. He was the one who everybody hated. He was a wild bad boy that nobody could deal with. All anyone wanted from him was for him not to be there. And the rage grew and grew. And then, as if by magic, the most perfect of square holes came along and he slid himself into it. Jimmy became one of the most dedicated of the infamous Young Derry Hooligans. Every day he hurled stones and abuse at the soldiers behind the barricades. But this time it was all different. Now he was accepted. He was no longer the wild bad boy who everyone wanted rid of. Now he was a defender of his community. Women took him in and gave him tea. They washed his clothes and gave him socks. The men ruffled his hair and slipped him sixpences and told him he was a bloody good lad.

So Jimmy threw his stones and petrol bombs further and harder than the rest of them. He was the one who dared go in the closest. He was the one who was once seen to laugh when a plastic bullet hit him in the thigh. It didn't go unnoticed. The IRA commanders up on the hill in the Creggan estate also saw Jimmy Madigan as a bloody good lad. Soon they were making use of his talents. He started by planting bombs in the shops in the town centre as part of the economic war against the city's ruling Protestant community. Next he was taken along on a post office raid when he got to carry a gun for the first time. Finally in 1974, at the age of 22, they gave him the address of an off-duty RUC man. Jimmy knocked on his door one Sunday afternoon and put six shots into his chest from point blank range when he opened it. The feeling it gave Jimmy was better than anything he had ever known in his life. As each bullet had thudded into the older man's chest he felt revenge for everything that had ever been done to him. It was as if the rusty old chains that he had heaved around for years were falling away from him. He felt the real Jimmy crawl out of the skin of the old one. The feeling was perfect. Clean. Orgasmic. And all he wanted was to do it again.

Once again it was noticed. Over the years they gave him more addresses. Jimmy never missed. He never hesitated. Never batted an eyelid. He knew no nerves. He just knocked on the door and put the target away. And with each successive killing he drifted further away from everyone else's reality.

Things went awry in 1979. A bar tender refused Jimmy credit in a pub in the Bogside. Jimmy simply pulled out a gun and shot him through the shoulder. His commanders met up to talk about it and concluded that Jimmy had become a liability. They thanked him but said that he wasn't welcome any more And once again he was back out in the cold. He went to the only place that was left for him. He joined the INLA. The INLA had by this time become a haven for many of those who found the traditional IRA too restrictive. The INLA was a perfect home for the hard men who didn't want to bother too much about the niceties of the war.

Now Jimmy was part of a team of men who saw the world through the same eyes. In 1983 they blew up a pub outside Ballycastle where it was known that soldiers sometimes went for a drink. They managed to kill two off duty soldiers. They also managed to kill five civilians. There was much talk in the press about murdering cowards and barbarism. Jimmy didn't care much

In 1987 they hit the headlines again. This time they gunned down four off duty RUC officers as they enjoyed their Sunday afternoon on the golf course. By now Jimmy was a known face. He was on everybody's top ten most wanted list. He was permanently on the run. By 1988 the Province had become too difficult for him. He fled to England and shaved off all his hair and played out the part of a skinhead. The security forces lost the trail. He formed up a small team with two others and in 1989 they achieved their great moment. Sir Ronald Stanley had been one of Margaret Thatcher's closest economic advisors right through the 1980's. He had never had anything to do with Ireland whatsoever. It was his place in the Iron Lady's heart that marked him down for the attention of Jimmy's team. They met Sir Robert and his wife as they pulled into the drive of their Surrey home one evening and mowed them down with in excess of 60 shots.

There was barely a word of support for the attack. Sinn Fein distanced itself. Even the INLA walked away from Jimmy and his colleagues. Thatcher was incandescent with rage. Jimmy's name moved up to number one on the list.

James had soon wiped the smile off Davie's face. The target information was terribly vague. It was not much more than a snippet. There had been a whisper that they had picked up. Jimmy Madigan had a woman. She lived on one of the estates on the outskirts of Dublin. It was a bad place. It was a place that the police avoided if at all possible. The IRA dished out what little law there was. It was a place that was impossible to stake out. Nobody would have a chance of getting close. Any kind of team would be clocked within minutes. They had no idea when Jimmy Madigan might visit his woman. It could be a week. It could be a month. It could be never. It was a complete bitch of a job.

Davie had travelled down the following week. The whole place was an urban nightmare. It was a huge sprawling concrete hell that made Ballymurphy look like Butlins. The address of the woman was on the sixth floor of one of the many grim blocks of flats. At least here was some kind of a break. There was a derelict block a few hundred yards away. It was all boarded up and completely uninhabited. That night Davie broke in and scouted it out. The place stank of urine and rotting food. There was evidence of recent inhabitation. Wet blankets. Old syringes. Used condoms. Crumpled up cans. Burnt out fires. Kids probably. Junkies. Homeless. It was a place of nightmares. He felt a sense of revulsion at the place. Silently he cursed James Hamilton and those he worked for. This was a task from Hell.

Their plan was simple. There was no way it could be anything else. Richard and Derek would take it in turns to wait and watch with Davie. They had been given no clue as to when Madigan may show. It could be a week. It could be a month. It could be anything. Similarly they had no idea about what time of day he would arrive. It could be before the break of dawn. It could be in the quiet of the afternoon. It could be in the dead of night. It was no accident that Madigan had evaded his pursuers for so many years. He may have been a psychopath, but he was careful and cunning. He never left anything to chance. Davie just hoped that the sheer nihilistic lawlessness of the estate would lull him into a sense of security.

There was only one factor in their favour. The flat where Madigan's woman lived only had one door. All there was at the back of the flat was a 100-foot drop to the broken glass and empty crisp packets. This made strategy comparatively easy. All they needed to do was to spot him going in. Once they knew that he was inside all they had to do was wait. He would have to come out sometime and there was only one exit. To do this they worked in shifts of four hours. One would watch whilst the other slept or read or listened to the radio in headphones.

Davie was in no doubt as to the task ahead when he and Derek took up their position. This was going to be his greatest test. This was all about endurance. He had talked it through with the others. What they were about to do would be unrelenting. They had no source of heat and soon the grey concrete walls of the empty flat seemed to radiate cold. They had to make the food and water that were carried in when the others changed their shift last for a whole week. Concentration was the key. It was only a matter of fifteen paces from the stairwell to the door of the flat. They timed how long it took when other residents made the walk. Somewhere between three and four seconds. That was what they had. In the midst of the endless 24-hour-a-day, seven-day-a-week tedium of the watch, they would have a mere three seconds that counted. Any lapse of concentration could mean failure.

After the first week Davie was not at all sure that he could do it. The hours seemed to drag on endlessly. On his breaks he found it hard to settle. He paced the bare floor endlessly and sleep was hard to find. He felt filthy dirty and could never get properly warm. He fought to try and stave off the growing despondency that crept into him. There were times when the walls closed in on him and the claustrophobia made him want to shout and scream and smack his head into the floor. They crapped into a plastic bucket and pissed into bottles. These were carried out once a week.

By the end of the second week he felt close to breaking point. He could not seem to clear himself of total depression. Day after day he stared out at the soulless misery of the place. He saw the gangs of kids hanging about, hating the emptiness of time; their pale thin faces filled with contempt at the cards that had been dealt. He saw the shuffling fear of the elderly as they slowly heaved their bags of shopping back to the sanctuary of their homes. He saw the bowed heads and sloped shoulders of men who had given up any hope of work. And on Friday and Saturday nights he heard the breaking of glass and the threatening shouts and the screaming abuse of fighting couples. The place made his heart ache.

He knew that he had come to the moment of truth. He sat back and closed his eyes and settled himself. He needed to organise the time. He needed to use the time. Turn the endless empty hours into something of value. The salvation was books. He compiled a list and a schedule. And slowly the days became easier. Once he finished his stint on the binoculars he buried himself in books that he had only heard about but never read. He took on Tolstoy and Dickens and Twain and Proust. The more he read, the more he wanted to read. Slowly but surely he turned his mind around. He forced himself to find the positive. If it lasted six months, there were plenty of books to fill the time. The world was filled with books, more than enough to fill a lifetime of four hours on and four hours off. Every day he spent an hour in the morning and an hour in the evening exercising as hard as he could. In the fourth week he had a book on yoga brought in and dedicated two hours a day to mastering its disciplines.

By the fifth week he was in a groove. He had discovered a new place. He came to appreciate the endless time. He felt the strength of his mind growing every day. He had faced crisis and come through the other side. The hours became meaningless. Time was a commodity that had no importance. He could wait. It was no longer a problem. He could wait for as long as was necessary.

In the end it was almost an anti-climax. Madigan came at four o'clock in the afternoon. They had worried that he may have been disguised. A hat, or a coat with the hood up. They had worried that positive identification could be a problem. It wasn't. Madigan came with the hood of his coat down. He was in no hurry. He strolled up to the door and waited for his woman to open up and went in. There was no question. No doubt. It was him.

Davie took up position on the gun whilst Derek packed everything away into bags and headed out to bring the car. The long wait was over. They had passed the test. All that was left was a short wait. It might be two hours, or five or ten. It didn't matter. Davie had learnt how to wait.

It turned out to be just under five hours. The woman came first. Then Madigan. Now he wore a cap and a pair of glasses. They were probably going to the pub. Or a curry house. Or wherever. It didn't matter. Madigan stood to one side as his woman turned to lock the door. The bullet took him straight through his heart. Davie knew that there would be no second shot this time. The body on the floor was hidden from view by the wall of the balcony. Davie didn't bother to see what happened next. He picked up the Barrett and made his way out. There were no alarms. They hadn't expected any. It was not a place where the police responded quickly to calls. It wasn't a place where anyone expected a man to be killed by a sniper firing from a range of 650 yards. By the time the police arrived to secure the scene, Davie and Derek were already on the outskirts of Dublin. By the time the victim was identified as the infamous Jimmy Madigan of the Bogside, Derry, they were over the border and heading up the coast of County Down. Davie stopped at a call box and dialled the number that had become familiar by now. He heard Hutchinson's voice at the other end.

"Snapdragon. Jimmy Madigan"

A week later Davie met with Hamilton in the same discreet restaurant.

"Well Davie, what can I say. People are awfully pleased you know. Awfully pleased. And impressed. I have a bag for you in the car. Lots of lovely money of course. Mind you don't spend it all at once. And a list. Five names. Pictures. Movements. Addresses. Number plates. Everything. Nasty bad boys all of them. Plenty for you to get your teeth into I should say. Now. I believe that the poor British tax-payer owes us a spot of Champers wouldn't you say?"

Brendan Conner looked older. The war was taking its toll on him. He hated the small council house in the town. He hated the constant security. He hated the hiding away. He was a countryman at heart. He missed the fresh air and the fields and the familiar work of the farm. He even missed his cows. He detested the melancholy that had settled over him. Life went on of course. It had been a good couple of months. They had taken out two RUC officers with a bomb under a bridge outside Newtonhamilton, and then a corporal from the Royal Green Jackets had fallen for a booby trap. But both of these victories had a hollow feel. Once again a sense of hope had been growing that the Ghost might have gone away. And once again the hope had been shattered. Nobody shed a tear for the demise of Jimmy Madigan. He wasn't one of theirs. He was a pain in the arse. A loose cannon. A raging nutter. As far as Brendan Conner was concerned the Ghost had done them a big favour by sending the likes of Jimmy Madigan to meet his maker.

The manner of the execution was a different thing altogether. Dublin for Christ's sake. The hardest, meanest, die-hard Republican estate in Dublin and the bastard still had the bottle. By now Conner had more than a grudging respect for the Ghost. The respect was fully-fledged. The man had guts. Real guts. And he didn't miss. Ever. Brendan often found himself wishing that he had been on their side. Christ. The possibilities would have been endless.

He nodded to Sean as he came in and joined him at the table.

"He's not gone away then."

Sean shook his head. "Did you think he would have?"

"No. I don't suppose I did. So come on Prof. Evaluate."

Sean's face was ageing too. There were lines now. Lines in the wrong places. There was little joy to be found in the tired eyes. He gave a shrug. "Things have just got a whole lot worse. A lot worse."

"Go on."

"We always figured that he had a line into the security services. But this is different. This isn't about the war. This is pure revenge. The Brits were desperate for payback for Madigan whacking Ronald Stanley. Any intelligence on him would be sent all the way to the top. And I mean all the way. Info about Madigan having a woman in Dublin wouldn't have come from some UDR man. This was prize, grade A intelligence on their number one most wanted. For the Ghost to be given it means collusion at a high level. A very high level. Madigan is no loss. Exactly the opposite in fact. That nutter was a liability. But the way he did it. Christ, it's frightening. The level of threat has just gone up a few notches."

"And still nothing we can do?"

Sean stared down at the greasy Formica table and shook his head. "No. Not a damn thing."

Chapter 10
War and Peace

February 1993

The morning shave was the worst part of Sean's day. He hated the reflection in the mirror. Over the last couple of years the hair loss that had started soon after his 40'th birthday had accelerated. He couldn't get away with words like sparse or thinning any more. The only word that worked now was bald. 45 years old and he looked nearer 60. He had lost the battle to try and moderate his smoking. He had made efforts to cut down and ration himself. On three occasions he had tried to give up altogether. It was hopeless. He never even made it past three days. Finally he had simply thrown in the towel. So what if he died younger than he should. His life was hardly worth living anyway. Better the cancer than a bullet in the back of the head care of the UVF. Once he had stopped worrying about it, his habit had spiraled to 60 a day. This gave his always pale skin a greyish tinge. He knew he didn't carry himself so well any more. A brisk walk meant coughing and no breath. Bald. Stooped. Wheezing. Gone. All shot to hell.

He gave himself a rueful grin. Stop whingeing O'Neil. At least you're still on your hind legs and walking about. There were plenty who weren't. Far too many. Faces from the past. Fleeting acquaintances. Men who had entertained them all with their singing from behind their cell doors in the Kesh. Men who he had briefly known in meetings in the back rooms of pubs or farms. Men who he had known as boys in the streets and parks of West

Belfast. All gone. All added to the list. The 700-year list of young men who wanted nothing more than a country to call their own.

For the first time in ages he felt a slight sense of optimism. At last the Brits were talking. Thankfully the hated Thatcher had been ousted by a coup within her party. In her place John Major had arrived. Initially they had not known what to make of him. Some saw him as a bit of a joke. He looked such a typical Brit wimp with his lank hair and big glasses and flat voice. But opinions soon changed. He immediately changed the whole tone. Instead of talking of endless war he started to hint at peace. Suddenly there was no more branding of the IRA as gangsters and criminals. Word had come to Sean that negotiations were under way. Nothing open yet, nobody senior, but talk all the same. Maybe at long last the nightmare was coming to an end. At least Gerry Adams had made it all the way to the top and seemed completely secure in his position. At least there was a man in charge who had spent his life with an eye on peace rather than permanent war. Maybe the time was getting close.

The radio was playing the morning news as he shaved. The Brits were having a hard time. The heady booming days of the 80's were a distant memory. The British economy was caving in. Unemployment was on the rise again and the pinch was being felt. It could only be good news. Hard times for the Brits meant that they would have to count their pennies. Costs would have to be cut. Sean's gut feeling told him that this was one of the main reasons for their new conciliatory approach. The bills for Northern Ireland were astronomical. Keeping a standing army of close on 20,000 men in their watchtowers and barracks didn't come cheap. The economy in the Province had more or less ground to a halt. The Brits were paying out a fortune in Social Security benefits and there wasn't much in the way of tax flowing back in the opposite direction. Any argument for keeping their colony for economic reasons was long gone. It had become a millstone around their necks that was costing them a living fortune.

Any strategic benefits that the Province had once offered had long disappeared. No longer were the great Belfast shipyards needed to fit a navy to police the Empire. The last shred of strategic significance had vanished in the early 90's as the Soviet Empire imploded. No longer was it crucial to retain safe havens to land thousands of American troops should they ever be needed to save the old country from the rampaging Russian hordes. Suddenly the six counties had become a mere burden. A colony not wanted any more. A bastard child that did little but humiliate and embarrass. And more than anything else, it was expensive. Endlessly, agonisingly expensive. No longer was Thatcher's remorseless, grinding hate of the IRA the driving force within Downing Street. Major the accountant was now trying to balance the books. Counting the cost. Preparing the bill. The Brits were ready to pack their bags. All that was needed now was a final nudge.

The big question facing the Movement was what kind of nudge it should be. The wrong kind of spectacular could backfire badly. The kind of action that was needed was something to bring them out of their corner to the negotiating table. The wrong kind of action would merely harden their resolve and prolong the pointless misery of the war. Sean had received word from Gerry Adams in January that he was to examine their options. Come up with something. Find the right buttons to press.

It was more easily said than done. The best kept secret in the IRA was that they were well and truly on the rack. The 90's had seen the Brits on top for the first time. The Movement was riddled with informers. Umpteen of their arms dumps had been discovered and either bugged or kept under surveillance. Almost all the best men were rotting away in the Kesh on long sentences. The areas where the IRA could move were few and far between. Belfast and Derry were boxed off. Tyrone had never recovered from Loughgall. In fact the war was more or less being waged from South Armagh. Even there it was getting harder all the time. The Army had erected a chain of watchtowers, which bristled with millions of pounds worth of sophisticated high tech equipment. Suspect houses and farms were under surveillance 24 hours a day, often from towers sitting on hills miles away. Car journeys were filmed and logged. Cameras and recording devices were hidden in hedges and old tree stumps. Big Brother had never had so many sets of eyes.

For the first time the Loyalist paramilitaries were out killing the IRA. It seemed that there was nothing they could do to respond.

The Loyalist murder gangs seemed able to operate with impunity. The Catholic communities were becoming restless. Every week brought another Loyalist killing and the IRA seemed unable to stop them. Morale was caving in. The once endless supply of volunteers was drying up. Young people were increasingly reluctant to join an organisation that was being torn apart by informers.

And then of course there was the Ghost. The mystery killer who had come from nowhere to haunt them all. He had become less active. There had only been one kill in nearly two years. It didn't matter. His very presence was enough. As long as he was out there somewhere the loyalists grew stronger.

Sean was perfectly clear as to the magnitude of his task. If they were to miss the window of opportunity that Major was offering they may never get the chance again. Somehow they had to show the Brits that they were stronger than was actually the case. They had to prove that they were still a threat. The problem was what to do and how to do it. He had started with certainties. The first and most obvious certainty was that the operation would have to be wholly planned and launched from South Armagh. All the personnel would have to be experienced men from the South Armagh Brigade. There was no-one else left to rely on. It was the last corner of the Movement that wasn't riddled with informers.

Once he had decided on the 'who' he had turned to the 'what' and the 'when'. It had to be big and brash. It had to hit the Brits hard enough to make them move on with the peace process. But somehow it had to fall short of outrage. For weeks he had rattled his brains and come up with a big fat zero.

Then all of a sudden, as he stared at his tired reflection with distaste, it hit him so hard that his razor took a slice out of his chin. The answer was in the news. The answer was in the flat depressed voice of the man from the Treasury who was being grilled on the plummeting economy. The answer was in the money. The way to hit the Brits where it hurt most was in their pockets. The voters never blamed their Government when another young soldier was gunned down in Crossmaglen. They blamed the guy who fired the gun. But when VAT on fuel had to go up because the economy was up the spout they blamed the Government every inch of the way. And if there was one thing that any Government hated above all else it was to be blamed by voters when they couldn't afford to change their car or take a holiday in the sun. Governments could be pushed into new directions once their pockets were under pressure.

He was smiling now. Smiling even though the blood was pouring down his chin and on to the clean shirt that he had only just ironed. Smiling even though it was stinging like hell. Smiling because all of a sudden the 'what' had jumped into his brain from out of the clear blue skies.

A few weeks later the men of South Armagh completed Sean's shaving mirror vision. On April 13th a 1000-pound fertiliser bomb exploded in Bishopsgate in London. The IRA had issued eighteen separate warnings in order to do all that it could to avoid casualties. As it turned out there was one, a press photographer who couldn't resist the chance of the picture of a lifetime. The building targeted was the NatWest Tower. When all the broken glass was swept up and the men in suits and hard hats had finished tapping numbers into their calculators the cost of the damage was astounding. The insurance industry was hit with claims in excess of a billion pounds. Shares in blue chip companies fell. Confidence was rattled. Lloyds names got hit. The City of London was well into a grinding period of recession and decline. The destruction of the NatWest Tower sent it reeling. The Government felt the pinch. Accountants gravely pointed out the bottom line to ashen-faced ministers. The Brits were well and truly nudged. The prospect of peace grew closer.

It had been nearly a year since Davie had met with Hamilton. A long year. A poor year. His father had died in the autumn of 1992 after a long and miserable battle with cancer. The upsurge in the family business following Davie leaving the army had given him a new lease of life for a while. But when the world economy had taken a nosedive at the turn of the decade, the demand for high quality classical furniture had all but dried up. This was compounded by the unusual strength of sterling, which made it all but impossible for them to compete with their American competitors. Seeing the workshop grow quiet again had taken away his father's flimsy will to fight the pain. He had just faded away.

The responsibility of the business weighed heavily on Davie. Had he not been able to feed in some of Hamilton's blood money it would have folded months before. He had made a fruitless trip to the States, which did no more than confirm his suspicions that the market had become impossible for them. When he returned in February he realised that there was no choice but to bite the bullet and close up. On a rainy Friday evening in March he closed the padlock on a business that had been part of the Shankill furniture for a hundred years.

His mum had gone old very quickly. The glue that had held together her existence had suddenly been corroded and the pieces started to fall apart. Davie did his best to manage but soon realised that it was impossible. He found her a home in Ballyclare and all of a sudden the house on Granville Street was an empty, gloomy place. In this it was in tune with the Shankill as a whole. If anything, the deterioration that had so upset his grandfather had accelerated. Unemployment had hit desperate levels. It had become a community eking out an existence on the meagre Social Security payments that came out from the iron grilles of the fortified Post Offices once a week. The only ones who prospered were the gangsters.

A new breed had taken control by now. They were younger men. Harder. More ruthless. They claimed to be defenders. They commissioned murals to try and give themselves a glory that their actions didn't deserve. It was drugs and protection and murdering innocent civilians. They never had a go at the IRA. Davie didn't think that they had the bottle. Too much like real risk. Much better to play the big men in the pub on a Saturday night and rake in the cash. It seemed as if the Long War had done no more than make the whole world bent. Once upon a time his people had built the Titanic. Now they were down to wearing baseball caps and peddling heroin. It disgusted him.

This acute sense of disillusionment was the real reason why the Ghost had gone quiet. Davie told himself that he had other things to sort out. His dad's funeral. Wrapping up the business. Finding somewhere for his mum. There had been lots to do. Things to sort out. He kept telling himself that this was the reason. But at times when he sat alone in the house listening to shouts of the kids in the street outside accompanied by the inevitable sound of breaking glass he had his doubts. The doubts were getting stronger. He had begun to wonder if it was worth fighting for. But then he would shake the doubts away. He would become angry with himself. Of course he would keep on. What else would he do? So what if a few hoodlums were making a mockery of what so many had been once so very proud of. It didn't change the big picture. It was still their home. It was still their place. And there were hundreds of thousands of decent, hard working Ulster people who looked to him to keep the IRA at bay. The fact that so many of the Loyalist soldiers had succumbed to the temptation of crime only made the task more important.

There was another reason for his inactivity. There was no great need for the Ghost to kill anymore. The power of the Ghost was the legend. Killing top IRA men was only ever going to make a marginal difference to the course of the war. What was important was that his people knew he was there. That they knew that somewhere he was out there and waiting. Always waiting. Always ready to make the enemy suffer. Making more kills than was necessary only put the legend at risk. He had no wish whatsoever to kill more than he had to.

It wasn't down to lack of opportunity. He had a ten man target list. He had carried out brief surveillance on all of them. There was nothing too difficult He could kill when it was needed.

This time James had chosen Glasgow. It suited Davie well enough. They met in the bar of a large hotel. James was waiting at a corner table when Davie arrived. His old friend was ageing well. He was still very fit and never seemed to lose his year round tan. When he smiled his welcome his teeth were white and even. Davie wondered what on earth his rank was these days. He wondered if James knew himself. By now he had created a murky little empire for himself. He worked under the loose banner of 'liaison'. He pulled together the threads of things that never officially existed. He was the link that drew together the various semi-secret arms of the Crown and he got things done. That was how he was known now. The man who got things done. Made things happen. Arranged for bad things to go away. Nobody really knew who he worked for or what he did. Nobody wanted to. And

James sailed through it all like a million-dollar yacht in a tropical bay. Always the smile. Always the easy graces. Always remembering the name of a wife or a son at Malborough.

"Davie. Bloody great. Grab a pew. Drink? Let me get it."

The waiter already had half an eye on him. He was the kind who was always ready with a tip. Proper toff. Could be a tenner. The drink arrived with appropriate subservience. It all amused Davie. The airs and the graces and the manners. Little did they all know. The ones at the golf clubs and the opera and the nice weekend parties. But he knew. He had been there on top of a rocky outcrop on a godforsaken island in the cold waters of the South Atlantic. He had seen James Hamilton kill. He had seen the gleam in his eyes. He had seen the passion in his face. He had caught a glimpse of the animal underneath the smooth skin.

Davie took a swig of his beer and lit up. James tut-tutted. "Isn't it time you chucked those things? Wouldn't want you leaving us early now would we?"

Davie shrugged. Mildly annoyed. He didn't really have the patience for it today. "So James. Come on. What's it all about?"

Hamilton arranged his cuffs and crossed his legs.

"You've been quiet of late Davie."

"Busy."

"No problem with the information I hope."

Davie shook his head. "No. It's fine. I've just had other things on. No great need at the moment anyway."

Hamilton sipped his gin. "I would like to ask a favour Davie. Bit like Madigan. Pressure from above and all that. You know how it goes."

"Do I?"

"Oh for Christ's sake Davie, don't be so fucking grumpy."

Davie smiled. "OK. I won't be grumpy James. Sorry to be so gloomy and Irish. Not the thing at all. I will be sweetness and happiness. Promise."

"Good. Splendid. Top man. Right. This NatWest bombing. Not good. Not good at all. People are rather upset. It really hasn't gone down at all well. You see the problem is money I'm afraid. It looks like it's going to cost an absolute fortune. The insurers are talking about claims over a billion quid. Now that is the kind of thing that really hurts. It means less schools and less hospitals and, God forbid, redundancies in the Civil Service. The Government is broke. They are a mile behind in the polls and they need every penny they can get to buy a few votes. So I'm sure that you can see a billion quid bill care of the bad boys doesn't sit well at all."

He paused for another drink and seemed to consider his words with care. Eventually he picked up his thread. "There's peace in the air, Davie. Not just the odd whisper and low level meeting. Things have changed. Maggie's long gone. We were all wondering what the new chap would be like, and to be honest he has come as something of a surprise. I suppose it has taken us all a while to see the truth. Mr Major appears to be exactly what he says he is. The man really is an ordinary decent human being who is rather keen on using all his efforts to bring peace to your troubled land. We all thought he would change his tune pretty quickly when the IRA dropped a mortar bomb in his back garden. But no. Not at all. He just climbed out from under the table, dusted himself down, and carried on as if nothing had happened.

NatWest has made things tricky. There are plenty who don't like the way that the wind is blowing one little bit. Every NatWest gives more power to their elbows. They want tanks in Crossmaglen, not cosy peace chats in country hotels in the Republic. People are worried that the opportunity might be lost. They want something done."

"And that is why I'm here."

Hamilton smiled brilliantly. "Absolutely Davie. Absolutely. We are pretty sure that the NatWest bomb had South Armagh written all over it. Now, it doesn't seem to make any difference how much money we spend on that wretched place, it still may as well be the dark side of the moon. We have watchtowers and bases and patrols and the busiest helicopter base on the bloody planet. And what do we get? Fuck all. Rumours. Whispers. Dead soldiers. A whole lot of bugger all. Now just so long as those boys limit themselves to killing the occasional squaddie or policeman we can more or less live with it. But when they start destroying very, very expensive buildings in London it is quite another thing altogether."

"So?"

"So we have a feeling that there might just be one man behind it. He's not one of the hard men. Quite the opposite. He's worse. He's the brains. We really don't know for sure. Not at all. Our suspicions are not much more than gut feeling. But we feel it is better to be safe than sorry. The job should be easy. He did three years in the Maze in the 80's for membership of the IRA. Before that he was a Literature Professor at Queens University. As soon as he got out, he went south. Moved to Monoghan and got a job as a teacher in a secondary school. Went for the quiet life. Never married. Lives on his own. Gets up. Goes to school. Goes home. Very, very ordinary. No security. Nothing. A walk in the park for the Ghost."

"Are you watching him?"

"Not really. We check on him every now and then. Politically it is seen as a bad idea to have men in the Republic at the moment."

"Bugged his house?"

"No. Same reason. The fallout would be too damaging if he found them. As I said, we don't have anything very solid. Just hints and bits and pieces. But the consensus of opinion is that there is enough. All in all, we would rather he wasn't with us any more. In fact we are so keen that he should not be here any more that we will pay £100,000 for the privilege."

Davie gave a slow smile. "A hundred grand on a gut feeling. Bollocks James."[1]

Hamilton gave an exaggerated shrug. "Don't ask me old boy. I know nothing. I just do as I'm told. You know that well enough. Anyway all I can do is ask. It's all in here. We will be grateful Davie. Very grateful."

Davie picked up the envelope and slipped it into his inside pocket. All around them there were men in suits working through their important meetings over glasses of mineral water with slices of lemon. An ordinary Tuesday lunchtime in the heart of a British city. Little do you know thought Davie. What would you think if you even knew half of the truth? One well-dressed man gives another well-dressed man a plain brown envelope. The second well-dressed man puts the envelope in the pocket of his jacket. The action was ordinary. Nondescript. Every day. This is how the oldest democracy in the world issues its death warrants. This is how it removes men it is unhappy with. And the price on the job is £100,000. And it is all done over gin and tonic and complimentary peanuts.

Sean took longer than was his custom to get back to the house. The school had been uncomfortably hot all day and the kids had been crotchety and ratty. He had stayed on for a couple of hours running a rehearsal for the up coming school play. By the time he walked out of the gates at six o'clock the heat of the June day had largely burnt itself out. There was a wonderful soft summer breeze which for a short moment chilled him as the sweat stuck his shirt to his back. For once the Irish sky above him was wall to wall blue, and he decided to walk the long way home. He made his way out of the town and picked up a footpath that looped its way around the north of the town. He chuckled to himself as an absurd thought hopped into his head as he made his way along a small path between blossoming bushes. It was just his luck to wind up as an Irish freedom fighter. Not only had he had to deal with everything the Brits and the loyalists could throw at him, to make things worse, it had always been raining. If only he had been somewhere else he could have been a freedom fighter in the sun. God knows there were enough options. He could have been an ANC fighter on the burning hills and valleys of Natal. Or a PLO man in the orange groves by the beaches of the Southern Mediterranean. Or even an ETA fighter in the vineyards of Spain. Christ the choice was endless. Nicaragua. East Timor. Kurdistan. They didn't know they were born. Lucky sods.

It wasn't just the perfection of the evening that had lifted his spirits. It was the news that was filtering through from the Army Council. Peace was getting closer with every day. Even the die hard ones were coming round to the idea. This time it seemed that it might just be for real. Of course it wasn't going to be a United Ireland. Any real hopes of that had died years before. What it meant was a fairer deal for his people and the chance of a United Ireland sometime in the future. It would not to be victory over the British State. That was never really on the cards. Once the Brits had gone stubborn and dug their heels in, there had never really been a chance. However it seemed that there was a very real chance that they would achieve victory over the hated Orange State. Peace would see an end to the hated monopoly of power that the Protestants had held for over 70 years. Never again could they marshal the forces of Burntollet Bridge. This time they would be forced to acknowledge that they had no choice but to share their space with their Catholic neighbours. Victory may well not have been complete. But it was still sweet.

What made it even sweeter was that it seemed as if they were about to pull a victory out of the jaws of defeat. The Movement had never been weaker. Their options were all but down to zero. All over the Province their Brigades were on the verge of being broken. All they had left were a few dogged fighters in the wilds of South Armagh, and somehow the few had managed to hang on for long enough. At least it had all been for something. All the dead. All the maimed and the injured and the mentally destroyed. All the broken men who had blinked at the light after years in the darkness of the Kesh. All the kids who had grown up in streets where rubber bullets were a part of everyday life. All the women who had announced the arrival of the Saracens with a crash of their dustbin lids. They had all been through a quarter of a century of constant torment but at least there was to be something at the end of it all. A chance. A new beginning. Enough.

As he meandered through the fields and the small lanes his thoughts turned to his own future. If peace was to come he could consider his own life for the first time in twenty years. It seemed a staggering prospect. He had almost forgotten what it was to have a life that was truly his own. He had avoided all attachments after Mary. It wasn't fair. He accepted that at any time he could be either shot dead or carted off for an endless stretch behind the wire. It would never be fair to subject anyone else to a life on these terms. It had meant that so many things were off limits. A wife. Kids. Friends. Holidays. Normal things. The very things that life was supposed to be about. Instead he had lived and breathed the Movement. The Cause.

Peace would change everything. Peace would turn his whole life into a blank piece of paper. And why not? So what if he looked like a bald old crock. He was still young enough. 43 was no age. The world would soon be his oyster. Just like it had been that day all those years ago when he had taken the bus across town from the Falls Road to the University. And for the first time in what seemed like years the old Sean O'Neil smile, that had once been so familiar to so many people, was back on his face.

By the time he actually made it home it was almost ten. The scenic route had turned out to be fifteen miles. It was more exercise than he had taken in years. His legs ached and he was hot through. It felt good to have the blood pounding around his arteries for once.

He unlocked the front door of his small house and stepped in. Damn. The bloody lounge bulb gone. For Christ's sake. He had only replaced it a few . . .

"Just stop exactly there please."

What the fuck . . .

"That's good. That's fine. I'm going to put the light on now. Stay completely still. Ready? OK."

The light showed him the man. He was standing in the middle of the room. Tall. About six two. Short cropped black hair. No grey there. Not very old. Probably about 30. Obviously fit. And very still. Still as a snake. Clearly powerful. No point even thinking about fighting. Ordinary clothes. Desert boots. Jeans. Chequed shirt. Golf jacket. And a revolver. Held very, very still. Aimed straight at his heart.

"That's good. Right. Let's do the formalities shall we? Take your jacket off please. You know how. Slowly. Very slowly. No sudden movements. That's good. That's fine. Good. Now your shirt. Good . . . trousers . . . don't moither yourself; I'm not a pervert. Grand. OK. Turn around slowly. Good. Shoes and socks. Grand. OK Sean. You'll do me. Put your shirt and trousers back on. Leave the shoes and socks. Sit down. That's it. Right there. Fine. OK. I've two pairs of handcuffs here. Put these around your ankles first. That's it. And now hold out your wrists . . . there we go. That's us. All done. I'll pour you a drink. I took the liberty of raiding the cupboard. Bit presumptuous I know . . ."

All the time Davie chattered on in a conversational tone. He poured a couple of stiff measures and dropped in ice, which was in a pudding bowl. He passed a glass to Sean who cupped it with his manacled hands and took a sip. All the time Sean stared directly into his eyes. He showed no emotion. He made the moves as instructed like a robot. All the time he tried to work it out? Who the hell was he? Could be anyone. Could have been sent by the Army Council. No reason why. A tout maybe? Or maybe he was a Brit? Special Branch? UDA? UFF? UVF? Not a lot of point in guessing. He would no doubt find out soon enough. One thing was for sure. Whoever it was, it wasn't going to be anybody good. He looked straight into the eyes of his killer to be and gave a small nod.

"Cheers."

Davie smiled "Aye. Cheers."

They were silent for a moment. Davie examined him closely. It was the hair that made it difficult. Or the lack of it to be more accurate. The face was changed too. Of course it was older. But there were more years on the face than there should have been. The man had lived the years hard. Hadn't they all.

Without warning he started to speak. "I knew there was something as soon as I started to read the file. Quite a file Sean. Hell of a file. Like a history of the Troubles. It's a 'been there, seen that' file. Burntollet, the riots in 69, interned in '71, Bloody Sunday, in the Kesh in '81, on the blanket, cell next to Bobby Sands, and then? Then, it's all quiet. A schoolteacher. A loner. Out of the loop. Out of the firing line. Or maybe not. The more I read it, the more a little voice in the back of my mind kept nagging at me. You know him Davie. You do. You know him."

He paused to light a cigarette and waved the packet toward Sean. Sean nodded. Davie lit him one and passed it over. He leaned back in the chair.

"It was driving be bloody nuts. And then it came after hours and hours. I was looking in the meat of the file. Looking for the connection and no matter how I looked it wouldn't come. And then it smacked me in the face. The answer. Clear as day. It wasn't the middle where I should have been looking. It was page one. The simple bit. The bit you barely notice. Name: Sean O'Neil. Date of Birth 27/2/1949 – Belfast. Address: 16 James Street West Belfast. 16 James Street. Something there. Something I couldn't quite reach. You're not even warm are you Sean?"

Sean shook his head. "Not remotely. But carry on. I'm enjoying the whisky and the smoke. At least it's civilised so far."

"Cast your mind back. Long way Sean. 24 years. You were the man with the wild hair back then. Remember that night in August? Bombay Street all on fire and the world gone mad? Remember Sean?"

"Aye. I remember." What was this? Where was it going?

" Remember the boy Sean? Eleven years old and daft as a brush. The boy had been told to stay in but he hadn't listened. Well they never do, do they? And the boy had shinned it down the drainpipe and met with his two mates and they had gone to Bombay Street to watch all the fun? But it wasn't a lot of fun. Terrifying more like. Out of hand. Men going mad. Chaos. And a petrol bomb. Remember the bomb Sean?"

Holy Christ. Surely not. No way. "Aye. I remember the petrol bomb."

Davie was smiling now. "The boy had never been to the Falls Road before. Eleven years growing up on the Shankill but he had never been on the Falls. And he was scared stiff when he was taken into the house where they had a picture of the Pope over the fire. And he didn't know what they were going to do to him because he was a little Protestant boy and they were Catholics and the whole of Belfast was on fire. But he was fine. The boy. He was fine because they were good people. They cleaned him up and calmed him down and later the man with the long hair took him home to his Ma and his Da. And his Grandad looked at the man with the long hair and there was respect for him. Remember Sean?"

"Aye. I remember. You're the boy, right?"

"I'm the boy."

"So how come the handcuffs and the gun?"

Davie chuckled. "Come on man, give me a bit of credit. Word is that you are one of the top intelligence men in the bloody IRA. I'm not going to take any chances am I?"

"Probably not." Sean was confused now. A few minutes before he had started to arrange his affairs in his head. This was it. After twenty years the moment had arrived. It was time for the traditional Irish bullet through the back of the head. It wasn't so surprising really. He'd had a long run. He had just wished it could have happened a few weeks earlier before he had got his hopes up for some kind of a future. But now? Now he was confused. This was bizarre. Surreal.

"I can see your brain turning and turning. Don't worry. I'm not about to cap you. Tomorrow will be another day. I'll take off the cuffs in a minute or two. But I need to equalise things first. Then I'll take off the cuffs. OK?"

"Sure. You're still the man with the gun."

"So I am. Do you know who I am Sean?"

"Not really. UDA? UVF? Special Branch? You tell me."

"I'm the Ghost, Sean."

The words hit him like punches in the chest.

"Christ."

Davie lit up a new cigarette from the one he was smoking. "OK. This is where things even up. Right now I'm the one with the gun and you're the one in the cuffs. I can whack you whenever I want. Pop, and it's done. Agreed?"

"Agreed."

"So we'll change it. Here's a gun for you. I'm Davie Stanton. I still live in Granville Street and I'm the Ghost. The file I have here comes from somewhere inside British Intelligence. They have a hunch that the NatWest bomb was down to you. They're seriously pissed off about it. And so they passed the file over to me. They want me to whack you. And then claim it for the UVF. And leave them right out of it of course. And just in case you're interested, they'll pay me £100,000 once you depart the land of the living. So that's it. You know it. You can see me off whenever you want."

He walked across the room to Sean and undid both sets of handcuffs. "The thing is that I owe you. I'm old-fashioned that way. My whole family is. But for you I would have been burnt to a crisp on Bombay Street before I was twelve. So I can't whack you. Hundred grand or no hundred grand. So there we go. No cuffs. The gun is away. And we're even. Another drink?"

Sean was completely stunned by now. It was too much to take in. He nodded at the offer and took the glass. It had always been a mad life, but this? This was just plain ridiculous. Crazy life. Crazy people. Crazy country. Only Ireland. It could only happen here in bloody rainy Ireland. And all of a sudden he was laughing. Laughing like he hadn't laughed in years and years and years.

Laughing so hard that the whisky jumped and spilled on his legs. Laughing so the tears welled up in his eyes and spilled out onto his pale, bony cheeks. Laughing because it was all just so plain bloody stupid. At first Davie just looked on with a look of mild amusement. But the laughter was infectious. It came over the room and got a hold of him. Soon he was laughing every bit as bad. And for Davie too it was a release that had been a long time coming.

At last it ran its course. Sean wiped at his eyes with his sleeve and coughed hard when he took a draw on his cigarette. "Jesus. It's been years since I laughed like that."

Davie nodded. "Aye. Same here. Not a lot of fun is it?"

"What?"

"The war. The long bastard war."

The words sobered Sean. "No. Not a lot. What about you? How come you fight?"

"Probably for the same reasons as you. My people. The place where I grew up. My family. Stories. Fear. Habit."

Sean looked at him with new eyes. So this was the Ghost. In his mind's eye he had always pictured a man who was a machine. Cold eyes. No heart. A clinical killer. Maybe even a psychopath. Never this man.

"The killing? How does the killing sit with you?"

"I'm OK. You?"

"I've never actually pulled the trigger. Never seen a man I killed close up. But there have been men dead because of me. It doesn't sit well. I don't really sleep. Haven't done for years. Too many faces. Too many men gone away. Hell, just look at me. I'm only 44 and I look 60."

Davie was grave. "I suppose that's just the way it is. If you believe in what you are doing. Someone has to take it on. I suppose we just hope it's worth it. You never married?"

"No."

"Because of all this?"

"Aye. Because of all this. You?"

"No."

They were quiet. They knew they were in the same place. They knew that they shared all the same doubts and sadness and regret. There was no need to say more. It was something that they shared.

It was something that words would never help. It was something that would never go away. They hadn't been forced. They had both made their choice. And now they were here. Here in a small front room in a terraced house in a small Irish town. The years had taken them far and wide but they had been drawn back together. They were enemies who didn't really have the stomach for it any more. It had been a long, long war.

Sean sat back in his chair and stared up to the ceiling. "So what now?"

"You have options. Option one, and I hope you decide not to take it, is that you go to the Army Council and tell them who the Ghost is. Maybe that is what you should do. Good of the Cause and all that. I'm not hard to find. You know the house on Granville Street. I won't be running. I'm too tired for that."

"Option two?"

"Your problems won't end if you get rid of me. I'm just a tool. The Brits are seriously pissed off with you Sean. If one tool doesn't do the job they'll just go and find another. If you stay here you're a dead man. The warrant has been signed. It will only be a question of time. All you can do is go away. As far as you can. Try and become harmless. Maybe they'll leave you be. They say peace is around the corner."

Sean stared into the space ahead of him. "Aye so they do. Will there be peace for the Ghost?"

"Who knows. It will depend on the small print. I'm not ready to leave my people. Not if there is still threat."

Sean nodded. There was no point in arguing. They both knew it. They were opposites. There could be no agreement. They would always be too far apart.

"What about the Brits? They won't be amused if you come back empty handed. What will you tell them?"

Davie shrugged. "I don't see a problem. They don't know my movements. I'll just say that I came down here and you were gone. Simple as that. That is if you are gone. That's down to you. If you stay then, yes, they'll be pissed off. It's your call Sean."

Sean smiled at him. "You're taking a pretty bloody big risk Davie. If I don't play ball it will be a race between the Brits and the Provies for who can whack you first."

"Then so be it."

"Well it isn't about to happen. I'll go. It's time I was out anyway. Twenty years is enough. Can I have that file?"

"Sure."

Davie tossed it over. He got to his feet and took a last look around the room. "I'll be away now." He extended his hand. Sean took it.

"Maybe there will be another time. When all the madness is done."

Davie smiled. "Aye. Maybe there will. You take care."

"You too."

Davie picked up the handcuffs and slipped them into the pocket of his jacket. He opened the door and left. He didn't look back. Sean stared at the closed door for a long time and then got up and started to pack.

Gerry Adams read the file without any obvious emotion. Once he had finished he closed it carefully and passed it back. "Go over it again Sean"

"There's not a lot to go over. It came in the post just like any letter. I opened it. Now it's here. I haven't the first clue who wrote the letter. Obviously there is someone inside Brit Intelligence with a conscience. Someone doesn't like cold-blooded murder I suppose."

Adams frowned and polished his glasses. "Stranger things have happened. You'll be leaving then?"

"Aye. I don't see a lot of choice. I don't much fancy hanging about and waiting for a bullet."

"Where will you go?"

"The States. There are a couple of colleges out East where I'll get work. I still have contacts from the 70's. I want to fly the Sinn Fein flag. Fund-raising and the like. No Army stuff though. That would be a red rag."

Adams nodded. "Fair enough. You've done enough. More than enough. You're a good man Sean. One of the best. You've helped to get us this far."

"How far are we Gerry? Is the peace real?"

"Probably. Maybe. Let's just hope shall we."

"Don't we always?"

Adams smiled. "Aye. I suppose we do."

A year later Sean was sipping a cup of hot coffee in the senior common room. He had been working at the University on the outskirts of Boston for six months and was well and truly settled in. At first he had wondered if he would miss the children and the routine of the school in Monaghan. He hadn't. It had been the opposite. As the time had passed he felt as if he was reborn. During his years in the IRA he had never been consciously aware of the constant threat that hung over him. It was something that had to be pushed to the back of the mind on a permanent basis. Death could come at any moment. He would never see it coming. It would come in a split second. A stranger in the street. The crash of sledge hammers at his front door. The hammer blow of a bullet in the back. It was something that he had more or less no control over. None of them did. It was the cloud they all had to live under. It was something that you either dealt with or it would slowly take away your mind.

It was only when he was away from it that he realised how the constant secret fear had eaten away at him. It was the fear that had taken his hair and all the youth from his face. It was the fear that had stripped the flesh off his bony body. It was the fear that starved him of sleep. It was the fear that had deprived his life of all joy.

For the first time in many years the old Sean was beginning to emerge from the shadows. He found that he had lost none of his verve when it came to teaching. The students that filled the hall to listen to him were wonderful. He felt that he could suck in some of their youth and hope and their optimism for a future that was worth having. He felt the years dropping from him like discarded baggage. He learnt to smile again. To laugh. To live.

One of his fellows came in and spotted him sitting quietly in the corner reading his book.

"Hey Sean. It's great isn't it? You must be over the moon."

Sean looked at him quizzically. "Sorry. I don't understand."

"The news! Haven't you heard the news?"

"No. I'm afraid I haven't."

"There's a cease-fire. Announced a few minutes ago. It sounds serious. Sounds as if they mean it. Peace."

Sean didn't really know how to react. It had been coming for months. Even the tension of the July marching season had failed to blow things off course. Somehow nobody had dared to believe that it could really happen. But it had. It actually, really had. It was August 1994 and at long last the guns had fallen silent. A quarter of a century had passed since he and Mary had made their way up to the police station on the Springfield Road and watched as the world had gone insane. 25 years of losing people he held dear. The images flashed through his mind. Mary. His dad. The raging flames of Bombay Street. The bodies on the ground in Derry. The army truck rising gracefully into the clear blue in perfect silence at the Narrow Water. The smiling face and long hair of Bobby Sands as he gave a thumbs up and walked through the rain of the yard to take a visit. So many faces. Images. All gone. So many years. All gone. The damn bust inside him. Walls that had taken years to build collapsed in clouds of dust and rubble. The icy control that he taken so long to master was all forgotten. And the tears came. They came in torrents. No control. They just came and came and his tired thin body was convulsed by the sobs. His friend leaned forward and took him to his chest. He held Sean's head to his chest as if he were a child. He gently patted him on the back and Sean clung to him as he clung to life himself.

Others came in when they heard the sound of the sobs. The colleague gave them a small shake of the head and they kept their distance. They stood to one side and watched Sean as he cried it all out. They watched 25 years of pain and loss come out of him. And for a few minutes they became a small part of 700-year-old pain of Ireland.

Davie had been expecting the visit. The week before, he had watched the television along with millions of others. A few miles up the road at Fernhill House the men who made up the Combined Loyalist Military Command announced their cease-fire. The statement was read out by Gusty Spence who had been the man who had taken the UVF to war back in the 1960's. Gusty had done his time in the Kesh and had emerged round and cuddly.

Gusty the cold-blooded killer was now Gusty the favourite uncle with a benign smile and a pipe. Gusty told the world that the loyalists were putting away their guns. Gusty apologised to all the families who had lost loved ones in the war. Gusty said it was time for peace.

For days Davie had tried to arrange his thoughts. Part of him was filled with an overwhelming relief. At long last maybe the nightmare was coming to an end. Maybe all the people of Northern Ireland might get their chance to join the rest of the world and live lives that could be considered to be normal. If so, it was something to celebrate. If so, he too could seriously consider starting to live a real, normal life. The trouble was that he couldn't settle with it all. He wanted to. Wanted to more than anything. His own cynicism angered him. Why couldn't he just be happy? Why was it so hard for him to find a bit of faith? Why always the dark clouds?

He had made his way to his grandfather's grave and stood there for a long time. He tried to find guidance there. For so many years of his life Peter Stanton had always been there for him. He had been his rock. His certainty. Now once again Davie sought the old man's certainty. He wanted to know that Peter Stanton thought it was going to be OK. He wanted to believe that it was real. Serious. That the era of hate had run it's course.

But he couldn't. All he could see was compromise. There was peace because the Brits had had enough. They had run out of energy. They had become scared that they would be out of step. The world had changed beyond all recognition. The Berlin Wall had crashed down. Nelson Mandela had walked out into the sunlight. Old rulebooks had been torn up. Having 20,000 soldiers on the streets and in hedgerows of Ulster was no longer politically acceptable. The Province had become an embarrassment. An expensive embarrassment. And now they wanted out at any price.

The cease-fire came at just the right time for the IRA. Maybe it had even saved them. They had been reeling. Another year? Maybe two? Victory had almost been in sight for his people. No wonder the IRA had leapt at the chance to negotiate. And they had got most things their way. There didn't seem to be any talk about them handing over their weapons. They were being given the chance to lick their wounds and regroup. Maybe the noises that they were making about peace were real. Davie just couldn't accept it. Leopards didn't change their spots. Not unless they had to. And it was still the same leopard underneath.

It was no surprise when John Hutchinson came to call. It was expected. Hutchinson seemed ill-at-ease. Nervous. Davie knew that he had always made the man nervous. He didn't want a drink. He didn't even take his coat off. He just wanted to get it over with and get away. Davie had no wish to make it easy for him. He just sat and waited until Hutchinson managed to find his tongue.

"I suppose you were expecting me."

Davie nodded.

"Aye, well. Well it's peace then. Well. So they say. Suppose we should celebrate. Good times to come and all that."

"If you say so."

"Aye, well, not me of course. Those in command. They have passed the word. No more operations. Nothing. Anyone carrying on has to answer to them. Full punishment routine. Unbelievable. Anyone who whacks a Provie will lose their kneecaps. Fuckers."

"So what are you saying John?"

"The UVF has to disown the Ghost. If you do anything, I can't claim it. I won't do anything about it. The Ghost is between you and me. I just can't make the claims anymore."

Davie slowly got up from his chair and walked to where Hutchinson stood. He went in very close so that his face was only inches away.

"You said it John. The Ghost is between you and me. Nobody else. Just the two of us. Make sure you never forget that John. Never. You know what will happen if you do forget don't you John."

Hutchinson couldn't hold his gaze. He had known it would be like this. He stared down at the floor and shook his head. Davie reached out and took his chin between his forefinger and thumb. He forced his head up so that their eyes were level.

"Not good enough John. I need to hear you say it. I need to see your eyes."

A croak. "I won't forget."

In the eyes there was only fear. Davie released his grip and turned his back.

"What will you do Davie? I mean about the peace and all that?"

Davie didn't turn around. "It just stopped being any of your business John. I think that completes our business. Good night."

Hutchinson stood awkwardly for a moment then opened the front door and left. Davie stared at the photo on the wall. Peter Stanton stared back at him. It was a Peter Stanton from many years ago. Peter Stanton with his friends. Smart and proud in their uniforms. Faces young. Eyes bright. Filled with the excitement of the great adventure to come. Peter Stanton on the day when he got on the boat to Liverpool, the first leg of the journey that led him to the horrors of the Somme. Davie wondered if his own war was really over. A small smile played on his lips when he replayed the conversation with Hutchinson. He had said that the Ghost was a secret that was theirs alone. It wasn't true of course.

There was Derek and Richard of course. He had already met with them. They had agreed that they would stand down. Take some time. See how things turned out. They all agreed that the peace needed to be given a chance. Maybe the moment had really come. Maybe there would never again be a day when the Ghost would have to fire the Barrett. Then there was James Hamilton. He had been moody and grumpy when Davie had told him that the Monoghan pigeon had flown the nest. He had wanted another notch on his rifle. He had wanted to prove to the men in the shadowy places that he was the person who could make problems go away. He had been annoyed because it was a small hiccup to his career.

And then of course there was one other. His kindred spirit from the other side of the tracks. The man who had once carried him from the flames to the house in James Street with a picture of the Pope on the wall. The man who could have become a friend. The man who might one day be there to share a pint and understand the endless sadness in his soul. The pigeon that had flown the nest. The man that he had not been able to kill. Davie wondered where he was. Wondered how he felt now that the guns were silent. Wondered if he had found any hope.

Chapter 11
Billy

June 1996

Davie watched the news unfold and felt the anger grow inside him. Three days and still nothing. It had been three days since the IRA had reduced the Arndale Centre in Manchester to a heap of smoking rubble. And still there was no fighting talk from Westminster. His sense of frustration had been growing for months. The peace talks had meandered on for years and finally ground to a halt. Predictably arms had been the sticking issue. The British Government had insisted that Sinn Fein would be excluded from the political process until they gave a firm commitment to decommission their arms. The IRA in turn had been adamant that it would never give up its arms until the British made real concessions.

The fragile peace had been blown into a million pieces in February when the IRA had planted a monumental bomb in London's Docklands district. The message seemed clear enough. The IRA had spat out the dummy. Give in, or get bombed. Surely the idiots in London would now see the lie of the peace for what it really was. All they were doing was giving the IRA time to take a long deep breath. Davie could feel it in his bones. Every minute that Sinn Fein spent sitting around the table talking, the hard boys in the background were getting ready for the next phase. When they had hit Manchester he had been convinced that the Brits would see that the time for talk was well and truly over. Surely.

They would have to be blind not to. It was the time to take off the gloves and let the IRA know who was in charge. He had watched the news and waited for the crackdown.

After three days it was fairly clear that there was not going to be a crackdown. Not now. Not ever. The Brits were broken. After so many years, their will to resist had been eroded. All they wanted was to find a way out. It didn't matter what it took; they were headed for the exit door. And if that meant leaving a million of his people to suffer the consequences, then that was just tough.

Peace had left Davie at something of a loose end. In one respect he was lucky. Far, far luckier than other men who had given their lives to the paramilitary units. At least he had no money worries. The payments from Hamilton had added up. He had banked them in a discreet account in Geneva and let them sit. He came away from the war with a £250,000 cushion to fall back on. It would have been £350,000 if he had sent Sean O'Neil onwards to the next life.

He had taken a long holiday and made his way around the world. When he had returned to Belfast six months later he found a city that was waking up after years of hibernation. Slowly but surely investors were starting to believe that the peace was real. There were cranes in the sky for the first time in 30 years. New buildings. New restaurants. New shops. Slowly the people of Belfast were coming to terms that peace might actually be real. Davie felt that they were so desperate to be convinced that they were learning the art of turning a blind eye. Never a week went by without the IRA carrying out several punishment beatings. Young lads lost their kneecaps or were hospitalised for weeks after vicious attacks with baseball bats and metal rods. Yet nobody seemed to care. Nobody wanted to care. All of a sudden the people of Belfast had developed a collective ostrich mentality. Heads were so far buried in the sand that the IRA seemed able to do as they pleased with impunity. Nobody wanted to rock the boat.

Davie decided that if nobody else wanted to do any rocking then he may as well have a go at it himself. He embarked on a career as a freelance journalist. He had never considered himself to be the artistic type. However he was confident that if he dug out the right stories, the content of what he wrote would compensate for the style. What soon made Davie stand out as a journalist was that he went into places where others didn't dare.

Soon he found that he was getting right under the skin of the IRA. Whenever there was a kneecapping or a beating Davie would be the first journalist on the scene. There were those who resented his presence. They would spit at him and scream abuse. But there were others who were more than happy to talk. Peace was slowly loosening tongues. Plenty of residents on the Republican estates were heartily sick of the violent control that the IRA insisted on maintaining. They saw the reporter who didn't listen to the threats as someone who would give them a voice. After a few months he had gained something of a reputation. He had no trouble in selling his pieces. In fact the papers soon started passing him stories to follow up. He had a weekly column and people started calling and writing in. He had embarked on his career thinking it would never be much more than a hobby. Within a year, much to his own amazement, he was earning a decent living.

He wondered how long it would take the Belfast Brigade to run out of patience. He was more than confident that they would stop short of killing him. The top men would never allow it. It would be political suicide. But a good kicking would surely come at some stage or another. Once again the adrenalin would flow through him as he drove into estates where the tricolours hung from the lampposts. The blood would pump through his limbs. He knew they would come. It was only a question of when and where. And when they came he would be ready.

As it turned out it was ridiculously obvious. He was following up a lead that had been phoned in from Andersonstown. When he pulled up outside the address the street was far too quiet. It was a little after seven on a sunny evening little after seven on a sunny evening. No kids. No women out gossiping on the doorsteps. No mums pushing prams. No men on their way to the pub. Nobody pulling weeds in the small front gardens. Not even a dog. Way too quiet. So bloody obvious. Amateurs. He found himself smiling.

They came out of an alley. There were four of them. Balaclavas. Combat jackets. Three baseball bats and lump hammer. Idiots. Davie was fast. One minute he was the helpless journalist in the tweed jacket climbing out of his car. The next minute he had a pistol in his hands. He had fallen into a firing stance. Arms extended. Perfect triangle from shoulders to wrists. Dead still. Legs braced. Like a man who had done it before a thousand times. The four of them pulled up short. Suddenly scared. Caught unawares. Looking at each other. Trying to decide what to do. Looking at the man with the gun. Looking into his face. Seeing the smile. A smile that told them that he wasn't kidding around. A smile that told them that he had done it before. A smile that told them that they were just second division and he was premier league. They hesitated and then they broke. They ran. And all along the street the curtains twitched. The smile never left Davie's face. He casually returned the gun to the holsster, got into his car and drove away.

Nobody reported it. Nobody said a thing. They never did. Not on Andytown. There were some who were livid. They let the men in charge know exactly what they felt. They were angry that one reporter had been able to make the boys run whilst everyone was watching. But there were others who raised a silent cheer from behind the net curtains. It was the cheer that is saved for seeing the bully humiliated. It was never reported but the word went about.

By the time the Docklands bomb ripped apart the cease-fire Davie had his own column. He was able to harangue the government for not taking a harder line. The paper loved it. They were able to say that the words of Davie Stanton were not the words of the paper. He was his own voice. He had every right to voice the opinions that many readers felt. He became an unofficial mouthpiece of Protestant Ulster. And he sold papers.

After Docklands he had met with Richard and Derek. It had been a good reunion in the old caravan out on the coast. They had agreed that it may soon be time. If the Brits didn't take steps it may soon be time. They had decided to wait. He had talked with them after Manchester. This time they agreed the Brits had to go in hard. If they didn't, then it was time.

It was three days now. Three days and still nothing. And that was all there would be. Nothing. Davie switched off the TV. He had given it long enough. He had watched the IRA lead them all a merry dance for two whole years. Nobody could say that he hadn't given peace a proper chance. They had left him with no choice. The cowards in London who allowed the IRA to dictate terms. The idiots in the UDA and the UVF who only cared about their little drug empires and protection rackets. All of them. They would all see his people sold down the river just so long as their own little worlds could stay intact. And all the while the IRA were gathering their forces and laughing their socks off. Well not any more. It was party over time. They would have to learn that there were still those who would stand and fight. And they would have to learn the hard way.

It was a strange road back to a war. A half-hour drive out of Belfast and along the motorway to Portadown. A drive through the small non-descript little town. Past the massive barracks that had once been a staging post for soldiers on their way to the badlands of South Armagh. Through the near deserted town centre. Through the grim estates of pebble-dashed houses. Sometimes the kerb stones were painted red, white and blue. Sometimes they were painted green, white and gold. A small town with a hundred flashpoints. Nearly every street was a sectarian riot waiting to happen. The peace had passed Portadown by. He could feel the hate hanging in the air. He could see it in the mean faces of the kids who hung around in small groups.

Edgarstown estate was different to all the others because the flags were newer. And there were more of them. There were probably more Union flags per square yard in Edgarstown Estate than anywhere else on the whole planet. He pulled up outside Robinson's Bar and locked the car door. By the time he turned around a small clutch of teenagers had gathered a few yards away. They fixed him with stares that said strangers aren't welcome here. Thin lips. Smirks. We're six. You're one. And you don't belong. They edged slightly forward.

Davie put his hands in his pockets and smiled. "If there is one scratch on this car when I come out, I'll find out who did it and pull his fingernails out with pliers. Understood lads?"

They saw it in his eyes. They all knew the hard men. They had grown up with them. It was nothing in particular. They came in all shapes and sizes. It was just something that they all had. They saw it in Davie Stanton. They shrugged their shoulders. They moved away. Nothing more needed to be said.

Robinson's Bar itself made little effort to offer a warm welcome to strangers. It wasn't a passing trade kind of place. It didn't cater for families. It was a place for the men of Edgarstown Estate to drink. The life expectancy of a customer in a Sinn Fein T-Shirt could have been measured in seconds. It was just turned 7.30 when Davie walked in and made his way to the bar. The place was hardly busy. Just another slow Thursday night. Eight men sat on stools at the bar. They weren't talking. A TV rattled away from an elevated position over the bar. Game show. Some eyes watched the screen without interest. Others stared vacantly ahead. Everyone seemed to be smoking. Three older customers were playing dominoes at one of the tables. If there had been a hum of conversation it would have probably dropped as Davie walked in. Instead he felt their eyes. Cold. Hostile. Suspicious.

The barman was idly polishing glasses. He made a play of carefully finishing the glass in his hand before acknowledging Davie waiting at the bar. When he eventually made his way over he didn't look at Davie. He started on another glass.

"Aye."

"Pint of lager."

The barman seemed to hesitate for a moment. His body language made it abundantly clear that he really would rather not. He was all reluctance as he filled the glass. There was no effort made to ensure a full measure. The glass appeared in front of Davie.

"One forty."

Davie dropped a couple of pound coins on the counter. He gripped the barman's wrist as he reached out for the money. The man's eyes widened in surprise. Surprise at what the stranger was doing. Surprise at the pain from the grip. He pulled back hard but it achieved nothing. The men along the bar stirred slightly. The game show was forgotten.

"I need you to pass a message. I need to meet Billy."

"Fuck off. I don't know any Billy." Half-hearted defiance. The man was frightened now. His eyes flicked to the other customers. There was a plea for help. None was forthcoming. Eyes dropped down. Beer mats were examined.

"Please don't piss me about. You know full well who I mean. Just pass the word."

The man nodded a tiny nod. Not his problem. He shuffled across to the corner of the bar and turned his back as he spoke into the phone. The conversation lasted two minutes. When he replaced the receiver he said. "Someone's coming" Then he went back to polishing glasses. Not his problem now.

They came after half an hour. There were three of them. They were all in their 40's. Still in their building site clothes. One opened a door to a back room and nodded for Davie to go through. Nothing was said. Davie drained his glass and did as he was bid. One stayed outside.

It was a small function room. The man who had opened the door waved Davie to a stool.

"Who the fuck are you?"

"Someone who wants to meet Billy."

"You out your fucking mind?"

"No."

Davie looked directly into the man's eyes. He waited for discomfort. It was a matter of seconds. The man was off balance now. Shuffling slightly.

"Well you're going fucking nowhere until you say who you are."

"Bollocks."

More shuffling. Davie continued. "I'm not armed. You can check if you like. You can tie my hands. You can put a blindfold on. Doesn't make any odds to me. All I want to do is meet with Billy. No way anyone else knows who I am. If he's not happy he can sort me out. It really is that simple. So call him."

The man pulled a mobile phone out of the pocket of his donkey jacket. He made the call from a dark corner of the dreary room. Back turned. Shoulders hunched. When he had finished he came to Davie.

"Stand up. I'm searching you."

Davie was searched. His hands were tied. A makeshift blindfold was tied around his head. They waited in silence for five minutes. Then he heard the fire door at the back of the room swing open.

"On your feet. We're going."

They bundled him into the back of a car. He was in the middle. Squashed by the two men who squeezed in beside him on the back seat. It had been easier than he had imagined. Well it seemed that way. There was still a chance that he was being taken out of town for a bullet through the back of the head. He doubted it. There was no reason.

In fact the drive to Billy's house took less than ten minutes. Davie was intrigued at the prospect of the meeting. Billy Wright had become something of a Last of the Mohicans figure to the Protestants of Ulster. At a time when all their paramilitary commanders had walked away from the fight and signed up for peace, Billy Wright had stood as a solitary, defiant figure. Davie had never met him. He knew him only by his reputation. Billy's life had started hard. One day before he was ten his mother left the house to buy a pint of milk and was never seen again. He grew up with relatives in South Armagh and most of his friends had been Catholic. He always claimed fond memories of these days. He had even played Gaelic Football. But the Troubles changed him. Relatives were murdered by the IRA. The final straw came when a lorry load of workers was stopped a few miles away. The Catholic driver was led to one side and the twelve Protestants were lined up and mown down. The whole of Ireland was stunned by the cold-hearted savagery of the attack. Billy Wright joined the youth wing of the Mid Ulster UVF.

By the 90's he had established a reputation that went far beyond his home town of Portadown. Under his leadership the Mid Ulster UVF became the most feared Loyalist paramilitary force in the Province. Along the way he acquired the nickname 'King Rat'. In 1994 when the Combined Loyalist Military command called a cease-fire, the men of Mid Ulster were alone in ignoring it. In Portadown the killing continued, and there were many who saw Billy as a hero who refused to be bowed. By the summer of 1995 Portadown had become the most likely flashpoint to shatter the fragile peace. On the 12th of July, 800 men of the Orange Order would always march from the centre of the town to the small church at Drumcree on the outskirts. For years the route of the march had been the cause of huge local tension. All the obvious routes took the marchers through

Catholic areas. The only solution was to re-route the march way out of the town. The Orangemen dug in their heels and demanded their right to celebrate their history and their culture. The Republicans demanded their right not to have the whistles and drums in their streets.

By this time there was a growing discontent among the whole of the Loyalist population. There was a feeling that everything was going the way of the IRA. There was a feeling that the Government in London was washing its hands of them. Somehow the march to the church at Drumcree became the final straw. If they were not allowed to walk down the streets of one of their traditional heartlands, then where would it all stop? Drumcree became a symbol. It was the line in the sand. It was where the rot had to stop. If they lost the battle to march to Drumcree, then all would seem lost.

In the lead up to the 1995 march, the spectre of Billy Wright hung over the town. If the authorities refused the Orangemen a route up the Catholic Garvachy road would Billy and his men force the issue with bombs and guns? There were frantic negotiations and in the end a shaky compromise was reached. The Orangemen were allowed to march the road, but they had to do so in silence. The whistles and drums fell silent and the road was lined all the way with Catholic residents screaming abuse. All the way the marchers were pelted with bottles and stones. When they made it to the far end of the road they were greeted like heroes by a vast crowd that had gathered from all over Ulster. They had hung on to their rights for another year. And the legend of Billy 'King Rat' Wright grew.

Once again the spectre of the July 12th march was looming large on the horizon. Once again the Catholics were hell bent on stopping it. Once again the Protestant community were marshalling their forces to make it happen. And Billy was telling the world that the march would go through no matter what it took to make it happen. By now his folk hero status was becoming something more than a thorn in the side of the authorities. He was a one-man nightmare to the peace process. He was a rally point for disaffected loyalists.

Davie was unceremoniously bundled from the car and pushed

roughly up a small path. He heard a door opening. Then he was inside. A hand pushed him in the chest and he fell back into a chair. It was soft. A lounge chair. A voice gave instruction. "Take the blindfold off."

It took a moment for his eyes to adjust. He was in a very ordinary living room. Neat. Pleasant. Clean. The man opposite him was not tall. He wore a white T-shirt and pressed jeans. He had short cropped hair and a small beard. He was watching Davie with interest. The three building site men stood menacingly behind the sofa.

"So. I gather you want to see me. Well, here I am." The voice was soft. Almost gentle. The face was thoughtful. Intelligent. There was no threat in the words.

"Thanks. We need to do this alone. Leave the hands tied if you like."

A small smile. "I was intending to." He nodded the three minders from the room. They left looking unhappy. Annoyed at being left out. Billy gave an open handed gesture. "OK. They're gone."

"You're sure that you're not bugged."

"Yes. We sweep every week. You can talk. A careful man. No names?"

"No."

"Well on you go."

Davie took the plunge. "I'm the Ghost."

Billy's eyes widened in surprise. He uncrossed his legs and leaned forward in his chair. Davie continued.

"I'm not much impressed with the way things are going. I think we've given peace a proper chance. It's not working. The IRA are taking the piss. It's time they get to know they can't have it all their own way. You know what I do. It's time for a message to be sent. The thing is, Belfast UVF won't claim it. I need someone to claim the kills. That's why I'm here. I think we see things the same."

Billy nodded. "How do you work?"

"Alone. I choose the targets. I take them out. Nobody knows until it's done. When it's done I call you. I give the word 'Snapdragon' and the name. If I say 'Snapdragon' and nothing else, it means I need a meet. I'll be outside Robinson's Bar the next day at six in the evening. You arrange for me to be picked up. You make the claim. I only hit senior IRA people. No civilians. I only hit the ones they have to give a funeral to. That's the only way I work. Take it or leave it."

"Oh I'll take it. No problem. How about targets?" Billy stepped across the room and untied Davie's hands.

"I have plenty." Said Davie as he massaged his wrists.

"Will you share?"

"No."

"Fair enough." Billy leaned back and made a steeple with his fingers. "One thing. Can you strike before the Twelfth? It would be good if you could strike before the Twelfth."

"Three weeks. It's tight. But I can see the logic. OK. I'll do my best. Can't say more than that."

"No. Course not. You'll have a drink?"

"Aye. A drink would be good. Can I smoke?"

"Sure. There's an ashtray on the table. Beer OK?"

"Grand."

They talked for two hours. Davie found him a confusing character.In some ways his impressive. Billy laid out his problems simply and honestly. His views closely mirrored Davie's. He had no wish for war, but he didn't feel that the way the peace was going gave him any choice. He felt that their people were being left in the lurch. He didn't believe a word that came out of the mouth of any of the Sinn Fein people. They just said anything to dupe the Brits. Once they had power it would all be very different. If they ever achieved control, there would only be suffering for the Protestants of Ulster. Someone had to make a stand.

Davie had no problem with any on this. It was why he had come. And yet there was another side to Billy that made him uncomfortable. It was an extremist edge that he had never known himself. At times Billy's inner passion would flare up through the quiet exterior. Davie had wondered about many of the rumours that he had heard. Rumours of a drug empire. Rumours of executions of innocent Catholics sanctioned on a completely random basis. He hadn't wanted to believe them. And yet now he was in the presence of the man it was hard not to believe the stories. Billy was a driven man. A man who had long since stopped caring about what was right and wrong. Only the result mattered for Billy.

This meant that his stand was attracting too many of the wrong people. He had become a magnet for the nutters. There were too many that were only interested in dealing drugs. Too many who wanted no more than an excuse to exercise their sectarian hatred. Billy had no particular problem with Catholics. He had grown up with them. His problem was with the IRA He said it was hard to keep discipline. There were too many cowboys who wanted to do their own thing under his banner. He said the Ghost was just what he needed. The people had always trusted the Ghost. The Ghost always hit the IRA where they hurt most. The Ghost would give respectability to the cause.

Davie couldn't help but wonder if he had made the right decision. Should he have come? Was this really the way that he wanted to fight his war? And yet where else was there for him to go? At least Billy was thoughtful. There was no doubt that he cared about his people with a burning passion. A frightening passion.

Davie had never been able to talk in this way with Hutchinson. He had always thought the man to be nothing more than a jumped up yob. A bully. A hoodlum. At least Billy was different. Davie had no doubt that he was a killer. He probably already had. But he didn't believe that he would take pleasure from it. Maybe here was a man that could do much for his people. Maybe. Or maybe he would make them hated. The problem was that there really wasn't any choice. Billy was the only game in town.

In the end they shook hands when it was time for Davie to go.

"It's up to you, but I think I should know your name."

Davie wondered about it. Maybe Billy was right. It was a time for trust. "Davie. Davie Stanton. Granville Street, Belfast. I'm in the book."

"The journalist, right?"

"Right."

Billy smiled. "You're a fair man Davie Stanton."

"Thanks."

Davie found it hard to believe that it had been seven years. His life was drifting away at a speed that he found it hard to come to terms with. Seven years. He was 38 bloody years old. Unbelievable. 38 years old and still fighting the same old war. Not that the seven years had done much to change South Armagh. He doubted if seven thousand years would do that. Only the weather was different. The last time the ground had been hard frozen and he had feared frostbite. This time the dawn was warm and beautiful. There had been a mist when the sun had started to light up the dawn but it was now already burned away. It was silage time in South Armagh. There had already been three solid days of sunshine and three more were forecast. The cut grass lay in the fields in neat rows ready to be picked up and pitted for winter. The mowers had wreaked havoc with the life of the meadows and kestrels hovered ready to pick up newly homeless field mice for breakfast.

One thing that was the same was the silence. The same timeless stillness was settled over the fields and the hedges and the small woods. There was a low buzz of flies. There had been a vigorous dawn chorus of birds. Now the world had settled into the silence of a summer morning.

Davie felt completely relaxed. He no longer even considered the prospect of missing. He was laid up on the edge of a small wood on a hillside that was seven hundred yards inside the Republic. He was using exactly the same plan as the one that he had employed in 1989. This time the farm that was in his sights was that of Brendan Conner. He had watched for three days and had seen no sign of Conner himself. He hadn't really expected to. Instead it was John Conner that he had watched. Conner had finished his ten-year sentence in Long Kesh the year before and had returned to the farm. Davie had no confirmation that he was still active. It was pretty well unthinkable that he wouldn't be. It didn't matter much. What mattered was that he was the son of the commander of the South Armagh Brigade of the IRA.

Every morning Conner Jnr had come out from his morning cup of tea just after seven. Davie had watched him make the slow circuits of the field with his tractor and mower. He had no doubt that this morning would be the same.

It was a simple shot. A little over eight hundred yards. No wind. Perfect visibility. Almost a formality. When the door opened he took his usual slow breath in and out. Seconds later the corpse of John Conner lay outside the back door of his father's house. The soldiers in the watchtower scrambled at the sound of the shot. Davie never saw what they did next. He was gone.

In the early afternoon the Mid Ulster UVF claimed responsibility for the execution of John Conner. They announced that the Ghost had undertaken the task of carrying out the execution. They announced that the Ghost could no longer stand by and watch the lie of the peace process. They announced that the Ghost was active again. The news sent a shiver of excitement around the Province. The Ghost and the King Rat were together. Now the IRA would know fear again.

On July 8th tensions in the Province rose another few notches. The body of a Catholic taxi driver called Michael McGoldrick was discovered a few miles outside of Lurgan. No organisation claimed responsibility but the word on the street was unequivocal. It had to be work of Billy Wright's Mid Ulster UVF. Davie caught a few whispers. The senior officers of the Belfast command were not happy. Not remotely happy. Strong words were passed down the line to Portadown. Billy was getting out of hand. Billy was becoming an embarrassment. Billy needed taking down a peg or two. The word was that Billy didn't give a shit what any of the people in Belfast thought. Billy would fight his own war as he thought fit. Billy thought that they could go and stuff themselves.

The McGoldrick killing bothered Davie. It had been a PR disaster. There was absolutely no evidence that McGoldrick had any kind of connection to the IRA. It seemed pretty obvious that he was a simple taxi driver who had been executed for no other reason than his religious faith. The torrent of condemnation that followed the killing completely undid the propaganda gains from the killing of John Conner. Davie felt like putting his fist through the wall. It never changed. Any step they ever managed to take forward was always lost by the actions of some cowardly psycho who got their rocks off killing completely innocent Catholics. He didn't want to believe that Billy had anything to do with it. If he had, it confirmed all of his worst fears. It bothered him for a whole night and the day after. He considered arranging a meeting but decided against it. Billy would have bigger fish to fry. The Drumcree stand-off was only a couple of days away. He waited.

Once again the Orangemen made it up the Garvachy Road thanks to a massive level of police protection. Once again the Catholic crowds pelted them with missiles. Once again there were rumours flying about as to what would happen if the march was stopped. Once again it seemed as if it were the threat of the Mid Ulster UVF that got the Orangemen down the road. The levels of sectarian hate in the Province were rising like the mercury in a thermometer in the noon day heat of a desert.

Davie arranged the meet a fortnight after the march. This time the car drove him out of the town to a small picnic site in the country. Billy was waiting at a wooden table. Davie thought that he looked older. Certainly thinner. There were deep lines on his face.

"Hello Davie."

Davie joined him on the other side of the table. "How's things Billy?"

"Been better. Yourself?"

"Not bad. The march went through then."

"Aye. Just." A smile. "I suppose we live to fight another day. Story of our people. We always seem to live to fight another day."

It was true. They never seemed to win. All they ever did was stave off defeat. Put another layer of sandbags around the bunker. Keep the ramparts repaired. Fight them off. Regroup. No surrender. Billy seemed to make a big effort to pull himself together.

"So. Davie. You wanted to meet?"

"Yes. I don't know if you'll like it much."

"So what's new?"

"You can probably guess. McGoldrick. I need to know. Was it down to you?"

Billy's eyes flashed with anger. It was only for a second, but it was bright. Vivid. Then it was gone. Replaced by calm.

"So, Davie. The question on everyone's lips. Who's asking? Journalist or Ghost?"

"Both."

"And what do you think Davie? What is your guess?"

"If I knew I wouldn't have come. I hope it wasn't down to you. I don't believe that it was. I need to know for certain."

Billy stared at him for a long moment. Then the tension drained out of him. "Course it was me. But it isn't how it seems. I'm getting a tonne of shite from those bastards up in the Belfast UVF. You'll have heard. They will do anything to avoid fighting the IRA. I had a mate lift one of their guns. I gave the order for the gun to be used to kill a Catholic. Not McGoldrick in particular. Any Catholic. It didn't matter much. I figured that the gun would be bound to have a history. Once the pellers put their ballistics experts on it they would tie the weapon directly back to Belfast. Give them a bit of heat. Force them off the fence." He paused and sighed. "Well it didn't work. The bastard gun was clean and everyone has pinned it on me."

"So you just topped a completely innocent man because of internal politics"

Billy looked up sharply at this. "If you have a problem why don't you just fuck off here and now. There are times when we have to do bad things. I didn't expect to have to tell you that. It's a fucking war Davie."

"OK. Calm down. Jesus Billy, I never thought you'd be so naïve."

Instead of calming down, Billy just got madder. "Don't you go calling me naïve . . ."

"Hey! Cool it. I don't mean anything. It's just you don't seem to be looking at the big picture."

It took Billy a great effort to calm down. He managed it. Davie was shocked at how highly-strung he was. "OK. Sorry. The big picture. Paint it for me."

"Just look at what you're doing Billy. You're making it easy for them. The Brits have hitched their wagon to the peace train. It's gone too far. If they can't make it stick, they'll wind up with egg all over their faces. They hate that. Hate it more than anything else. So, it means that you are making yourself public enemy number one. You're going beyond the stage of just being a nuisance. You're the spanner in their wheel. And they won't be liking it. So what will they do ? They'll do what they always do. Black propaganda. Make you into a bogeyman. Billy deals drugs. Billy's just a pscho. Billy's homicidal. MI5 are the best in the business. And what do you do?: You just make their job easier.

Come on Billy. Wise up. You know how it all works. It's just that we're used to them doing it to the other side."

There was surprise in Billy's face. "You're serious aren't you?"

"Very. You need to get used to it. It's the Brit way. They will try and demean you, humiliate you, brand you as a maniac, a psycho, it's how they work."

"There's more."

"Go on."

"I'm getting rumours from Belfast. From the UVF command. They're going to throw me out. After all these years and they're going to throw me out."

It wasn't unexpected. The Belfast UVF had got a taste for the niceties of politics. The debating chamber was a more comfortable place to fight the war. "So what do you intend to do?"

"Split. I'm not giving up. No way. I think most of the lads will come with me. We'll form a new outfit. LVF. Loyalist Volunteer Force. How about you? Will you come along?"

"UVF. LVF. Makes no odds to me."

"Good. I thought you would. No surrender then."

"Aye. No surrender."

It happened the following week. The Belfast UVF issued an ultimatum. They announced that Billy Wright was to be stood down from his position in the Mid Ulster UVF. Billy was true to his word. He renounced his old comrades. The LVF was born. He vowed to keep up the fight.

On September 1st things came to a head. The UVF command were raging mad at the turn that events had taken. They issued Billy with an ultimatum. They gave him 24 hours to leave Ulster. If he ignored the ultimatum he would be executed at the earliest opportunity. Billy gave them the two fingers. It enraged Davie. It always had. It could be accepted that the IRA would want to target Loyalist leaders. It was even just about acceptable when the Brits did it if it suited their political ends. He just couldn't stand it when they did it to each other. There were always fine words. Always big talk about defending the freedom of Ulster. But in the end it was only ever about turf. And money. And petty power games played out by men who had done no more than been born in the wrong place at the right time.

Then suddenly it hit him that in fact a real opportunity had been placed in his lap. One of those rare opportunities to kill several birds with one stone. It was how it always was in the nasty little war that he had fought for so many years. Like making ground over tough terrain. Sometimes you had to go back to find a way forward. Sometimes the route back was the right way.

Three days later he shot dead John Hutchinson from the eighth floor of a disused block of flats. It was ludicrously easy. Easy because this was home ground. It was the ground where he had grown up. The ground where he knew every alley and bit of waste ground. 800 yards and clean through the heart. Clean and simple.

"Snapdragon. John Hutchinson. The Ghost hereby warns the leadership of the Belfast UVF to stay clear of Billy Wright. Any who attempt to carry out their death threat will meet with the ultimate sanction."

Later he watched the hysterical TV coverage. Grave faced pundits told the cameras that the peace process was in danger of falling apart. Officials of the UVF said that John Hutchinson had been one of their finest. He had given his life to defending the community of his birth from the relentless march of the IRA. But they declined to answer any questions about the death threat to Billy Wright. And Davie had smiled to himself when he saw the fear in their eyes.

And inside he felt pleased that he would never have to worry about John Hutchinson. Hutchinson had always been the itch that would never go away. He had been a necessity for a while. But he had always been a liability as well. Davie knew that the man was scared to death of him. But that was never enough. There was always a chance that someone would offer enough money or cause enough pain for him to tell what he knew. Now he would never tell. He would take the secret of the Ghost to the grave. Now it was just the two of them. Davie and Billy. Two mixed up guys pushing 40 trying to hold back the tide.

And then he remembered that there were more than two. Somewhere in the shadows was James Hamilton. How was he taking it all? For so many years The Ghost must have been the brightest feather in his cap. Not now. The Ghost had become the loose cannon. A lasting embarrassment from the days where that kind of thing was considered to be OK. But things had changed. The days of Maggie were long gone. No more open cheque books. No more anything goes. It was all about peace now. Peace and looking good in the eyes of a suddenly liberal world. What would James be told to do about the Ghost? Was it a mess that he would be ordered to clean up? Clean up and bury in a place where it could never be found. Maybe. Probably.

And of course there was one other. He often wondered about Sean. He had heard nothing of him since the night in Monaghan. He hoped that he had got out. He hoped that he was far away. Sometimes he envied him. That night he felt that he had found a kindred spirit. In the midst of all the hatred and the killing he had found a man much like himself. A victim of history and duty. A decent man who was born in an indecent place. A victim of his postcode. Maybe one day they would meet again. There was a part of Davie that hoped they would.

The Irish bar in the heart of Boston was Friday night busy. It was filled with a new breed of Irish Americans. Once it would have been all policemen and firemen and labourers. Now it was all sorts. There were as many who wore the designer suits as those in the clothes of working men. They had become so much more American than Irish. They clung to their Irish roots and sang the songs and drank the Guinness. Their Irishness had become a label. It was no more to them than Armani. These places always made Sean feel like a fish out of water. He never wanted to join in the songs. He was always the sad looking bald one sitting apart from it all. Sometimes there were those who noticed the ironic smile on his lips. But they never guessed. They never guessed that such a non-descript little man had once sent a four tonne truck full of Paras sailing high into a blue summer sky.

There were some who knew him from the Sinn Fein meetings. They had heard him speak and saw him in a different light. By now his speeches were calmer. More reflective. He seldom raised his voice. The old long-haired firebrand of the late 60's was no more than a distant memory. But he could make them think. Most of the time his fellow Sinn Fein officials were rattled by him.

They said that he was always losing sight of the big picture. He was always forgetting that it was his job to make the Yanks put their hands deep into their pockets. Fire them up. Stoke the embers of their guilt.

Sometimes Sean did as they wished. He could bring the tears to the eyes of middle class America as well as the best of them. When he switched on the melancholy there wasn't a dry eye in the house. But he didn't do it often. More and more his words were about the cancer of sectarianism. He told it like it was. He painted pictures of burning streets. Pictures of poor families packing their meagre belongings and moving away under the threat of death. Pictures of little empires ruled by gangs of thugs. It wasn't what anyone wanted to hear but he told them anyway. He told them that there would never be peace unless the people of the North learned to come to terms with each other. He told them that the only way forward was to forget history. And everyone hated it. It wasn't what anyone wanted to hear. They all wanted goodies and baddies. White hats and black hats. Heroic lads of the IRA and the wicked, scheming murderous Brits. They wanted it to be simple and straightforward just like it was in the movies.

But Sean always got his place on the platform. It was owed to him. Nobody really knew why. They didn't really want to. All they knew was that he had a past. So they always gave him his place. He had become an anomaly. A man out of step with the times. Pessimistic in the face of everyone's optimistic. Melancholy in the midst of designer cheer. A dark corner in the light. A sad little figure from the rainy terraced streets of the Lower Falls in the midst of the shining high rise blocks of corporate America. A relic.

Tonight he was waiting on an appointment that he was rather looking forward to. He had received a call from Brian Docherty three days earlier. It had been nearly twenty years since they had last met when Brian had met with Sean in the bar on the West Coast of the Republic and told him that the leadership wanted a Spectacular. Astonishingly Brian had survived the series of disasters that had rocked the East Tyrone Brigade in the 80's. Now, like Sean, he was out. He had done his bit. He too was a Sinn Feiner. As soon as he had been given the trip to the States he had been keen to look up Sean. There didn't seem to be many of the old guard around any more. They were either rotting away in the Kesh or out of things altogether or six feet under the turf of Milltown Cemetery.

It was Sean who spotted Brian as he came into the noisy bar and looked around. His gaze passed over Sean twice. When Sean squeezed through the bodies to where he waited at the bar he still didn't recognise him. Only when he tapped him on the shoulder was there any recognition.

Sean smiled at his old comrade's look of consternation.

"I know Brian. I know it every morning when I look in the mirror. I went and got old. How the hell are you?"

Brian regained his balance. Christ but he looked awful. It was hard to comprehend that it was the same man. Only the eyes and the smile. It was all that was left of the Sean O'Neil that he had known all those years before. They bought drinks and sat in a corner. For a while it was just niceties. Sinn Fein talk. What old comrades were doing? A little bit about old times. They kept taking it in turns to fight a path through to the bar.

At last they got to more serious business. Brian was still very much in the loop. He told Sean that things seemed to be going well. The Docklands bomb had given the Brits a real rattle. They had come scurrying back to the negotiating table. Everybody was sure that peace was coming. It could only be a matter of weeks. It would happen in the summer of 1997. That would be the date. Just a few weeks and the guns could be buried for good. They were having a few problems keeping everyone in line. The only operations that were getting sanctioned were against economic targets. The leadership were determined to avoid own goals. All they had to do was keep up the financial pressure and it would come.

There were a few rogues about. There always were. Brian was pretty certain that the Movement was bound to split. There was no way that everyone would go down the road of peace. He just hoped that it wouldn't be too many. A few they could deal with. If it were more than a few, things would be tough.

"So what's the main worry?" Asked Sean

"The bloody INLA. They aren't showing any interest in the peace. You know how they are. Bloody nutters the lot of them."

Sean smiled. "Some things never change."

"We had a strange one last week. One of the INLA lads changed sides and came over to us. We debriefed him and came up with a problem. He told us that the Brits had passed them a name. The guy was ex 14th Intelligence. They gave them the lot. Names. Dates. Places. The guy was a player all right. Loughgall, the bloody lot. You may have heard of him. Davie Stanton. He writes that column for the paper. The fucking voice of decent Orange Ulster. Anyway, he must have got right up the noses of the Brits. They want him gone. Typical. Passed the whole thing over to the INLA. We don't really know what to do. To be honest, most people would like to see him topped. Why not? We owe the bastard. The trouble is that he's too high profile. Column in the paper. Decorated in the Falklands. Apparently his Granddad was something of a folk hero. Old UVF man. Back in Carson's day. Came back from the Somme with a VC. He got blown away a few years back by one of our bombs on the Shankhill.

The publicity would almost certainly backfire. It would have the Orangies up in arms if we took him out. Try telling that to the INLA. They don't give shite. Never have. Mad buggers all of them. Sean? You alright?"

Sean's face was far away. It took him a moment to come back. He saw Brian looking at him quizzically.

"Sorry about that. I was away. Just thinking I'm glad it's not my call any more. All I have to worry about is the morning lecture and how to lift a few dollars from good old girls who had a great Granddaddy get off the boat in 1900."

The young journalist leaned back in his chair and shouted down to where Davie was sitting at his computer. "Davie! For you. Line 5"

Davie pressed the button and lifted the phone to his ear. "Hello."

"Davie?"

"Speaking."

"Is the phone safe?"

Who the hell was it? Belfast voice. Something familiar.

"Maybe. I wouldn't hang my hat on it."

"Ring me on this number. Five minutes. Bring plenty of change. It's Sean."

Sean. Sean O'Neil. An American number. What the hell was going on? He grabbed his jacket and made his way outside. There was a bank of pay phones across the street. He dropped into a newsagent. He bought cigarettes and pocketed a handful of pound coins as change. He thrust a cigarette into his mouth and dialled out the number.

"Hello."

"It's Davie."

"You good to talk?"

"Fine. Pay phone."

"OK. Listen up. I heard a whisper. The source is sound. The Brits have passed all your old files to the INLA. Army. 14th Intelligence. The lot. They want you dead Davie. You need to get out."

A chill settled in Davie's stomach. It was James. He knew it in his bones. James Hamilton and his favourite games. Bastard. He took a hard pull on his cigarette.

"What do you mean Sean? Out of the country?"

"If it was just the INLA then that would be OK. They'd never find you if you went to ground. But it's not them you need to worry about. It's the Brits. They'll find you eventually. Out of the country isn't good enough."

Davie could follow the logic. It would be very hard indeed to get away from the Brits. Not if they really wanted to find him.

"Any suggestions?"

"Just one. You'll probably think I'm nuts."

Davie pushed the receiver into his ear. "Go on. I'll take anything I can get."

There was a pause on the other end of the line. "Get yourself into the Kesh Davie. It's the one place on the planet where you'll probably be safe. The Brits would never get to you in there. It would be a publicity disaster. Find a way of getting yourself put away. Peace is coming. You'll be out in a year or two. Everyone will. It's part of the deal. Give it time to blow over. Things soon change."

Davie considered it. On the surface of things it was a crazy idea but he could see the logic in it. Maybe it was indeed the only place on the planet that was beyond the reach of James Hamilton.

"It seems that I'm back in your debt Sean."

A chuckle. "Aye. That it does. Best of luck to you."

"Thanks Sean."

He stood for several minutes listening to the dial tone in his ear. He spent several hours weighing up all of his options. No matter how he looked at things he couldn't get away from Sean's logic. Portadown might have been an option. But they had got Billy now. He was away. Of all things they had banged him up on a charge of menacing behaviour. It was a joke, but it had been enough for the judge to get him off the streets. He had fought a battle inside the Kesh and had eventually won the right for the LVF to have their own wing in H6. Without him the LVF was not up to much. There would be no real chance of sanctuary in Portadown. It was straight choice. He could head overseas and try and use the funds that James had paid him for the Ghost killings. Maybe there would be enough to find a way to disappear.

The idea held little appeal. He barely considered it. That night he opened up the padlock on the door of the workshop for the first time in several years. The electricity had been long cut off. As he swung his torch around and the light lit up the dust and the cobwebs he was filled with memories of his father and grandfather. He pulled one of the workbenches out of the way and started to lift floorboards. Underneath were the guns that Peter Stanton and his great grandfather had brought from Larne on that night in 1914. Carson's guns. Still as good as new. Covered in oil and gleaming in the light of the torch. They had sat there under the floorboards for 95 years. Davie shook his head. What a crazy place. Crazy, crazy place. He pulled out two of the Lee Enfield rifles and a box of ammunition.

He carefully replaced the padlock and dropped the rifles into the boot of his car. And then he started to drive. He drove up and down the streets of the Shankill and the Falls Road. He drove through the sad divided place where he had lived out his days. His mind wandered over the collection of events that constituted his life. On a normal night he couldn't have driven the streets for more than half an hour without being stopped and searched. He chose the streets that were closest to the interface where the high peace fence separated Catholic from Protestant. At every roadblock he expected a soldier to step out and wave him down. But things were already changing. The news was full of the talk of peace. The soldiers were all thinking of home. There was little urgency about them. He cruised through roadblock after roadblock.

In the end it took just over two hours. At last he was waved down. The squaddie must have been about eighteen. He had acne on his chin. He had the accent of the Black Country. He asked Davie to step out of the car. He asked Davie to open the boot. His eyes nearly popped out of his head when he saw the guns. Davie found it hard not to laugh as the young soldier covered him with his gun and screamed for the sergeant to come.

It took three months as they processed him. They all looked so confused. They read their notes and shook their heads. How could it be? Scots Guards. Crossmaglen. Mount Tumbledown. 14th Intelligence. Loughgall. A thriving antiques business. A widely read newspaper column. And caught at the top end of the Springfield Road at three in the morning with a couple of hundred-year-old Lee Enfields. It was mad. Crazy. They all wanted to know how it could be. They wanted Davie to explain. To enlighten them. Instead he just smiled politely and informed them that he was a volunteer in the LVF and that he was fighting for the freedom of the people of Ulster.

The court case caused a mild flurry. The media were hungry for news by this stage. The cease-fire was now a few months old and the novelty of nothing happening was starting to wear off. They liked his story. They wrote features about him. They dug out pictures. In one paper they had a picture of him in his full uniform as he graduated from Sandhurst. Next door was an old picture of Peter Stanton ready for his trip to France. How could it be they asked? How could this man who distinguished himself so in the service of the Crown fall so low? Where on earth was he going with two antique rifles in the boot on that rainy night in Belfast when peace was about to break out? For a while there were all kinds of theories flying around.

The Court turned out to be a damp squib. Davie wore his best suit and stood up straight and tall, as he pleaded guilty in a strong clear voice. The Judge took no time at all about it. He found David

Stanton guilty of being a member of an illegal organisation and of being caught in possession of illegal firearms. He sentenced David Stanton to ten years. It was all over before it had started.

There was a sense among those who had come to the court that they had been cheated. They had hoped for drama and the whiff of conspiracy. Instead it was all over in a matter of minutes. Just before Davie was led away from the Dock he spotted the smile. James Hamilton was near the back. He was wearing one of his trademark suits and his arms were folded. A beaming smile filled his handsome face. Davie returned the smile in kind.

When their eyes met there was only coldness.

They were waiting for him as he came on to the wing of H6 in Long Kesh. It was a very different place to the one that Sean had known eighteen years earlier. Once the hunger strike was over and the ten men dead were buried, the British had given their concessions one by one. By the autumn of 1997 the H Blocks were unrecognisable from the nightmare zone of the Blanket Protest. The cell doors were never locked and the warders simply gave the inmates a cursory inspection twice a day. All the prisoners wore their own clothes and could organise themselves and their time as they saw fit.

Billy stood out in front with a wry grin on his face. Behind him was a motley bunch of men who made up the ranks of the LVF inside Long Kesh. Davie returned the smile.

"Hello Billy. Thanks for claiming me."

Whenever a prisoner was sent to Long Kesh for a political offence, it was up to the commander in the block to claim the man as one of their own. Billy hadn't really known what to do in Davie's case. Once he heard that Davie had pleaded guilty to membership of the LVF he decided that it wasn't much of a secret any more. Claiming him had been no problem. What Billy really wanted to know was just what the hell was going on. He didn't want to let on to the other prisoners who were watching the new arrival with interest. He walked up to Davie and gave him a playful punch on the arm. "Well somebody had to take you I suppose. I wouldn't have wanted to have seen you stuck with any riff-raff. Come on. Come in here and I'll fill you in on how things are."

He led Davie to his cell and closed the door. Davie sat down on the bed and Billy took a chair at the small table in the corner. The smile was gone now.

"For fuck's sake Davie, what's going on? I couldn't believe it when I heard. Two Lee Enfield rifles in your boot? Were you trying to get caught or something? All I could think was that you must have been pissed."

Davie leaned back against the concrete wall and lit a cigarette.

"Of course I was wanting to get caught. Christ Billy. Give me a bit of credit will you. I'm not that daft."

"So why?"

Davie blew smoke up towards the fluorescent light on the ceiling. "I got a whisper. The Brits had passed all my details to the INLA. They lined me up for a hit. This seemed the safest place to hang out for a while."

"What did they tell them? Not the Ghost stuff surely."

"No. No chance. The Brits will bury all that stuff in as deep a hole as they can find. It was all the rest. The Army. 14th Intelligence. All of it."

Billy let out a low whistle. "The bastards. The cold hearted, devious bastards."

"And then some."

They were quiet for a while and then Billy chuckled to himself.

"It's bloody ironic though."

"What?"

"That in order to steer clear of the INLA you wind up coming here."

"Why?"

Billy gave a short bark of a laugh. "You've not heard then. The INLA are our neighbours. Seriously. Right across the yard in the next block. I had a word with the screws about it last week. They've got some really bad boys in there. Last week Clip McWilliams and John Kennaway came in. It's nuts. There we all are either side of the fence. The only bastards still at war with each other in the whole of Ireland. I asked them why the hell they are doing it. I told them. Told them it was plain stupid and they should move us to another block."

"What did they say?"

"Said they couldn't. Said it would cost too much. Said that the budgets were being cut to hell, what with peace and all. I suppose it'll be OK. Just insults and stones and stuff."

"Who's on the wing here?"

"A bit of everything. There's a few of our people. They sent in a few of the UFF lads who refused to agree the cease-fire. Bit of a mixed bag. Good lads by and large. It's no great hardship. We try to keep everyone busy. Lessons. Drill. Bit of training. You know the kind of thing."

"Aye."

"Don't worry about it. The time will soon pass. They reckon we'll all be out in a couple of years. The war will wait. It always does."

Davie lay on his bunk and stared out of the small window. Outside it was one of those December mornings when the day barely seemed able to find the energy to get light. A few snowflakes fluttered across the gunmetal grey of the sky. His head was throbbing slightly. The day before there had been a Christmas party on the block and they had broken out the moonshine. It had been a half-hearted affair. They had all tried to make it something, but it was never anything more than a sad little affair. The last few months had been hard on all of them. The IRA had once again announced a cease-fire and this time it really did seem like the real thing. The peace process was picking up momentum with every day that passed. The Tories had finally been kicked out of office and their New Labour successors were driving forward for peace with the zeal of people with no skeletons in their lockers. There was a carnival atmosphere across the Province.

All of a sudden the LVF seemed to be yesterday's men. They had become out of step with the mood of the times. They were the dinosaurs. It was hard for Billy to keep a sense of purpose inside H6. All of them felt that with every day that passed they were being left further behind. An air of gloom had settled over them. The party had not done much to alleviate it.

As he stared vacantly out at the snow Davie wondered how many men had done the same before him. So many of them. Men from all sides of the tracks - Provies, Officials, INLA, UVF, UDA and now his own LVF. All of them fighting the endless little war for their own ends. Sometimes it was all about great dreaming visions of a United Ireland or socialism for all. Other times it was down to settling niggling little scores among neighbours that had festered for years. How many? Thousands and thousands. Moving along the conveyor belt of the Kesh. And now he was one of them. Sliding through the slow days. Reading. Time in the gym. Staring up at the sky from the yard. Not thinking about the time. Just letting it drift. Just treading water. Biding time. Waiting for the next chapter in his life.

Billy stuck his head through the door.

"How's the head?"

"Bloody awful. You look chipper."

Billy smiled. "Aye. Got a visit. See you later."

Billy made his way to the end of the block where the corridor met the cross bar of the H. The warders rattled their keys and clanked the heavy locks open. It was Jackson. He was all right. Billy usually had a crack with Jackson. But not today. Today Jackson wasn't for talking. The skin seemed tight on his thin face. Billy shrugged. Probably because of Christmas. Everybody seemed to have their 'domestics' at Christmas.

The others were the same. All of them quiet. Tense. Up tight. So much for the Christmas cheer. They were all as miserable as sin. Billy held his hands out for the cuffs to be snapped on.

"Fucking Hell lads, cheer up. It might never happen."

No laughter. No smiles. Nothing. What the hell was going on? They led him out into the yard where the minibus waited to take him to the visiting block a few hundred yards away. He had a bad feeling now. Really bad. There was something not right at all. He glanced up at the watchtower on the corner of the yard. Empty. Strange. He checked the tower at the opposite corner. Empty. What the hell was happening?

The sliding door of the van was already open. There were two lads waiting in the back. He knew them slightly. He nodded. They nodded back. The bad feeling was all over him now.

Footsteps. Footsteps running across the gravel of the yard. A voice. Shouting. He started to pull himself off the bench seat. A figure crowded into the space of the sliding door. His heart seemed to stop dead in its tracks. Eye to eye. Just four feet away.

It was Clip McWilliams. Clip McWilliams with a huge grin on his face. Clip McWilliams with a rifle in his hands. For a moment Billy felt paralysed. Then he tried to force himself forward. He pushed his hands out. He tried to kick at the gun. Then the blows came. One. Two. Three. Hard bruising thumps to his chest and his shoulders. Four. Five. The sound had caught up with the hammer blows and the flashes from the muzzle of the gun now. The sound of the shots roared around the inside of the van. Six. Seven. He was falling back now. Back down to the dirty metal floor of the van. Eight. Nine. It didn't seem to matter any more. No point in fighting it. It was done. Ten. Eleven. Just a case of a short wait. The blackness was on him now. Just as he had always known it would be. It was coming in great waves. There was no pain. No real suffering. Just the blackness of death. His brain was barely flickering now. There were only hints of thoughts. Shreds of memories. Then the blackness swallowed him completely.

40 minutes later he was dead.

Something died inside Davie that day. The day they gunned down Billy. He had leapt from his bed and tried to haul himself up to the window to see when the sound of the shots split the quiet winter air. For a while he had been boiling with rage. All of them had. Especially as the rumours started. No men in the watchtowers. A fence A fence cut the day before. Two men over the roof with guns and nobody to see them. And Clip McWilliams and Sonny Glennon handing their guns in as cool as you like. The sheer audacity of the whole thing took the breath away.

The Brits wanted their peace and Billy had just become too big a thorn in their side. The solution had been easy. Just tell the INLA that they would be happy to turn a blind eye. Let them transfer Clip McWilliams onto H6 and allow the guns to be smuggled in. Let the fence be cut. Leave the towers empty and let the dirty work be done. Unbelievable. But true. True because Billy was filled with holes and dead. The whole of Portadown had ground to a halt for his funeral. There was a spate of tit-for-tat killings, but it soon blew over. The British were masters at the long game. It was a short-term embarrassment but it would all soon be forgotten. And by and large everybody was happy to see the back of Billy 'King Rat' Wright. There was a rare unity in the celebrations. The IRA were happy. The INLA were cock-a-hoop with themselves. The UDA and UVF were glad to see the back of him. And the Brits could move along serenely to the peace that would at last get them out of the mire.

All the will to fight drained out of Davie. What was the point? The odds were impossible. The whole of the bloody planet had turned against his people. They had become everybody's bad guys. They were up there with the Boers and the Serbs and the Iraqis. Nobody cared a damn what happened to them. Their time was over. Now it was time for everyone to move on whether they liked it or not. It was all too much. He'd had enough. For day after day he just stared out of the window of his cell and brooded.

The letter came two months after Billy's funeral. Air mail. American stamps. He opened it with a flicker of interest.

Dear Davie,

Please accept my sympathy. I have been where you are now. I will never forget the days and weeks that followed the death of Bobby Sands in 1981. Bobby was both a great man and a great friend. I have never learned to properly come to terms with his loss. I know little about Billy. I dare say all the stuff in the press is probably as wrong as it was about Bobby. I guess that you were close and now you too must learn to come to terms with it. It defies belief that men are still behind the wire in that wretched place after all these years. My time eventually ended and so will yours. I wouldn't insult your intelligence by saying that a normal happy life is waiting for you. That would be wrong. However I can confirm that a life of sorts is available. I have one. It's OK. So keep the faith. Time passes. And thanks to the likes of me and Bobby at least you get to wear your own clothes!

Ciao,
Sean.

For the first time in weeks Davie smiled. It wasn't much of a smile. There was nobody there to see it. Just a flicker. He folded the letter carefully and put it in his breast pocket.

He pulled his knees up to his chest and watched a pair of crows as they flapped across the grey Irish sky.

Part Three
Terrible Beauty

Chapter 12
Rage

Autumn 2002

Bru Dempsey was having a bad day. A really bad day. It had started well enough. It had started with a massive fry-up in the café and a few pints in the pub. It had carried on fine as the ten of them had piled into the back of a mini bus and made their way across town to Ibrox. They had gone through all the well-rehearsed rituals of an Old Firm Match. Their bus was decked out on Union Flags. They hung out of the windows on the M8 and screamed abuse at car loads of Celtic fans. They swilled down cans of beer until their bladders nearly burst. By the time they reached the stadium, their voices were already raw from singing.

It was a ritual. Their ritual. And they enjoyed it at least four times a year. The bitter Old Firm rivalry had been at the very heart of Bru's life for as long as he could remember. His dad had first taken him to an Old Firm game when he was four years old. It had been all very different then. Most of the crowd had been standing up. His dad had found him a place where he could sit on a wall. There had been no corporate boxes then. In fact football on the whole had been on its uppers. It was only when the Glasgow rivals played each other that the stadium was ever full. But that day, the sheer unrelenting noise and violence of the occasion had rooted itself deep inside him. From that day onwards his bedroom wall was all Rangers. From that day onwards his club moved to the forefront of his life.

Even at five Bru was a big lad. He had earned his nickname because of his passion for drinking Iron Bru. All the way through his school days his size had marked him out. He was never the brightest star in the firmament when it came to his schoolwork. It never seemed to matter much. His mum and dad certainly were never bothered. He had little interest in being a star of the classroom. The playground was always his preferred environment. The playground was the place where he could stand out. Here he was always the hard man. The best fighter. The 'cock of the year'.

As he got older the fighting spread beyond the playground. And, more often than not, Rangers was the Cause that he fought for. There were always fights among the kids from his school and the Catholic school a few hundred yards down the road. Sometimes these were chance affairs at bus stops or outside newsagents shops. Other times they were managed. Things would be arranged and groups would gather on areas of waste ground to fight it out.

It wasn't anything that he ever questioned. Hating the Catholics was something that he had just grown up with. His dad hated them. His grandad hated them. It was something that was carved in stone. It was never something that was ever debated. There didn't need to be any particular reason for it. It was just the way it was. The way it always had been.

The 90's was a golden decade for Bru. He kept growing and by the time he was twelve he was the apple of the eye of all the coaches at the local boxing club. He won his fights and he got talked about. The men in the bars would consider it over their pints on a Saturday night. Too soon to tell of course, but maybe. Maybe he would go all the way. Maybe in a few years time they could all go up to the Kelvin Hall and watch him fight for a title. The boxing was only a part of his fighting life. The other part was lived out on the streets.

And the 90's was an uninterrupted golden era for his beloved Rangers. Title followed title. Butcher, Gough, McCoist, Goram, Laudrup, Gascoine. It seemed as if there was an unending conveyor belt of greatness in those heady days. It was a time when Celtic never got a look in. A time where defeat was unknown. A time where life didn't seem like it would get much better. He stopped growing when he hit six four. By the time he was eighteen he was getting paid for his nights in the ring. Sometimes five hundred quid. Sometimes a couple of grand. Designer clothes. A different girl every week. And he kept on winning. So did Rangers.

The wheels came off with the New Millennium. He made it to his night at Kelvin Hall. The night that the men in the bars had wondered about for years. He didn't fight for a title. He was just the under card. But it was still a step up. For the first time the television cameras were there. And half of Burnside turned out to watch the big man take another big step forward. And it all went wrong. The opponent from Wolverhampton was three inches shorter, twenty pounds lighter and about a hundred times quicker. Bru barely saw a punch. Within a minute the jabs were draining the energy from his legs. There was nothing that he could do to stop it. He floundered around the ring like a great wounded buffalo. Within twenty seconds of the second round it was all over.

People were embarrassed with him for a while. The talk in the bars was different now. They had seen it all before. There were lots who looked as if they had it. Big enough. Strong enough. But in the end it was always down to class. It didn't matter how big you were if you didn't have the class. And they had all seen it that night in Kelvin Hall. Bru didn't have the class. The lad from down south had made him look silly.

He kept on fighting. Mostly the bare knuckle stuff now. The money was OK, but now he only won half the time. He had lost most of his self-belief. Now he was getting hurt. Sometimes badly. But there was nothing else. He had no qualifications. He had always assumed that fighting would give him a living.

As Bru fell from grace, Rangers fell with him. Martin O'Neil came up to Celtic Park and everything changed. Now it was Rangers who became the whipping boys. One by one the great faces left or retired. They were replaced by a group of foreigners and a Dutch coach and none of them seemed to have the heart.

The lid came off after the first Celtic win at Ibrox in years. Bru and the lads had finished their night of sorrow drowning in a city centre nightclub. A group of Celtic fans were singing loudly in a corner. Bru lost the plot. He waded in smashing a broken bottle into every leering face he could find. For a few moments the place disintegrated into a chaotic brawl, and Bru was right there in the middle flailing his bottle that was now soaked red.

An hour later he was in the cells. A month later he was in Barlinnie Prison. He stayed there for two years. When he got out in the summer of 2002, he emerged into a world that didn't suit him at all. It seemed that most of his mates had either married and settled down or moved away. He was unemployed and unemployable. The days dragged by. At least things were looking up on the football front. The arrival of Alex McCleish as the new manager in the spring had reawakened hope amongst the Rangers faithful. Celtic had still strolled to the league title, but Rangers had lifted both cups in titanic encounters with the old enemy. The new season looked a whole lot better.

The bubble was popped as early as September as a rampant Celtic demolished Rangers 3 – 0 in the first Old Firm game of the season. By the time Bru took his seat at Ibrox for the second encounter Rangers were already trailing their rivals by seven points. It was only November but it was already make or break. And things started well. Really well. In the seventeenth minute the blues burst up the field and took the lead. For a while Bru forgot all the troubles of his fast disintegrating life. Rangers moved up three gears and pinned the green shirts back into their own half. Pressure. Near miss. Corner. Pushing. Penalty. Groans as Ferguson put it wide. And then, within seconds of the half time whistle, the hated shaven head of Henrik Larsson put Celtic back on level terms.

The second half turned into a slow, lingering nightmare. Celtic scored twice more. Rangers barely got a kick. By the time the final whistle went the blue seats of the home supporters were nearly empty. Bru felt the rage grow inside him as he made his way from the ground. Behind him the Celtic fans sang and sang. Mocked and mocked. Rubbed it in. Not just a win. A win, and a ten point lead, and the league more or less over and done with before Christmas. They were celebrating a humiliation. Not just for Rangers. It didn't seem that way to Bru. It seemed like they were singing to him alone. Rubbing it in.

They drove back to Burnside and fell into the pub. Bru drank mechanically. He was in no mood to talk. Others kept a distance. There was something about Bru that wasn't quite right any more. Ever since he had come back from Barlinnie. He was like an unexploded bomb. Fair enough, it had been a rough time for the big man. But still. Better to stay out of the way. He was trouble waiting to happen.

Four of them left at ten o'clock.

As he made his way slightly unsteadily down the street Bru spotted a familiar figure. It was Lenny O'Donnell. He and Lenny had been sparring partners for as long as Bru could remember. They were the same age and had moved through school at the same time. Lenny had been at St. Theresa's, the Catholic school a few streets away. They had been having run-ins from the age of seven. Bru had got the better of most of them. Lenny was wearing his Celtic shirt and was eating a tray of chips with two mates.

Bru never hesitated. Not even for a nano-second. The frustration of the day burst over. The frustration of his life burst over. He was running. Pounding down the pavement. His three mates looked at each other for a couple of seconds then followed. There was a gap of 50 yards to close. He willed O'Donnell and his friends not to move. He willed them to stand and fight.

When he was twenty yards short of them the scene started to change. There were more or them. Lots more, coming out of the chip shop in a rush. They were soon six. Then nine. Then twelve. Bru sensed a faltering in the footsteps behind him. His three friends who were fifteen yards behind stopped. Then turned. Then fled. For Bru it was too late. He was big and he was strong but he had never been fast. If he tried to run they would catch him in no time. He was stuffed. No choice. He never checked his stride. He launched himself into O'Donnell with his fists and boots flailing.

It didn't last long. They had him down within seconds. Kicks rained in on him. He covered himself as best he could and took it. It wouldn't last for that long. Just a kicking he told himself. Grit your teeth and take it. But he soon realised that it was going to get worse. Much worse.

They dragged him into an alley. Into a backyard with dustbins. A cat scuttled over the fence at the back. There was litter everywhere. He tried to get to his feet. Hopeless. Too many. All kicking. Down again. Down and trying to make himself into a ball.

Now they were pulling him out of the ball. Pulling at his arms and legs. Opening him up. He writhed but there was not much strength left now. A feeling of complete helplessness was starting to take him over. Bastards. Lousy fucking Fenian bastards. And there was fear now. Real fear. Fear the like of which he had never known before. Fear that sapped his strength. Fear that took away his ability to struggle. Fear at the leering figure of Lenny O'Donnell who stood over him. Fear at the pleasure written all over O'Donnell's face. A handful of greasy chip wrapping was pushed into his mouth. He could feel his eyes bulging. Bulging like they were going to pop clean out of the sockets. He wanted to scream, to roar, to howl, but instead the cold grease on the paper made him want to gag.

O'Donnell was smiling now. A devil in a green and white shirt. He was saying something but Bru had been kicked too many times to hear him. His head was just a bucket of noise. Static. Pain.

One of the lads was running back up the alley. He had been somewhere. An errand. Christ. What was going on? They were pulling at his trousers now. Pulling them down. Down over his thrashing legs. Now his pants. Oh for fuck's sake. No way. Please Christ no. But the begging was all in his mind. All he could do was thrash and writhe as O'Donnell crouched down. There was a sudden hot feeling all around his groin. His penis. His testicles. And O'Donnell was laughing now. All of them were. Laughing as if it were the best joke there had ever been. His pants were back up now. And his trousers. What had they done? What the fuck had they done? O'Donnell was talking all the while. Talking and grinning but Bru couldn't hear a word. Then O'Donnell was waving something in his face. What the hell? What was that? Then he knew. He knew exactly where the lad had been sent for his errand. He had been a few yards down the street to the newsagents that stayed open to eleven on a Saturday night. He had been to buy a tube of Superglue.

They left him in a heap in the yard. Slowly his hearing came back enough to register the gurgling of the drain as the rain lashed down. He was soaked through. Moving was almost impossible.

His limbs were on fire. He managed at last to crawl. He crawled out of the alley through the litter and the chip papers. He made it to the pavement before he collapsed. A passer-by found him ten minutes later.

Davie looked around the room with familiar distaste. He seemed to have lived out great chunks of his life in rooms like the one where he now sat. Bare rooms. Miserable rooms. Government rooms where the budget never ran beyond cheap paint and gallons of disinfectant. Rooms to wait in. Rooms where you sat and waited to be told what was next. There had been so many of these rooms during his days in 14th Intelligence. Miserable rooms off miserable corridors. Strip lighting and lino. Functional. Never comfortable.

This time it was a hospital waiting room. Ten feet by ten feet. The chairs had green plastic cushions. There was a small coffee table made from chipboard with twelve month old copies of 'Hello' magazine. A moronic looking young girl who didn't look as if she had eaten in six years grinned up at him from the well-fingered cover. He leaned back and rested his head against the wall and closed his eyes. As ever the pain was chewing at him.

The pain had started eighteen months before. At first he had thought that it was food poisoning. He stayed in bed and tried to force the pain away with whisky. It faded, but it never went. It lasted for too long to be food poisoning. He wondered if it was something in his diet. Maybe. Everyone seemed to be getting food allergies these days. He spent months trying different regimes. He took every vitamin that he could find. He took garlic and cod liver oil and went on the wagon. Sometimes it got better for a while. But each time it got worse it was worse than the time before.

He had put off the doctor. He didn't like doctors. He never had. But in the end the pain was too much to deal with. The doctor had pushed and poked and shaken his head. He didn't know. There would have to be tests. And there were tests. Lots of tests at the hospital. Nothing we can say straight away Mr Stanton. We'll have to wait for the results Mr Stanton. Do you have anything for the pain? Take these. They are very good. They'll help. It should be less than a fortnight. You will get an appointment card. In the post. Try to take it easy. Try not to worry.

Taking it easy was no problem. That was all there was these days. Taking it easy. He had been let out of Long Kesh in 1999 as part of the Good Friday Agreement. The two-and-a-half years behind the wire had sapped him of his strength. He tried to avoid it. He exercised. He read. He did all that he could. But he could never seem to find the heart after Billy. In end he just sat and did his time.

He could not come to terms with the pointlessness of his life. The Peace was a joke. A sick joke. The Peace was a fudge job that was designed to give the Brits an excuse to walk away. And all the parties agreed to it. It wasn't what any of them wanted. But people were tired. They'd had enough. It was better than nothing. There was no victory, but there was no surrender either. It put off the moment of truth for a while. It gave breathing space.

For a while he tried to resume his career as a freelancer. It didn't last long. Nobody wanted to know him. Not when the word got around that he was fresh out of the Kesh. Not when they heard he had been on the LVF wing. Not when he was associated with those nutters. Drug pushers. Maniacs.

For a while he would scan the columns of jobs in the evening paper. Then he gave up. Who would want a man with his CV? Good exams. Good degree. Three years a soldier. A five year black hole covered by the Official Secrets Act, a couple of years as a journalist and two and a half years in Long Kesh in the LVF wing. He came to terms with being unemployable. A man who had skills that nobody wanted any more. A worn out relic of a war that everyone was trying to forget as fast as they could.

For a year he had waited for a bullet. Would James Hamilton want to dot his I's and cross his T's. If he did, then there was nothing that Davie could do about it. He made a few enquiries into his old friend. It was no surprise to find that the Hamilton career was still locked in fifth gear. It was Brigadier Hamilton now. Military Intelligence. James's face kept popping up on the internet search engines. He was a man for the cameras in Kosovo. Smooth as ever. The well-groomed face of British peacekeeping. He was young for a Brigadier. He was on the fast track.

After a year Davie accepted the fact that the bullet would never come. In a way the acceptance was a disappointment. His life had lost all direction. He had no family. No job. No hobbies. He was driftwood. A relic.

He eventually gave up looking for a job. He joined the biggest club on the Shankhill. He signed on. He stood in line and put his name on the dotted line with all the others. The young girl had wriggled nervously in her seat when she had perused his CV. She had given him a brave smile and told him that they would do what they could. But it was not easy, she said. Times were hard, she said. What she neglected to mention was that employers were not queuing up to take on ex-paramilitaries.

There was one area where he could have easily found work. Within a week of his release he got word from the Shankill UFF. They could use a man like him if he wanted in. There would be money and a good place at the bar on a Saturday night. They always wanted good men. Experienced men. Men who had been around the block a time or two. And there was lots of work. Protection work. Drug work. Once Davie would have lost his temper. Once he would have backed them up and told them exactly what he thought of them. But he had felt far too tired. Too old. Too washed out. He had just shaken his head and walked away.

For two years he had done nothing. He spent his time sitting in the house gazing at the TV. Sometimes he would walk for miles and miles across the city. Sometimes he would take the bus down to the old caravan on the coast. He slowly disappeared into himself. And then the pain had started.

The door opened and a nurse came in. She had a clipboard and short hair. No smile. Too many hours to smile. "Mr Stanton?"

"Yes."

"The doctor is ready for you now."

The consultant's room was rather more cosy. There were certificates on the walls and watercolours of the North Coast. There were photos of smiling children. There was a flourishing rubber plant. Out of the window there was a fine view of Belfast. The doctor had an avuncular, tweedy air about him. He had bushy white hair and pens lined up in his breast pocket.

Davie sat and the doctor opened a brown file and frowned. He entwined his fingers and leaned forward with his elbows on the desk. Davie noticed that there were leather patches on the elbows of the jacket. It was something that you didn't see much any more.

The old man weighed his words for a moment. A brief shadow of regret flitted across his eyes. Davie knew then that what was coming was not going to be good. He saw that the man was struggling to find a place to start. He decided that the best thing was to help out.

"Maybe the best thing to do is to just tell it straight Doctor. Best for both of us."

The doctor nodded. "OK. Fair enough. The news is bad Mr Stanton. Very bad. You have cancer of the bowel. It is well advanced. I expect that there has been pain for some time?"

"There has."

Again a nod. "I fear it is too far advanced. We can try treatment of course. But I must warn you that there is little likelihood of success."

So here it was. How ridiculous. It wasn't Crossmaglen. It wasn't Tumbledown. It was a small room on the fourth floor of the infirmary. A bullet called cancer. The cloak of death was wrapping itself around him. He felt almost detached as he studied his emotions. He felt more or less nothing. A vague despondency. Nothing more. He had been expecting something like this.

He looked up at the doctor. "How long?"

"It's not easy to say. Six months. Maybe a year. You look strong. I would say a year."

"How will I be?"

"The pain will get worse I'm afraid. Not dramatically. Slowly. We can help you with it of course. I will leave you to consider things. Treatment is an option of course."

"Treatment means sickness, right? Time in the hospital. Months of it."

"Correct."

Davie gave a small shake of his head. "No. I don't want that. I'll say no. Thanks. But no."

The doctor looked understanding.

"I'm very sorry Mr Stanton."

Davie got to his feet and extended his hand. "Yes. Of course. Thank you. I'll be going now."

The doctor looked at the closed door for a few minutes before opening his next file. What a very strange man. It was almost as if he had been glad. Very strange.

It took Bru a month to get out of the infirmary. The net result of his injuries was three cracked ribs, a broken wrist, any number of bruises, and an unholy mess in his nether regions. With each day that passed on the ward, his rage grew and festered. It hadn't taken long for the nature of his main problem to get around. Soon there were sniggers and amused glances. It had been all of them. Doctors. Nurses. Fellow patients. At first he had been tempted to lash out and give it to them. But he hadn't. Instead he turned the rage inside. Before the beating his life had become directionless. Not any more. No way. Now he had all the direction that he needed. It was a direction that would lead him to Lenny O'Donnell in particular and anyone in a green and white shirt in general.

It was December before he was back on his feet. There had plenty of time for him to come up with his plan. Endless hours on the ward. Hours through the nights when he was too warm to sleep. Hours through the day in the midst of the smirking and the giggling. He came up with a plan that had the virtue of complete simplicity. It needed little preparation. It was based on a single piece of vital intelligence. On Thursday nights Lenny O'Donnell played for the pool team in the Fiddler's Rest.

At eight o'clock on the next Thursday evening Bru was waiting in the car park at the back of the pub. It was a cold night and the sky above was clear. It promised to bring the first real frost of the winter. He had found a good place to hide in a fenced in area where the wheelie-bins were stored. There was a window that looked into the area at the back of the main bar where there were two pool tables. A little after five past eight he spotted the figure of Lenny O'Donnell chatting with two other players.

Time. No point in putting it off. Just do it. He reached into his jacket pocket and took out his lighter. He lit the soaked cloth that he had stuffed into the top of a king size whisky bottle filled with petrol. He took the bottle in his left hand. He used his right hand to smack the window with a small lump hammer. He didn't bother to look through to see what the reaction was inside. He simply tossed in the bottle and started to run. He had only covered a few yards when he heard the thumping sound of the igniting petrol. He didn't look back. By the time he was a hundred yards away he could hear screaming. He was in his car and well away when the first items appeared on the radio news.

Reggie McAlister was one of the lucky ones. He was on the home team. The draw had just been made and he wasn't on until the third game. He had gone for a piss. Then he had gone to the bar to get a round in. He had just turned with the tray of drinks when the petrol bomb had ignited. The force of the blast had thrown him back against the bar. The drinks had gone everywhere. Once his ears began to adjust, the scene in front of him took his breath away. There were four men on fire. He reacted remarkably well. Instincts that he would never have suspected kicked in. He grabbed overcoats from the pegs and dived onto the first of the men. Others followed suit. Their actions stopped what were serious burns from becoming life-threatening. The landlord soon put out the rest of the flames with fire extinguishers.

The screaming was soon an awful sound. All four men were writhing with the pain. Lenny O'Donnell was the worst. His face was barely recognisable. McAlister found others to help and held the victims to the floor. They got ice from the freezer and did what they could to cover the wounds with freezing bar cloths until the ambulances arrived. McAlister was a hard man but he was badly shaken. He had seen his fair share of injuries in his time. Hell, he had inflicted a few himself. But this was different. This made you want to throw up.

The ambulance came first. Then the police. Statements were taken. People in the bar were asked about motive. The same answer came up time and again. It was obvious, wasn't it. Everyone knew about The Fiddler's Rest. The Fiddler's Rest was a Celtic pub. This was the work of some Rangers nutter. The police filled their notebooks. They photographed the scene. They checked the area outside the window. They should have investigated a little more deeply. Had they spent a bit of time looking into the four men who were raced to the burns unit, they might just have made the connection. They might just have put two and two together.

They didn't. They put it down as a random sectarian attack. No prints. No sighting. No chance. They hoped that they would get a whisper at some stage. After a week the Republican community of Burnside started to cry foul. The police didn't care. The police were sweeping the thing under the carpet. And their anger grew.

Two Saturdays before Christmas, McAlister tapped into the anger. He gathered together fifteen men and they attacked the Unicorn pub with baseball bats. They wore black balaclavas. Witnesses inside the pub told of their manic rage as they hit out at anything that moved. Fifteen of the customers spent the night in hospital. One of them never came out. He was Angus Rogerson, a 68-year-old pensioner who died at five o'clock the next morning of a massive brain haemorrhage.

This time the motive was clear for all to see. The Unicorn had a large picture of the Queen over the bar.

It was raining when Davie came out of the front door of the infirmary. For a moment he considered taking a taxi home. To what? The cold emptiness of the house seemed barely tolerable. Instead he walked. He walked through the winter rain like a man in a trance. He didn't think much about where he was going. He just walked.

He didn't really know what to make of the news. In many ways he was lucky. He had no family. No great responsibilities. He wouldn't leave much of a hole when he died. There were a few that would care, but not many. In many ways the news was a relief. For months he had found the prospect of the rest of his life to be a painful subject. At least it was all taken care of now. There were no great decisions to be made. Just one really. Should he see out his time and deal with the pain that the next few months would bring? Or should he get it over and done with quickly? Take a short cut with a bullet through the head?

The question rolled around his brain as he walked. He was wet now. The driving rain had penetrated his coat and the sweater underneath. Wet and cold but it didn't seem to matter much. He was beginning to feel a little better now that he had shovelled away much of the clutter from his thoughts. He liked the idea of the single decision. He smiled as he remembered words from his English A level. Good old Hamlet. To be or not to be. Absolutely bloody right. That was the question. Take the pain or eat the bullet.

He was at the bottom of the Shankill now. It was deadly quiet. It was no afternoon to be outside. He stood for a moment and stared down the street as it wound its way up towards the grey hills that overlooked the city. How changed it all was. Many of the old terraces had been demolished. In their place were new maisonettes. No doubt in the eyes of the architects and the planners the open spaces that surrounded the small new estates would give the residents somewhere to have picnics or throw Frisbees. How pathetic. The grass was littered with empty bottles and assorted garbage. There was a small playground. Nothing worked. All trashed. The roundabout was daubed in graffiti. He kicked at the floor in distaste. Needles. Just dumped on the floor next to the see-saw that had been smashed in the middle.

It was what they had come to. The proud Loyalist people of the Shankhill. The ones who had followed Carson all the way to Thiepval Wood. This was how it had all ended up. Junkie needles in the playground. Young people who had grown up through the Troubles into a peace that was a lie. No jobs. No ideals. No future. And instead of trying to provide leadership the paramilitaries provided heroin.

He wandered across the waste ground and came to a square of murals. It was a strange place. In their wisdom the authorities had demolished a square of terraces and done nothing with the space in the middle. Only the houses were gone. The streets and the kerbstones had been left in place. And the lampposts. Every kerb was carefully painted red, white and blue And every lamppost.

The streets that remained backed onto the empty space on three sides. This meant that the square had about fifteen gable ends looking on to it. Every one carried a mural. The desolate place had become a Loyalist gallery. He sat down on a low wall and struggled to light a cigarette.

In a way the murals painted the story of his life. Maybe it was the story of all their lives. There was Carson. All those years before. His thin determined face with the strong eyes as he looked up from the table in the City Hall as he signed the Covenant in 1912. The same Covenant that his grandad had signed. What would they have made of things now? A few months before Belfast had elected it's first Sinn Fein Mayor. Unthinkable. Unimaginable. A Catholic in the citadel of Carson's state.

Two along was the mural they had painted of his grandad. The artist had used the old photo from the lounge wall. A young Peter Stanton stood tall and heroic in front of a backdrop of the Somme. The Victoria Cross that in life he had been so reluctant to wear took pride of place in his line of medals. "Peter Stanton. 1898 - 1987. He never surrendered." Davie had often wondered what Peter would have made of the mural. He would have probably hated it. It wasn't his thing. Davie had always rather liked it. There were plenty of faces that stared from the gable ends of terraced streets all over Ulster who had no right to be there. Tin pot little terrorists from both sides. If anyone was worth a mural it was Peter Stanton.

And then of course there was Billy. The sight of him staring out from the wall gave Davie a stab of sadness. Billy might have been one of the best of them. Cut down by the Brits because he refused to compromise. Because he wouldn't accept second-best for his people. Part of Davie wished that he had been in the back of the van with him that day. The last five years had been barely worth living. And now all there was to wait for was death.

The sight of the next mural made him chuckle. Little did anyone know. The Ghost was about to become a real Ghost. He remembered how they had laughed when the mural was finally finished. The three of them. Him and Derek and Richard. They had stood and completely cracked up. On the wall the cartoon Ghost held a sniper's rifle over its head in triumph. At its feet lay the bleeding figure of a masked man. In the background the flag of Ulster flew at full mast. The caption read "The Ghost. 1987 - ?". Underneath was the promise "There to haunt the IRA forever."

The Ghost hadn't haunted a soul for five years. And now it would never haunt again. What had the killings achieved? For a while it seemed as if the legend of the Ghost might have actually done something to turn the tide. For a while in the early nineties it had seemed as if the IRA were really on the brink of defeat. But then the desperate truth of the situation had really emerged. Without the British his people had nothing. Once the British had lost the will to carry on the fight his people had been left defenceless. If only their own leaders had been of a better calibre it might have been different. If there had been another Carson maybe they would have been able to hold back the tide.

But Billy had been their last chance of another Carson. And Billy was gone. Everybody was gone. All that was left were the drug dealers and the gangsters. His people had all but given up. There were some who fought. Futile little weekend battles over a few yards of housing. And every time they fought they looked worse in the eyes of the world.

He shuddered when he remembered the fiasco at the Holy Cross School. The whole world had looked on. All over the planet heads were shaken in disgust. And why not? What the hell else were people expected to do at the sight of a mob of middle-aged men in masks swearing and spitting at five-year-old schoolgirls. For what? Because they didn't want then to use their road to walk to school. And then some moron had thrown a blast bomb. A blast bomb. Of all things. They had actually thrown a blast bomb at five-year-old kids. Even now, eighteen months later, he found himself seething with anger.

The cameras had played out the whole episode to a disgusted audience. And instead of apologising there had been those who had actually tried to justify it. Unbelievable. And all of a sudden everyone had started to hate his people. Their whistles and drums and orange sashes and bowler hats became the symbols of shame. Contempt. Loathing. These were the people who threw bombs at little schoolgirls. Irish Serbs. Irish Boers. Irish Nazis. To make matters worse, various lunatic far right groups from all over the world started to affiliate themselves with the UDA and the UFF.

And all the time Gerry Adams and Martin McGuinness smoothly smiled their way through their press conferences. All of a sudden they were senior statesmen in nicely cut suits. They spoke the language of the new Millennium. They were sensible and educated and thoughtful and reasonable. They played well wherever they went. And of course everyone liked them. Everyone was taken in by them. They showed the world that leopards could indeed change their spots. These were not the kind of guys who would throw bombs at schoolgirls. No way. These were the men of peace. The men who had ended 30 years of suffering. They had become everybody's good guys.

For Davie these thoughts were a stuck record. The events of the last few years had eaten away at him. It had been one thing after another. An endless series of idiotic blunders on his own side. Blunders carried out by ignorant buffoons. In a world that was now dominated by the sound bite and spin and slick PR, these blunders had catastrophic implications. Every year the world looked on with distaste as a small group of skinheads hurled stones at the police barrier at Drumcree. This was how his people were now seen. Swearing skinheads and grim faced men in bowler hats. It was the only time on the news that they ever got.

It didn't seem to matter what the Republicans did any more. They could beat lads with metal rods and nobody cared. They could take the kneecaps from teenagers and nobody cared. They could try out their new generation of weapons with the guerrillas of Colombia and nobody cared. It was always shrugged aside. Just a small minority. A few nutters who had broken away. Nothing serious. Even when they had broken into Castlereigh and stolen 30 years of secrets, it barely warranted more than a few inches of news space. They had managed to get hold of the name of every Special Branch officer, every informant, every secret file and nobody seemed to give a damn.

For months Davie had sensed the enemy getting stronger. Behind the smooth façade of Sinn Fein, the hard men were out there, quietly marshalling their forces. All the time the clock was ticking. Time was running out. He didn't believe the reassuring words from the smooth politicians. The IRA hadn't all of a sudden become nice people. Nice people didn't take the kneecaps of those who chose to disagree with them. They were simply waiting. And they had all the patience in the world. Little by little the British were pulling back. The watchtowers of South Armagh were being dismantled. Most of the barracks were closed. Every year there were less troops in the Province. The RUC had been dismantled and the new Police Force of Northern Ireland seemed powerless. In a few years there would be nobody left to stem a new assault.

Once again his eyes were drawn to the mural of his grandfather. Thank god he hadn't lived to see how things had turned out. Maybe the bomb of the Shankill had been a blessing in disguise. At least he had missed the worst of it. Defeat he could have lived with. But there had been no defeat. Instead there had been surrender. Surrender of the worst kind. Surrender form a position of strength. Surrender because a new generation couldn't be bothered any more.

The mural's cartoon image of Thiepval Wood took him all the way back 36 years. He closed his eyes and allowed the rain to pour down his face. Out of the mists of the past he found the voice of his grandfather. One day there will be time when the people of Ulster will need you Davie. One day. Well nobody could ever say that he had not tried his best. In his own way he had fought the IRA as hard as anyone. But a war needed more than individuals. It needed armies. And armies needed people behind them that cared. Otherwise all that any of the soldiers could ever achieve were a series of futile gestures.

Maybe that was all his life had been. 44 years of worthless defiance. Years of fighting for a cause that nobody cared about any more. A war that could never be won because the vast majority of the army had simply thrown its weapons to the ground and made its way home. Maybe that was all it had been. Just a waste. A huge, empty, monumental waste.

He opened his eyes and found three lads in front of him. They wore the new uniform of the Shankill young. Trainers. Tracksuits. Baseball caps. Always baseball caps. There was something about baseball caps that really got on his nerves. He saw the violence in their thin pale faces. It was the violence that they had grown up with. All they knew. All that anything was about. It was where things had come to. Be violent. Get what you want. That was all the Shankill was now. A sad, tired, filthy no-go area. Too much trouble for the police to bother about. A haven for thugs.

"Give us your money."

Just a simple statement. The law of the jungle. Three of us. One of you. Give us your money. The faces on the murals seemed to look on with interest. So what now Davie Stanton? What do you do now? You who were one of the big men? He smiled at the thought. He must look so pathetic to them. Just a middle-aged man too long in the rain. Sat on the wall with his eyes closed and the rain pouring down his face. Probably pissed. Just a sad old bastard. An easy shake down.

So come on Davie. What do you do? You've got 30 quid in your pocket. Are you going to turn it over? Anything for an easy life. Give the little bastards your cash and slink off home and top yourself. That's what it all comes down to. Poor Davie. Davie with terminal cancer of the bowel. Davie who fought as hard as he could and still wound up on the losing side. Poor, poor Davie. Isn't it sad. Such a shame. Such a wasted life. No wife. No children. No nice house. No happy ending. Sad, pathetic Davie Stanton. This is where you are. This is how it all ends. So give them the money Davie. Give it all up. Stick your hands in the air. Surrender you sad bastard. The faces mocked him. The voices from the past mocked him.

"One fucking chance mister. One chance. Empty your fucking pockets."

There was a knife now. A Stanley knife. Slowly the sorrow and shame turned to anger. No way. No way was he going out like this. Not while there was still breath in his body. He stood up slowly. He never let his eyes move from the one with the knife. He eased off his soaking jacket and wrapped it around his left arm. He sensed them begin to tense. This wasn't in the script. They glanced at each other nervously. And Davie Stanton smiled. His hair was plastered to his forehead and his sweater was all wet. His face was now lined with all the pain that had eaten at him for months. He spoke very quietly.

"You try. You die."

He stood perfectly still and waited. They shuffled. He knew they wouldn't come. No chance. All mouth. All bluster. They would never come. They didn't. They backed off. Slowly. Resentment written all over their faces. Five yards. Ten. Then they turned. They tried to walk cocky. They kept glancing back. And they saw that the man had never moved. He just stood there in the pouring rain and never moved a muscle. He just stood and smiled that weird hard smile. They had no idea who he was. All they knew was that he was one mad looking bastard.

As he watched them slope away Davie knew that his decision had been made. He wasn't about to put a bullet through his head. He had a few months yet. A few months left to fight his war.

He pulled on the soaking jacket and took a last look at the faces on the murals. In the end his gaze was drawn to the image of the Ghost. Maybe there was still time. Time for one last battle.

The smile never left his face.

The next day, just like so many times in the past, he made his way down to the old caravan on the coast. The weather got even worse. For three days it barely got light at all. The beach belonged to him and him alone. He spent long hours striding along the drenched sand; head bent to the wind. For the first time in months his brain felt as if it were fully engaged. The ideas leapt around searching for order. The basics were easy. There would be three of them. And they would have six months. Six months before the black cloud of death came down to swallow him up. Six months to turn back the tide. There was no point in thinking of anything long term. No time. All there was time for was something outrageous. Something spectacular.

Slowly but surely the pieces of the jigsaw started to drop into place. On three occasions he stopped in mid stride and howled out loud into the wind as he saw the road that he needed to take. By the end of the third day he knew it. All of it. Of course it was outrageous. And the chances? Not great. Maybe one in three if he was lucky. But not bad. And success would turn the tide. Maybe turn it so far back that it would never come in.

That night he went to the pub in the village to use the phone. The landlord seemed surprised. It had been a long time. Years that had taken their toll on Davie. His face had grown thin and pale. His eyes were set deep and ringed with grey. He knew when he looked in the mirror that he had the face of a man who did not have far to go. People were beginning to notice. He saw it in their eyes. A shadow of embarrassment. An instinctive sense of death.

He made his calls to Derek and Richard. There was surprise in their voices. It had been a few months since he had spoken with either of them. There was surprise, but there was no hesitation. He had never doubted for a moment that there would be. They would come tomorrow. They would come before seven.

Again he saw the shock on their faces. They tried to make it like old times. They brought the beer and the curry. But their efforts were strained. Davie could sense their anxiety. He decided that it was time. Time to stop pretending.

"OK lads. Enough foreplay I think. Time for the nitty-gritty. Sitting comfortably? Good. Then I shall begin. Number one. I've seen you looking. You're both too polite to say anything. Yes. I look like a bag of shite. No way round it. I have terminal bowel cancer. It was diagnosed last week. They say it is too far advanced to be treatable. Basically, I'm fucked. I've got six months. Maybe a year."

He felt quite moved by the sorrow and shock on their faces. They had been with each other a very long time. It was nearly forty years since they had played soldiers in his bedroom in Granville Street. They were all that each other had. None of them had ever married. None had kids. All of them were cut loose and adrift. All that they had was a sense of immortality. And now that was all broken up. Davie had always been the leader. The strong one. The one who would made the decisions. And now he was not going to be there any more. He could see that they felt they should say something. He could feel their struggle for the right words.

"Don't bother trying to work out what to say. It's a bastard and that's that. No point worrying it to death. I didn't know what to make of it myself at first. I wondered whether I should eat a bullet. Just get it over and done with. But it didn't sit right. I don't feel as if I'm done yet. I don't feel that we're done. Not yet. So crack a can. Sit back. This is the gospel according to Davie."

He opened a can himself and lit up.

"This is my picture of Ulster in five or ten years time. More of our people will have moved away. The population will be about 55 percent us and 45 percent them. They will be able to see a majority on the horizon. Our people will be spread out all over the place. They will have their people concentrated. Belfast will be theirs. And Derry of course. And Newry and Cookstown and Dungannon and Armagh. They will be calling most of the shots in Stormont. And behind the scenes the IRA will be fully armed.

They will be able to push our people out of their homes at will and there will be fuck all that we can do about it. The Brits will all be gone and there is no way on earth that they will be coming back. And it will be pay-back time. They will control everything. That is what I see coming and unless something is done now there isn't a hope in hell of stopping it.

So that is the place that I came to. Six months left. Six months to turn back the tide. One last battle. Interested?"

They both nodded. Intrigued now. He knew that they would be. Like him they had nothing much else. Davie ploughed on.

"The way I see things, there is one problem that overshadows everything else. Everybody loves the Republicans. They have managed to make themselves all warm and cuddly. Adams and McGuinness have nestled themselves under Nelson Mandela's coat tails. They have become the men of peace. Reason. Nice suits. Smiles for the cameras. Statesman. And there's no point in fucking around here. They're good at it. Shit hot. To make it worse, the better they get, the worse our lot appear. We are the bad guys. Thugs in baseball caps, bullies, drug dealers, Fascists in bowler hats.

This is the biggest thing that has changed. Everybody falls over for Sinn Fein. Everybody wants to buy it. Of course they do. We all like happy endings. The world wants to see Ulster as a Disney wonderland where the sun has started to shine after hundreds of years of rain. Well that's all very nice unless you happen to come from the Shankhill. Everyone wants to forget all about us. They don't give a shit about us. We either doff our caps to the Peace or we can get stuffed. Every time we try to show a grievance we screw it up. We wind up throwing blast bombs at schoolgirls. And everyone hates us even more. And Gerry Adams looks grave and shakes his head with sadness at how our people behave.

So. Where is the solution? Well, there isn't much that we can do to make our lot behave better. We've been down that sorry road before. How many times did we lose all the benefits of a Ghost kill because some idiotic cretin went out and whacked an innocent Catholic civilian? So there's no way forward there. Instead we need to turn the thing on its head. It is all really quite simple when you think about it. We need to make the world hate the IRA again.

We need to turn them back into the bogeymen.

That will be the scope of the operation. The time scale will be six months. The 'What' bit. Next up is the 'How' bit. That's the part that is bothering you. It's all over your faces. How the fuck can we manage it? Three of us? Three of us to change the course of history? Big ask. Hell of an ask.

Well, it's not as impossible as it seems. Remember 1968 when the IRA blew up the power and water? Big outcry. Prime Minister forced to resign?"

His two friends nodded.

"It wasn't them. It was all a set up. It was my Grandad's idea. It all came out of course when some dickhead from the UVF had a few too many and got himself blown up. But by then it was too late to matter. O'Neil was out and Faulkner was in. The result was all that mattered. Well that is exactly what we are going to do. The Ghost will come back to haunt them. Hit them. Niggle at them. Pick them off. And the whole world will sit back and wait to see if they will respond. And Martin and Gerry and all the nice guys at the front will shake their heads in sorrow whilst in the background the bad boys will start getting itchy fingers. And the Ghost keeps at it. Getting under their skin. Taunting them. And people begin to wonder if they really have changed. They will wonder just how long they will be able to turn the other cheek and smile for the cameras. And the Ghost will mock them. He will remind them of what the people said in 1969. IRA. I Ran Away.

The tension will build. The media will pump itself up. And just when it seems as if they might just be able to restrain themselves, they lash out. They produce a Spectacular. This time they don't attack the Brits. This time they throw all their pent up anger and rage straight at us. The Prods. The Orangies. The enemy. And what they do is so indescribably awful that the world draws back in horror. How could they? How could anyone? And there will be no doubt because they will call the press and claim the responsibility and they will use the right code."

There was a gleam in his deep-set eyes now. They could see that he had crossed some kind of line. He had gone into a new place. A harder place than before. A place where the cost didn't matter any more. Only the result. Part of them felt the chill of the place. Part of them felt a surge of excitement.

"What will happen will be so big, so awful, so damned evil there will be no avoiding it. There will be rage. And West Belfast will go up like a bonfire. The whole of Ulster will be one big riot. And the only answer will be for the Brits to send the troops back in to sort it out. It will take months to settle things down. Maybe longer. The bad boys of the IRA are being held on a very short leash. Once things blow there will be no holding them back. By the time they find out that it wasn't the IRA at all it will be far too late. The soldiers will be back on the streets and the bad boys will be back, firing their guns at them. And now that they have all the stuff that they stole from Castlereigh, it will take a very long time before the Brits manage to get the IRA back in a corner. That's what it's all about. Buying time. Bring them out into the open. Start up another shooting war. And maybe the next peace will be better for our people."

They were all quiet for a while. It all took some digesting. It was huge. Monumental. At last Derek found a question.

"This Spectacular. I can see the theory. The question is how will we do it. I know the peelers are all at sea at the moment. But they're not that far gone. There is still massive security around any event that might cause a sectarian flashpoint. Just look at how things are at Drumcree. It won't be easy to get through them. The IRA have never really managed it. How can you be sure that we will do any better?"

Davie grinned at him. "Very good. I'm impressed. Come and sit at the front of the class. You've found your way right to the heart of the matter. How to commit the ultimate outrage in a place wrapped up tight as a duck's arse. The answer. You don't. You go elsewhere."

"Where?"

"You find a target that is as Orange as anything in Ulster. You find a target in the middle of a city that is riddled with simmering sectarian tension. Gentlemen, I give you Glasgow. Gentlemen, I give you the Orange Walk in Glasgow on 12th July 2003. Gentlemen, I give you an IRA bomb that will make Omagh look like a £10 box of fireworks."

The reality of it hit them both in the face like a bucket of iced water. Richard muttered. "Jesus Davie. They're our own people"

The eyes were hard now. Far away. Deep in the other place that he had found.

"It's about sacrifice. It always is. Yes, people will die. Hundreds of them. And some will die hard. People will lose limbs. People will go blind. There will be women and children. It will be a horror. An outrage. And it will be done by us. It is merely a question of how strong we are. We weigh the odds. A few hundred die and a million have a future. Is it worth it? Our people know all about sacrifice. Remember the fifteen thousand that fell on the Somme. They paid for our future with blood. The debt isn't paid back. We still owe it. All of us. Now let's not piss about here. It's easy for me. I'm a dead man walking. You lads will have to live with it. There will never be a night when you don't wake up in a sweat. It will never leave you. It is no little thing. It's make-the-mind-up time. In or out?"

"In." Said Richard.

"In." Said Derek.

They crossed the line. They joined him in the place of darkness that he had found.

Chapter 13
The Road to an Outrage

The years had been kind to Brigadier James Hamilton. That much was apparent to Davie the moment his old friend opened the front door of his Kensington house. He wore baggy cord trousers and a cotton shirt. The permanent tan was still in place. And he was still fit. No middle-aged bulge around the waist for James Hamilton. It was still a rare event for him to lose on the squash court. He still swam for at least an hour every day. The only concession to the ageing process that Davie could detect were a few lines on the face and a thinning of the sandy hair.

The last time that Davie had visited the house James's parents had lived there. It had been when they were at Sandhurst together. Christ, it seemed like centuries ago. Davie remembered that James had mentioned his mum and dad had moved to the country and passed the house on to him. He had worried a little on the flight into Gatwick that James might have sold the house. He doubted it. Having the Kensington address would be important to his old friend. He chuckled as he made his way up the street. The place must be worth millions now. James could have bought about six whole streets in the Shankill on the proceeds, if he had chosen to sell.

For a moment James Hamilton's face registered confusion. No recognition. Wariness. Then it dawned on him. Surprise. Concern. Alarm.

"Christ Davie, it's you."

"Aye. It's me. You look like you've seen a Ghost."

He had never seen James so hesitant. So completely ill-at-ease. Well of course he was. It amused him to sense the thoughts racing around behind the handsome face. After all, here was the man that he had personally sentenced to death five years ago. So what was this? Was this the moment? A pistol and a shot he would never hear.

"It's OK James. I'm not here to top you. Aren't you going to ask me in then?"

"Yes. Of course. Sorry. You just took me by surprise. Bloody hell Davie. I can't believe it. Come on. In you come. Let's get a drink."

Inside it was all Tatler. There was a Tatler wife in the lounge who was introduced as Elspeth. She shook hands languidly and smiled with a row of pearly white teeth. Only in her eyes was distaste. She struggled dutifully through the obligatory small talk. The smile never left her lips but her eyes constantly flicked anxiously to James. Who on earth was this dreadful man? Belfast he says. What on earth is he doing here? Davie sat and sipped his whisky and enjoyed the whole thing hugely. He had chosen his clothes deliberately. Tired old combat jacket. Jeans. Heavy work shoes. His hair was long and uncombed. His pale face was stripped down to the bones. Two days of stubble.

James tried to see beyond the outer layer. There was something else. Something more than just the extra miles on the clock. Davie had always carried a sense of threat about him like a cloak. Now it was barely hidden. Now he was like an armed weapon. The eyes. Those bloody eyes. They were as dead as stone. James Hamilton was no stranger to the company of killers. He had lived among them for the whole of his adult life. He was one himself. But Davie Stanton gave him goose bumps. Time to get him out of the way. Every syllable of Elspeth's body language demanded it. What the hell did the bloody man want?

They moved to the study. It was a place of leather chairs and soft light and no expense spared. Davie pulled his cigarettes from his pockets and raised an eyebrow.

"Yes. Sure." Said James and he pulled an ashtray from the drawer of his desk.

"Still use them?"

James hesitated then took one. "Technically, no. But fuck it."

They lit up. James was still ill-at-ease. Davie could see that he was trying to think what the hell to say. Whether to mention the unmentionable. He made the decision for him.

"It wasn't very nice was it James?"

"What wasn't?"

"What you did. Giving all my details to those lads in the INLA. And there was I thinking we were mates."

Hamilton stared down at the cigarette between his fingers for a long moment. When he spoke his voice was unusually anxious. "I don't expect that you'll believe me, but I had no choice. Orders of course. People wanted things cleaned up. The decks had to be cleared. Evidence removed. You know how things are when peace comes. They want all the unpleasant stuff buried as deep as it will go."

"Oh I know James. Only too well. And I was an embarrassment. A serious embarrassment. But don't give me all that orders shite James. The Ghost belonged to you. Only you. You would never have shared. There was only one man who would have made the decision to remove the Ghost. It was a choice. Me or your career. It didn't come as any surprise. I was waiting to be honest."

"How the hell did you find out?"

"Let's say that I have a guardian angel."

Again silence. Eventually James picked up the tired thread of the conversation. "It was clever what you did. The Maze was probably the only place on earth where you were safe."

"Billy wasn't."

"No. I suppose he wasn't. Look Davie, let's stop pissing around. If you're not here to whack me, then what is it?"

A surge of temper had brought back the old James. Confident. Arrogant. Demanding control of the situation. Once started he was soon backfiring on all cylinders. "Anyway, what the fuck is going on with you Davie. Just look at you. You look like a bloody corpse. Skin and bone and your eyes half way to the back of your skull. You can't be hard up, surely? I paid you hundreds of thousands of pounds. You should be on a beach somewhere. The bloody war's over. Enjoy yourself for once."

Davie just smiled and lit up another cigarette. James was about to carry on but Davie waved him back to silence. "Answers James. Answers. I have cancer of the bowel. Terminal. They say I might have a year. Maybe six months. It has taken the weight off me. But don't worry. I've been putting your money to good use. I spent a few grand of it only a few days ago. You see the pain was getting a bit hard to deal with. Hard to function properly. So I went to my friendly local UFF man and got something to take the pain away. Far away. Far enough away for me not to worry about it. Maybe you can guess the magic cure. It's the new cornerstone of our Shankill economy. Who needs linen mills and shipyards anyway. Heroin is a whole lot less bother than building the Titanic. Good old Heroin. A few bags a day takes all the pain away."

The colour drained out of the face of James Hamilton. He was in the presence of death. Death was waiting deep in the dark staring eyes. Fear leaked through him. Davie continued.

"So James. You asked why I am here. It was clever of you to guess that it wasn't a social call. I'm afraid not. It's business. There are things that I need."

"Go on."

"I have a wee list. Nothing that should present too much of a difficulty for a Brigadier in Military intelligence. Want me to make a start?"

There was indignation now on the face of James Hamilton. "Don't be so bloody stupid Davie. There is no way. No way in hell. Things have moved on. No bloody way. I think it's time that you left actually. Come on. This little meeting is ending right now."

"Sit down. Calm down. Here. Play this."

Davie tossed a cassette onto the leather top of the desk. James picked it up and looked at it with suspicion. "What is it?"

"Just fucking play the thing." There was a new edge to Davie's voice. James shrugged and leaned over to set the cassette up in his stereo system. At first there were only background noises. The subtle sounds of a discreet corner in an expensive restaurant. Then James heard his own voice. Clear as the air on a crisp frosty morning in January. And slowly his shoulders sagged as he listened to his own words from fifteen years before. The words described senior members of the IRA. They described movements and locations and the amounts of money that the Government was willing to pay for these men to be removed. After a few moments he reached over and switched the cassette off.

When he spoke his voice was tired. "You bastard Davie. You wore a wire. You bastard."

Davie laughed. "We're all bastards James. We always were. Your arrogance was always going to be your undoing. You were sure that I was just another thick Paddy. Well, I'm afraid you got it wrong. I decided that a little insurance was in order. Something for my old age. A little nest egg. Well, the time has come for me to cash it. It's Judgement Day James."

"It's no use to you Davie. You can't print it. Nobody would touch it."

"Don't take me for a fool James." Again Davie's voice snapped with anger. "Those days are long gone. All I need to do is post it on the Internet and it's in the public domain. The Irish papers will jump at it. And the Americans. They'll love it. And you'll be fucked James. 100 percent fucked. The fall guy. I can just hear the army statements. Can't you? Rogue officer. Loose cannon. Always acted alone. Never kept his superiors informed. It will all land on you James. Every last ounce of the shit that will fly. You know what will come. Court Marshall. Big long sentence. Complete disgrace. You know how it works."

There seemed to be many more lines on Hamilton's face now. The reality of the situation was sinking in. He was cornered. No point in trying to fight it. "What do you want?"

"That's better. Number one. Five files. IRA Battalion commanders and above. Just like before. I don't need paying this time."

"OK." That wasn't too bad. He could get that.

"Number two. I need Semtex. About 200 pounds. I need two detonators. Something hand-activated from a few hundred yards. I need a couple of guns. Nothing fancy. Something semi-automatic. And I need a mortar with ten rounds."

James laughed. "Don't be idiotic Davie. How the bloody hell do you expect me come up with that. I'm a Brigadier in

Intelligence. I can't just go around requisitioning hardware. You know that."

Davie smiled. "Of course I do James. I don't expect you to get the stuff for me. I just want to know where to go and collect it. The Semtex and the detonators need to come from an IRA arms dump. The guns and the mortar need to come from a Loyalist dump. I need the locations and all details on what surveillance is in place. Simple."

James nodded. That was not impossible. He could do that. "Go on."

"Number three. I will need the latest IRA code. I expect they still change it every two days or so. I will need it at 24 hours notice."

Hamilton's brain was racing now. Semtex from an IRA dump. 200 pounds of it. And detonators. And now the code that all the media would recognise for the IRA to claim responsibility for a bomb or a killing. The pennies rolled into their slots.

"Christ Davie. You're going to blow the peace out of the water. What the hell are you about to do?"

"That's 'need to know' James. You don't need to know. You complete your side of things and we're quits."

"How do I know I can trust you?"

"Because you have my word. Unlike yours, it means something."

"Why Davie? Why are you doing this? Why can't you just leave the peace be?"

"Peace!" He spat the word out like a mouthful of sour milk. "Don't give me fucking peace James. A nice peace for the fucking Brits. A nice peace for the fucking Provos. A nice peace for the hoodlums in the UFF. Well I don't buy it. I don't buy it because my people are the forgotten ones in all of this. Nobody gives a shit about us any more. We are just an embarrassment. Well fuck that James. Not while I'm still here. Your lot might want to forget what you still owe us after the Somme. You always do. Same with the Aussies and the Kiwis and the Canadians and the Indians. The British way. Use them and throw them away. Well not us. Not this time. Not on my bloody watch."

Davie was shaking with anger. James had never seen him this way before. This was a new Davie Stanton. He had crossed the line to the place where only the end mattered. It was the place that other men had found. Kamikaze pilots. Suicide bombers in Tel Aviv. The ones who steered the planes into the UN towers. They were the ones who allowed their belief to become the very core of their being. And Davie Stanton had joined them. It was there in the deadness of his eyes. James felt cold now. Icy cold. But he knew there was nothing he could do. The choice was a simple one. Go along with it or see his life destroyed. Ten years in a military prison. Maybe more. No way. He wasn't going there. He slowly settled himself. "When?"

"As soon as you can. It shouldn't take you more than a week. We'll meet in the old restaurant a week tonight. Eight o'clock."

"OK. Eight o'clock. I'll be there."

James returned to the study when Davie left. There was coldness in the room. It was as if evil had left its mark. An evil that he was a part of.

Bru Dempsey was delighted when he heard the news of the attack on the Unicorn. It was fine by him. It was what he had wanted. The Fenian bastards had decided to play. No problem. If they wanted to play that was fine. He was happy to play. Keen to play. Eager.

On the day after Boxing Day, Celtic played Kilmarnock at home. It wasn't much of a game. The league leaders ran in three goals without ever playing at their best. The routine win that kept them ten points clear of their rivals from across the city. Bru was past caring much about results on the pitch. He was playing a bigger game now.

Two days before the game he had broken into the back door of a disused three story tenement half a mile from Celtic Park. He had stashed twenty petrol bombs by a second floor window. Twenty minutes after the end of the game the crowds filled the street below as supporters made their way back to their cars. Once again Bru's plan was remarkably simple. He removed the board that covered the window and lit the bombs one by one. Once he had five burning he tossed them down into the street below. He didn't bother to light the remaining fifteen. He merely tossed them into the flames. The whole exercise took him a little over 25 seconds.

By the time anyone in the street even began to try and work out what had happened he was in his car and driving away along with thousands of others. He stopped and made a call to the Glasgow Times from a pay phone.

"This is the First Battalion of the Glasgow UVF. Today's action was retribution for the death of Angus Rogerson at the Unicorn pub in December. No surrender."

The call made him feel good. The call made him feel great. All his life he had been reared on tales of the UVF. They all had. The UVF were the ones who fought the real war against the Fenian bastards. They didn't mess about. It wasn't just a punch up on a Saturday night for them. They killed the bastards. Shot them. Bombed them. Never gave them an inch. There had always been the hard accents of Belfast in the bars around Ibrox. They had often looked at these guys with awe. Who were they? Were they UVF or UFF or Red Hand Commandos? On two occasions he had taken the ferry from Stranraer with a car full of mates to join the crowds at Drumcree to throw stones at the police lines. And now he was one of them. He felt as if he had come of age.

Pictures from the street were beamed across the world. Two supporters were killed, one of them only ten years old. Over a hundred were hospitalised. City officials pronounced shock. Police spokesmen promised to leave no stone unturned. Men in high places demanded to be updated on all information available on the Glasgow UVF. In response the Special Branch could merely shrug their shoulders. MI5 shared the same boat. Nobody had ever heard of the Glasgow UVF. Nobody even knew it existed. Calm was pleaded for. Community leaders promised to do all they could. No effort would be spared to stop an escalation of the violence between the two communities.

Within a week graffiti started to appear on walls all over Glasgow. 'Glasgow UVF' to start with. Soon it was simply 'GUVF'. The police looked under every stone they could think of. There was no doubt that everyone was talking about the GUVF. It was the talk in every bar and workshop in the city. Everyone was talking about it but not a soul knew a thing. As the days passed and no suspects were rounded up the tension rose a few notches. The only ones arrested were kids with aerosol cans who sprayed the walls of the city. None of them knew anyone in the GUVF. They just knew they were there. They just thought they were cool. Dead cool.

Davie could hardly believe his eyes as he read the reports. He had picked up the news of the attacks on the Unicorn and the Fiddler's Rest. These had been seeds of ideas that had germinated as he took his long walks on the rainy beach. The attacks had offered a starting point. A small, smouldering flame that could be fanned. Instead, it seemed that the flames needed no help. They were spreading all by themselves. Glasgow UVF! It made him laugh. Idiots. Morons. Who the hell did they think they were? Jokers.

When a fortnight passed and nobody was arrested he began to wonder. It made no sense. There was no way that they could be that well organised. Unthinkable. He had expected the Special Branch to be through them like a dose of salts. He was wrong. He could see it on the strained faces of the policemen who had drawn the short straw and had to face the Press every afternoon. They hadn't a clue. No idea. Well, thought Davie, it takes one to know one. There was no GUVF. It was one man. One solitary maniac who was leading them all a merry dance. A Glasgow Ghost. And of course Ghosts should stick together.

By the end of January his own plans were well advanced. James had come up with the goods. Once again he had files to work with. Five of them. Big men. Big men who thought it was all over. Big men who thought they could have it all their own way. They had started to do their watching. All of the men were careless. They had forgotten all about precautions. Not one of the hits would be difficult. Not to start with. It would be tougher after the first. But that was nothing new. The Ghost had never missed in the past.

The arms dumps had presented no problem. It had all been just as James Hamilton had said it would be. He had told them how long it would take for the security forces to react. He had predicted fifteen minutes for the IRA dump down in the Republic. He had been wrong. The Irish Police had long given up being alert. It was 40 minutes before their officers reached the scene. Davie and his team had needed only ten minutes to remove the

Semtex and the detonators. The UVF dump on the Antrim Coast was even easier. The Police Service of Northern Ireland took over an hour to investigate.

Reports shot around the Province and over the water to London. Frantic contacts were made between all sides. Questions were asked. Answers were demanded. Who was responsible? What was happening? 200 pounds of Semtex was a serious amount of gear. Tempers were lost. Favours were called in. Information was demanded. Tables were thumped. And nobody knew a thing. Not a bloody thing.

The worst moment for Davie was taking the Semtex across the water. They had wrapped it half an inch thick with cling film and packed it into several old pieces of furniture from the workshop. For the first time in years the old van was driven out and onto the Shankill Road. One or two pedestrians looked on in surprise. They were of an age to remember the time when they had seen the 'Stantons of Shankhill' logo every day. Maybe they were opening up again.

It was the sign on the van that helped at the docks. It was all very different from the time when Davie had smuggled the Barrett into Ulster. This time there was a full scale alert on. Two hundred pounds of missing Semtex had set alarm bells ringing all over Britain. The police and their sniffer dogs were out in force. No vehicle escaped their attention. But they weren't looking for a van from the Shankhill. That was a long way from the top of their list. They were looking for hauliers from Armagh and Derry. They were scanning for once familiar faces from old files. Republican faces. They stopped him. They gave the back of the van a quick check. The dog had a cursory sniff. And they moved on. His whole body was drenched in a cold sweat. It had been the moment when everything could have fallen apart. The moment of absolute risk that couldn't be avoided. Derek and Richard had tried to persuade him that they should drive the van. But he had refused. No way. If anyone was going to get caught it would be him. He had nothing to lose.

The checks in Stranraer were much easier. The Scottish police were happy to trust the expertise of their colleagues in Belfast. He was through in a hour. Two hours later he reversed the van through the doors of 'Ayr Furnishings Ltd'. He had never bothered to dismantle the old shell company. There had been many times when he had been on the brink of doing so. For some reason he never had. Maybe it just seemed like too much bother. Maybe something told him that the day would come when he needed it again. Everything was on direct debit. Rent. Rates. Water charges. A modest electric charge. He had just let them run. The figures barely made a dent of the money in his account. Every year his accountant filed figures for a company in moth balls. And now after sixteen years he opened the door for the first time.

It was as if time had stood still. As he got out of the van and breathed in the stale air his mind wandered back to the last time he had stood in the workshop. What a different world it had been. He had been a different man too. He had never been stronger. Fresh from the mountain air of Montana and ready for war. It had been a time when he had really believed that the war would be won. The IRA were falling apart at the seams. The loyalists and the security forces were squeezing them like a tube of toothpaste. Just a few more years. That was all it had needed. Just a little while longer and they could have won. Instead they had been betrayed. Instead the British had thrown in the towel and taken the easy way out. And now he was back. A dead man walking. A man counting down his last days on the planet. A man with just enough energy for one last battle. So many years and one last chance.

There was a ludicrous pile of mail on the mat by the door to the office. Sixteen years of junk. For some reason his eye was caught by a letter on the top. It was barely dusty. Hand written. Recent. He picked it up and the postmark confirmed that it had been posted a fortnight before. He opened it with mild interest. Inside was a hand written letter that had been photocopied. As he read, a slow smile spread across Davie's face. First it had been the GUVF. Now this. Fate was smiling on him. The Gods were throwing him favours.

TERRIBLE BEAUTY

James McCreadie
'McCreadies'
86 Sauchihall Street
Glasgow
G1 7DL
0141 332 6754
james@mccreadies.co.uk

17th January 2003

Dear Sir,

I am trying to locate a piece of furniture for my wife's birthday in August. It is a Welsh Dresser of a particular design. I gather from your entry in Yellow Pages that your company specialises in this kind of item. I am sending this letter to several companies in your field. If you have a piece that matches my specifications please contact me either by telephone or email. I will require a viewing before negotiating a price. The item can be delivered to my business premises in Glasgow where we have a large basement and good unloading facilities.
I look forward to hearing from you.

Best regards

James McCreadie.

Davie looked at the photo carefully. It was extraordinary. He made his way into the workshop and pulled away a large dust sheet. Underneath was a dresser that matched the photo in almost every respect. He had bought it years ago. Paid a fortune. It needed a lot of renovation. But it was still magnificent. Nearly half a tonne of beautiful oak. He had forgotten all about it. It had just sat there under the sheet for a decade and a half waiting for its moment to arrive. And the moment had arrived. The last piece of the jigsaw.

He set up his laptop in the office. He logged on and created a letter head.

Ayr Furnishings Ltd
Unit 27
Blaylock Industrial Estate
Ayr
KA13 4FT
01292 645 349
d.stanton@btinternet.com

3 February 2003

Dear Mr McCreadie,

Thank you for your recent enquiry. I have the type of dresser that you require here at the workshop. I will take some photographs and email them to you in the next couple of days. Should you find the photographs satisfactory then we can arrange for you come down and view the piece.

Best Regards

David Stanton
Managing Director

The piece was easily worth ten thousand pounds. James McCreadie knew it only too well. Davie could see that he found it hard to keep the glee from his face when he found out that he could have the dresser for six thousand. Davie confirmed that the deadline was the end of July. McCreadie confirmed that he would take the delivery at his shop on Sauchihall Street where it would be stored in the basement until his wife's birthday in August. Davie assured his client that this allowed plenty of time for the piece to be fully refurbished. They agreed that McCreadie would return to inspect the dresser at the end of June when they would arrange the final delivery details. McCreadie wrote out a two thousand pound cheque as a deposit then shook hands and left.

It was the first week of February and outside the very first sniff of spring was in the air. The clock was now ticking. It would tick quietly away for a further four and a half months.

TERRIBLE BEAUTY

The first battalion of the Glasgow UVF bit the dust in spectacular fashion in the third week of March. Despite the best efforts of the Strathclyde police, Special Branch and MI5, the GUVF had remained a mystery to all concerned. There had been many hours of high level meetings on the subject. Older hands suggested that the whole thing was a myth. Maybe it didn't exist at all. Maybe it was no more than a single cracker acting all on his own. By and large these voices were ignored. Everyone was still very much in September 11th mode. They were at war against a murky conspiracy of global terrorism and they were perfectly convinced that the GUVF was yet another cog in the wheel. They were men with the problems of the world on their shoulders. Civilians being burned to death on the streets of Glasgow was bad enough. Looking bad in the eyes of the Americans was much, much worse. If they couldn't manage to clean up a mess in their own back yard then how on earth could they expect a seat at the top table of those running the great crusade.

What was beyond doubt was that things had been a lot tighter at street level. Bru had scouted around diligently to try and find a new opportunity, but it was hard. The problem with the petrol bomb approach was that it needed him to be there personally to light the bombs. So long as it was a surprise attack this didn't matter greatly. However, with the new blanket police presence all over the city, this plan of action was made almost impossible.

By this stage Bru was well on the way to losing the plot. The unbelievable success of his last attack had gone to his head. He felt indestructible. He was a superman. He was quite convinced that nothing was beyond him. It became clear that it was time for him to move up to a new level. What he needed now was a bomb. A real bomb. A proper bomb. Just like the ones that the UVF had used in Ireland.

He could feel that he was maturing as a fighter now. He actually spent two whole days in the library trawling the internet. He astounded himself as he dug deeper and deeper into cyberspace until he found sites constructed by like-minded men that told him all about how to make a fertiliser bomb. He drove far and wide collecting the various ingredients and found a disused basement to get on with the task.

THE ROAD TO AN OUTRAGE

The internet can be a wonderful thing for all kinds of research, but it comes with no guarantees. There were several flaws in the instructions that Bru had so lovingly written down. The result was that he blew himself into a thousand pieces on the second evening. To all intents and purposes the First battalion of the Glasgow UVF was gone. All that was left was the graffiti artists and a few young stone throwers. The investigators and the forensic teams who swarmed over the basement like flies didn't see it this way. To them the bomb making was a sign of escalation. Sophistication. Of a move to a new and more dangerous level. The old hands believed that the solitary cracker had blown himself away. But they kept it to themselves. There was far too much excitement for anyone to want to listen to anything they had to say.

The older hands in fact had an ally. Davie had always shared their opinion that the GUVF was a one-man show. The reports of Bru's demise came as a mild disappointment. Nothing major. It had been something of a bonus all along. It meant a small tinkering with the plan. They had contingencies in place

The Ghost team went into action on the mainland for the first time on the last Thursday in April. They had bought a small cottage outside Ardrossan on the Ayrshire coast. It provided a useful base for both the workshop and the city of Glasgow itself. It was the kind of place where people kept themselves to themselves. Nobody paid them any attention. As they worked through their preparations there was a new mood among them. In the past there had been an excitement, almost a lightness. They would often keep themselves going with humour. The war had always been a good crack.

It was different now. They all knew that this time they were entering a whole new zone. They had no doubts that what they were about to do was right. It was the only way. But it was also evil. No longer could they draw comfort from the fact that their targets were dedicated terrorists who deserved everything they got. This time they were about to kill innocent civilians. Lots of them. There was no other way. But it was hard. Really hard. They became quiet with each other. Withdrawn. Mechanical.

The way Davie was made it tough on Richard and Derek. He never said anything. He didn't have to. They could see the cancer eating away at him piece by piece. The weight was melting off him and the pain was etched deep into his face. To start with he had only needed one bag of heroin a day. By January that had become two. By the end of April it was four. Each day took him further away. He was like a robot. He barely spoke any more.

Initially Davie had tried to fight it. But he didn't have the energy. The pain sapped him. Drained his resources. It was endless. Interminable. All he could do was to strip himself down. He peeled away the layers of his being one by one until all that was left was the mission. One goal. Nothing else. Just a few months and then there would be peace. A blissful release. An end to his war.

It was Friday night. They were in the kitchen. Around the table. They were drinking mugs of tea and watching the clock. The minutes dragged by miserably. Each of them was quiet. Each was trying to deal with his own thoughts. At last it was seven. Time to move. Time to step over the edge.

Davie forced a smile onto his face. The new distance that was between them hurt. They had been together forever. They were close as men could be. And yet now they were drifting. Sliding apart.

"So. This is the moment lads. Speech time. You can still walk. You have done nothing yet. There's still time. After tonight it will be different. After tonight we will be guilty. It's different for me. I'm a dead man. I won't have to live with it. You will. All your lives. And it won't go away. It will never go away. So this is the time. You can walk away right now and I will understand. Seriously. You don't need to do this. After this we will be hunted men. Hated men. We will be like the ones at Enniskillen or Omagh or Lockerbie. You don't have to come with me on this. That's all. All I want to say."

Richard and Derek glanced at each other. It wasn't much of a decision. Had they wanted out, they would have taken the chance already. Davie had little doubt that they would be with him. They didn't have the cancer of course. But what else did they have? Like him, they had lost their lives to the cause. No wives. No kids. No mates. Nothing. Only the war. Always the war.

Nothing was said. They just nodded and started to get ready. It was time to step over the line.

The Red Bull was a Celtic pub. It had always been a Celtic pub for as long as anyone could remember. There was live Irish music every Friday night and the place was always packed. Friday 27th April was no different. The whole pub was singing along with the band. Out of the two hundred and thirteen people in the pub, only a couple saw the front door open and the man in the black mask step over the threshold. One of then lived to tell the tale. It was unlike anything he had ever seen before. The door opened. The man stepped in. Black mask. Green combat jacket. Jeans. Army type boots. Nothing was said. He just stood there for a couple of seconds. Like a statue. Then he lifted up his gun and started to fire. Just like that. No words. No warning. He just fired. The witness said that it seemed as if it went on forever.

In fact it had been less than twenty seconds. The high velocity bullets smashed into the packed bodies. By the time the dust settled and the news lines buzzed with the story, the scale of the horror emerged. It was beyond belief. Beyond imagination. In that twenty seconds sixteen died and 36 were injured. Responsibility for the attack was claimed by the GUVF in a letter to the Daily Record.

The police tracked the CCTV film and discovered the car that had driven the gunman away. It was in a lock-up garage across the other side of the city. The owner of the lock up told the police that it had been a cash deal. He told them that the man who rented the garage had an Ulster accent. He told them he had long greasy hair and a motor bike jacket. He told them he had worn sunglasses the whole time. There were no prints in the car. However there was a gun. It was in the boot wrapped in an old blanket. The forensic experts had a field day. They positively confirmed that it was the gun that had fired the shots in the Red Bull. They also cross-referenced their ballistic findings with their colleagues in Belfast and discovered that the gun had killed twice before. The gun had fired the bullets that killed a Catholic postman in the Ardoyne in 1986. It had also been used in the execution of an IRA man as he made his way home to the Turf Lodge Estate in West Belfast in 1991. Both killings had been claimed by the UVF.

The bit that wasn't made public was that the arms cache in Antrim had been under surveillance by the security forces. The surveillance had been systematically downgraded in the years after the Good Friday Agreement. There were no cameras. No microphones. Certainly no watchers. Instead there was an alarm system which had worked perfectly well. The bells had rung for the first time in years at the local police station. It had caught everyone unawares. Response time had been poor. Shocking in fact. It had taken them over an hour to make it out to the cache. They had confidently expected to find evidence of a digging fox or badger. Instead they found that the cache had been closed back up. They checked the contents against their lists. There were two semi-automatic Armalite rifles missing along with a quantity of ammunition. One of the guns was in the boot in the lock up garage. Also missing was a mortar and twenty rounds of ammunition.

It was the mortar that kept people awake at night. Guns were bad enough, especially when they were used with the kind of devastating effect that had shocked the world at the Red Bull pub. But a mortar? A mortar was a completely different thing. What the hell could they be planning to do with a mortar? The old hands were suddenly very glad that they had kept their mouths shut. So it hadn't just been a lone crackpot after all. Anything but. All of a sudden there was a connection. The worst kind of connection.

After endless agonising the decision was taken to keep the news of the mortar from the public. Things were already bad enough. Despite a queue of politicians and community leaders pleading for calm, things were fast getting out of hand. Both communities were at each other's throats. In the week that followed the Red Bull killings there were several incidents. Two Loyalist pubs were attacked with petrol bombs and the weekend saw the worst rioting that the city had known in living memory.

There was rage in London. The Police Service of Northern Ireland were told to get their collective finger out. Doors crashed in all over North and East Belfast. Every UVF man on the files was pulled into Castlereigh and interrogated. Every informer was grilled. Every stone was turned over. But all there was to find was a whole heap of nothing. Nobody knew a thing. They shrugged their shoulders. They leaned back in their chairs and smoked. All there was a big echoing void.

It was 4 a.m. on the Morning of May 7th when the mortar riddle was at last solved. The weapon was fired from a piece of wasteland 850 metres from Celtic Park football stadium. After exhaustive interviews with the residents of the area, the police were able to establish that the ten rounds had been fired in just under two minutes. They concluded that whoever had been in control of the mortar team must have been professionally trained. The first shot hit the roof, tearing a great hole. Three of the shots landed squarely on the pitch leaving small craters. The remaining six shots all hit the terracing. The damage bill ran to over a hundred thousand pounds. The damage to the city was incalculable. Before the mortar attack it had become hard enough to keep a lid on the sectarian tension that was sweeping the city. The attack blew the lid clean off. Rioting was now a nightly occurrence. The police had to draft in reinforcements from all over Scotland. By the end of May there had been two more fatalities as well as countless casualties and damage to property.

Things started to get tense between the Government in London and the new Parliament in Edinburgh. The issue of troops started to be discussed. It was becoming clear that the police were finding it hard to hold the line. The TV pictures that were sent out across the world were doing no good for the image of Great Britain Plc. As May turned into June everyone's fears escalated. The coming of summer would mean the kind of warm nights that always fanned the flames of riots. Even worse, July heralded the start of the Loyalist marching season. The decisions that had caused such turmoil to successive Governments in Ulster now had to be taken by the authorities in Glasgow. Banning marches would inflame the Loyalist half of the city who would see it as an impingement of their Civil Rights. Allowing the marches to go ahead would similarly inflame the Republican community. It was a no win situation. In the end, the powers that be compromised. The marches would be allowed, but only with unprecedented levels of security.

Apart from the frantic enquiries of the police, the situation in Glasgow by and large had little effect on things in Ireland. All this changed on the twelfth of June. At six in the evening Seamus McBride was executed by a sniper. McBride was the IRA's commanding officer for the North Derry brigade. He was shot as he walked out of his house in the Bogside. The sniper had fired from the old walls of the city from a distance of over a thousand yards. A few hours later the BBC received word from the Ghost.

> *This evening at six o'clock, Seamus McBride was executed in Londonderry. This action was carried out by the Ghost. The Ghost now acts alone. The Ghost acts only for the loyal population of Ulster. The Ghost will no longer accept a peace process that is a betrayal of his people. All senior officers of the IRA are now targets. The executions will continue until the interests of the loyal people of Ulster are better looked after. Today's action was carried out in the name and memory of Sir Edward Carson. No surrender.*

A week later Gerald Keenan was gunned down as he parked up his truck in his boss's yard in Newry. Keenan was the long time Quartermaster for the South Armagh brigade. Once again the Ghost claimed responsibility for the kill. Not that there was any need to. The shot had been fired from a distance of 1,300 yards. Nobody had any doubt as to who had fired it.

That night there was full-scale rioting in Belfast. The same old crowds swarmed at each other down the same old streets. Soldiers struggled to keep them apart. Shots were fired a little after one in the morning. A boy of fourteen was admitted to hospital and found to be dead on arrival. The Government moved two extra battalions of troops to the Province in an exercise that they promised was merely a precaution.

Sinn Fein joined all the other parties in pleading for calm. Gerry Adams tried to address the crowds in West Belfast but he found it hard to make himself heard. Soon the same question was on everybody's lips. How long would the IRA hold back? How much would they be willing to take? Events both sides of the Irish Sea seemed to merge. The Ghost and the GUVF were the vanguard of a Loyalist backlash. Things had gone the way of the Republicans for long enough. Now the Loyalist population were venting their rage and frustration at what was happening to them. For too long they had lacked leadership. Now it was all changed. Now the Ghost had come back. It had seemed as if it were too late for any of them to dare to hope. It had seemed that this time it was really over.

But they had seen these bad times before. Always in the past a saviour had emerged. Once it had been the Apprentice Boys of Derry who had barred the gates of the city to King James and his army. Then Carson had raised the great army of the UVF to fight against Home Rule. And now the Ghost had returned. Just when there seemed to be no hope and no will left to fight, the Ghost was back to show them the way. The Republicans had seen it all before. A thousand times before over hundreds of years. The Loyalists were starting to march again. And again the Republicans looked to their defenders to come out and stem the tide. Sinn Fein pleaded for calm. Sinn Fein promised to do all it could to help the authorities to calm the situation. But the pressure was rising. All over Ulster local IRA commanders were getting calls. The questions were always the same. How long are you going to stand by and let this happen? Remember 1969? When will you get out there and defend the community?

June slipped into July and the pressure gauge was stuck in the red zone.

Sean cursed the nagging sound of the alarm. He reached out and killed it. Six o'clock. Once upon a time getting up early had been easy. Not any more. Now he felt he could happily sleep until ten every morning. As far as his work was concerned there, he could have happily slept in until after eight. However for months now it had become his habit to rise early and spend a couple of hours on the internet to check the news from home.

He set his computer to the BBC and switched the volume high so he could hear the news as he arranged his coffee machine. He had a cigarette half way to his lips when the newsreader's voice stopped him dead.

. . . Last night 48-year-old Patrick O'Hara was killed in the Andersonstown Estate in West Belfast. The rogue Loyalist gunman known as The Ghost claimed responsibility for the killing. In a statement to the Belfast Telegraph he claimed that O'Hara was in charge of the IRA units based on the Andersonstown estate. O'Hara served a ten-year sentence between 1982 and 1992 for his part in an attack on an army

patrol in 1981. A spokesman for Sinn Fein refused to confirm that O'Hara was still an active member of the IRA. A statement from the Police Service of Northern Ireland confirmed that the killing had been undertaken by a sniper and that the fatal shot had been fired from long distance. The shot was fired a little after eight o'clock last night and once again there was major rioting in several areas of Belfast. There were two shootings in the Ardoyne area of the city and . . .

Sean sank down into his armchair and completed the task of lighting his cigarette. The words still floated out of the speakers of his computer but they evaded his attention. For months it had been the same. Words from his past. His youth. A life that he thought that he had left far behind. Swarming crowds of rioters pelting policemen with bottles and bricks and petrol bombs on the Falls Road. And the Ardoyne. And Andersonstown. And Ballymurphy. As if the wheel of time had taken 30 years to come back to the same place. Extra troops sent. Plastic bullets fired. Men dead on the hard streets where all the shops had closed down.

And then the Ghost had come back to haunt them all again. Everyone was talking about him now. As the scenes of chaos in Belfast and Glasgow were beamed across the world every night there was a media frenzy about The Ghost. Who was he? What was he? Where had he been? Why had he come back? What was he going to do next? Reporters beat a path to the square of murals at the bottom of the Shankill Road to conduct interviews with local residents in front of the old mural of the Ghost hidden beneath a white sheet.

Everyone was rattled. Politicians from all sides wore the expressions of men under the cosh. Brits, Sinn Fein, Unionists, all the same. All struggling for something to say. All desperate for some positive spin. All trying to find a brave face. All pleading for calm and common sense. All being completely ignored. All discovering the hopeless limits of their authority. All incapable of keeping the crowds off the streets.

It was eating Sean alive. He felt as if he were covered in a million ants. What the hell was Davie up to? Why? Always why?

Why was he doing this? Why now? Why at all? Why was he taking his people back to war when it seemed as if there was a chance of peace? And there were only two people who knew him. One was a soldier in the British Army. One was Sean O'Neil. Sean O'Neil a 53-year-old lecturer in Irish Literature who had found peace and a degree of happiness after so many years of pain.

But what could he do? He could make an anonymous call to the police. He could tell them that the Ghost was Davie Stanton of Granville Street, Belfast. It was what he should do. On several occasions he had actually picked up the phone and been ready to dial. But for some reason that he couldn't begin to understand he had been unable to dial the number. The second option was even worse. The second option was to contact the Army Council and come clean. He would have to tell them that he had known the identity of the Ghost for nearly a decade. No matter how hard he would try to explain there would be no sympathy. None at all. The Council was never famous for sentiment. It would be a bullet in the back of the head and a quiet grave somewhere in the rolling hills of South Armagh.

He had put it off. Put his head in the sand. Hoped it would just go away. He wanted no part of any of it. He liked the life that he had found for himself. He liked his flat. He liked Boston. He liked the fresh untainted enthusiasm of his pupils. He liked being able to walk the streets and not have to feel the prickle at the back of his neck. He liked the normality of his existence. He had done his part. Surely he had. Years and years of it. He had made just about every sacrifice that could have been expected of him. Surely it was enough. Surely he could leave it now.

The sound of the phone jumped him out of his skin. He dragged himself from his chair and picked it up. The voice on the other end was like a bucket of iced water running down his back.

"That Sean?"

"Yes."

"It's Brendan."

Jesus.

"Hello Brendan. Long time."

"Aye. Long time. I'm sorry about this Sean. Honest. The Council met last night. We need you back Sean. Gerry wants you back. Fuck it, I want you back. It's all tits up over here. Fucking crazy. It's getting hard to keep the boys in line. They nearly voted to go back to war last night. It was close Sean. Really close. We only just held them back."

Sean chuckled. "You mean you were on the side of peace Brendan. My, my. Things have changed."

O'Conner's chuckle bounced back over the Atlantic. "Aye, well. Age brings responsibility you know. I'm Chief of the whole fucking thing now you know."

"I heard. Belated congratulations. What do they expect me to achieve?"

"Miracles. That's where we've got to. We need a miracle. And you're our miracle man Sean. Just like always."

"Any miracle in particular? Or just miracles in general?"

"In particular. Find the fucking Ghost. Stop the fucking Ghost. Stop the bastard before the whole place burns to the floor."

"Give me two days. Same old farmhouse?"

"Aye. Nine o'clock. The lads will collect you from the hotel in Dundalk."

Sean stared down at the phone for ages. In a way he felt better. At least the decision had been made easier. They had asked for a miracle. Little did they know.

Chapter 14
A Terrible Beauty is Born

Sean pulled his collar up to try and keep the rain from finding its way down the back of his neck. July in Belfast. Nothing much had changed. Above him an endless army of grey clouds marched east. It had rained from the moment he had stepped off the plane. Wet. Cold. Miserable as only a Belfast summer could be. Welcome home Sean.

He struggled to get a cigarette going. He was only a few hundred yards from the house on James Street where he had grown up. And yet this was only the second time in his life that he had stood on the Shankill Road. The first time had been 34 years before. It had been sunny that morning when the soldiers had escorted him to Granville Street. 34 years since he had taken a pale faced eleven year old boy back to his Ma and his family. And now the boy had grown into a man. A man that it was his duty to hunt down. A story from West Belfast. Maybe the craziest story ever to come out of a crazy city. His city. His home.

Just a few yards from the Falls to the Shankhill. From James Street to Granville Street. Just a few yards and yet so much hatred. Both the streets looked the same. The same bleak terraces that could be any old industrial city in northern Britain. The same, but so very different. A foreign country. Enemy territory. Every nerve in his body told him that he was behind enemy lines.

The street was in a woeful state. There had been yet another riot the night before. The debris of urban warfare was strewn everywhere. Broken glass. Rocks. Bricks. Burnt out vehicles. Probably there would be bloodstains on the pavement. A few hours before, the whole place had been a mad swirling chaos of noise and people. Now it was quiet. Empty. Threatening.

He saw the old church across the road. It hadn't been a real church for a long time. For years it had stood empty and forlorn until Don Lawrence had commandeered it to open up his youth centre. Sean had met Don twice. The first time had been in the Kesh. On two occasions they had shared the same waiting room as they waited to be led in to see their visitors. Don was serving a ten-year sentence for the attempted murder of a Sinn Fein councillor on behalf of the UVF. They had shared a few moments of good-natured banter. It was how it had been in the Kesh. Inside they were all soldiers together. Outside they would happily kill each other. Inside they were all men behind the same wire.

They had met for the second time a year earlier. Don had come out of prison a Born Again Christian. He had rejected violence and thrown himself into the work of the Lord. In 1996 he had persuaded the local authorities to allow him to open up the old Church as a youth centre. Over the years it had become popular. The youngsters of the Shankill were more than happy to spend their time at 'Don's Zone'. The God stuff was a bit of a bore, but he retained plenty of credibility from his days in the UVF. He made sure that he never pushed the Lord down their throats. Giving them somewhere to get off the street was good enough for him. He figured that it would probably be more than good enough for the Lord as well.

In 1998 he had his autobiography published. 'Hate to Hope – UVF to Jesus' made quite a stir in the Province. Sean had read the reviews with a smile on his face as he remembered the big red faced man from Long Kesh. He ordered a copy and loved it. The pages rolled by with tales of the Belfast that he had known as a young man. Religion had never played any part in Sean's life but he still found the book oddly uplifting. When he read that Don was due to tour America to promote the book he had got in touch. He had persuaded Don to come and give a lecture at the University and it had been a thumping success.

A TERRIBLE BEAUTY IS BORN

They had sat up late that night and worked their way to the bottom of a bottle of Bushmills. It had been a healing night for both of them. They both carried scars on their consciences. Wounds that refused ever to heal. They had both been responsible for death. They both buried their pain far from the light. It was a night when the pain could be shared. A night when they had spoken of things that few would ever understand. A night when the sectarian lunacy of their lives seemed so very futile.

Sean tossed his half-smoked cigarette into a puddle and opened the old door of the church. It wasn't particularly busy inside. Most of the kids would still be tucked up in bed having had a late night rioting. There were a few blasting away on Playstations. A couple were playing a half-hearted game of pool. Don was at the far end of the room clutching a mug of tea as he read the paper with a frown. He looked up in surprise as Sean approached him.

"Bloody hell. Sean O'Neil. You're a long way from home."

Sean smiled. "And which home would that be?"

"Either of them. James Street is further away than Boston. What the hell. Good to see you. Come on, we'll go in the office."

Don chattered away as he cleared papers off a chair so that Sean could sit. He boiled water and made tea and sat down behind his desk.

"So. Is it a social call that brings you onto the Shankhill, Sean? Dangerous ground for a man like you. It wouldn't go well if anyone recognised you."

"I don't think that's very likely. I had hair in those days. Nobody notices sad old bald guys in raincoats. It's sort of social. Sort of business."

"Well get on with it then."

Sean got out his cigarettes and raised an eyebrow. Don nodded. "Yeah. No bother. Here. I'll have one of those. Supposed to be giving up, but, well, you know."

Sean took a pull of smoke and pitched in. "I'm on with a book Don. Troubles stuff. A men behind the mask thing. Who we were. Why we did it. Where we came from. Not just my lot. Your lot as well. All of us. You know the kind of thing."

"And?"

"Well. I want you to be one of the men. And I want some help. Obviously I never mixed much with the lads in the UVF and the UFF. We didn't tend to socialise. Happen you could help me out. Make me a few introductions. Open a few doors. There's one in particular. Maybe you know him. Davie Stanton. He used to write a column in the paper. Good stuff. Well written. He went down on a five for possession in '97. Went onto the LVF wing. I tried his house but he's not there. The neighbours said he's not been around for a while."

Lawrence was frowning now. Uneasy. "Why Davie Stanton?"

Sean winced inwardly. It wasn't going as well as he had hoped. "Well, there's the newspaper stuff of course, but there is something else. Remember Bombay Street? August 1969?"

"Aye. I was there."

"So was I. we were probably throwing bricks at each other. I got one on my head. Split it clean open. When I looked I saw that a young lad had chucked it. He was only eleven. I was about to give him a good smacking when a petrol bomb went off. It set his arm on fire. It brought me to my senses and I managed to put the flames out. His hand was all burned, the poor little sod. I took him back to my Ma and she patched him up. The next morning when things calmed down I took him home to Granville Street. I've always wanted to catch up with him ever since. Especially when I read his stuff in the papers."

Don reached over to the packet of cigarettes and lit one before leaning back in his chair and staring up at the ceiling. At last he spoke.

"You're a shite liar Sean. Really shite. Want to tell me the truth?"

Sean wasn't particularly surprised. The cover story had only been thin at best. It had proved too thin. He looked deep into Don's eyes. There was suspicion there. But not hostility.

"I can't. Sorry. But I can't. I need to ask you a question. We talked a lot about peace that night in Boston. I think you meant it. In fact I know you did. I meant it too. All of it. But do you believe me Don?"

Lawrence took a long time. He took his eyes away from Sean's. He stared past him to the door of his office. At last he came to a decision. "OK. I believe you. We have to believe sometime."

Sean blew out a long breath in relief. "Thanks Don. I'm not here for war. Not any more. Not ever. I don't want to find Davie for war. It's for peace. I can promise you that. I hope it's enough."

Don leaned forward with his elbows on the desk. "There's not much to tell I'm afraid Sean. He left home sometime in December. A couple of lads saw the old van on the street. The family used to have a pretty big business you know. 'Stantons of Shankhill'. Ran for over a hundred years. They were into all sorts. In the old days they used to do the bars and the wardrooms on the big ships. Then they got into furniture restoration. In the end the recession did for them like everybody else. That's why the lads were surprised when they saw the old van on the street. It must have been locked up in the workshop for over ten years. There was a bit of talk in the pub about it. Speculation. Maybe they were opening up again. But it soon died down. Nobody has seen the van since. And nobody has seen Davie either. The Stantons are quite a famous family round here you know."

"Really? How come."

"Well the business of course. But then there was Peter Stanton. Davie's grandfather."

Sean frowned for a moment. Then it came back to him. The old man in the house in Granville Street.

"Aye. I met him. That morning. When I took Davie home."

"He was one of the greats. He joined the UVF as a lad in 1912. A Carson man. Ulster will fight and Ulster will be right and all that. Went to the Somme with the 36th Ulster. Came home with a Victoria Cross. He was your real genuine hero. There's a mural of him down the road. He bought it in 1987. He was trying to help a young lad after a bomb. He knew full well that there would probably be a second bomb. But he wouldn't leave the lad to die alone. The second bomb got him. The whole of the Shankill went to the funeral."

Sean could remember it vaguely. He remembered the pictures on the news. The old grainy black and white photo of a smiling Peter Stanton on his way to the Somme. It had never clicked back then. He had never realised that it was the same man he had met in Granville Street.

Lawrence chuckled softly. "I'll tell you what, he was some lad you know. Remember back in '69 when the UVF bombed the water and the electricity. We got the police to blame it on the IRA to put Prime Minister O'Neil under pressure, made him resign. Remember it?"

"Aye. I do."

"Well, that was all Peter Stanton's idea. He must have been pushing 70 at the time. The operation to bomb the sub-station was run by a lad from our street. John Hutchinson. Got whacked by the Ghost when the UVF put a death sentence on Billy Wright. Remember him?"

"Aye."

"Well he was the local UVF chief at the time. Peter Stanton sold the idea to him and John sold it to the top men. When he told Peter that he had got a green light the daft old bugger insisted on going along. He didn't trust Hutchinson not to fuck the whole thing up. Thought he would get pissed up and botch it. Insisted on going. Planned the whole thing. Got the job done. 70 bloody years old and still active! Aye he was some man . . ."

It was like a lump of ice in Sean's chest. A big lump. Big enough for him to find it suddenly hard to breathe.

He knew.

A sharp bright light bulb flashed on in his head. The answer. The answer to all the questions he had asked himself for months. What was Davie Stanton doing? What was the Ghost doing? Why? Why now? Why war again? And now he knew. He knew it exactly and it turned his stomach to liquid.

" . . . you OK Sean?"

"Yeah. Fine. No problem. Bastard indigestion. My landlady at the B&B must have thought that I needed fattening up. She gave me an Ulster Fry to feed an army and I'm paying for it. None of us are getting any younger are we Don?"

Lawrence laughed. "Are we buggery."

They chatted for a few more minutes. Sean didn't want to give anything away by leaving too soon. When he felt that enough time had passed he glanced at his watch. "Ah well. Better not hold you back. I can imagine that lot out there will get up to no good if you leave them too long."

"That's right enough. Actually they're not bad. Most of them are all mouth. I like to think they keep me young."

Sean held out a hand and they shook. "Good to see you again Don. Keep up the good work."

He was about to open the door when Lawrence called him back.

"Actually Sean, there is something else. I'd forgotten. Something a bit weird to be honest. I don't even know if it's true. It was just a rumour that I heard. Just a whisper."

"Go on."

"The week before he left, Davie Stanton went to the UFF. He bought heroin."

"Heroin!"

"Aye. Lots of it. Ten grand's worth. He promised it wasn't to sell on. Said he wouldn't step on any toes. Ten grand's worth of heroin and he was gone. As I said, maybe it was just a rumour."

Sean shook his head. He left the church and walked very slowly down the Shankill Road. The lump of ice was bigger now. His whole body felt cold despite the fact that the sun had at last emerged from the clouds. There were more people about now. A few council workers were getting on with clearing up the mess. Shoppers were making their way along the pavement with carrier bags. Clutches of young men exchanged war stories from the night before. He was so lost in thought that he nearly bumped into a ladder.

"Hey you daft bastard! Watch where you're going."

The man at the top of the ladder was angry. Of course he was. He was a good fifteen feet off the pavement as he fixed a new Union Flag to the lamppost. Sean gave the man an apologetic wave.

"Sorry about that mate. I was in dreamland for a minute."

He received a grunt by way of acknowledgement. There were new flags out all along the street. In the midst of the litter and the broken glass and the boarded up shops there were hundreds and hundreds of brand new Union flags. Brand new flags that came out all over Ulster once a year. Brand new flags that came out to celebrate the Battle of the Boyne when King Billy routed King James and his Catholic army in 1690. On July 12th 1690. July 12th. And today was July 9th.

He spoke to himself under his breath. "Sweet Jesus Davie. That's when you'll do it. The 12th. The bloody 12th."

Instinctively he quickened his step. There was little time. Three days. He had three days.

He took a moment before picking up the bedside phone in his guesthouse. It was such a crazy long shot. It was almost certainly hopeless. And yet it was the only hope that he had. At last he tapped out the number that had waited patiently in a locker in the back of his brain for 32 years. The number that had been given to him in a bare room in the police station in Portadown. He finished tapping and braced himself to hear the unobtainable tone. It never came. Instead there was ringing. But ringing was nothing without an answer. Two. Three. His hopes started to fade. Six. Seven. It was stupid to expect anything else. Nine. Ten

"Hello." Surprise in the voice. Surprised that the phone had rung at all.

Sean's mouth was dry as ashes. "I want to speak to Mr Edwards. I want to talk about the 'terrible beauty.'"

"Just a moment please. Will you hold?"

"I will."

He imagined the confusion at the other end. He pictured men rummaging through dusty old files for the long forgotten code. Surely Edwards would be long gone by now. How old had he been back in 1971? Late 30's. Maybe even 40. That would make him nearly 70 now. He'd be long gone. Pruning roses in his garden somewhere like Bournemouth. Another Cold War warrior with memories that few would ever believe. The minutes drifted by with silence in his ear. MI6 obviously didn't go in for canned music. The voice returned after seven minutes.

"I'm afraid Mr Edwards isn't here right now." Sean felt a sickening collapse of hope. The voice continued. "We have located him. Could you call again in an hour? He will speak to you then."

"Yes of course. Goodbye."

"Goodbye."

The hour dragged by with miserable slowness. Sean lay on the bed and tried to concentrate on reading the paper. He couldn't. His mind was racing. He had barely dared to hope that Edwards would still be out there. But he was. Sean had no idea what his position would be. If he was still working at nearly 70 years old then he would surely be very senior. Maybe he had indeed retired and they were merely dragging him in. What was important was that he was still there. There was still some hope. This time the call was answered on the second ring.

"Hello."

"I would like to speak to Mr Edwards please. I would like to speak about the 'terrible beauty.'"

"This is Edwards speaking. Which means that you must be Mr Sean O'Neil."

Sean smiled. He'd done it. Pay dirt. "You know Mr Edwards, Easter 1916 was the favourite poem of a very great friend of mine. One of the best friends I ever had. You'll remember him. Yeats could have written the poem about him,

> *MacDonagh and MacBride*
> *And Connolly and Pearce*
> *Now and in time to be,*
> *Wherever green is worn,*
> *Are changed, changed utterly;*
> *A terrible beauty is born.*

It was Bobby Sands. Whenever he recited those lines I always got to thinking about you Mr Edwards"

There was a silence at the other end of the line for a moment "Not our finest hour Sean. You were both in H6 if I recall correctly."

"We were. You followed my career then?"

"Of course. With the very greatest of interest. I must say I had long given up ever hearing from you. But never mind. Here you are. What's 32 years between old friends. What can I do for you?"

"We need to meet."

"I see. How soon?"

"Yesterday."

"That soon. Well tomorrow is probably a better idea. Where shall it be?"

"I'll come to you. London. I'll take the morning flight. Early afternoon wherever it suits you Mr Edwards."

"Well, I suppose since we've waited so long we might as well do things in style. Lunch at the Dorchester all right?"

Sean couldn't help but laugh. Typical Brit. They never changed. "I never dine anywhere else when in London Mr Edwards. I'll be there for one o'clock."

"Splendid. I will have a table reserved."

Sean recognised him straight away as the waiter led him across the floor of the restaurant. He had aged well. His hair was completely white but there was still a young man's brightness to his eyes. His attire was impeccable. A three-piece charcoal suit. Snowy-white shirt. Official looking tie complete with pin. Cuff links. He rose to his feet to meet Sean with a warm smile. They shook hands.

"I took the liberty of ordering a bottle of wine. I hope you don't mind. I can assure you that is really rather good."

"I don't mind in the slightest Mr Edwards."

"Now please. If we are to enjoy each other's company over lunch I think we should drop the Mr Edwards It is frightfully formal and it isn't even my real name. Please call me Sebastian."

A penny dropped into a slot in Sean's mind. He grinned. "That isn't entirely correct now is it. I believe that it's actually Sir Sebastian. Sir Sebastian Heathcote if I'm not mistaken."

Heathcote raised an eyebrow in surprise. "I see that you have been keeping up Sean."

"Well, I try. I was wondering whether or not you would have retired. No need was there. If I'm not mistaken, you're the man in charge."

Heathcote filled their glasses. "I suppose that I am. Within reason. In the end I am a mere civil servant. The politicians call all of the shots of course. But I cannot complain about how my career has panned out. Now Sean. Let's order some lunch."

The waiter came and went and Sean found it quite amusing to mentally tot up the bill that would be presented to the British tax-payer.

Once the waiter had scuttled away Heathcote leaned forward. "Now Sean. How would you like to do this? Would you like small talk, or should we get straight on with things."

"Oh I think we should pitch straight in. I'm going to tell you a story Sebastian. It might well be the strangest story you have ever heard. Maybe you'll believe it. Maybe you won't. I need you to believe me because I think that we both have just over two days to stop a catastrophe."

The old man leaned back in his chair. "Then please begin. I always did love a good yarn. Especially when it's told by an Irishman."

Sean took a sip of wine. "In August 1969 I was on Bombay Street. It was the night of the pogroms when the Loyalists burned the Catholic houses to the ground. A young lad threw half a brick at me. Before I could belt him, a petrol bomb went off and set his arm on fire. I put out the flames and took him back to my Ma. She patched him up and I took him back to his home in the Shankill the next day. His name was Davie Stanton.

"OK. Fast-forward 25 years. By this time I was a teacher in a secondary school in Monoghan. I was also the Intelligence Officer for the South Armagh Brigade. I left school one evening feeling pretty good about life. The Brigade had just successfully bombed the NatWest tower in London. It had been a perfect operation. A billion quid's worth of damage and no casualties. It looked like it would be enough to push John Major into peace. I went for a long walk through the countryside and dreamed of how things would be if there was peace. When I got back to my house I was in for a bit of a shock. A man was waiting for me inside with a gun. He tied me up and I prepared myself to meet my maker.

"Well, as you can see, I didn't meet him after all. The man told me that he was The Ghost. He had a file all about me. The file had come from inside Military Intelligence. All his files did. He told me that he had a contact in the Army who supplied him with targets. Only senior people. Everything that he needed to know. The where. The when. The who. And they paid him for his trouble. They had offered him £100,000 for ridding the world of my good self. It's nice to know your own value in such precise monetary terms.

"This is where things become rather extraordinary. You see I was familiar to him. My address. James Street, West Belfast. It was familiar to him because I had taken him there when he was a frightened little boy with a burnt hand. He told me that his family understood what it was to honour a debt. I had once saved him. So it was only fair and honourable for him to do the same for me. He gave me two options. I could either reveal all to the Army Council, which would have meant his inevitable execution. Or I could get out. Right out. He pointed out that even if he was out of the way, the Brits would probably send somebody else after me. He let me keep the file. I told the Council that it had been sent to me anonymously. And I got out. Right out. All the way to Boston.

Fast forward again. This time to 1997. I received a visit from an old comrade in Boston. We sat in a pub and swapped tales about the old days. He told me about how things were at home now that peace was almost complete. He told me about the case of an INLA man who had come over to the IRA. The lad told of how the INLA had received the file of an ex 14th Intelligence man from a Brit. Guess who. Davie Stanton. Whoever had given him his target list was obviously wanting to clear the decks before the guns fell silent. At the time Davie was making a bit of a name for himself with a column that he was writing for the paper. That was why my old mate brought it up.

I called Davie at the newspaper. Told him what I knew. Told him that the tables were all turned. Now it was his turn to be on a British death list. I gave him some advice. I suggested that the only place on the planet that he would be safe from the Brits was inside the Kesh. He took the advice. He was arrested for driving around Belfast with some old rifles from 1912 in the boot of his car. He got ten years and that was that."

He took some more wine.

"So Sebastian, as you can see, there is a bit of history between the Ghost and me. 30 years of it. Imagine how I felt when the Ghost started killing again. There I was out there in Boston with my nice flat and my nice life and my nice job. A million miles from West Belfast. Just getting used to the idea of peace. I knew full well what I really should have done. What I should have done was contact the Army Council and come clean. But the Army Council would have not been very pleased when I told them that I had kept the identity of the Ghost to myself for ten years. A couple of times I nearly picked up the phone and tipped off the police. But I didn't. I have no idea why. I just didn't. Couldn't do it. Couldn't do it to him. In the end the decision was made for me. I got the call. Come back Sean. They want me to perform the miracle. They want me to catch the Ghost."

Heathcote's eyes were wide by now. He barely noticed as the waiter placed their starters in front of them. Sean placed his napkin on his lap and continued. "What had been nagging at me was 'why'? Why on earth was Davie doing this? What had changed? What the hell did he hope to achieve? Where was it all leading? I didn't really know where to start. I decided that the best place as usual was the beginning. I went round to the house on Granville Street. Nothing. A neighbour told me that Davie hadn't been there for months. I hadn't expected anything else to be honest.

"So I called on a mate. An ex-UVF man on the Shankhill. I spun him a yarn that he didn't really believe but he told me a couple of things. Davie's family had a joinery business for years and years. It was quite a concern in its day. It closed down in the early 90's when the recession hit them. Apparently the old van was seen driving down the dat about the time that Davie disappeared. Not much there I know. There was one other thing. Something strange. Really strange. The week before he left town Davie Stanton bought ten thousand quid's worth of heroin off the UFF. Very weird but I don't suppose that there is much anything there either.

"It was something else that my mate told me that made all the pieces fall into place. Do you remember when the UVF bombed the water and electric supply stations back in '69? They pinned it on the IRA and it raised the stakes high enough for the Prime Minister to have to resign. Remember?"

"Yes. I recall it well."

"The whole idea was dreamed up by Davie's grandad, Peter Stanton. He was a big hero on the Shankhill. Won a VC on the Somme. A real UVF legend. He actually led the operation to bomb the electricity sub-station when he was nearly 70."

Heathcote shook his head. "Sorry Sean. You've lost me now."

Sean pushed his half-eaten starter to one side impatiently. "OK. This is how I see it. I have been looking at the statements that the Ghost has issued after each of the killings. He says that he is acting alone and on behalf of the people. He says he is acting in the name of Sir Edward Carson. No surrender. Now this is classic Loyalist mythology. Whenever God's children are threatened with annihilation a saviour will emerge to rescue them. King Billy. Carson. The Red Hand. All that stuff. Well the Ghost is assuming the mantle. So I ask myself what is the threat this time? It's right there in his statements. The Peace. The Peace that seems to be all one way traffic to many Loyalists. The Peace that only benefits the Brits and the Republicans. Look at what's been going on the last couple of years. Drumcree, Holy Cross, a Sinn Fein Mayor in Belfast Town Hall. The Loyalists feel deserted. Abandoned. Betrayed. And the reason? The reason why it is all going so wrong for them? The Peace. The Peace is the enemy. Can you see?"

"Yes. I think so."

"So. Let's assume that is the way that Davie feels about things. Let's assume that he sees that the only way to save his people from Republican domination is to end the Peace. Declare war on the Peace. To end a peace, you need to start a war. But it takes two to fight a war. And of course Davie will want the war on the right terms. He wants the soldiers back on the streets of the Falls and Andytown. He doesn't want a war just between the Republicans and the Loyalists. He wants the old war. The Republicans on one side. The Brits and the Loyalists on the other. Just like it always was. So Sebastian, how does this happen?"

Heathcote was catching up fast. Very fast. "The Republicans would have to be provoked. Severely provoked. Provoked so badly that the boys get the guns out again. So that's why he has been assassinating senior IRA officers. He is trying to get the IRA back fighting."

Sean nodded. He decided to ignore the fact that he was in the Dorchester. He rummaged in his pockets and pulled out his cigarettes and lit up. "I don't think it ends there Sebastian. That would be leaving far too much to chance. Maybe the IRA would refuse to be provoked. Maybe they would respond, but only in a restrained manner. Worse than that, there would actually be a degree of sympathy for their striking back. No. I don't think Davie is willing to take a chance on what the IRA are going to do."

Heathcote slowly laid down his cutlery and was suddenly very pale. "Oh yes I see now. You think he is about to take a leaf out of his Grandfather's book. He's about to commit an outrage that will be blamed on the IRA."

"Yes."

The old man suddenly seemed to age further. "And it will be something terrible. Something so terrible that the whole world will shrink back in horror. Oh yes I can see now. Only too well."

Sean dragged hard on his cigarette. "I think it is worse than that. What day would you choose for the IRA to commit the ultimate outrage against the Orangemen?"

"The 12th of course."

"Of course. The 12th. Within a few weeks of the execution of three senior commanders. And today is the tenth Sebastian. I think we have two days."

The waiter arrived with their main courses. Heathcote waved him away. "Sorry. We won't be needing any more food. Thank you." The waiter looked confused for a moment, and then he shrugged his shoulders and made his way back to the kitchen. Heathcote was getting to his feet. Suddenly he was an old man in a big hurry. "I'll book you a room here Sean. Give me a few hours. I'll start the ball rolling. I'll be back early evening. Don't go anywhere. We need to work together on this."

As soon as he had completed the formalities at the reception desk he turned to leave. Sean stopped him with a hand on the shoulder. "There's one thing I thing you should check. It could be another clue as to why he is doing this. I've been rattling my brains about the heroin. Diamorphine. The ultimate pain killer. Maybe Davie's in pain. Big pain. Pain that means he hasn't got long left. Maybe this is the last fling of a dying man. Check his medical records Sebastian."

Heathcote nodded and left. Sean made his way to the luxury of his room. There was nothing he could do but think. Puzzle. Try to work it out.

Richard smiled when the car that he was following turned into the same estate as the night before. He had been watching the depot of the haulage company for three weeks. Each night he would wait for the wagons to come home at the end of their day and park up. He had watched the drivers collect up their paperwork and check in at the office. He had watched them come out and make their way to their cars. He had followed them to their homes. There had been a couple of other candidates who would have been OK. But this one was perfect. Perfect because two young girls of three and four years old had rushed out of his house to greet him. Perfect because a pretty young wife waited on the doorstep of the house to give him a hug and a kiss. Perfect because when he watched the house for two days through the week, it became clear that the pretty young wife didn't work. She stayed home and looked after the little girls. Perfect.

He turned into a small close and did a three point turn. All done. All in place. He switched on his radio and headed back to the house near Ardrossan. He found Derek alone at the kitchen table.

"Things go OK?"

"Aye. Fine. Piece of cake. Where's Davie?"

Derek pointed up at the ceiling. Richard nodded. Davie had been spending more and more time in his room. Both of them could see that the pain was getting worse all the time. They could see how hard he tried to hide it from them. They could see that he was only just managing to hang on.

Richard went up the stairs and tapped on the door. "Aye. Come in."

Davie sat up. He had been lying on the bed. His face was completely grey. He had lost almost all of his weight by now. He was just a shadow of the big strong man that he had always been. The pain was all over him. He attempted a smile. It wasn't convincing.

"How did it go Richard?"

"Yeah, good. Perfect. It will be fine. How's about you. You hanging on in there?"

"Aye. Just about. Only two days now. I'm good for two days."

Richard nodded. He knew it would be the case. Davie would complete his last mission no matter what it took. When it came, death would be like a holiday in the sun for Davie Stanton.

Brigadier James Hamilton was working in his study when the doorbell rang at nine o'clock. Elspeth was out with friends. He tossed his pen down with irritation. He wasn't expecting anyone.

He opened the front door to find Sir Sebastian Heathcote and two unmistakeable heavies on his doorstep. Strange. He didn't know Heathcote well. He knew of him of course. The head of MI6 was well enough known in his circles. But they had only met twice. Both times fleetingly at civil service drinks parties.

"Sir Sebastian. This is unexpected. Please. Come in."

They went into the drawing room. Heathcote sat. The minders discreetly positioned themselves either side of the room. James could feel a quickening of his pulse. This wasn't good. Not good at all.

"Can I get a you drink Sir Sebastian?"

"I don't think that will be necessary. Sit down please."

Not good. Bad. All bad. James sat.

"I have spent this afternoon examining your career Hamilton. Extensively. In detail. I can assure you that there is little point in you spending any time denying the facts that I am about to go over. They are all confirmed. Co-operation is the only option for you. Co-operate and things may go better for you."

James controlled himself. It was a moment that he had always feared. Maybe even expected. "Go on."

"From 1988 to 1994 you ran an agent in Ireland. He was an ex-Scots Guardsman. Ex-14th Intelligence. David Stanton. I gather that you graduated from Sandhurst together."

"Correct."

"During this period you supplied Stanton with comprehensive details on several senior targets in both the IRA and the INLA. Stanton executed several of these targets. You arranged for him to receive substantial payments for each of these killings."

"It was authorised. All of it. From the top."

"Authorised, yes. Written down, no. It was always your baby, Hamilton. You must have realised that it would be yours to hold if the time came."

"Possibly."

"Over recent months you have re-established contact with Stanton. You have supplied him with more details of senior IRA officers. I also believe that you have supplied him the location of IRA and UVF arms dumps. Will you confirm this please."

James got up. He made his way across the room and poured himself a very large scotch. He dug in the back of a drawer and pulled out cigarettes. He lit one. His mind was racing. How the hell had they found out? It didn't matter much. They knew. Heathcote was too confident. God knows how, but they knew. He struggled for options. There were none. All he could do was go along with it. Co-operate. Cut the best deal he could get. He sat down and took a careful sip at his glass.

"I presume that there are options."

Heathcote nodded. "Two. Number one. If I am happy that you are co-operating fully, then you will be allowed to resign your commission and the matter will be closed. Number two. If I am not happy, you will be court marshalled and sent to prison. You should know that it was not my decision to offer you these choices. It was a political decision. Nobody has the stomach to dig about in the dirty laundry from the bad old days. If it was up to me, I would send you away to rot."

James nodded. At least there were options. His army days were over, but there were other things in life. "OK. I'll co-operate. Stanton contacted me in February. He wanted several things. I supplied them. Five files for senior IRA men. An IRA cache. A UVF cache. There is one more item. He will be calling me tomorrow evening for the up to date IRA code. I am to be in between eight and nine. That's all of it."

There was a look of acute distaste on Heathcote's face. "Why?"

"Blackmail of course. Davie wore a wire. Back in the old days. I had underestimated him. He had recordings. All of it. Names. Addresses. Cash payments for corpses. I knew that it wouldn't matter that I was acting with complete authorisation. Nobody would have admitted it. They would have hung me out to dry. You know that. So I gave him what he wanted."

"You're a bastard Hamilton."

James laughed. "Of course I am. We all are. But Queen and Country always wants men like us. Men to get things done.

Heathcote was in no mood to continue the conversation. He felt soiled. "These men will stay here. You will not leave the house. You will wait and take the call tomorrow evening. There will be technicians to trace the call. I will call you with a code to give Stanton. If you try anything these gentlemen are fully authorised to shoot you. I will bid you good night Brigadier Hamilton."

Sean was climbing the walls by the time he heard a tap at the door a little after eleven. The day seemed to have aged Sebastian Heathcote. He threw down his jacket and loosened his tie. He nodded at the offer of a drink.

"Well?" Said Sean.

"I've covered a lot of ground. Filled in a few gaps. It looks as if you are right. We have the army contact. He didn't tell us much that we didn't know already. He gave Stanton a list of five targets. All three of the men who have been executed were on the list. He also gave locations for two arms dumps. One was a UVF site in Antrim. We have already linked the weapons from the site to the recent activities of the Glasgow UVF. The gun used for the Red Bull killings came from the dump. And the mortar was used for the attack on Celtic Park."

Sean realised that his mouth was hanging open. "So the GUVF was Davie all along?"

"Possibly. We think the first killings were down to someone else. We think Stanton has only become involved recently. We have tracked the van. It was taken on a Stena ferry to Stranraer on February 3rd. CCTV isn't great up there. All we could discover was that the van headed north. However we think we know where. Inland Revenue records show that a David Stanton is the sole director of a company called Ayr Furnishings Ltd. It was established in 1987. There was a modest turnover for a few years. Then nothing. Every year the accounts are filed. No sales. Basic expenses. Rates. Water. A modest loss each year. It appears that the company is in mothballs. We have the warehouse under surveillance. Special Branch will be raiding it as soon as we get a warrant. It should be the early hours of the morning."

Sean's face was screwed up in thought. "First the GUVF. Now a company in Ayr. The van got off the boat in Stranraer and headed north. It looks like Scotland then. Glasgow."

Heathcote nodded. "That is our interpretation. The actions of the GUVF mirror those of the Ghost. They seem to be designed to inflame sectarian tension between the communities. And it's worked."

"Oh aye. It's worked all right. And there is a big Orange Walk in Glasgow on the 12th."

"Yes."

They were both quiet for a moment. Sean broke the silence.

"You never told me what went missing from the IRA cache."

"Two hundred pounds of Semtex and two detonators."

"Two hundred pounds! Sweet Jesus."

"Sweet Jesus indeed. We have been hunting high and low for it for weeks."

"So you need to get the march stopped."

Heathcote leaned back in his chair and seemed suddenly tired. "I've tried. No go. The whole thing has caused a political storm. I'm getting it in the neck from MI5 and Special Branch for interfering with their territory. The army have shut up shop. The politicians daren't do a thing. Everybody is telling me that what I have is circumstantial. Just a theory. Nothing concrete."

"You're joking."

"No. I'm afraid not. The march will go ahead. Oh there will be massive security of course. But it will not be stopped."

Sean slumped back on the bed and stared at the ceiling. Heathcote continued, speaking quietly. "We got Stanton's medical records. You were right again. Last December he was diagnosed as having bowel cancer. It was well advanced. Too far advanced for effective treatment. He was offered treatment of course. He declined. They told him he didn't have long to live. A year at best. Six months at worst. And they told him that there would be pain. Terrible pain."

"Hence the heroin."

"Hence the heroin."

Sean lit up and tried to put the pieces together. "OK. Let's see what we have. Two hundred pounds of Semtex. A massive bomb. Somewhere in Glasgow. How big is the march?"

Heathcote shook his head. "It's a nightmare. The Orange bands march into the city from all over. They come together at Glasgow Green. It covers just about the whole city."

"What about the call tomorrow? Will you be able to trace it?"

"Maybe. If he talks for long enough. Doubtful I would say. Even if we trace it we are unlikely to learn much."

"What about the detonators. How do they work."

"Manually. Effective up to five hundred yards."

Sean nodded. "So he'll be there. Up close. I don't think it will be five hundred yards. He'll be right next to it. So we need to find out where. Find out where and I might be able to spot Davie. If I can spot him maybe I can talk him down."

Heathcote looked astonished. "Come on Sean. That is hardly likely. If we find him, we take him out. It's as simple as that. There will be no messing about."

Sean shook his head. "Too risky. His finger will be on the button. If you shoot him it will almost certainly get pressed. Do anything and it will get pressed. You have to let me talk to him. It will be the only way. Unless you can find the bomb and diffuse it. What else have we got? There must be something else we can try."

Heathcote shrugged. "We're doing what we can. The Special Branch are looking for men with Ulster accents. We might get something in Ayr Furnishings. I have been onto the FBI. They have the technology to check emails. I gave them some key words. Stanton. David. Shankhill. Ayr Furnishings. It's a long shot to be honest. I tried to make them understand the urgency. Maybe they'll play ball. I'm not holding my breath. We won't hear a thing until the day after tomorrow."

"The 12th."

"Yes. The 12th."

Sean sighed. It all seemed hopeless. "So what do we do?"

"I think you should go up to Glasgow tomorrow. Book in somewhere in the centre. I will wait here until our army man gets the call. Then I'll join you. All we can do in the meantime is hope to get lucky. At least most of your mission is completed Sean."

"What do you mean?"

"He will not have the correct IRA code. If he does succeed with the bomb the truth will come out. And, if you are right, he will kill himself in the process. You can report back to the Army Council with positive news. The Ghost will be gone."

It didn't seem much like good news to Sean. All he could see in his head was the devastation of two hundred pounds of Semtex exploding in a packed street. It would be the worst terrorist atrocity ever seen in Britain. The death toll could run into hundreds. He couldn't help but feel that it would be down to him. For ten years he had known the identity of the Ghost. And he had done nothing. He had buried his head in the sand and pretended it was none of his business. He had allowed Davie Stanton to come to this point. He had been in a position to stop him and he had done nothing. If the bomb went off and hundreds died he would have to live with it. He didn't know if he could.

Derek had stayed up late. He knew that it was stupid. One more night and it was time. He should have been in bed. He should have been resting up ready for the operation. But he was finding sleep hard to find. In the moments before drifting away his mind would be filled with terrible pictures. Bodies without limbs. Mothers screaming over the corpses of dead children. Gutters filled with blood. No matter what he tried he couldn't drive the images away. So he avoided his bed. Instead he sat in a chair in the kitchen and killed the long hours of the night by watching the TV. In the end he would dose. Sometimes he got four hours sleep. Sometimes it would only be an hour. Sometimes Davie would come down and make coffee. They didn't speak much. There wasn't much to say. They were each consumed with their own demons. Talking wasn't going to help.

He could feel his eyelids growing heavy. He had lost track of the American cop film on the screen. It was old. Early 70's. Big collars and long hair. His eyes were almost closed when a movement brought him back awake. There was a computer screen next to the TV. For weeks it had shown exactly the same picture. It was the unmoving view of the inside of the Ayr Furnishings warehouse. Before they had left the premises they had set up a web cam. Nothing had moved on the screen for day after day, night after night.

But there was movement now. Lots of movement. The blurred shapes of men in black boiler suits with guns. He stood up slowly.

"Fuck."

Minutes later the three of them watched as more men came into the picture. Uniformed police. Men in suits. The urgency had gone out of them now. They knew that the warehouse was empty. It would be a while before they discovered the web cam. Then they would be able to trace the number. It would all take time. Too much time.

"Looks like it's time we were off." Said Davie. There was barely any strength in his voice.

"Who are they?" Asked Richard.

"Peelers. Obviously. Special Branch by the looks of them."

"How much do they know?"

Davie shrugged. "Can't say. They must know about me I suppose. No way they can know about the bomb. They won't find anything at the warehouse. They don't have time. We're OK. No worries."

An hour later they were gone. Six hours later the front door of the cottage flew in. The Special Branch took the place apart. There was nothing to find. Just an empty cottage. The trail was cold.

James Hamilton drummed his fingers on his desk and waited. It hadn't been the best of days. Elspeth had demanded to know who in the name of hell were the two men in the house. He had told her that it was army business. He had told her that she didn't need to know. It had been a huge row. She had locked herself away in their room and not emerged until noon. She hadn't said a word to him all day. It had suited him well enough. He had retreated to his study and done his best to read. All the while there was always one of the men in with him. They just sat there. They didn't say a word. They just sat and stared.

The technicians had arrived at seven and bustled about with their equipment. James had simply sat and watched. Nobody was speaking. Heathcote arrived at quarter to eight. He confirmed with the boffins that all was in place. Then he sat. He didn't seem inclined to speak either. James felt like a leper. It didn't bother him too much. It would all be over in a few hours. Resigning would be a drag. But not the end of the world. Then he would go away for a while. Somewhere hot. Somewhere he could do a bit of sailing and decide where life could take him.

The phone rang at twenty to nine. Everyone in the room jumped except James. He annoyed them by waiting seven rings before picking it up. Time to light up.

"Hello."

"Hello James. It's Davie. You got it?" He was shocked by the voice on the other end of the line. It was flat. Dead. Devoid of any life.

"Yes. I have it."

"Go on."

James paused for a second. They had asked him to prolong the conversation for as long as possible. "Are you sure you want to go through with this Davie?"

Silence. Five seconds passed. Then the voice was back. A flicker of anger now. Coldness. Hardness. Those who listened felt a prickle of fear. "Don't fuck me about James. Just give me the code. Give me the code and we're all done."

"What about the tapes?"

"As I said before, you have my word. You'll just have to trust it."

"Bluebottle. The code is Bluebottle."

"So long James." The line was dead.

Heathcote looked to the technicians. All he got was a shake of the head. "Sorry boss. Not long enough to be precise. It was Glasgow. Somewhere central. We'll trace the number in a minute or two. Hopefully the CCTV might give us something. They waited half an hour. The cameras found the man who had used the call box. The images were worthless. He wore a large hat and a long coat. They were able to track him for a while. But then he went into the Metro and he was gone.

The hat and coat were found on a platform just after dawn. Davie Stanton had vanished.

When the call had been traced Heathcote asked the technicians to leave the room. He also nodded the two minders away. When he was alone with James he spoke. His voice was quite emotionless. Flat.

"I will expect you to have submitted your resignation within the week Brigadier. So long as that happens then the matter is closed and it will stay closed."

James nodded. At least it was over and done with. All he wanted now was for these people to leave his house. Heathcote made as if to get up from his chair, then he seemed to hesitate, as if he had suddenly remembered something.

"Maybe there is one more thing that I should mention. I have been working on this case with an Intelligence Officer from the IRA. I dare say he may be familiar to you. His name is Sean O'Neil. Once upon a time you offered the Ghost £100,000 to assassinate him. I will be sure to pass on all your details to him. I dare say that the Army Council will be more than a little bit interested in the identity of the man who gave the Ghost his targets." Heathcote's handsome face broke into a wide smile. "I do hope that you enjoy the rest of your life Brigadier. Try not to spend too much time looking over your shoulder. In the end it will make your neck ache."

All the colour had drained from the face of Brigadier James Hamilton.

"You bastard."

"We're all bastards Brigadier. Didn't you say so yourself?"

Heathcote arrived at Sean's room at four o'clock in the morning. Outside the window the sky was starting to show the first signs of light. Dawn was an hour away. Sean hadn't even attempted sleep. He saw the strain in Heathcote's face immediately.

"Nothing?"

"Not really. He made the call. Somewhere in the city centre. We picked him up on the cameras for a while. It was far too late. He's long gone now."

"Nothing else? No movement on the march?"

"No. There was nothing incriminating either in the warehouse or the house in Ardrossan. No evidence. Just a theory. Not enough."

"So it goes ahead."

"It does. All we can do is wait. Maybe the FBI will come good. It's the last hope now."

"When?"

"Hard to say. My contact promised no later than late morning. It's a bloody long shot Sean."

Sean nodded. They were all out of options. There were just a few hours left. A few hours and it would be too late. All he could do was wait. And pray.

Robert Strong looked up from his bowl of Cornflakes with surprise. The doorbell was ringing. He glanced down at his watch. It was only ten to eight. Who the hell was ringing his bell at ten to eight on a Saturday morning? Maybe the postman. He got up. As soon as he had opened the door an inch it flew in at him. He hit the floor hard. Before he could even think of reacting, there was the cold end of a gun being pushed hard into his forehead. Behind the gun was a man in a black balaclava. Another man passed them and ran up the stairs. He tried to get to his feet. Upstairs was where his wife and children were. He was pushed back down hard.

"Now you be calm. Stay still. Absolutely still. Stay still and you stay alive. You and your wife and those two lovely girls."

The voice was Belfast. Belfast and a balaclava mask and a gun. What the hell was going on?

He felt like he was hyperventilating. His mind couldn't come to terms with what was happening. He strained his ears to hear what was happening up the stairs. It seemed to go on for hours. All he could do was lie there as the man in the mask pushed his head down into the carpet with the barrel of his gun.

At last the second man came to the top of the landing and said "OK."

His captor stepped back. The voice again. Hard. Uncompromising. "Right. On your feet. Slowly. Don't even think of fucking me about. Up the stairs. Go. Now."

They were in the front room. His wife. His girls. Their hands and ankles were tightly bound with thick tape. The same tape was wrapped over their mouths. Their eyes stared back at him with raw terror.

"OK. This is the situation. You will be going into work as usual. I will be following behind. When you get to work you get your truck just like any day. You take it to Queen Street and you wait. I'll meet you there. One wrong move and you don't see your family again. Not ever. You understand?"

Robert nodded. He didn't think he could speak.

"Good. We're not animals. You do as we say and your family will be fine. You'll be fine. Just do as we say. It's all you have to do. Try anything and you die. They die. You all die. Understand?"

Again he nodded.

"So let's go."

He took one last look at the terrified faces of his wife and girls. He managed to speak. "It's OK. Everything will be fine. I promise. Everything will be fine."

A TERRIBLE BEAUTY IS BORN

"Come on. Let's go."

An hour later he pulled up on Queen Street. The man had chosen the street well. It was deserted. He had been worried whether he would be able to find a place to park his big artic lorry. It wasn't a problem. He parked and waited. It hadn't taken him long to work out why they wanted him. They wore masks and they came from Ireland. There was only one reason why men in masks from Ireland would go to the trouble of holding his family at gunpoint. It was because of what he drove.

Robert Strong's tanker was filled with a full load of 32,000 litres of unleaded petrol.

Sean left the hotel at eleven. It was a lovely July morning. The sun was strong and the people of Glasgow were in festive mood. For weeks a cloud of violence had hung over the city. It was as if they had all made the collective decision to try and forget all about it for a day. It was a day of colourful summer outfits and ice creams and skateboards. Sean felt completely helpless. He wanted to stand in the middle of the road and scream at the thousands of Saturday pedestrians. But all they would see was a mad ranting Irishman. They would laugh. Nudge each other. Assume that he had spent too long in the pub. An old Irish nutter.

He had no idea where to go. All he knew was that Davie would strike somewhere in the centre. It wouldn't be a blast somewhere down a side street. It would be right bang in the middle. All he could do was walk aimlessly. Scanning faces in the crowd. Searching for the face of the man he had only ever met twice. Seeking a recognition. A chance in a million. A miracle.

Every few minutes he checked the mobile phone in his pocket to make sure that he had a signal. Half past eleven now. He cocked his ear. There it was. A sound that he had grown up to hate. A sound that made the hairs on the back of his neck rise up in anger. It was still a distance away. But it was there. Coming closer. It was the sound of the thumping of a lambeg drum. Soon he would hear the whistles to go with it. The sound of a marching Orange band. How far? Maybe half a mile. Maybe even a mile. How long? Half an hour? 40 minutes?

A feeling of sick despair was growing inside him. All around

419

him there seemed to be thousands of children. Smiling faces. A day out in the sunshine. Their whole lives stretched out in front of them. Too young to have learnt about hate. Too young to be sucked into the war. His war. His endless war of hate.

He could almost feel the presence of Davie. He would be somewhere within a few hundred yards. Waiting for his moment. Waiting to commit the ultimate outrage. Waiting to join the ranks of the most hated men in history. He wouldn't know that the plot had been unravelled. He would have no idea that what he was about to do was utterly futile. Instead of rallying his people, all he was about to do was to make them universally despised. How could he have possibly come to this?

He nearly jumped out of his skin as the phone rang. Heathcote's voice was breathless. "Sean, we've got it. The FBI have come through. We have emails from Ayr Furnishings to a James McCreadie. He is the owner of 'McCreadie's'. It's a clothes shop on Sauchihall Street. He purchased a reconditioned Welsh Dresser from Ayr Furnishings for his wife's birthday in August. It's a big piece. It weighs over half a tonne. Ayr Furnishings made delivery of the piece to the shop on July 3rd. It is to be stored in the basement until the birthday."

"Where on Sauchihall Street?"

"Half way. I have a bomb disposal team on the way to the back door now. I'm going to try to get the street blocked immediately."

Sean held the phone away from his ear for a moment. The sound of the drums was loud now. Close. Just a few hundred yards. At the top end of Sauchihall Street.

"Too late Sebastian. The March is already on the street. Do anything now and he'll hit the button. I'm on my way. I'll be there in five minutes. Keep your men back. There's no other way. You have to trust me."

He hit the end button before Heathcote could respond. And then he was running. Colliding with the pedestrians. Curses. Shouts. And soon his lungs were on fire. He hadn't run like this for years. The sound of the drums was loud in his ears now. Whistles and drums. The nightmare sound. The sound of hate.

He was on the street now. The crowds lined the pavement two and three deep. He stared up at the shop fronts. All the usual names. Burger King. Next. M&S. Allsports. Where the hell was it? The marching band was in sight now. The crowds on the pavement were cheering and waving their Union flags. The sun beat down on the men in their bowler hats and bright orange sashes.

Sean felt as if he couldn't breathe any more. His chest was burning hot. W. H. Smith. Where the hell was it! There! He saw it. Just a few yards now. 'McCreadies'. An old-fashioned sort of a sign amidst more garish neon. A big window full of dummies in summer clothes. There was a sale on. A blue dress. A red trouser suit. And a figure by the wall. Back from the crowd on the pavement. Dark glasses. A coat too heavy for such a warm day. A baseball cap pulled down low. Surely he was too small. Davie was a big man. Straight back. Wide shoulders. Strong. This man seemed stooped. Almost broken. Painfully thin. His clothes hung off him. It couldn't be. And yet there was something. Then the man looked up. The face was different. Thinner. Pale. Like a dead man's face. But it was him. It was him.

Davie couldn't believe the pain. It was all over him. It was beyond anything he had ever imagined. He had decided to leave the heroin. He needed a clear head. He had taken his last fix the night before. Now he knew it had been a mistake. Without the shield of the heroin the pain was becoming too much. What made it worse was that he was beginning to suffer from withdrawal. It was all that he could do to stand up. He had to lean on the wall to keep upright.

Two passers by had already stopped to check that he was OK. He could see the shock in their faces. He could barely speak. Neither had been convinced. He told them that it was just a migraine. He told them that his son was playing in the band and he didn't want to miss it.

He could feel his vision beginning to fail him. He kept screwing his eyes shut. It was no good. The waves of agony were breaking through him. He couldn't hang on much longer. He raged at himself for being so stupid. Why the hell had he not taken a fix? Idiot. Stupid. He dug as deep as he could. Come on Davie. For God's sake. Just a few minutes now. It's nothing. Just a few lousy minutes and then it's all over. Silence. Blackness. Peace. No more pain. No more war. Only silence.

He checked his watch. 12.23. Seven minutes. Seven lousy minutes for Richard and Derek to do their part. Seven minutes for the whole of the March to fill the street. Seven minutes and he could turn the tide back for his people. He closed his eyes again. Seven bastard minutes. 420 seconds. Seven minutes at the end of a whole lifetime. A picture of his grandad jumped into his thoughts. He saw him crawling back up the field from Thiepval wood. Crawling even though he had been shot twice. Crawling through the heat of the French sun. Crawling through the corpses and the men screaming for their mothers. Ignoring the pain. Focused. Getting through it. Making it. Beating the pain. Beating the fear. Seven minutes. Nothing. 400 seconds. Nothing. Seven minutes . . .

"Hello Davie."

His eyes sprang open. A man. Bent with his hands on his knees. Face all red. Finding it hard to get his breath. Bald. Thin. Out of condition. Familiar. He screwed his eyes to make them focus. His voice was tiny when he spoke.

"Sean. Is it you Sean?"

"Aye Davie. It's me. Jesus. I can hardly breathe. Too many fags." Sean tried to suck oxygen into himself. Davie's face was a mask of confusion.

"What are you doing here Sean?" He felt dumb. Stupid. As if the terrible pain was eating away at his brain.

"It doesn't seem as if we can stay away from each other. You look like shit Davie."

Davie couldn't believe it, but he laughed. Despite the howling pain he laughed. "You don't look so clever yourself. What the fuck are you doing here Sean?"

"I've come to tell you not to do it Davie. It's all over. The Brits know all of it. They've got Hamilton. It was the wrong code he gave you. Nobody will believe it was the IRA. They will know it was you. It is you they will blame. You and your people. You don't want that Davie. All you'll do is make the whole world hate your people. That's not what you want." He had to stop. He had to breathe. Suddenly he was consumed with coughing.

Davie looked at him with dumb astonishment. The realisation of what Sean had said was seeping in through the pain. It was impossible. Impossible.

"How? How did you know?" His voice was like a child.

Sean's eyes were streaming tears from the coughing. "It doesn't matter how Davie. I just found out. That's all. I just found out."

Richard checked his watch. 12.26. He glanced over to the figure of Robert Strong. They were parked up a hundred yards down the road from Ibrox Stadium. "OK Robert. You're going to pull up right outside the main entrance. As soon as you stop you're going to get out and run like you've never run before. You'll have two minutes. It will be enough. There is going to be one hell of a bang. I will call and tell my mate to leave your family. He will leave the house. You'll go home. And you can all live happily ever after. OK?"

"OK."

"So let's go."

Strong parked the tanker by the famous old red brick stand. He never even looked at Richard. He jumped out and ran. Richard followed him out. He ran hard for the corner of the street. Once there he checked his watch. 12.30. Show time. He pulled the detonator from his pocket and pressed the button.

The old stand was enveloped in a towering sheet of flame. A notable football landmark was reduced to rubble.

The sound of the blast carried easily over the few miles to the city centre. Davie looked up. There was still a bemused look on his face.

"What's that Davie?"

A tight smile appeared on Davie's face. "That's Ibrox Park. Home of good old Glasgow Rangers. A grand target for the IRA. But I don't suppose anyone is going to see it that way now."

He pulled his hand from his pocket. He stared down at the detonator. Sean stared with him. His finger caressed the small red button. When he spoke it was more or less to himself. "That's my signal. The plan. Hear the blast from Ibrox. Press the button. Die. Time to die. It's my signal."

He looked up. His agonised eyes found Sean's eyes. They held the stare. Sean was becoming frantic. Davie was gone. Way gone. Somehow he needed to reach him. "Think of your Grandad Davie. He wouldn't want this. He wouldn't want your people to be hated.

Think Davie. Picture him. Picture what he would tell you. This isn't his way."

Davie fought to put order to his thoughts. Everything was just a mess. A complete mess. "But that's why I'm here. It's all for him. Him and all the others. All the men on the Somme. I'm calling in the debt. They owe us, Sean. They have to be reminded that they owe us. Surely you can see that. Now I want you to go now. Fuck off. I'll give you a minute. A minute is enough. Fuck off. Run. Get out of the way. I've no fight with you Sean."

Sean was angry now. "Oh no. No fucking way Davie. I'm not making it easy. You want to push that button, then you push it. But I'm going nowhere. You push that button and you can take me with you. Me and all these people. Come on man. Open your eyes. Look at them. Women. Children. They are your victims. Show some courage Davie. Look around. Look at the ones you are going to kill. Maim. Dismember. Look them in the eye before you do it."

He was shouting now. Heads were turning. People were moving away from them anxiously. Faces stared in at them. Amused. Curious. Anxious. Two old men having a row. Davie hadn't wanted to look at them. He had concentrated on looking past them. Through them. Ignoring them. Making them not seem real. Extras on a film set. Cardboard cut outs. But now he couldn't. Sean's voice was biting into him. Goading him. Needling him. Forcing him to meet the eyes of his victims.

Ordinary eyes. Ordinary faces. Strangers. Young and old. Staring at him. Some looking concerned. Not out of fear. Out of the way he looked. So pale. So sick. So close to death. And they had no idea that he was about to take them with him. Hundreds of them. And Sean. All of them. For nothing. For rage. For anger. For hate. Always the hate. And he knew that Sean was right. He knew that this wasn't what Peter Stanton would have wanted. This was not the way of his people. This was not the way of all those who had died. This was not the way.

He turned to Sean. There were tears in his eyes. Tears of shame and pain and sorrow. "I need you do one thing for me Sean. One last favour. I'll give you the detonator. In my pocket there is a gun. A pistol. I want you to shoot me Sean. I can't take this pain any more. I want out now. No more war. Just peace. Silence. Will you do it Sean?"

Sean nodded. The crowd moved back a few feet. Nobody was really sure. Maybe they were both drunk. Or mad. Or both. Davie passed the small box over. He lifted his hands clear of his pockets. Sean reached over and took out a pistol. Now the crowd fell back in panic. All around them was the thundering beat of the drums and the high pitched noise of the whistles. It was all happening too fast for the onlookers. It was just too strange. Not real. Street theatre.

Sean slipped off the safety catch and looked into Davie's eyes. The pain was draining away now. A small smile played on his lips. It was over. Sean knew that he would do it. He was filled with an almost unbearable sorrow. But he knew he would do it. Davie gave him a small nod.

"Bye Sean."

"Bye Davie."

The shot sent the crowd running and screaming. They got all mingled up with the marching band. Policemen came crashing onto the scene. They found Sean sitting on the pavement. The gun was thrown to one side. He was cradling Davie's shattered face in his lap. His trousers were soaked in blood. His face was like nothing they had seen before. Tears were pouring down his thin cheeks.

It was the face of despair. A sorrow so deep that they were reluctant to step forward. They had never seen such despair. Total. Utter.

Sean never saw them. He saw nothing. Just a great emptiness.

THE END

Other titles available
from Glenmill Publishing

One Man's Meat
by Mark Frankland

"Frankland turns crisis into drama"
Sunday Telegraph

November 1997 and British Farming
is being ripped apart by the BSE Crisis.
Vast areas of the countryside are facing devastation.
Finally one man decides that enough is enough.

Sir Alistair McIntyre, owner of the vast McIntyre
Holdings Corporation, makes the fateful decision to
save the Beef Industry. He hires a team of Mavericks
who claim to be able to solve any problem.
Their prize is massive. So is their task.

As their campaign gathers momentum
thousands of angry farmers at last start to fight back.
The story sweeps across the globe at breathtaking speed
from Argentina to Matabeleland,
from the windswept Scottish hills
to the shanty towns of Brazil,
from the Cabinet Room in Downing Street
to the Boardroom of a Supermarket giant.

Every step of the way the team are sucked into ever
greater danger until their path inexorably leads them
to the lair of one of the most dangerous men on earth . . .

To order a copy complete
the order form at the back of the book
or tel. 0776 149 3542

£5.99 plus £1.00 P&P

Red Sky in the Morning
by David Cherrington

"Red sky in the morning, shepherds warning . . ."
Harry Sinton mumbled to himself noticing the sunrise.
Minutes later he was standing over two lifeless
bodies, clutching his shotgun, and shaking in disbelief.

Harry Sinton was a quiet man leading a quiet life
on his farm in his quiet piece of England,
until one fateful morning when he stumbled across
a gang of thieves stealing his machinery.
Within seconds two thieves lay dead,
a third was running scared,
and Harry Sinton could not believe what he had done.

Red Sky in the Morning is a gripping tale
of how a single incident can transform a life.
As the story sweeps to its climax, the reader,
like the jury, has to make some hard judgements . . .
Who is the victim?
How far can any of us go to defend ourselves?

*"The story is enjoyable, thought-provoking and so strongly
written that it seizes the reader's attention in the first chapter
and holds it in a vice-like grip until the final moments."*
Charlotte Smith, Hampshire Chronicle

*"A gripping read, the more so because it is so chillingly
close to the fact. Mr. Cherrington's book raises
controversial questions about how far anyone has the right
to go to in order to defend themselves and their property."*
Angela Turnbull, Salisbury Journal.

**To order a copy complete
the order form at the back of the book
or tel. 0776 149 3542**

£5.99 plus £1.00 P&P

The Cull
by Mark Frankland

£1 from every copy sold will be donated
to the Daily Record Anti-Drugs Campaign.

*'Everyone who has lost a child to heroin will want to be Jack Sinclair.
Tragic, thrilling, captivating'* **Simon Houston, Daily Record**

'Mark lifts the lid on Drug Town' **Sunday Post**

Will Sinclair is dead. It seems as if he will be just another
statistic. Another young man dead before he reaches twenty.
Another Scottish junkie unlucky enough to shoot up a bad bag
of heroin. A few column inches in the local paper. Ten seconds
on the radio news. And then he will be added to the long, long
list. Just another dead junkie

But this time it is different. It is different because Jack Sinclair
will not accept his son's loss with resigned grief. He refuses to
forgive and forget. He was once Major Jack Sinclair of the
Scots Guards. In three tours of Northern Ireland he learned all
about fighting an unseen enemy. Then there were rules.
Regulations. Restrictions. Red tape. His war against the drugs
gangs who killed his son will be very different. This time the
gloves are off. This time he has a free rein

As Jack Sinclair lights his small fire, the story sweeps from the
empty wilderness of the Galloway Forest to the war-torn
streets of West Belfast, from the mean council estates of South
West Scotland to the Cabinet Room of 10 Downing Street. And
the fire becomes an inferno.

**To order a copy complete
the order form at the back of the book
or tel. 0776 149 3542**

£5.99 plus £1.00 P&P

Hot Property
by John Peel

For each copy sold £1 will be donated
to the North West Cancer Research Fund.

'A rich seam of humour in the Cumbrian fells'
Developing a small piece of land in Cumbria should
have been a straightforward affair for Nick Kennedy,
an ambitious London lawyer: but he was not to know
of events that had taken place eleven years earlier.

Nick is banned from driving, and so we find the
enigmatic Charlotte behind the wheel of his beloved
Porsche. Together, they embark upon a journey
with many unexpected twists and turns: a journey
that develops into a roller coaster ride of emotions.

As Nick begins to unravel a web of deceit, plagiarism
and greed, the machinations of a hard up, ageing pop singer,
a convicted embezzler, a tramp and even his
distinguished boss, threaten his career and ultimately,

his freedom . . .

To order a copy complete
the order form at the back of the book
or tel. 0776 149 3542

£6.99 plus £1.00 P&P

The Drums of Anfield
by Mark Frankland

"A fantastic adventure book for all young
football lovers – even one as young as me!"
Sir Tom Finney

Once in every generation a great new star emerges
into the world of football. Out of the slums of Sao Paulo
came Pele. Out of the bullet-scarred streets of Belfast
came Georgie Best. Out of the shanty towns of Buenos Aires
came Maradona. When Liverpool's veteran captain,
Tony Hobbes, suffers a crippling injury and receives a long
ban for violent conduct, he decides to take his son to Africa.

He expects to find lions and elephants amidst the Dark
Continent's endless wild plains. Instead, far away in the East
of Uganda under the shadow of the Mountains of the Moon,
he finds a boy called Simon Matembo. He knows that the
boy's talent is so huge that he could become the greatest
of them all. He knows that this boy can take Liverpool back
to the great days. But first he has to find a way to take him
back, and to do this he must overcome many huge challenges
from the tribe, the club, and even the forces of nature.

"Anyone who loves football will love this book.
Football is about passion, unrelenting excitement
and, more than anything else, it is about dreams.
Exactly the same can be said about 'The Drums of Anfield".
Gerry Marsden, from 'Gerry and the Pacemakers'

"Genuinely hard to put down", **FourFourTwo Magazine**

To order a copy complete
the order form at the back of the book
or tel. 0776 149 3542

£4.99 plus £1.00 P&P

Order Form

Name --

Address --

Telephone --

Email --

Please send me ----------------- Copies of

Please send me----------------- Copies of

I enclose a cheque for ----------------------

Please make cheques payable to:
'Glenmill Publishing'

Return this form to:

> Glenmill Publishing
> Glenmill
> Dumfries
> DG2 8PX

Or Telephone   0776 149 3542